"You're dyin

He tried to jerk his hands from the bed. The scarves held fast, tightening more around his wrists. "I feel sick. My stomach . . . my stomach's . . . "

"Hurting?" she asked. She leaned forward a little to look him in the eyes. "Is there pain yet? I'd be interested to know what it feels like."

"Listen, you bitch, I don't know what kind of game you're up to, but I don't like it! I ought to get up from here and beat the living hell outta you."

"You're dying," she said coolly. She was surprised how complacent she sounded, how detached she felt.

"What are you talking about?"

"You won't beat the hell out of me or any other woman again. You won't hound them, use them, abuse them, or screw them. Not anymore."

⅊ WIDOW ⅁

Widow

BILLIE SUE MOSIMAN

BERKLEY BOOKS, NEW YORK

WIDOW

A Berkley Book / published by arrangement with
the author

PRINTING HISTORY
Berkley edition / April 1995

ISBN: 0-425-14683-9

BERKLEY®
Berkley Books are published by The Berkley Publishing Group,
200 Madison Avenue, New York, New York 10016.
BERKLEY and the "B" design
are trademarks belonging to Berkley Publishing Corporation.

PRINTED IN THE UNITED STATES OF AMERICA

10 9 8 7 6 5 4 3 2 1

For Matt Bialer,
who is always on my side,
and Melinda Metz,
who encourages me to follow my obsessions.

❧Prologue❧

Perfection was the key. If she could manage to create a flawless environment, it might prevent any further descent into the chaos that had intruded itself into Kay Mandel's life.

The flowers were arranged with Japanese economy in a black vase on the entry hall table. The tablecloth on the gleaming dining table was freshly ironed, precisely centered, the china and silverware for two placed across from each other. Dinner was her husband's favorite. Rib-eye steaks broiled to medium rare, scalloped potatoes, artichoke heart salad.

The children, Gabriel, two years old, and Stevie, four, had been bathed earlier, fed their dinners, and now sat playing with plastic blocks on the floor of the immaculately clean den. They were quiet, always eager to please their mother. Good children. Perfect sons.

Kay checked her hair in the mirror on the living room wall. She patted a stray black strand into place just above her right brow. Did her eyebrows need plucking? They were all right. She looked her best in the white summer dress and the sandals with little heels. The white offset the naturally dark olive complexion. The sandals brought attention to the lovely curves of her legs. She knew her legs were good because Scott told her so. He preferred miniskirts on her for that very reason.

She wet her lips nervously, frowned. Was he late? Late meant he might come home in a foul mood. She glanced at her watch. Ten after six. Just ten minutes late, it didn't mean anything. Not yet.

His moods had been swinging violently between euphoria and depression for over four months. He might come home ecstatic over something at work she didn't understand. Or he might enter the front door wearing a pained look, unable to speak except in monosyllables. Yes, no, not now, stop, go away.

When it all began—suddenly, inexplicably, without any cause that she could discover—she searched for some meaning. Was it his job? It was not, he claimed. Was it her, something she had done or left undone that upset him? Or was it the children, the routine of married life, some sort of midlife crisis? Not likely, he told her, I'm too young to be middle-aged. Then what? What could be wrong? Would a massage work, more frequent sex, a hot bath, another drink?

Nothing helped. At wit's end, she suggested he see someone.

"Me? *See* someone? Why don't *you* see someone," he had screamed that night, frightening the children so that she hurried them into their pajamas and into bed.

Stevie had asked, "What's wrong with Daddy?" Kay couldn't answer her son. She tucked the covers beneath his arms, leaned down to kiss his forehead. "Go to sleep now. Tomorrow's another day." Yes, it was. Tomorrow Scott might feel better. Tomorrow it was possible her children would not have to ask her unanswerable questions.

"What do you think is so wrong with me I need to *see* someone?" he had asked upon her return to the den. "I know what that means. It means you think I'm going crazy. Well, I'm not. Do you hear me? I'M NOT."

But all evidence pointed to the conclusion that he *was*.

What about the nights he argued with her over nothing, then slammed the bedroom door in her face, and when she entered anyway, she found him sitting on the side of the bed loading and unloading the Smith and Wesson .38? He had bought the gun for protection against burglars, he told her. There had been a rash of break-ins in the neighborhood the year before. In some other neighborhoods a plague of "kick burglaries" was becoming commonplace. Two or three young men wearing ski masks or hoods kicked in the front door even when families were at home, and proceeded to loot and pillage.

Yet Scott wouldn't let her touch the gun. He didn't really *approve* of guns, he said, they simply should have one on hand. Just in case.

"What are you doing?" Kay had asked when she found him with the gun and the ammunition box lying open on the comforter, shiny brass cartridges scattered around, ominous signposts she could not decipher.

His stare was one she did not recognize. His eyes didn't reflect any emotion she had ever seen before. They were hateful and suspicious, callously weighing thoughts she was not privy to. The look chilled her so that she wrapped her arms around herself to keep from shivering. When he had no answer forthcoming, when he continued to stare at her with those cold, reptilian eyes, she backed from the room and slept on the sofa, an afghan thrown over her legs, tossing and turning throughout the night, wondering if he was still loading and unloading the gun in the other room.

She didn't know what to do. She didn't have any women friends to ask about the behavioral change. She had dedicated herself to being the best wife, mother, and housekeeper she knew how to be. She didn't make friends easily, didn't feel she needed them. Her own family was enough.

It was an archaic way of life these days, no woman even called herself a housewife anymore, but Kay liked the title and didn't much care what the new feminists thought of her. She had married Scott Mandel after one failed miserable marriage when she was too young to have been married at all. She had never had ambition for a career of her own—despite the two years she had been a club dancer—other than motherhood. Even that had taken a while. She was twenty-four before she conceived and twenty-five when she gave birth to Stevie.

It was all perfect. There was love. There were children and a nice home and shopping and caring for the family. It was idyllic.

Until now.

* * *

At six-thirty Scott came through the front door. From the way he walked and the determined look on his face, she knew he had slipped into another mood. Not euphoric or depressed, those moods she had grown used to, but something else, something new she intuitively feared.

He headed directly for their bedroom. She paced herself behind him, unconsciously wringing her hands. "Dinner's ready. Are you hungry? Would you like a drink first? Scott?"

He opened the clothes closet door and walked into the spacious dressing area. She came to the doorway and watched as he felt along the top shelf between shoe boxes and extra pillows for the gun. She was somewhat relieved to see he did not haul down the cartridge box. She had contemplated doing away with the weapon entirely, but was afraid of the fight that would ensue if she did.

Just the week before she had called a telephone hot line and anonymously explained the situation she now found herself in. She was referred to another number, another agency, but she did not make a second call. The first one had left her shaky and feeling stupid. Couldn't she control the atmosphere in her own home? Didn't she have the wherewithal to make her husband happy again without outside interference?

"I've made your favorite . . ."

He turned on her, the gun in his hand, the barrel pointing toward her belly. She flinched, ground the knuckles of one hand within the grip of the other. "Back away," he said. "I'm going to end all this."

"End what? What are you talking about?" Blood exploded in her brain, trampling through the veins in her temples like mad horses. The initial pain of a migraine headache made her wince. "Scott, put the gun back."

"Get out of my way or you'll be first. I don't really want to hurt you. I think you ought to stay behind to handle all the arrangements. It's not in *your* blood."

He pushed past her and left the bedroom, leaving Kay to trail him. *Not in her blood?* What could he mean? What arrangements?

He paused to look around the perfect living room, the vacuumed silver-gray carpet, the sofa and easy chair a soft shade of mauve, the accent pillows plumped just so, the paintings they had picked out together for the walls. She came to his side, her eyes pleading with him, praying he would listen.

"Scott, what do you mean not in my . . . ?"

He moved away from her as if he hadn't heard, moved purposefully down the hallway to the back of the house, toward the den.

Where the children played.

Now panic caused clarion bells to gong and clang in Kay's head. *Gabriel. Stevie. NO.*

"Wait, Scott, stop. . . ." She hurried behind him, hands outstretched.

He stepped into the den and strode directly to where the boys sat together on the carpet, gaily colored blocks scattered about their feet. They looked up, interested in the gun in their father's hand. Was it a toy for them? Stevie started to rise to his feet and Scott pushed him down again. He put up the palm of his free hand in a gesture that said "Stay." He turned to point the gun at Kay. "Don't come any closer."

"What do you want, Scott? Please don't scare the boys this way. Let's go back to the bedroom and talk about it. Let's try to—"

"Too late for talk, Kay. Too late for everything. I have to do this. Don't you see? I have to. It has to end here, with me." He gestured at the children with his gun hand. "And with them."

He turned the barrel of the revolver toward Stevie's confused face and pulled the trigger. Brain matter spread over and stained the carpet with streaks of red. Stevie fell backward to the floor with a thump.

Baby! Her baby! What had Scott . . . ? What was he . . . ? Kay screamed and rushed the remaining few feet to grab at her husband's hand.

Too late.

He swung the barrel toward little Gabriel's stunned face.

Gabe said, "Daddy, don't . . ." Scott pulled the trigger a second time. The reverberation was magnified so that it filled the house, it filled the world. Gabriel was flung back across the floor as if he had been hit by a great blast of wind. A large portion of the back of his head disappeared.

Scott threw off Kay and immediately put the gun into his mouth. He did not smile or flinch or say good-bye or explain himself.

As she watched in horror, he pulled the trigger and blew his brains across the den walls. His body fell across those of his dead children.

There was a keening in the air. Kay crawled to the bloody bodies and tried to gather them all into her arms to rock, to rock, to rock, to put back together again, and to rock.

One

Charlene had nicknamed the woman Shadow because she drifted around the place behind other patients like a shadow dogging their heels. Shadow did not speak and she did not respond to conversation. Sometimes she began chewing her fingernails until they were down to the quick and bleeding. The nurse had to tie her into a wheelchair then, or into the bed, to keep her from gnawing the flesh right down to the bone. When this occurred, Charlene, a patient known throughout the ward as a nurturer, spent a lot of free time sitting beside Shadow and patting her on the hand, talking in a soft voice, telling her it was going to be all right, really it was.

A year passed this way and then one day Charlene sat on the floor next to Shadow prattling on about this and that when suddenly Shadow tossed her head and her eyes focused on Charlene's face. "What?" she asked.

Although Shadow's unused vocal chords were rusty and the word came out of her mouth as if she were spitting gravel, Charlene understood. She reached out and caught Shadow's hands in her own, tugging at her until her face was but inches away. "Did you say something, honey? Did you really speak to me? Is that you in there, Shadow?"

She shook her head. Her name wasn't Shadow. Her name was something else entirely, she knew that, and soon it would come to her what exactly that name was. "What?" she said again, more plainly this time. "Where . . . ?"

Charlene jumped to her feet and went whooping around the big open room. She grabbed some of the other women and told them the news, she rushed to the nurse's window and announced it, she slid across the waxed tile floor like a baseball player stealing second base. When she returned to where Shadow sat on the floor, legs crossed, looking confused, there was a small group of women crowding around. "Get outta the way, give the lady some air, don't be scaring her now."

Some of the women moved aside and let Charlene sit down as if it were her divine right to take up the place of honor. She scooted very close to Shadow and took hold of her arm and held it close protectively. "They're just surprised, sweetie, that's all. You can't blame us for acting this way. You haven't said a word in months and months, not since you were brought in here. It's just a miracle is what it is, a real-life, hot-damn miracle. Some said you'd never come out of it, some said you'd never speak again, ever, and some I can name thought you were playing a game."

Shadow's face crumpled. Tears leaked from the lower lids. "I don't know . . . ," she began, "I . . . want . . ."

"What you want, sugar? You want to see the doctor? He'll be coming along soon. I told them you came out of it and they'll be falling all over themselves to get to you, don't worry. They're gonna be real surprised, but a happy surprise, you know, because it's been soooo long . . . oh, you poor thing, so terrible, you poor little thing. . . ."

Shadow buried her face in her hands and wept as if her heart were broken. Charlene took this as an excellent sign. Highly preferable to the mindless vegetative state the younger woman had suffered for so long. She put her arm around Shadow's heaving shoulders and pulled her close. For once she didn't have any encouraging words to say.

Stingy Betty crept along the floor on her hands and knees. She plucked at Shadow's hospital-issue slippers. Charlene reached out to swat her hand. "You leave her alone. You want to make her crazy again, is that what you want? Here." Charlene kicked off her own slippers. "Take mine instead. Leave Shadow alone for now, I never seen such manners in all my born days, what are you, trying to prove something here?"

More women swarmed around until the crowd completely surrounded the two women sitting on the floor. Some gibbered and motioned to unseen beings, some wept with Shadow, heartbroken, and some laughed inappropriately. It took Barclay, the orderly, the on-duty nurse, a woman the inmates affectionately called Skeeter, and Dr. Shawn to clear out all the women so that Shadow could be extricated and walked down the hallway to Shawn's private office.

Charlene stood at the wire gate waving. "Don't worry," she called. "You're going to be all right now. No one's going to hurt you anymore, sweetie, you gotta believe that. Remember, okay, what I said, about being fine and getting well and making a new start. . . ."

Her chatter followed the patient and the doctor until more doors were opened and closed against her.

Dr. Shawn sat beside Kay Mandel on the sofa in his office. He wanted nothing to appear threatening, nothing adversarial.

"Hello. Didn't they call you Kay? I'm your doctor, Kay, and I've been waiting a long time for us to be able to talk together."

"Yes. Kay. Ka . . . Katherine. That woman. She called me Shadow, I don't know why."

"Hmm." The doctor waited for the questions. There should be questions she needed answering. He had taken more interest in her case than any other in his career. Not often did he find himself challenged by a patient. There were so many he simply could not help, so many the state had to write off. There were so far gone that they had to be maintained, chemical dependents, and shunted aside in order to care for the patients who might still have a chance. He had always held out hope for Kay Mandel despite her yearlong catatonic state. She was relatively young, no history of past mental problems, and he felt the trauma she had undergone might eventually let go of her. As today it had.

Now to step carefully, to take it slowly, to give her every chance of recovery. He might save this one, return her to society, if not whole then at least enough so to function and to find some kind of life beyond institution walls. Even doctors needed an occasional triumph. It had been some time since he could count anything he had done as victorious in the Marion State Mental Facility. It wasn't the sort of place where success was assured. And it was for that reason that he stayed despite the low pay and the lack of stature a psychiatrist was afforded on the staff. He had to make a difference.

"Where am I?"

Shawn smiled at her. He said as gently as he could, "Marion State. Austin, Texas. You were transferred here from Houston immediately after—"

"But why? Isn't Marion a . . . it's a . . ."

"State mental hospital, yes. It is."

"I was crazy?"

He noticed her use of the past tense. It buoyed him even though it was not yet true that her psychosis had been put behind her. "You were traumatized, Kay. Do you remember what happened?"

She frowned, shook her head. Her long black hair moved slightly, her bangs fell loose across her forehead. He thought she could still be an exceptionally pretty woman with a proper diet, a little sun.

She asked, "Where's Scott? The boys? Have they been here to see me? Did I do something wrong?"

Her voice was squeaky and high. Shawn needed to back up, let her discover the past in her own time, at her own pace. "I'm so glad you're able to talk about things with me now, Kay. It's been almost a year. Next month, I think, makes it a year. And you haven't spoken to anyone until now. How do you feel? We're here to help you, you understand that, don't you?"

"But why am I here? Why didn't I speak before, can you tell me that? I don't remember . . . anything. God, my throat hurts. Can I have a glass of water?"

Shawn went to the adjoining bathroom and ran a glass of water from the sink. While she drank he said cautiously, "That's all right, you don't want to rush it. Your memory will return eventually. You have a lot to catch up on. The important thing is that you're no longer catatonic. You were in a trancelike state caused by a traumatic event. It will take a while to sort it all out. I want you to take it easy, don't be surprised if there are missing blocks of time, they'll come back to you more easily if you don't try too hard." He was glad she wasn't insisting on knowing about her husband and children. It was much too soon for revelations.

She set the glass on the table and lifted her hands in front of her face, puzzled. She turned them back and forth, peering finally at the fiercely bitten nails. There were raw sores and dark scabs along the nail rims where she had ripped them off completely. He had only last week given the order to remove the bandages. Her hands looked pretty sorry still.

"Who did this?" she asked. "It hurts."

"You did it, Kay. You were just . . . worried. Your hands will heal."

"I couldn't have done this. I've always had long beautiful fingernails. I always polished them with clear nail polish because Scott didn't like . . ." She paused in midsentence and let her hands fall into her lap. Her gaze took on a faraway look. It was the hundred-yard stare that he was used to seeing during months of silence. Shawn waited, hoping she could not yet see behind the curtain of memory to that night when she lost all she owned in the world. Had she had any family at all to come visit her, he thought she might have come out of shock sooner. It was infinitely sad that she was left alone, everyone in her life now dead. Most of Marion's patients had *someone* who cared, but Kay Mandel had no one. Except Charlene. It was a good sign when one patient took responsibility for another. He did not hold out any expectations that Charlene Brewster would ever be fully well again, but it was encouraging that she seemed to care so much for the lost waif who had wandered into the open ward a year ago.

While he waited he watched Kay Mandel's face for a change in expression. The big round white clock on the wall ticked off minutes and still she did not respond again to his voice. He sighed, helped her stand, led her to the ward bed, asked the nurse to watch over her closely. When he hurried down the hall to a meeting with other staff members, he wanted to be able to tell them Kay Mandel had spontaneously exited catatonia, that she was well on her way to recovery, but the truth was she might not be. She might not speak again for another year. He just didn't know.

Charlene sat beside Shadow's bed soothing her with a torrent of words. "So see, I get everybody's story who comes in here, and then if they get shock treatment and they forget, well, I can tell them their life stories, give them back the past. I figure that's the least I can do, maybe what I was meant to do being here and all, can't get out, except now and then, you know, but they picked me up that time on the streets down in Houston, said I was carrying a duck around in my arms and talking to God and stuff, but hey, I'm better off here where it's safe, you know, where I *know* these people won't slit my throat, or mug me, they'll just hassle me with their stories so I can remember for them, and like I say, I don't mind that, I figure that's my job, since I don't have a real job, I might as well do what I can. They don't give me electroshock 'cause I don't get violent, see, so I got this good memory, honey, the best, it's like photo . . . uh . . . graphic, kind of, and . . ."

On and on, a cascade, a typhoon of words and words and words that flooded Shadow's brain and kept her from thinking at all.

She had not slipped back into the gray world. She was biding her time until the dark came and she could be alone, away from Charlene's battering voice, though she understood that the woman cared for her and was merely trying to help. It was the *relentlessness* that bothered her, though she would rather bite off her tongue than say anything to stop Charlene's recital. She had the idea that already she had done something or seen something that stopped people, stopped them in their tracks, horrified them so badly they never moved again, ever, and she would not chance doing it again. She didn't know whether Charlene needed all those words or not, but it seemed that she did, and it would not be Kay who interrupted the lava flow.

Finally the day waned and the darkness crept over the sills of the wired windows. Charlene hardly drew breath, but dinnertime came, and she wandered away, never giving the words a break, swamping the other women with them as she joined in line for the cafeteria. "Betty, put down your bag of stuff, we're going to eat. Marta, that's a mighty fine smile you got on your face, you got a secret we don't know? Hey, Shere, wanna play a game of checkers later?"

Kay was left alone on the bed, the place empty and the night coming on. Lights flickered to life in the nurse's station, wheels rattled carts down some far hallway, voices drifted and died.

Scott liked clear nail polish. He had made fun of her red nails that time and she, feeling ashamed for not somehow guessing his preferences, had sponged off the scarlet polish and thrown away the bottle of Revlon Watermelon Red.

Where was Scott now?

She knew.

Sounds told her. Big sounds. Blasting sounds. Sounds that boomed and ricocheted in her brain.

She reached for the place where the sounds came from. It was in her home. Not here in this place of women who spoke too much, who made repetitive hand motions, who had not had their hair done in ages, in this place where a doctor was interested in her and kind, with gentle eyes, but careful, too, treating her as he would a fragile bit of glassware he might drop.

In her home. The sounds.

In the closet. The gun.

On her knees holding . . .

She shut her eyes and the tears came again, so many, so heavy that she couldn't think for them. She felt her fear rolling into a burning ball, scorching her lids, lying bundled and hot behind her eyes. Her chest heaved with the pain of it. She pulled her legs up and wrapped her arms around her knees. She tucked her chin down and clenched her teeth and still the tears wet the pillow.

They were dead. Her family was dead. Scott took her children and he took himself.

What could she do? What could she have done?

How was she going to live?

Damn him, damn him to hell forever. He had taken her perfect life and torn it apart. It was gone now, ripped from her. There had been no mercy in it. No salvation. No life left behind for her.

The nurse came and gave her an injection. She swam toward blackness with both arms flailing to get her there. She would die from her memories if it were not for the hope of a chemical oblivion.

❧ Two ❧

He watched her for weeks from the shadowy interior of his parked car. She worked the late shift at Laguna Liquor Mart.

That she was to be his victim was a happenstance. He had entered the store to buy a bottle of Chivas Regal to take with him to the beach in Galveston. To drink alone. To get drunk. There had been six serial murders within a year in Houston, none of them committed by him. He knew the modus operandi thanks to the thoroughness of the two Houston newspapers and television camera teams. Beheading with a sharp knife and, recently, since the killer was stepping up the viciousness of the attacks, a severing of the body limbs, which were taken away from the scene of the crime. But knowing the method and what was expected of him so that he might copy the killer did not provide a likely victim or a fail-safe plan to get away with murder. Therefore, the Chivas.

He took the bottle from a display shelf and walked to the counter. There she was. Waiting to ring up the order, smiling her pretty Hispanic smile, totaling his purchase on the cash register, handing him change.

He took in the white blouse she wore, the size of her breasts, the sweep of hair from the sides of her face, held back with a metal barrette at the top of her head. Loose curly tendrils trailed close to her ears, whispering past silver shell earrings that seemed molded and pressed into finely shaped earlobes. Small, delicate hands the color of creamy coffee lifted the bottle and set it gently into a brown paper bag. She wore three rings. A plain silver band on her right hand, a gold ring with a yellow stone, and a gold nugget ring on her left. One of her front teeth was turned slightly so that it hooked her top lip when she smiled. Her lower lip was full and, without lipstick, red as cranberry. She appeared to be in her midtwenties. Lively, courteous, conscientious. She was *his*.

He could not explain, were he asked, how he knew it must be her. These things just came to him. The timing was right. He felt pressed to find someone. All the victims thus far had been around her age, pretty like her, dark complexioned, working class. One of the other six had also been Hispanic. *Perfect.*

Hurrying out to his car after that first meeting, gleeful and no longer requiring the quart of alcohol, he drove off the parking lot and across the street to a closed strip shopping center. He backed into a space in front of Pilgrim's Dry Cleaning and waited. He could see the front of the Liquor Mart and was not so far away he could not recognize the cashier.

He followed her home. He came back late the next night to the liquor store. And as many nights as he could afterward. Memorizing her walk, which shoulder she carried her purse on, how long it took her to unlock the car door when she left after closing.

She was always alone. She always parked her car at the right end of the building in the last slot or, if it was unavailable, as close to the storefront as possible. She came to work five days a week at four in the afternoon and stayed until closing at midnight. The manager locked up and left an hour later.

He obsessed about the clerk, wondering who lived with her. There were two other cars in the drive at her house when she returned home between midnight and one each working night. An old Caddy with a busted left taillight, and a cherry red Chevy truck with a black toolbox mounted below the back window. She might have a boyfriend. She might have two. He fantasized a ménage à trois.

He wondered what kind of lingerie she wore, what she slept in, who her friends were. He imagined her life and, imagining, fell in love with her. You could not kill what you did not love.

Tonight was the night. He knew her as well as he was going to at this distance. At twelve midnight he parked in front of the dry cleaning store. He watched the front of the Laguna Liquor Mart, his pulse hammering in his throat, his palms beginning to sweat. He wore navy slacks and a matching short-sleeved shirt. Nothing memorable or outstanding.

It was a warm April night and he could feel the sweat crawling down from his temples like worms wiggling from out of his hair. Madly chirping crickets made a racket in his ears. He supposed they were down in the drainage ditch that bordered the shopping strip. Making passionate love. Performing acrobatics. Singing arias. Some damn noisy thing.

He couldn't see the stars for the city lights, but the moon was quartered, high up in the sky, a bitter lemon-peel yellow.

Time to go. Minutes ticked by. Time to go and he was paralyzed. It never failed. When it was important that he make the first move, he stalled, worrying incessantly over minor details. What if someone accompanied her to the car tonight? What if the manager left just as she did? What if a squad car cruised by to check the place? He had to be ready to turn aside suspicion if anything unexpected occurred.

He forced himself to open the car door and step out, eyes focused on the Laguna Liquor Mart. She was coming. He could see her moving purposefully down a long aisle through the store to the double glass entry doors.

Hurry. Hurry now.

He crossed the street between passing cars, face turned from the oncoming headlights. Entering the parking lot, he kept the wide-blade hunting knife in his fist at the side of his thigh, out of sight. He walked casually toward the lighted store. All business, no hint of delay now that he was in motion. Every molecule dancing with anticipation.

He was still three parking spaces away from his desti-

nation—her car—when she came from the store, slinging
the black leather bag over her shoulder, car keys in hand.
She stepped off the curb into the drive-by lane and crossed
it. She hadn't raised her head yet, hadn't seen him. She
almost always fiddled with the key ring, shaking it around
until she found the key that would unlock her car. He made
it through the three spaces. He circled the rear of her dirt
brown Nissan Maxima just as she found the ignition key
and looked up, noticing she was not alone.

Her steps never halted, but they slowed, and she frowned
at him. Her shoulders went back, her head tensed. A pro-
tective hand gripped her shoulder purse.

He smiled. "Hey, you closed already?"

She nodded, angling a little away from him, still making
for the Maxima's door. "Yes, I'm sorry." She wasn't looking at him now, her mistake. She wanted to ignore him,
pretend he wasn't there. He took the opportunity to move
in even closer.

She wanted into her car, locked and safe, of course she
did, he knew all her thoughts, *all* of them.

"Damn," he said. "And they wanted another twelve-
pack of Miller Lite back at the party. I thought y'all stayed
open all night." Friendly. Nonthreatening. Just a party kind
of guy.

She had the key in the door lock, but was having trouble.
She didn't want to present her back to him, and standing
the way she was, trying to keep him in sight from the corner
of her eye, she wasn't able to turn the key quickly enough.
"We're *closed*," she said. Then she swore softly and the
key turned and the little latch inside the Maxima shot up
with an audible *click*.

Her hand went for the door latch. His hand went for her
mouth. He held her against his chest, tight, the knife point
around front, pressed dangerously into her left breast. If she
moved, the blade would cut into pliant flesh.

"Easy . . . easy. Get in and crawl over the gearshift."

She hadn't struggled except for a second. He could feel
her heart pumping against the knuckles of his knife hand.
He could feel the round softness of her breast and the hot

place just below it where her ribs began. "Open the door. Get in and climb over to the passenger side like I asked. Don't scream. I'll kill you if you scream."

Only one out of ten ever disobeyed him. They had been told fighting back got them killed. They had been correctly advised.

She managed to open the door. He held her mouth, keeping the knife to her breast, and bent with her into the seat. He brushed briefly against her buttocks and suddenly could think about nothing but having sex with her. She felt so warm, like a furnace against his skin, and her scent was faint rose. Then he let her go, but reluctantly. She scrambled over the gearshift, her shoes clacking like Spanish castanets against the steering wheel and console. She was crying. But not screaming.

He slid into the driver's seat and reached over, jerking the keys from her trembling hand.

"We're going for a little ride."

He had to do it outside of Houston where he wouldn't be interrupted. These types of murders took time. They were grisly. Messy. Demanding.

He knew all of Houston and the cities outside its environs that were attached to the city limits as if by busy umbilical cords comprised of strip shopping centers, fast-food franchises, and supermarkets. He drove her from Pasadena onto Interstate 45 north, took the 610 Loop to 290 west. He already knew a place, a killing place, one of his own, outside of Hempstead not far from Houston. Secluded. Beautiful in its ghostly serenity.

She talked to him, trying to swallow down rising panic, offering him her money, her car, submitting to him if only he wouldn't . . . if only he wouldn't . . . He didn't respond. Then she began to cry again, the effort causing her to heave and hunch and hold onto her stomach and he told her, "Shut up, I have to drive. Don't make this harder for yourself than it is."

They always cried. They always begged. Once in a while, but not often enough to suit him, they were crazy wild and hysterical. There was never any variety in a woman's emotions.

He turned down a country road heading north, away from Hempstead. He had to watch for the turnoff. He knew it by a curve in the road, a big live oak growing in a lonely field. There was a place, an abandoned farmhouse, weedy, overgrown, gray, and falling down. Site of multiple murders over a period of many years. *His place.* Cattle grazed the fenced pastureland behind and on each side of the old house, but there wasn't another dwelling for miles.

He parked behind the house, driving through weeds taller than the Maxima's windows. He told her to get out. He marched her up broken and creaking steps beneath the lemony moonlight to a black opening into the house. The back door was missing. There was a strong smell of damp wood rot, a smell of night air gone stale and bad inside the yawning empty room. She pleaded that he not hurt her; rape her, okay, but no, don't hurt her, please; she'd do *anything* for him if he promised not to harm her. Oh, God.

He said he wouldn't. She wanted him to lie and he did.

Inside, he thought it not in his interest to put off the inevitable longer than necessary. The serial killer's rationalization for these murders was not his. He copied the crime itself, but he could no more re-create the original killer's motivations than he could fly to the moon by flapping his arms. His main pleasure came from adding to a string of murders without penalty. It was the most perfect, orgasmic lift in the universe to work inside a pattern already laid out. A certain gender, certain age, certain type, certain manner of death. It was pattern that mattered, duplicating it. He was a student faithfully executing the lessons taught by a master, a Tintoretto influenced by the staggering talent of a Michelangelo. The serial murderer he copied might be into necrophilia, cannibalism, sadomasochism, dismemberment, or mutilation. None of those variations particularly moved him, even as he was called upon to perform them in order to match some of the profiles he had imitated over the years. However, these additions did not repulse him either. He was like the physician called upon to stitch a jagged tear in a person's leg at a car accident, even though his specialty was plastic surgery.

Whatever was called for. That is what he did.

Before she could even turn to face him with a fresh barrage of tears and hoarse whispery pleas, he plunged the knife into her back between the shoulder blades and rode her with his weight down to the bare wood floor.

Now she screamed.

It had taken most of the night. Hours. Undressing her dying malleable body. Sucking her silent dusky lips one at a time into his mouth, discovering the places where she had patted the rose scent—behind each pierced ear, in the crook of her arms, behind both fleshy knees. Talking to her while light drifted and died in the brown eyes, testing her death to be sure it was real before cutting off one arm, both legs, her head. Burying those parts in the makeshift graveyard that held an abundance of such body pieces from times past. Hiding again the shovel under the crumbling carcass of a fallen sweet gum tree. Wrestling her slick torso into a black plastic garbage bag he had brought along in his back pocket. Hoisting her into the trunk of the Maxima.

At the hand pump that brought up rusty iron water from the well near the back of the house, he bathed off the blood, feces, and urine that slimed his body. He put on his clothes. There was a blotch of dried blood on his blue shirt, from the first stabbing frenzy of her back, but he could wash it at home.

He knew they would find a way to identify her by the one arm he left attached to the body. So far, in the six preceding killings, one identifying body part was left intact. Probably for identification purposes. Or to fulfill some mangled fantasy the killer had invented.

It was barely light, the city hunkered down in a fog-shrouded dawn, freeway lights blinking out, when he drove the Maxima south of Houston into Pasadena and parked it in the end slot at the Laguna Liquor Mart. The air reeked with the rotten-egg scent of chemicals from the oil refinery plants, but he took a chest full of it as if it were sweet honeysuckle air.

He made it home before the freeway work traffic crush, before six A.M.

Suffused with adrenaline, he was able to pass the day without sleep or mishap. And through all the long hours of this sleepless day he walked around patting his belly, snapping his fingers, smiling to himself. He was a full man, replete, confident, and radiant, thrilled at his accomplishment no one would ever know or guess.

No one except the serial killer he had one-upped. Another fool of a man who could never speak of the treachery done him.

◊ Three ◊

Detective Mitchell Samson walked down the block in the inner-city neighborhood watching all the shadows. Neon flickers from the many club signs along the sidewalk did little to alter the dark night's dangerous possibilities. Grotesque shapes loomed in the alleyways and staggered toward him, their faces limned in sulphurous yellow, emerald, and vermilion. Mitchell kept his head down, but his attention sharp. It was not a good place to be late at night.

He saw Big Mac leaning against a telephone pole on a street corner at about the same time the bag lady snitch saw him. Homeless, broke, unemployable, Big Mac lived on handouts and by trading street news with the cops. Mitchell felt in the breast pocket of his jacket and withdrew a bill. He had it folded and waiting just in case he saw Big Mac. There but for the grace of God, he often thought. She could be me. I could be her. We're old friends.

"Hey, Samson, how's life treating you?"

"Where'd you get that T-shirt, Mac? I didn't know you went in for headbanger music." Mitchell reached out and stuffed the folded twenty into the woman's shirt pocket.

"Aww, I don't like nothing like that. Some kid gimme this shirt. Pretty colors, though, ain't it?" She pulled the oversize T-shirt out from her emaciated chest and looked down at the wild collage of colors spraying out from the faces of a band she had never heard of before. "I kinda like it."

Mitchell moved on down the sidewalk, Big Mac at his side. The woman ate all her meals at McDonald's, and Mitchell believed that was why her color was pale as oyster shell. Her arms were sticklike, her knuckles thick with arthritis, but she possessed a jittery energy, the kind someone dancing on the edge of survival needed to keep herself dry, warm, and fed.

"Heard anything on that gay bashing happened down here last week?" Mitchell asked. He didn't really expect to get anything for his money. He just knew Big Mac needed a hamburger. She looked wolfish, under deep strain, the lines in her face digging woeful trenches toward underlying bone.

"Might've been some kids outta the neighborhood. Seen a carload of 'em down here about that time. Waving bats out the car windows. Calling people faggots and names like that. Not that there ain't some flaming fags here, but, you know, what's the problem with that? Cain and Abel might have been fags, what do we know, right?"

"Any idea where the kids came from, what part of town?"

"Some say they're from up north, maybe the Woodlands."

That surprised Mitchell. The Woodlands was a planned development built with nature in mind, houses surrounded by trees, the complex's research, university, and corporate buildings hidden behind massive green forests. The domain of the wealthy, the educated. Made them feel ecology conscious living in a place named one of the top three designed communities in America. Could it also be the breeding ground for skinhead fascists? Or maybe it was just a few boneheads out for a joyride. Too much beer. Too few brains.

"Well, you see that carload of kids again, you give me a call. We need to keep an eye on people carrying bats."

Big Mac began angling across the sidewalk in front of Mitchell, pushing her shopping cart ahead of her. She stepped into the street. McDonald's beamed yellow bright across from where they walked. "I'll do that, Samson. Thanks for the dough. I was so damn hungry, I thought I was gonna start eating shoe leather. If I had any." She glanced down at her worn rubber-soled sneakers and laughed.

Mitchell tipped an imaginary hat and kept walking.

He slipped in the door of the Hot Spot at fifteen after eleven. It was a weeknight, Tuesday, and the clientele were few. One drunk sat hunkered over a draft beer in the corner booth.

Two younger men, blue collar types dressed in jeans and plaid short-sleeved shirts, sat together at the long bar sipping whiskeys and calling out to the dancer when they thought she needed more encouragement to swing her bare tits.

Mitchell took his usual table and ordered an Irish coffee. The bartender already had the pot brewed, waiting. Mitchell regularly hit this place on Tuesday nights. He always ordered Irish coffees. He stayed until twelve or one in the morning, until after a dancer called Jezebel came on, and then he moved on to the next topless bar on his list, one right down the block where the dancers were younger and firmer and earned quite a bit more money for dancing in a G-string for horny men.

The coffee came steaming with whipped cream on top. Sometimes bartenders dropped in a sprig of mint, but not here at the Hot Spot. What did he want, class or naked women? He wanted the naked women. He did. His day wasn't complete without them.

He stirred the light cream into the liquid, savoring the smell, wondering for the hundredth time if maybe he wasn't getting too infatuated with the drink, the way he had become enamored of the dancing girls. This was a worry. If he turned into a lush, his job might fall into danger. Or was it already in danger? How would he know something like that?

He shrugged, took a small swallow of the doctored coffee, and felt it go down real smooth, like honey that coated the tongue and swelled the taste buds. Before he reached home tonight, he'd be half-drunk. So be it. There were lots worse things to be half of than drunk. Like hungry and having to depend on handouts.

The girl in the pink center-stage spotlight was no longer a girl, but she could move. The platter player, the deejay, called her Babycakes. She was nobody's baby, but she'd make a helluva birthday cake surprise. She could move like a boa constrictor, and did so, sinuously, wrapping her long white legs and arms around a center pole in the stage. She rocked to the beat of an old blues song, humping at the pole, leaning back all the way until her head reached the floor. Her breasts, not young, not that large, but real, not silicone-injected biscuits, slipped up her rib cage, nipples standing, teetering on their mounds of flesh. God! There had to be a God, given nipples like that.

She looked right at Mitchell and he looked back, sure she knew his game. He wished to hell she'd tell him what it was. He'd be most grateful for that.

She lifted her torso oh so slowly and unwound from the pole. She did a few dance steps, a few bumps and grinds for the boys at the bar, who gave her appreciative whistles, and then she moved to the back of the runway and, peeking with a smile from the curtain, disappeared as the last strains of music died.

Mitchell drank the coffee, asked for a refill. His waitress was the girl he watched dance on Friday nights. She now wore a red baby-doll pajama top over her G-string, but it did nothing to camouflage the voluptuous figure. You could see all the way through the material as if it were gauze, or a red spiderweb. That was a jolly thought. Imagine those legs on a spider. Those tits. That ass.

Every time she brought him a drink he tipped her another dollar. Off him she made a dollar every twenty minutes or half hour. Not good. Not bad. But it was acceptable. He wasn't rich, they knew that. They even knew he was a cop, a clean one, which explained why he wasn't rich. The whole damn street knew he was on the force. But they didn't fear him. He wasn't out to bust anyone. He was just another one of those guys who liked to watch the female body undulate to the music. He didn't proposition them. He didn't even make any remarks. He just watched.

And that was his secret, The Secret, as Mitchell Samson thought of it. His buddies at the station didn't know about his late-night encampments in Houston's inner-city sleaze joints. They probably would have been stunned, if not properly indignant. Mitchell? Got a thing for the topless girls? Not Mitch, Jesus no. Not good old dependable quiet laid-back Mitchell, gimme a fucking break. The only cops who knew were from Vice. And they didn't care one way or the other. If they happened by a place where he was, their eyes slid over him without pause. Girls were his thing, they didn't give a damn.

But Mitchell's precinct homeboys didn't know, and if he had anything to do with it, they never would. Also, Patty didn't know. His fiancée. Though he wasn't quite sure how that had come about—that engagement business. He had been married once, and once was all one man should have to try to find out he wasn't the best marriage material on the planet Earth. But nevertheless, someway, he had proposed. Kind of. And Patty accepted. And she thought he was bringing her an engagement ring one of these days. Just as soon as he could remember to go to a jewelry store to shop for one. What with all his time taken up with his work, she might give him a little time, a little leeway to produce the package.

As he sipped another Irish coffee, Mitchell figured he could hold out on the ring thing for another couple of months at least. Who could afford a diamond anyway? Had Patty ever looked at those price tags? He thought she probably had. Some women knew these things demanded sacrifice, monetary and otherwise, and wanted them made. Have to secure the goddess's favor, whatever the cost. Not that he blamed her for that. They all wanted the same things anyway. Was she supposed to be different?

As for getting married, really tying the knot, well, he'd have to see. Patty was sweet and all, hell, she was top-notch, any man's catch. Smart, three diplomas hanging on her wall, on her way up at the Housing Authority, on a first-name basis with the mayor, but . . .

But what? he pondered. Every time he turned around there was a but. Life was just chockful of them. But for the grace of God he was not homeless and beaten down. But for his misgivings, he might really marry again. But for the sake of his old dog, Pavlov, he might sometimes even admit to fleeting bouts of true loneliness. But, but, but.

Jezebel came onstage and all those anxious thoughts swiftly vanished from mind. Jeze was something else again. Not as full bosomed as his waitress, not as young and firm as the girls he would see at his next regular hangout, but damn she was a man's kind of woman. Legs, man; would you look at those legs, they made his eyes want to fall from their sockets. Beautiful ankles, the dip between foot and calf *just right,* the curve behind her knee smooth and pure as French vanilla ice cream, the thighs thick but luscious, the hips like magnolia blooms, milky, soft looking without appearing loose. Waist not more than twenty-two inches around, he'd have to swear. And eyes. Dark, liquid, suggesting darker nights and darker deeper sex than he had ever experienced.

Oh, he knew it was illusion and lie. All of it. From the flesh to the paint, from the lust in the sometimes dilated, drugged-out pupils to the swish of the unclothed buttocks, but it was the best lie and the best illusion and it caused him to swell where he sat, which is what he was supposed to do, which is what her dance was supposed to accomplish, and accomplish it did. Magnificently.

He smiled, a gentle curving upward of his lips, enjoying the titillation overwhelming him. Jezebel. The reason he came here on Tuesday nights. So untouchably beautiful and full of promise, so ethereal that she might be an angel with tattered wings dropped onto the stage, soaked through with aquamarine spotlight, her eyes casting about in the dim club for a man's look, any man's, to judge if her performance was getting through.

He did not sip the coffee while she danced. He hardly breathed. He ignored the men at the bar who thought, as he did, that she was really something, really special. And when she finished her set, having drained from him whatever tension it was that brought him back week after week to watch her, Mitchell Samson stood from the table, dropped another dollar beside his cup, and wandered outside into a limpid midnight world. He had to adjust his erection. It was too painful the way it lay, though now the blood and fantasy feeding it were slowly washing away, sand from a shore.

He still had two hours to kill at Chez Tigress. Where the girls were younger, though no more beautiful than Jezebel.

And the bartender never failed to drop the sprig of mint into his Irish, whatta guy.

❧Four❧

The wind outside the window rustled a mass of green bushy hydrangea leaves against the windowpane. The woman in the bed turned off the radio and listened, decided what had made the noise, and spent some time looking at her empty water glass.

"Son? I hate to bother you, Son, but could you refill my water pitcher?" Her voice was high and a little breathless as she called out from the back bedroom of the house.

Son squeezed shut his eyes. He reached up and massaged his temples before raking his hand down over his face. His lips silently mimicked his mother's words. "Son? Fill my water pitcher? Will you, Son?" Being a gifted mimic, if he had been speaking out loud, his voice would have sounded almost identical to his mother's.

He swiveled the office chair around from the computer at his desk, and stood. "I'm coming, Mother. I'm coming, I'm coming," he breathed into the dimly lighted room, looking around, orienting himself so that his anger might leak out enough to allow him to pass inspection when he went to her assistance.

The hallway that led to the bedroom was dark. If he wasn't so damn economical, he'd turn on a light. That's what he was thinking just as he stumbled on a fold in the carpet runner. He cursed beneath his breath, halted, and waited, counting backward from ten. Nine, eight, seven, six . . . He stooped and felt for the fold, smoothed it flat, his exasperation growing. I will *not* turn on a light.

She was lying propped up like a duchess in her four-poster bed, all those lacy and crocheted pillows at her scrawny back. There must be a dozen. That's how she spent her bedridden days—sewing, crocheting, piling her bed with the efforts of her nimble fingers, the only part of her that still worked without giving her pain. The pillows were ugly. They were useless. And the thread cost him too much money.

She smiled when he entered the room. Son tried to smile back, but he wasn't a smiler. His mouth didn't work well when people watched him. He hoped there was warmth in his eyes. If she picked up on his resentment, she'd run her little game of martyrdom on him. Next time she wouldn't call when she had to go to the bathroom until it was nearly too late, and she might accidentally wet her gown. She had done it before, by God. *Then* he'd have to help her change. Bring a fresh nightgown to the bathroom, stand outside to walk her to bed again. Why didn't she let him get things done on time? Why did she always wait until there was a skim on the water or her bladder was full to bursting? Didn't she know that only made him feel worse than if she'd asked his help when it was really needed?

"I'm sorry to call you away from your work, Son. But this water . . . it's been here since yesterday and . . . well, there's a coat of dust on the top of it."

"I should have changed it before now. It's my fault." He gripped the thick glass handle of the pitcher and was about to turn. Glancing down at the water, he saw there was indeed a film topping the water level. Dust, just as she said. He hated dust. It was time he thoroughly cleaned her room again. Wasn't it just three days ago that he . . . ?

"It's not your fault," she said. "I'm too much trouble. I think we should hire someone to help, Son. It's not fair you have to do so much work because of me."

"No strangers in the house!"

He clamped his mouth closed and swallowed hard. His eyes had flashed, and he could see by the surprised look on his mother's face that she had seen it.

"I didn't mean . . . ," she began.

"No, Mother, it's all right. I just don't think hired help would be worth it. You know what it's like with other people around. I can't work. I can't concentrate. That one girl we tried, remember how sloppy she was? I found empty potato chip bags beneath your bed. I didn't tell you that, did I? You thought it was because she took naps, but she was a pig, Mother. And she never wiped the sink when she washed her hands.'' He did turn from her now, renewed anger creeping into his face at the thought of the day nurse he had let into the house to care for his mother's needs. Slob. Take the money and run. ''Besides,'' he said, passing from the room to the hall, ''I don't mind doing for you. You know that.''

He thought he heard her sigh. He steered the hallway by moving toward the light coming from the kitchen. The air was fresher here outside Mother's room. Her ancient flesh was ripening, filling his nostrils with an undeniable stench of decay.

He mustn't think that way. He must go to the kitchen sink. Clean the pitcher. Fill it with ice and water from the tap. Wouldn't take long. It wasn't that bad, the chores he was forced to do for his mother. They were just *endless*. Not difficult or beyond his abilities. He cooked for her, he cleaned, he washed her clothes and ironed them, even her sheets and pillowcases. She had to have someone do it, and he'd be damned if he'd let her think he couldn't measure up to the task. He was her son. Her last remaining relative. She was eighty-two. He had been a child produced in her midlife, planned and wanted and loved. He *knew* she loved him. How could he not do his duty when she was now old and sick and helpless? What son could turn his back on his own mother?

The ice trays fought him. He ran water over them and cracked them into the sink, the clacking sounds grating on his ears. Finally they gave up their bounty and he filled the empty pitcher to the top.

He carried the water back to his mother's bedroom. She was tired, dozing. Her eyelids raised slowly as he came into the room. Her old gray orbs were shiny and filmy as the water had been, yet she followed his movements. She always said he was like a cat burglar, that sometimes she didn't know he was in the room when she was asleep. Son took that as criticism and snapped back, "Should I knock first before I enter then?" She had given him that hurt look and turned away her face. She had said no, that's not what she meant. She never said what she meant, it seemed to him. She was always skirting around the issues, confusing the meanings. How was he supposed to read her mind?

"Your water," he said. "Shall I pour a glass for you?"

She shook her head. "I can do it." She groaned, trying to lean near the bed table to reach the glass.

"Let me, Mother. If you'd let me do things for you, it would be easier for both of us. I don't mind, really." He filled the glass and held it out to her waiting hand. She drank as if she had come from a week's walk in the desert.

That burned him up. She had gone without water because it was scummy; he had been remiss in his duties. She had been without a drink so long she was parched and she never called him. Goddamn it, why did she do that anyway? He could throttle her sometimes. She was long-suffering and making a fool of him.

"Are you hungry?" He looked at the Timex on his wrist. Eight o'clock. He had fed her dinner, hadn't he? He brought his hand up to his temple, trying to think. Surely he'd given her something to eat. He had taken a bologna-and-cheese sandwich to his computer around six. He ate while he worked. But before that, he had brought her—

"I'm not hungry, Son. The soup was delicious. I was just a little thirsty. Thank you. You're a good boy."

Her lips were wet from the water, glistening, catching the rose light from the lamp with the frilly flowered shade. It looked for just a second to him like blood on her mouth.

Crazy. She was driving him crazy and didn't even know it. At least he had brought her dinner. He remembered now. The chicken-vegetable soup. That was good for an old woman, wasn't it? He probably should have made a green salad, too. He was *not* a good boy.

"Then I'll go back to work. Anything else you need while I'm here?"

She reached out a thin, blue-veined hand and shook her head. He took her old thin fingers into his cupped palms.

Her skin was cool and dry. He wondered if her heart was pumping the way it should. Her extremities were always so cold. He'd bet ten bucks her feet beneath the two quilts were icy as a mountain stream. She had a weak heart. A *diseased* heart. Too old and feeble for the surgeons to operate. She took medicine that kept her alive, kept the battered, broken, tired old organ beating. For how long? Oh God, for how long would he have to be her nursemaid?

"You go," she said, withdrawing her hand from him. "I'll be asleep in minutes. I'll listen to the talk shows on the radio a while."

He nodded, reached for the On knob of the radio before she could make the move. He adjusted the volume, leaned to kiss his mother's papery cheek, and left her alone.

Maybe he should install an intercom in the house, he thought, making his way through the rooms to his study. Or at least give her a bell she could pick up and ring. She didn't like calling out for him. She hated imposing on his time. She was so sweet. So good. So . . .

She was so awful, weighing a hundred and four pounds, nothing but bones in a sack of sagging skin, not enough energy anymore to get up from bed and go to the toilet alone. Soon she wouldn't be able to wash herself. Or make it down the hall to the bathroom. Then there would be bedpans and maybe IVs and piss bags hanging off the side of the bed. There might be baby food jars and protein supplement powders to mix and hours where he couldn't leave her alone.

He found himself standing in the middle of the study staring at the blue screen of his computer, his hands clenched, his brow dimpled with sweat.

"I'll listen to the talk shows," he mimicked, his voice low and frail and feminine. As if that was news to him. She *always* listened to the talk shows. Strangers' voices, her best, most dependable companions.

He stared fiercely at the computer screen. How could he work anymore when she interrupted him this way? How could he be expected to create a puzzle for his amateur sleuth to solve when he never had a block of time to himself where he could *think?* The publisher wanted this book, the fifth in the Eddie Lapin series, by September. He had exactly one chapter written and it was June already.

He sat down in the swivel chair and faced the screen, his hands positioned on the keyboard. CHAPTER TWO headed the page. What came next? Below the chapter heading the cursor blinked, blinked. Waited. Blinking. True, he needed something to copy. So far he had just reintroduced Eddie and established the setting. He had not yet brought in the dead body and the suspects. No one knew or noticed, not his agent, his editor, or his small but dedicated following of readers, but every one of his books were stolen works. He had a whole wall of old novels from which to choose his plots and characters. He carefully changed enough so that his work would be hard to recognize as being plagiarized from other works in print, but they were nothing more than rehashed, updated stories from books that were published in the thirties and forties. Books by authors long dead, authors no one had ever heard of or remembered.

He was just about to pull down one of those dusty old mysteries when Mother had called for water.

Now he wasn't in the mood, wasn't in the mood at all. She had destroyed his concentration completely. Not meaning to. She was thirsty. He shouldn't blame her. She was sick, she was old, she was incapable of walking to the kitchen without help. She was his *mother.*

But she still managed to screw up his days and nights just as if she were a badgering, hateful, spiteful old thing pulling him down. To hell with ''didn't mean to.'' Fuck ''didn't mean to and couldn't help it.''

He pushed away from the computer desk and found to-day's newspaper where he had dropped it that morning on the library table in the center of the room. He unfolded it, turned to the page where they carried the police reports. His pulse rate stepped up. He could feel the blood noisily racing in his head.

One breaking and entering.

A brawl and shooting at a bar.

Reported rapist loose in southwest Houston.

His blood slowed. His breathing took on an even, easy rhythm. No serial killings yet.

It wasn't time. The killer, whoever he was, would come. In a city as big as Houston there was always one at work somewhere. He just had to wait, had to notice the pattern. He liked to get in on it before the police or the media picked up on the fact they had a serial killer on their hands. He very much liked being in on the ground floor.

That smile he didn't think he had in him wound its way from his dark interior to his lips and transformed Son's round, dour face into that of a cherub. Every mother would have loved him had she witnessed that genuine, sweet smile.

Five

Charlene wouldn't let Kay go. "Can I call you sometimes? You'll have a phone, won't you? Will you come to visit me? If I get out soon, can I come see you?"

Kay felt guilty. She liked Charlene, believed whether it was true or not that it was Charlene who had saved her from a lifetime in that shadowy world where she had walked with ghosts. Now she was leaving the state mental ward and Charlene had to stay behind. The reality of it caused Kay to pinch the top of her nose to keep from crying.

She had asked Dr. Shawn if she could take Charlene from the hospital, be responsible for her. But he said no, that was too much of a burden; she would need all her resources to survive out in the world. Besides, he said, Charlene Brewster wasn't ready. Maybe she would be in another month or so, but not yet. She periodically was set free, but invariably returned to Marion State when life got too rough out on the streets.

"I'm going back to Houston," Kay said to Charlene. "I don't know if I can visit that often."

"Oh, hon, I know how hard it's going to be, I shouldn't have even asked, but I'm gonna miss you, and if I could just call once in a while . . ."

It occurred to Kay that once on her feet she could then help Charlene, repay her for part of the debt owed her. "When I get a place, and when they let you out, you come down to Houston, and we'll stay together."

"You mean it? You really mean it? Honest to God and cross your heart, you mean it? I'd have a place to stay and everything? I can cook, you know. I can cook real good.

And I could clean up and wash the clothes and do anything you wanted me to do.'' Excitement at the prospect heightened Charlene's color from pale ivory to blushing pink. She jiggled on the balls of her feet as if she were about ready to sprint across the room whooping out the news. "I've never had a roommate before. Not even a real friend. I could be a good friend, Shadow, you know I could, you know I was your friend here. I wouldn't get in your way and I'd never fight with you . . .''

This litany would have gone on had not Kay stepped forward and put her arms around the other woman to stem the flow. "I know, I know," she murmured. "Don't worry, you're going to be all right here. And I'll find us a place. You work hard and be good and I'll do the rest.''

Charlene stepped back from the embrace, her facial tics easing, her nervousness falling away from her like a caul pulled free. "You're the best person I ever knew," she said. "I don't think I ever knew anybody good as you.''

Kay smiled. "That's not true, Charlene, but I'm glad you think it anyway. We're going to be great partners, wait and see.''

In the car with Dr. Shawn on the way to the bus station, ticket clutched tightly in hand, Kay watched the hospital grounds slide past the windows. She had felt so confident when she talked with Charlene about the future. Now facing the reality of that future made her uneasy.

"I don't know how to be a maid," she said, blurting out her anxiety. "I'm scared of being on my own.''

"Now, now, don't panic, Kay. I've talked with the manager of the best maid service in Houston, and she's promised you a job. You're going to do fine, just fine.''

But a maid? Kay thought. What sort of job was that? Yes, it would pay a little more than the minimum-wage jobs she might find on her own, and she wasn't too good to clean someone else's house, that wasn't it. She just feared the prospect of this new life that had dropped her so suddenly toward the bottom of the social scale. How should she behave? What if the people didn't like her or they found out she'd been in Marion for over a year? She had offered a home to Charlene. Someway she'd have to live up to that promise. She would find some way to survive.

Once the doctor drove them off the hospital grounds, a bright, buoyant confidence took over where she had just been entertaining thoughts of failure. She straightened in the seat, and when Dr. Shawn looked over at her, she smiled. She sure didn't want to waste another year of her life. She would let the hospital help her find work and make her plans as she got onto her feet. She could use the money from the job to have her hair styled. She could join a health club, get herself into shape. She wouldn't have to remain a maid all her life. Was she too old for dancing? She glanced surreptitiously at her reflection in the car's side mirror. She looked younger than her true age. She looked sallow, too, and a little haunted. Frightened. She'd have to lose that look.

"I'll do all right," she said, breaking the silence. "The important thing is to get myself together."

"That's right, Kay. That's what I wanted to hear. You're a capable young woman. Your life isn't over."

She wanted to argue that point but chose not to. It was men who continued to ruin her. They deceived, betrayed, and murdered her love and her children. As soon as she was on her own in Houston she meant to call her mother-in-law in New Orleans. Scott, in ten years of marriage, had never taken her to visit the woman. His father was dead, and he was an only child, so she thought it extremely odd they never went to see his mother.

It wasn't that far to New Orleans from Houston. She suggested they go there on vacation or at Christmastime, but he always managed to lure her elsewhere. Canyon Lake and a camping trip in the hill country of Texas. Canoeing down the rapids of New Braunfels. Once they went to Disney World in Orlando. But never to see his mother. All she had known of the woman were the infrequent telephone calls that came once every two or three years. And then Scott spoke to his mother in grave tones, carrying the extension phone with him into the bedroom for privacy. Mrs. Mandel had never seen her own grandchildren. Had she been at the funerals? Had anyone attended them?

Before anything could be set at peace in her life, Kay had to discover the source of Scott's madness. It had something to do with *his blood,* that's what he said to her. And now she knew it had something to do with the mother he deliberately neglected and kept separate from his life.

As the car moved through downtown Austin, Kay closed her eyes a little and let the exterior world shimmer and blur. She missed her home. She wished she were returning to it, but no, she never could have gone home again, not with the boys' bloodstains on the den carpet, or would they have taken it up by now? She would never know. Shawn had softly explained to her that she had lost the house. Repossessed due to her illness and because there was no one to make the mortgage payments. Scott's life insurance policy didn't pay on suicide. The state had taken over and buried her husband and sons. Everything had been sold to pay off debts. She had nothing. Not a checking account or any savings. Not property or insurance money. Nothing. She could draw a small check from Scott's pension fund, plus Social Security, but it wouldn't be enough to live on.

Shawn was an old-fashioned gentleman who made her sit in the passenger seat until he came around the car to open her door. He walked her into the bus station. When he said good-bye and wished her luck, he took one of her hands and pressed a prescription bottle of Valium into it. Though she protested she didn't need the tranquilizers, he said go ahead, keep them, you might need them after all and it's better to be safe than sorry. He asked her to call him if she needed help or advice. He waved at her window as the bus pulled away from the station. She took the prescription to the bathroom at the back of the bus when they were two blocks from the bus station. She flushed all the little tablets down the toilet and put the empty bottle back into her purse.

He had told her she was strong. She didn't feel strong. She felt physically weak, almost ill, her stomach full of butterflies like a girl leaving home for the first time, her hands shaking. She put her thumb into her mouth and chewed at the nail. Caught herself and jerked it out again. No. She shouldn't mutilate herself like that. People would think she was nuts.

She'd find something besides the maid's job in Houston to keep her mind off the children. She would go to the gym and, no matter what it took, get her body in shape again. She did a mental assessment of her body and thought it wasn't bad. She had never been overweight, and bearing the children had left no stretch marks on her fine skin. Not so much luck as a strict regimen of exercise during pregnancy, keeping the weight down, and using oils on her expanding belly. Maybe she could find a nice little apartment and decorate it in mauve and gray. . . . No. She wouldn't decorate it to look like her lost home. She'd let Charlene decorate it, that's what she'd do. She'd find a job and make some money, Charlene would keep house.

Regrets. So many of them. She should have forced Scott to talk to her about his mysterious relationship with his mother. She should have called someone when he began acting strangely. She should have gone to school before the children were born so if something happened to Scott, she could support her family. And she had done nothing, but let it happen. It was as much her fault, almost, as it was Scott's. She had never prepared herself for life, and even less for loss and misfortune. She had *known* they didn't give jobs—had she needed one—to mothers and housewives. They had no need of them at all. Women hardly ever did those jobs anymore, except on a part-time basis. She had let herself become an anachronism. She was about as worthless and unneeded as an extinct species.

The thumb crept back to her mouth and she gnawed on the nail as the miles rolled past.

She was just a little scared, that's all. And that was natural. She wasn't backing out now. She had plans. If she took them one at a time, she could handle anything. Other people found a means for coping after suffering tragedies and deaths. She wasn't so different.

She blinked at the sudden, coppery taste of blood and jerked her thumb from her mouth.

She laughed and the man across from her flinched in his seat by the window. He looked over, frowning. She frowned back until he turned away.

All right, so she wasn't altogether one hundred percent absolutely normal and sane, and she had a compulsion to bite the skin from her fingers, and she was scared shitless, but . . . but . . .

She could still find a way to live.

The next time her thumb moved up to her lips, she put her hands beneath her hips and sat on her burning fingers.

Houston wasn't far now. Here I come, ready or not.

She daydreamed about a little apartment with a balcony full of flowers, her new job a nice, easy one where they paid her enough to cover all her expenses, and life began taking on some kind of shape and meaning again. Charlene was there with a feather duster and a recipe book. Somewhere a wise person waited to tell her all about what had happened that day and why. God whispered in her ear at night that the children were safe and free of pain, free of fear and suffering. Scott was there with God and he was being taught what he had done wrong, where he had erred, and he was sorry, he was prostrate with grief for his sins. All she had to do was move forward through the days and the days took care of her. The questions were going to be sorted and answered. She would find new spirit and hope. Life was bountiful again and the future was more than a black deadly wall waiting for her to run into it.

That's what she had to think.

So she wouldn't lose her way again through the fog.

Before the bus reached Houston, her hands were once again free, and she gnawed at the pinky finger of her right hand.

By the end of the day Kay had a room in a cheap boardinghouse near downtown Houston, not far from the bus station. Twenty-five bucks a week, bath down the hall, no one could use the kitchen. She unpacked her few things, carefully setting out the two silver-framed photos of Gabriel and Stevie on top of a rickety chest of drawers. She ate a cheese sandwich and tomato soup in a downtown diner, and when she paid, she asked for five dollars' worth of quarters. Outside the diner she stepped into a telephone booth that was open to the traffic and held the receiver close to her ear. She called Information and found her mother-in-law's phone number. Her hands shook as she dialed it. It rang once, twice, three times. Her palm began to sweat and she changed the phone to her other ear so she could wipe her hand on her skirt.

A bum passed close by and saw her pile of quarters on the phone stand. He held out his hand to her. She made a face at him and shooed him away with her free hand.

On the fifth ring the phone was picked up on the other end. "Mrs. Mandel?" Kay asked.

"Who? Who do you want?"

She had to speak louder. The evening traffic was horrendous. "Is this Mrs. Mandel? Scott's mother?"

"It is. But my son is dead. What is this about?"

Kay shuddered. "This is Kay."

"Hey?"

"Kay. Katherine Mandel, your son's wife."

"He killed your kids," she said without pause, but her voice lowered as if in respect for the dead. "I thought he might, it was always in the back of my mind, and I was scared all the time for them."

Mystified, Kay said, "Why didn't you ever warn me? What was wrong with him? You've got to tell me why he shot my boys and then himself right in front of my face, did you know he did that? He said it was because of something in his blood. What did he mean by that, can you tell me? I have to know why he did it."

"His father died a raving maniac, took a shotgun to himself, pulled the trigger with his big toe. Scott was just a little boy, five or so. Scott found him in the garage where he did it. I was at work. Neighbors had to call the ambulance. Later Scott's cousin Brucie got cancer and blamed his whole family. They found them stabbed to death in the kitchen. My sister-in-law, her husband, and Brucie's two brothers and one sister. Piled them up in the middle of the kitchen floor, how do you like that?

"But me, it wasn't me. None of my side ever did nothing crazy like that, let me tell you. We come from Georgia, good stock, and except for my granddad who was supposed to have shot a couple of niggers worked with him on the WPA, there never was any mental defectives on my side. I expect that's what Scott was talking about in the blood and all. And it was, too. He done the same thing his father did. I wanted to tell you about it, but he wouldn't never let me talk to you."

Kay hung on to the phone as if to a lifeline, the blood draining from her face. She felt faint. The bum was back hanging around the glass side of the booth, beckoning to her, pointing at the quarters. "I have to go," Kay said, fearing she might fall to the floor of the booth and be vulnerable to robbery by the bum or anyone else who happened by this busy street. A man riding in a pickup truck leaned out and whistled at her. She wiped sweat from her forehead. "I have to go now."

"It weren't my fault," Mrs. Mandel was screaming over the receiver. "I told Scott to be careful, he had bad genes in him, he might do something terrible someday, but he never listened to me, he wouldn't even let me come see my own grandchildren, I had to wait until they were in sealed caskets going into the ground, that awful Texas ground—"

Kay hung up and pressed her face against the booth's wall. The glass was cool to her feverish skin. She turned, stumbled from the booth. She had to remember where her room was, where she lived now. She halted, remembering she'd left the rest of her change in the booth. When she turned she saw the bum scuttling away into a weedy overgrown acre that separated the diner and an apartment complex. To hell with it.

Afternoon had shaded rapidly to evening while she had listened to Scott's mother, and now a ribbon of lights from the traffic showed her the sidewalk. She had to get to her room. She had to forget what Mrs. Mandel had told her. She hadn't been able to think directly about what Scott had done ever since she'd come back to herself in Marion State.

She had walked around the edges and peeked at it from out of other thoughts that crowded her mind, but she never took a good look at it head-on. She couldn't. Not and stay sane.

She *knew* what he had done, and she *remembered* the sounds of the gunshots and the color of the blood, but she never allowed herself to see all the pieces together, never approached that scene in her memory too closely because it would swamp her with grief and submerge her with sorrow. She would never climb from that pit if she went into it again.

The first man in her life was a liar and a cheat. She married a man twenty years her senior when she was just seventeen. Her mother said don't do it, you're making a big mistake, it won't work. But he was wealthy, she was poor. He offered her a home, a future, security. All the wrong reasons, and she had suffered the consequences. After a year she suspected him of philandering—late business meetings, out of town trips, cooling ardor—and she called him on it. "You think marriage means fidelity?" he had asked, laughing at her. "Not for me, Kay. I'm way too old for that sort of thinking."

When next he left their Memorial home she broke the windows, destroyed every beautiful object in the house, smashed the furniture, and ripped the carpet from the floorboards. The divorce was final before the ink could dry.

Then she had married Scott Mandel, a man who seemed honest and loving but was hiding the secret of a history of suicide and murder. While she was working at Babe's, a high-class exotic dance club that drew the businessman and his clients, Scott had come through the door with some coworkers. They left without him. After a few months of dogged pressure, some movies, the theater, quiet dinners, she decided to chance it again. Scott wasn't wealthy, he was closer to her age, and he promised to be faithful.

He never told her there might be a problem. He let her have their children without telling her. He harbored the idea that one day he, too, would go insane and kill, but he never tried to prevent it, and he carried his secret so long, with such utter deceptiveness, that she never had a clue. Not until the end.

Was that the reason he had chosen her, a young girl who danced in a topless club, a girl without education or experience of the world, so that she would never decipher what it was that made him tick? He wanted someone stupid, someone who might overlook his reluctance to see his mother, someone who was gullible and willing to do anything he wanted, agree to anything he said.

She hated him now with a fury she could barely contain. She buried her fingers in her clenched fists as she walked, head down, following the sidewalk, ignoring the traffic and the occasional catcall from the open car windows of passersby. There was no way to get back at Scott. The release she had felt upon destroying her first husband's home allowed her to retain a shred of dignity. She had paid him back for the pain he inflicted. But with Scott, there could be no act of revenge.

She shook her head furiously, hair whipping her cheeks, tears of pure frustration running down over her chin and into the hollow of her neck. If she could get hold of Scott now, she'd kill him herself. She would have killed him without hesitation had she known what he was planning to do to her children. She didn't care if he was responsible legally or not, if he had been insane or not, she blamed him for everything, from the day he walked into Babe's until the day he shattered her fairy-tale life. The boys were all she really had, all she had really ever wanted. Being a mother fulfilled her like nothing ever would again. He never should have fathered her children! He never should have taken the chance!

Hate and rage burned her cheeks and made them red. Her blood pressure soared, and her clenched hands shook at her sides as she stalked to the nearby boardinghouse that smelled of old women and unclean sheets. Up the stairs, into her room, closing the door, she stood still, wishing she could lash out at someone or something to release the building fury that bubbled close to the surface of her mind. She rushed across the tiny room and grabbed the pillow, began beating it relentlessly against the sagging mattress of the bed. She beat it until the pillowcase tore and the pillow went flying across the room to land with a smack against the wall.

Standing there holding the case bunched in her hands, she glared into the darkness and saw red, the red of blood, the red of murder, the red of betrayal and lies and dying young.

Had a man, any man, stepped into her room at that moment, Kay Mandel would have turned on him and clawed open his throat with her nail-bitten and savaged fingers. Nothing in the world would have been able to stop her. It was men who left their women to raise children alone the way her father had left her mother. Men who took mistresses and thought it their divine right to do so. Men who took up guns and . . .

Men who were the enemy.

❧ Six ❧

Kay arrived at the Severenson Maid Service offices promptly at nine when her appointment with the manager was scheduled. There was a brief interview, but the job was already really hers due to Dr. Shawn's earlier phone calls to the company. Kay filled out the W-2 forms, papers for health insurance, and was told her pay was seven dollars an hour, time and a half for overtime.

She was put into another room, a small cubicle with one chair and a television with a video recorder sitting alongside it. There for the next hour she watched dully as the duties of a Severenson maid were detailed. An actress in a maid's uniform went through the motions. Kay thought she wasn't having much fun. Greeting the client at the door, making sure the uniform—traditional black with a white skirt and white cap—was in order, no gum in the apron pocket, no cigarettes, hair put up off the neck, shoes clean and shined. If there was a list left by the client, the maid was supposed to do those chores first, what Severenson called "special chores, always done in good humor and with an obedient smile." That did not negate the fact she was responsible for cleaning toilets, tubs, doing one load of laundry, vacuuming, dusting, bed making, and general tidying up. The video hurried the actress through these chores, showing just the beginning of them, and then the results. A perfectly clean and orderly household. Sparkling like new. A glory to behold.

Kay yawned but watched the tape through, and outside in the outer office again was given two uniforms, two caps, two aprons. Size seven. She was to begin tomorrow. She was paid every Friday. She was not to be late to a client's home, and she was not to fraternize with either the woman or the man of the house. Her job had sharp parameters, these to be met precisely by Severenson rule and regulation.

Kay hated it before she left the personnel office. She knew how to endure, however, and that was part of the plan. She realized she was too old for dancing again, her competition being eighteen- and twenty-year-old women with unsullied bodies, with bellies tight as the skin of basketballs and breasts as big as softballs. Yet if there was a minuscule chance of dancing onstage again, she would prefer it to being a maid. At least dancing was something she knew, it was familiar. And in some way she instinctively understood, dancing in a G-string demeaned the voyeuristic men more than it did the dancer. Cleaning the beautiful residences of Houston's rich made her feel like a slave. There was no advantage in it, no power over men.

At the first house she was sent to, Kay was greeted at the door not by a grown person, but a child. A little boy hardly tall enough to have opened the door. He stood there in navy blue short pants and a crisp white shirt, staring at her with big liquid brown eyes. "Hi," he said. "My mother's in the bathroom."

Kay froze. He was the first child she had seen since her own children had died. There were no children in the section of Marion she had been kept in. No children on the bus to Houston. No children at the boardinghouse, not with all those old women living on their retirement checks. For the first time since the horror of Gabriel and Stevie's death, she faced a child, a boy child who reminded her strongly of her own dark-haired sons. She could not speak or move. She could not swallow or draw breath.

She wanted to die.

A tall woman wearing an orange sundress and an orange headband to match placed her hands on the boy's shoulders and pulled him toward her into the entranceway. "Oh, I see you're right on time," she said to Kay. "I've always been able to depend on Severenson for good people. Please come in. This is Andrew. Say hello, Andrew."

"Hi," he said again, giving her a mischievous smile.

"My mother isn't in the bathroom now."

"Oh, Andrew! You'll have to forgive him, he's at that stage where he says anything that comes into his head." She stooped to admonish the boy. "That isn't polite to tell strangers when Mommy is in the bathroom. All right?" He nodded, and she stood to usher Kay inside and closed the door. The house opened out from the tiled entrance into a modern, airy cathedral space with a two-story ceiling and a balcony overhang that looked over the living area.

"Andrew and I will be gone until noon or one. If you finish by then, you can lock the front door from the inside on your way out. I don't have any special things for you to do, just, uh, you know, clean it up the best you can."

She waved a bejeweled hand around the room at the scattered stacks of magazines, newspapers, two empty cups and saucers on the wood-and-brass coffee table. Kay had lived like this once, privileged, her home more a thing to show off to business partners than a place for living. Her first husband had come back to find it wrecked. And it had certainly served him right. She wondered idly if this woman ever checked up on her husband's late hours at the office, his "business" trips.

Kay had not yet said anything, she had not been able to. She kept seeing her sons, holding them, cherishing them, loving them. She saw them laughing, bathing, playing with their toys on the den floor. She couldn't withdraw from the past when the past held her so rigidly in its grasp.

"Do you think you'll be able to find your way around? The cleaning supplies are in the kitchen on the counter, I set them out for you, and in the downstairs bathroom, again on the counter so you could find them. All right?"

Andrew had sidled over to where Kay stood mute near the coffee table, and now he took the loose fingers of her right hand into his own. She glanced down at the touch and her smile was beatific. "He's a beautiful boy," she said to the mother. "Such lovely eyes. Brown."

The woman wasn't listening. She had found her purse on the entrance table and the keys to her car inside. She was gesturing Andrew to hurry. "We've got your piano lesson and then we have to meet Daddy for lunch. Hurry up now, we don't want to be late.''

When the front door closed, the latch snicking shut, Kay shook herself as if she were coming in from a rain shower. She didn't know how long she could stand this. She wondered if every child she saw would affect her so keenly, or if it would be just boy children. What about little girls, or babies? Did everyone she might clean for have children? How could she bear it if they did?

Rage again filled her, coming up from her gut to her torso and finally suffusing her brain until the room turned red. She blinked, unclenched her fists. She made herself walk through the house to the kitchen for the cleaning products. She did a load of dishes in the dishwasher, cleaned the white counter, mopped the red-tiled floor. She had to finish before noon. She wanted out of this house and away from another meeting with Andrew. Next time she might break down and weep. She might lose her job. She might never come out of this as a survivor. Damn it, if she would let that happen.

Severenson sent her to other homes the rest of the week, but she realized she'd be servicing the one with Andrew in it every Monday, regardless. The four other homes she cleaned did not upset her quite as much. One of them had three teenage girls living in it with their parents. It was a tougher job, but at least she didn't fight off waves of nausea thinking about her sons. Two of the houses were occupied by professional couples too young and too work oriented to think about bringing children into the world. The fourth house had a single mother who seemed to be at work all the time, leaving her three-year-old daughter in the care of an elderly aunt. The little girl tugged at Kay's heartstrings, but not nearly as badly as Andrew did.

It was Andrew who reminded her too much of her loss, and it was Andrew who made her feel tortured every minute she spent in his home, even when he was not there. In his room she would catch herself immobile, staring at his bed made in the shape of a racing car, or find one of his Tonka toys on the carpet and stand holding it like a talisman until her eyes burned. In the boy's closet she could spend an hour touching his little shirts and trousers or holding his pajamas close to her face so she could inhale the baby scent he had not yet lost.

With her first week's paycheck, Kay started going to an exercise club not far from downtown. It wasn't as good as the Houston Racquet Club or some of the more expensive exercise arenas in the city, but they had enough equipment, and the men didn't bother her as long as she didn't look at them much. One of the employees, a muscle-bound hunk with surfer blond hair tried to put the make on her the first time she came in, but she took him aside and whispered, "If you come on to me one more time, if you even raise your eyebrow my direction, I'm going to the management and report you, then I'll ask for a full refund of my membership fees. They won't be happy with you. Do you fully understand what I'm saying to you?"

He steered clear of her after that, though he still stole looks her way when he thought she wouldn't notice.

She had to take buses everywhere she went or sometimes, when it wasn't far, she walked, but she meant to remedy that soon. She had her eye on a used Toyota in a car lot she passed on the way to the diner. If she scrimped and saved, if she remained in the run-down boardinghouse with the old ladies, ate sandwiches two and sometimes three times a day, she'd be able to get her body into shape and still save enough for the car.

She called Charlene at the end of the first month she was out of the hospital. "I'm getting it all together," she said, hoping she sounded happy. "I have a job, which I hate." She laughed a little to soften her words. "But this job will afford me the things I need to get out of it. I'm getting a car in another month so we'll have transportation. It isn't much, about ten years old, but it's a Toyota and they run forever. So, how are you doing? Are you all right?"

Charlene babbled on and Kay stopped listening after ten minutes, but she held the line and waited patiently, glad she had someone who *wanted* to talk to her. "I'll call you again next month. If they start talking about letting you out, call me at the boardinghouse, I'll give you the number, okay?'' What Kay didn't say was that she hoped Charlene didn't get out until things were more under control. They needed the car. You couldn't get around in Houston without one. The Metro Transit System worked, but it took a lot of time to get anywhere, and the men on it seemed to think they were destined to flirt with every pretty woman they saw. She spent all her riding time brushing off men and giving icy stares that would have shriveled the hottest desire.

Kay also needed another place to live. She worked out like crazy, every day after work until eight or nine at night. She had one pair of cheap black spandex pants and a top that she bought at the Woolworth's store downtown. She had to wash out the set every night in the hall sink at the boardinghouse, then hang them in the window of her room to dry overnight. After a month she had saved two hundred dollars toward the purchase of the car, and her muscle tone was coming back in her arms and legs. She stood five feet six, weighed a hundred and twenty. Her waist needed a little work, had to get those inches off, so she switched from sandwiches to salads and cups of yogurt. She still had to have her hair cut and styled.

Every night when she returned to her depressing room with the peeling cabbage-rose wallpaper and the veneered chest of drawers, she stood looking at herself critically in the strip of mirror nailed to the closet door. With the overhead light on, she examined her face for telltale signs of aging. No wrinkles. No deep crease lines yet. She was blessed with good bone structure that would shield her from looking her age for a few years to come. Her hair was thick and lush, but she worked at it, brushing the shoulder-length tresses a hundred times every night before bed. She washed it with beer and lemon juice. She used the best conditioners. It was beginning to shine like wet slate and have the bounce of health when she flung her head.

She sucked in her little round tummy and sighed with despair. Had to get that flat again. Do more sit-ups and bend-overs. Her buttocks had not sagged, driven by gravity earthward, not yet. They rode high without leaving a smooth line sloping to her thighs. She soaked her feet in Epsom salts, rubbed lotion into them, trimmed her nails. She couldn't do much about her hands yet. At any time when they weren't working inside rubber gloves with cleaning solutions, she found them slipped into her mouth where she gnawed at the stubby nails. Maybe if she dipped her fingertips in Tabasco sauce. It was a thought. If that didn't work, she would simply go to a salon and have them put nail wraps on.

She had to be perfect. She could not, would not, dared not be a maid the rest of her life. She could not continue seeing Andrew—or any other male children—who tore at her heart and dazed her with fresh sorrow every time she looked at them. It would kill her. Or cause her to kill some-one else.

The feeling was frightening and awesome in its intensity, but she had trouble being around men now. It had started with the job, the same as her reaction to the children. When there was a man in the house, she fought an urge to jump him, to wrestle him to the floor and plunge a knife through his heart. Any man, it didn't matter, but usually she felt this sudden craving to destroy when the man was a father of small children. She had less animosity toward the father of the teenagers in the house where she cleaned once a week.

But still it was there, that feeling of losing something that held the world in check, losing it to the point that she might pick up something and hurl it or smash it . . . or stab it clear through flesh and bone.

It was crazy, she knew that. But it made perfect sense at the same time. Fathers were irresponsible. They never loved their children as much as mothers did. They were stick figures who moved through a family with the role pulled over their heads but not their hearts. They could not be trusted. They might do something irredeemable at any mo-ment. Kay suspected all of them of child abuse or incest or hidden motives aimed toward children that involved sexual gratification or violence.

Once she stood on the stairway leading down from the balcony in Andrew's house and saw his father enter, a briefcase tucked under one arm. He scooped little Andrew up into his free arm and laughed in his face. She stood stock-still, her breath caught tight as if inside a steel cage, while she watched the father carry the boy through to the living room sofa and dump him unceremoniously into the cushions. Andrew laughed, thrilled, but Kay knew in his heart he must have been terrified. So high up! Such a long drop! Such a terrible hazard to endure! What if he had fallen from his father's arms onto the parquet floor and busted open his skull? What if he had rolled from the cushions and fallen into the sharp glass corner of the end table?

That father was irresponsible and unheeding of his son's safety. Kay took a deep breath finally and walked down the stairs one at a time, watching her step, keeping her eyes from the now-tousling father and son in their act of play. She moved past a sideboard where her fingers reached out and slid along a silver candelabra, on past to the base of a thick-necked pottery vase painted with green vines winding around it. She paused, listening to the sounds behind her, the laughter and giggling, but there were possibilities those sounds could change to screams of slaughter. She wanted to yell, "Don't trust him, Andrew! He might kill you! He's so big and strong, he might hurt you! Run from him while you have the chance!"

As she stood quietly, fingers brushing the vase, the father took up Andrew again and marched past her into the kitchen. In passing he said, "Hello, Kay, how are you today?" Then he said to his son, "Let's get a bowl of ice cream, whatta you say, champ? You won't tell Mom, will you?"

Kay turned her back, whipping around so fast her black taffeta skirt swished against her thighs. She ran to the hall closet and grabbed her purse, snatched the maid's silly white hat from her hair, and was out the door on her way home without saying good-bye.

She worked harder and harder at the health club. They told her she was going to pay, she was pushing too hard, too fast, but she didn't care. It felt good to have pain, to lose herself in it. At night she lay on top of the sheets and stared at the cracked ceiling overhead stippled with shadows from the streetlights. Her back and stomach hurt, her legs and shoulders, her neck and arms. But she was looking good. Better than she had in ten years. No one would ever know she had been the mother of two children.

No one would ever have guessed.

Mitchell Samson walked into the Hot Spot at a quarter after ten on a Saturday night when the place was packed and jumping. He found an empty table close to the men's room. He ordered the Irish coffee and turned his attention to the stage. He'd never seen the place this lively. What the hell could be the new attraction? She must be a knockout.

Not the girl onstage. She was Babycakes and the regulars knew her. Great and sexy, but no Jezebel.

He scanned the room and gauged the temperature. It was pretty steamy and rising. Guys were after the girls who served the tables. "Wanna go out with me after this joint closes? Want to make some money, honey? Want to make it with a real man?" All the old lines, all the old brushoffs. The dancers had to wait on the customers between gigs, and they had their hands full tonight.

He turned his gaze back to Babycakes, who was winding up her dance. He hadn't noticed a new girl advertised on the posters in the glass cases outside the club. It had to be that, though. This place never pulled such a crowd, even on a Saturday night. Maybe she was so new they hadn't done any publicity photos yet. Could be.

Interesting. Word had spread fast along the street. He had been in here just the week before and it was deader than roadkill.

Babycakes walked offstage with her tits swinging, her shoulders squared, and her G-string riding high. Mitchell admired her bravado in the face of whatever young woman had come along to draw the crowd. He put his hands together to clap for her loud and hard. The crowd joined in.

Good. The girl deserved some appreciation, that was obvious.

Could his favorite, Jezebel, have made it by word-of-mouth and drawn this mob? Is that who was about to part the curtains and mesmerize them the way she had him? That rankled. She was his devotion. He didn't much want to share her.

A song by Prince came over the music system and the men took a collective breath and held it. Mitchell had his cup of Irish halfway to his lips when she walked down the runway like Queen Cleopatra taking her place before her subjects. *Walked.* She didn't dance out. She didn't slink. She didn't vamp. The platter player said, "Gentlemen, we are proud to give you Shadow, the sensation of the nation, the dark side of the wild side. Only the Shadow knows which way the wayward wind blows. . . ."

Mitchell lowered the cup to the table with a shaky hand. He checked to see if his mouth was hanging open and it was. He shut it with a snap, his gaze glued to the stage.

Shadow did it all wrong and it worked anyway. It worked like gangbusters. The men who had come to see her, even those who were now drunk, didn't pull any stunts. They might have been statues, all turned to stone and gone to heaven. Faces softened, eyes glistened, jaws went slack, and eighty male heartbeats drummed as one, in love. Or lust. Or both.

She was a dark doll. She moved just slightly to the music, and she never looked at the audience. She kept her long lashes downcast. Her hands roved over breasts and waist, slid down hips and thighs. She took the center pole as if it were a lover while men ground their teeth and drew their muscles tight to keep from leaping onto the stage to carry her away. Shadow might have been alone in her own bedroom thinking the most exquisitely private sensuous thoughts for all the attention she gave the room full of men.

Mitchell couldn't believe his eyes. Her loveliness was something absolute and indisputable. She was a goddess, something come to life from myth. She was a queen, not flesh and blood. She had the movements, smooth but careful, that made the men lean forward toward her. She was of medium height, but not small, perfectly proportioned, the breasts behind the veil of pink nylon round and tilted, the nipples shockingly large. Skin the color of lightly stained birch, flawless, smooth, reflecting a soft sheen like the finest polished wood.

He watched her long hair sway, the black color so deep it could mirror a face on its surface. He watched her while she ignored the room, and when the song, a long one, drowned in its last note with a wail from Prince, she vanished, the curtains trembling from her passage through them.

Mitchell blinked. He looked around at the other entranced men. They came to their feet and a thunder rose from their stomping and clapping. He sat perfectly still wondering if he had seen what he thought he had seen. Of all the exotic dancers he had watched in this city over the years, he had never experienced such a loss when one left his sight to disappear behind the curtains.

"My God," he breathed. "Jesus jumping Christ."

Who and what was Shadow? A miracle of some sort, that's all she could be. An Eve walking the depths of the underbelly of the entertainment world.

Was she real?

He gulped down the Irish coffee and ordered another. He sat at the table, as did the rest of the audience, for the next four hours hoping to see Shadow again. He *had* to see her to be sure he had not been dreaming. But she did not dance another set and she did not wait the tables. They closed the place at two. Mitchell came out into the night with a stumble.

The dancers after Shadow were a blur, a distraction to him. He had drunk way too many whiskey and coffees. He was, by Jiminy and glory be, drunk as a goddamned skunk, hey, hey, whatta you say?

He called for a cab from the corner phone booth, knowing it was going to be a bitch to come down here on a Sunday morning to pick up his car.

At home, he had to fiddle with the door and the key for

ten minutes to make anything work. Pavlov almost knocked him down, butted his legs, whacked him with his back end, and Mitchell didn't even scold him. The dog, a well-trained boxer who could hold his water longer than a camel, barked to go out. Mitchell said, "Shut up, you crazy mutt, I gotta get some sleep," then promptly fell fully clothed onto the sofa.

After whining for a full five minutes to no avail, then sniffing at Mitchell's face before backing off at the scent of alcohol, Pavlov climbed onto the sofa and curled over his master's legs like a rumpled blanket.

He'd just have to hold on till morning.

⚜Seven⚜

She thought of herself as Shadow now. Kay? Katherine? That was another person in another life. Light years in the past. Buried in the graves of her children.

So when the manager, Bertram, called her back from the private exit door leading to the alley where her parked Toyota waited, she corrected him. "Call me Shadow," she said. "That's my name." She liked and had adopted the name because Charlene had given it to her. It fit her like no other could.

"Yeah, that's what I meant to say, sure you're Shadow, sure, baby. That was some performance tonight! Had them with their tongues hanging out. Now you could do a little more shaking and stroking, you know what I mean, but essentially, you got what it takes. I knew that the first time I saw you. I can spot 'em, don't think I can't. I ain't seen a crowd like this in years."

"Let me do it my way or I don't do it," she said, pushing open the door. "And since the boys liked me so well, I expect another fifty dollars a week."

"Now hold on one goddamn minute, I never said—"

"Fifty. Or I walk." She sucked in the night air, smiling to herself, glad to be out of the smoke-filled atmosphere of the club. Cheap perfume. Sweat. Stink. Bottom of the barrel stink. Some people said they loved humanity. What was there to love but the stink of them? Pawing, fawning sons of bitches, the whole lot. Men. They brought misery and pain and left behind bad tastes in the mouth and memories that broke your heart.

She was glad they hadn't known, though, how scared she was out on the stage. It was her second performance

and she had to psych herself but good to go out on that
garishly lighted stage wearing what she wouldn't be caught
dead wearing at home. In her *real* life. It was nothing like
the dancing she had done before in the elegant atmosphere
at Babe's. That was a class place that attracted a class clientele. The Hot Spot was about a hundred levels below
Babe's, down there in the stink, floating like scum in the
swill. She had tried the better places, but despite her work-
outs and muscle tone, despite her new stylish cut that let
her black glistening hair swing free around her face and
shoulders, they thought they just couldn't use her, sorry,
she was one helluva nice-looking woman, though, they'd
say that for her.

Well fuck them and their backhanded compliments. She
never really believed she could dance the better clubs anyway. She might not look thirty, but she also didn't look
eighteen either. She had a choice to make. Either continue
working for Severenson Maid Service and running into
families with children where she had to control her wild
urges to attack the fathers, or take a job dancing. Wherever
they would let her. There was no choice. Not unless she
wanted to go to prison for murdering an absolute stranger
just because he might accidentally drop his son or accidentally knock him aside when rushing out the door for work.

Charlene told her she could do it. Charlene believed in
her when no one else did. "You've gotten yourself all
dolled up," she said. "I don't think I've ever seen anyone
so pretty."

Before Charlene came from Marion, Kay was able to buy
the Toyota and move from the boardinghouse. A girl she
met at the gym told her about a place that needed a house
sitter. The girl worked as an apartment-locating represen-
tative, and this thing had come up, but no one wanted to
take it because of the house's reputation. Kay asked what
reputation was that, maybe she'd be interested. She needed
something cheap.

"How's free sound? That cheap enough?" The girl
brushed streaked-blond hair from her eyes, reached over,

and gripped a couple of weights, her biceps popping and straining.

"Free? Like no rent?"

"It's free because the owner can't get anyone to stay in it. He just wants someone to be there while he's out of the country—off in Spain somewhere . . . Lisbon? Anyway, he's afraid the place is going to get trashed. Vandals, drug dealers, squatters—all that. It's already happened twice and cost him an arm and a leg to redo the place. He doesn't want any money out of it, the guy's rolling in dough, he just wants house sitters. Think you might do it? I get a commission anyway, the guy's paying us to find someone."

"Depends. What kind of reputation are you talking about? What kind of house and where is it?"

"Well, the reputation, see, is that the former owner was killed in it."

A flash of gunshot and blood crossed Shadow's vision momentarily. She swallowed, tried to concentrate.

"He was a queer, some kid killed him. But there aren't ghosts or anything, right? It's a mansion, a real mansion, honest. Big as a hotel. You could throw parties in there like you wouldn't believe."

Shadow wasn't interested in parties. She was interested in free rent, though. "So where is it?"

"Out in Seabrook. Near the water."

"God. That's way out. I'd have to drive forever."

The girl shrugged and put down the weights. When she bent over cleavage showed from the rim of her silver spandex top. The blond surfer walked by, head cranked her direction until Shadow gave him a look.

"Yeah, that's out of town, but it's a neat place, you ought to go check it out. I can't take it, I have a lease, but it's a real deal. All you have to do is keep it clean, don't break anything, and pay the electric bill."

"I can go look, I guess. When's the owner coming back?"

"Not for a year at least, maybe longer."

Shadow toured the house, loved it, and moved in the next weekend. She had a place for Charlene, and she didn't have to spend a bundle of money getting it. She didn't even have to lay out money for furniture.

There was just one problem. The mansion spooked Charlene. She thought it was cold and gloomy. It had too many rooms and echoed every time she walked through it. She mentioned voices, but Shadow tried to turn the conversation away from that.

She told her to look at the funny side of it. "What's funny about this mausoleum?" Charlene wanted to know.

"Well, we don't have much money, we're driving a ten-year-old Toyota with rusty rocker panels, but we get to live in a mansion big enough for ten families, and rich enough to please a millionaire."

Charlene made a *humph*ing sound, but she soon settled in and stopped complaining. It *was* better than nothing, she admitted. It was *lots* better than being locked up in Marion.

Living fifty miles out from the center of Houston, Shadow had to give up the exercise club. Instead she ran every day (around and around the mansion), and did sit-ups until she was soaked with sweat and blistering the walls with profanity at how much it hurt. She bought weights, an exercise table, and a stationary bicycle.

She hated driving the long distance in to the dance club, and the job was, to say the least, not one hell of a lot better than cleaning people's toilets for a living.

"Exotic dancing," Charlene said one day. "It pays great and you don't have to diddle with the guys if you don't want to."

"It's not as much fun as you think."

Charlene's eyes grew misty and she took on a faraway look. "Just about any kind of job has some fun in it. I wish I knew how to dance. I can't even follow the rhythm for a two-step. I always stepped on Louise's toes in the rec room. She hated being my partner."

"Dancing's dancing. It's no big deal. I'll teach you how to do the two-step one day."

Charlene brought her gaze back to Shadow's face. "You will?"

"Sure. Why not. Then you can go out to some shit-kicking country dance place and get some big ole cowboy with a ring of keys dangling from his back pocket to waltz you around the floor."

"Now you're kidding me."

"Not about those cowboys. They really do carry big ugly goddamn key rings."

Charlene laughed.

Shadow settled for five hundred a week to start out at the Hot Spot. She was told tips from couch and table dancing were all hers, but she couldn't trust herself to get that close to the patrons. She didn't want them touching her, or even trying to. All the moves came back to her after a couple of nights, but she was still a little stiff and shy. No one had seen her bare breasts except Scott for ten years. It was difficult to parade around undressed again after leading a normal life for so long.

The thought brought her up sharply. Normal life. How normal could it have really been when her husband carried the seeds of madness and destruction around in his brain like a cancer waiting to spread? Still. For a while, she had been deceived into believing she was living a normal life. Maybe that was the shame of it; it surely was why the shock was so complete.

Bertram said she'd have to do longer sets, but for right now she was on trial. She knew she'd get the extra fifty a week she had asked of him. And if she danced more than once, she'd up it another hundred, maybe two. "Sky's the limit, hon," Charlene told her. "You make them money, they pay to keep you."

On the way home to Seabrook, she picked up some Chinese from a Hunan restaurant. It was eleven-thirty when she walked into the mansion. She breathed in the scent of industrial-strength pine cleaner. It reminded her of the maid's job. She never thought she'd be able to look at a toilet again without thinking about cleaning under the rim.

She wrinkled her nose and went searching for Charlene. She found her in one of the four bathrooms down on her knees scrubbing tile. Shadow suspected that's how she spent all her waking hours—cleaning. It was Charlene who would have been a good maid. Here she had a big place to keep up. She'd stay busy. She might not start talking to unseen beings and hearing voices in her head if she had something to keep her occupied.

"Chinese! I love Chinese takeout. Did you bring chopsticks? I can eat with chopsticks, you know, and fortune cookies, did you get fortune cookies? Honey, I tell you, this is turning into a sweet deal. I almost believe I won't have to go back to Marion for a while, what with all this luck."

They camped around the big glass coffee table in the cold, cavernous living room and ate from the white cartons.

"They like you, don't they?" Charlene asked. "I told you they would. It's this sexy look you got. And that cut you got for your hair, it's perfect. You tried table dancing yet?"

"I don't want to do that." She stabbed an egg noodle with her fork and, holding her head back, inelegantly dropped it into her open mouth.

"Why not? They ain't allowed to touch you. They touch you, the management throws their asses out the door."

"I don't want to get that close. They're all a bunch of slime buckets and horny assholes. They wouldn't be in places like that if they weren't."

"You're there. And you ain't no slime bucket."

"I might be." The image of a bucket of slime flashed in her mind and it amused her so much she thought everything about their conversation funny as hell. She took a bite of an egg roll and grinned big so Charlene could see the cabbage leaves dangling from her bared teeth.

"You are not. You are the sweetest, kindest, best—"

"I'm a slut of the sluttiest kind." She tore off a piece of egg roll and slapped it to her forehead where it would stay stuck if she tilted backward just a bit. She stared at Charlene innocently, egg roll on her head.

"You are not. You're just the prettiest little—"

"I am the Whore of Babylon." She grabbed up some of the red sweet-and-sour sauce from the chicken entrée and smeared it onto her lips and cheeks.

Charlene couldn't help it, she couldn't be serious any longer. She burst out with a laugh that echoed overhead against the two-story ceiling and bounced off the yards and yards of white marble-tile floors.

Shadow pretended to ignore the mess she had dripping from her face while she took up a fortune cookie and cracked it open to delicately retrieve the little slip of paper inside. Charlene fell back onto her elbows she was laughing so hard.

Shadow arched her neck to keep the clot of egg roll from sliding past her eyebrow into her eye. She read aloud her fortune, "You will dance naked for money and men will leave slobber trails at your feet."

Now Charlene lost it completely and rolled between the coffee table and the white leather sofa. "Stop it, oh God, stop it, you're killing me. . . ."

Shadow swiped a trail of red sauce from her cheekbone and licked her finger. "You are a bona fide crazy person," she said.

Charlene's laughter turned into howls. She held her belly in place she laughed so hard. "I know! That's what they've been telling me for years," she screamed. "And I'm going to piss myself, too!"

"That's what I said. You're a bona fide pissy-panted crazy person. I always knew that."

Eight

At home Son lived a sedentary and withdrawn existence. When his mother insisted, he might sit with her and talk a while, but she knew he wasn't comfortable with idle chit-chat so she asked this of him less often as her health failed. Now confined most of her hours to the bed, she needed his company more—this was something he understood—but he possessed no road map to show him the way through the quagmire of what he thought of as her petty, daily concerns.

He went over this particular resentment now as he sat, like a prisoner held fast by invisible chains, in an over-stuffed easy chair across from her bed.

"How is the new book progressing?" she asked.

She fancied herself his source of encouragement and alleged to take great pride in his creative achievements. The problem remained. He had nothing to say to her, really, that he hadn't already said a hundred times before, and his fund of patience grew leaner the longer he felt obligated to sit in the chair, bound by her infirmity. "It's progressing slowly."

"Where are you sending Eddie Lapin this time?"

"Maybe to England."

She clasped together her spindly hands. "To England! London, you mean, like Sherlock Holmes?"

"No, Mother, to the moors. Off to the bleak, forbidding moors where heather grows and neighbors kill their neighbors."

"Well, that's still delightful. I'm sure your editor will love it, Son. It sounds like a perfectly grisly place for your detective to solve a murder."

"I suppose so." He counted the open crocheted flower petals in a doily spread over the chair arm. Five in each flower. Why hadn't she chosen six or four, why five? Why any at all? What was the purpose of a doily anyway? It was positively Victorian to have them draped over chair arms and backs, spreading like creeping lichens over table-tops and shelves. When she died he would—

The curious thought made him blink back sudden tears. He didn't hate her. He didn't want her to die. Not his own mother. He *loved* his mother. She was in all ways perfect and she had been good to him. How could he be such a shit and go about thinking of what he'd do when she died? Look how she cared about his livelihood and his interests.

Look how much time he was spending counting cro-cheted flower petals and wishing to be anywhere, anywhere at all, but here with her.

"I don't have it all worked out yet." He cleared his throat and swept the idea of what life would be like without her from his thoughts completely. "I don't know who the murderer is." *I haven't gotten that far into the book I'm copying.*

"Who are the suspects?" She had taken a fat pillow from her back and plumped it to press just behind her bony hips. He thought her color was good today. She wasn't as pale as usual.

"There's a mine worker and a handyman carpenter. There's the maid at the rectory. And there's a woman who is visiting from London, hoping to marry the local barrister."

"Why does she want to do that?"

He waved the question off with a hand. "I don't think it's her. She's too obvious. I expect it will have to be the rectory maid. She's incredibly jealous of the dead man's relationship with her Catholic priest. That's how she thinks of him—as belonging to her."

"She's in love with him then? Oh, that's so sad."

"Did you love my father?" He hadn't known he was going to ask that. He had heard over and over again from her that she had loved his father at one time. "At one time" never satisfied him. What happened to make her stop loving him, why didn't she ever tell him that? He deserved to know the details. The man was dead for all he knew, and he had never had the opportunity to meet him. He deserved all the details of their life together because he had been so cheated.

"I loved him at one time," she said carefully. He noticed her gaze had wandered from him to the wall just over his left shoulder. In order to lie to him more easily?

He sighed and began, little by little, bunching up the doily into his fist.

"Son, he was as good a man as he could be. He was thrilled when I found out, after trying for so many years, that I was going to have you." Now she was looking at him again. Perhaps some of this was truth.

"So why did you leave him months after I was born if he was a such a good man?"

"He became progressively . . . unkind."

"Unkind? Did he beat you or something?"

She shook her head and the cap of tight curls clung in place like a helmet. When she didn't continue, he prodded, "How was he unkind? You never told me that before."

"He couldn't help it. None of it was his fault. He was a nervous man. You have to remember that neither one of us were young anymore. A baby in the house . . . it just . . . he couldn't . . ."

"He hated me."

"No, Son! He never hated you."

"Then what happened? I think it's time you tell me, Mother. Past time."

It was her turn to sigh. She brought her gaze level with his and spoke softly. "He had a nervous condition."

Son shook his head, puzzled. "What does that mean? He had a nervous tic? He snapped his fingers at the dinner table? He paced floors?"

"Don't be flip. When I said 'nervous condition' I meant something quite a bit more serious and you knew what I meant." The scold left her voice when she continued. "Your father was prone to rages. I didn't know it until after we were married a while. And the rages were prompted by something no one could figure out. He lost his temper all the time. He had no control over it. Out of the blue he'd become thoroughly enraged, shouting at the top of his lungs so the neighbors could hear . . . smashing things . . ."

"He didn't hurt you?"

"He took it out on objects around him, never me. Your crying, and babies cry, they can't help it, but your crying sent him into cataclysmic anger. He would go through the house breaking chairs and china and anything else that got in his way. I'd try to soothe you, but the noise he made and his shouting frightened you so that you cried all the harder."

"What happened?"

"I left him. One day I packed our things while he was at work and I . . . left him."

"He never knew where you went?" He knew this part of the family history. They had skipped town, which at the time was Sacramento, California, and taken up residence in Houston, Texas. She was afraid his father would follow them. She lost touch with him forever.

"He never found us," she said. "Sometimes I think I should have tried to stay longer."

He thought so, too. Maybe then he might have met his father face-to-face.

"But he was too violent," she continued. "I was scared all the time. In the beginning he'd apologize and say he had had a bad day, he didn't know what was wrong with him, he wouldn't do it again. Yet the next day something would anger him and off he'd go, stomping around the house like a bull. It wasn't a good environment for a child. I did my best, Son. I'm sorry."

"Why didn't you ever tell me before? It would have made things more understandable."

"Do you want the truth or a convenient lie?"

He had the doily balled tight in his fist, knuckles showing white. "I want the truth, Mother." *Don't lie to me. You've been lying to me for years now.*

"I . . . I was afraid. I had to wait to be sure his condition . . . that you didn't . . ."

"What?" Though he was not so stupid that he didn't see where she was headed and what she was going to say to him, what he *expected* her to say; it caused flashing lights to go off in his brain, powder kegs of brilliance that numbed him.

"I didn't know if perhaps you had inherited—"

"You thought I'd be like him, didn't you? You wouldn't tell me because you had to see if I'd grow into a violent man, too. It was more than any 'nervous condition,' wasn't it? He was insane, or near enough to have been handed a medical certificate saying so."

Her gaze wandered away to the window where the hydrangea had shaken out great purple heads of blooms. "I didn't know what to think. I was . . . worried."

"Well, are you satisfied I'm not like him? I don't break things and I don't shout." Then he laughed and she turned back to him. "I just solve murder mysteries for a living. That's pretty violent."

She smiled now with him. "I love you, Son. If I could have given you your father, I would have endured almost anything. But it was hellish, it was a nightmare, and I couldn't subject you to that kind of household. You were my responsibility. I owed it to you to get us out before it was too late."

He kept his thoughts to himself about that. He would rather not discuss her motivation. He knew she needed his approval for it, however, so he stood from the chair, dropping the balled doily into the seat behind him, and he went to her bed. He cupped her old face in his big hands. He could smell the powder she sprinkled on her nightclothes. Prince Matchebelli's Windsong. Sweet, floral, heady. He kissed her lightly on the forehead. "Mother, I love you, too. You've always done your best."

Now he was released and free to clean the house. He must wash her clothes. He had a basket of ironing to finish. Tonight he must finish scanning *Death on the Moor* so that he could find out if it was the rectory maid who killed the victim.

On the way down the hall he again tripped on a fold in

the carpet. He dropped to his knees and beat it into submission, the sound a muffled tattoo in his ears. Finally it
spread out flatly along the wood floor. He'd find carpet
tacks and the hammer. He'd pound the damn thing down
before he broke his fool neck.

With anger boiling inside, he thought that it was possible
he was more his father's son than his mother ever suspected. In fact, he had to admit that it was a certainty.

It explained his own impatience, his volatile nature
(which he was careful to keep under wraps when around
his mother), and maybe it even explained his darkest of
secrets. But he wasn't sure of that.

Not that it mattered.

A man was what he was, born or bred, and nothing on
all of Earth could change it. Although life was a mystery
written by the cleverest of authors, Son knew most people
were preordained to function just one specific way and no
other.

Besides, he thought, fumbling through the hall closet for
his toolbox, who would want to change anything?

"I love you, Son," he whispered at the hammer he held
close to his lips. He grinned at the sound of her high, old
lady voice coming from his mouth.

He could have become a ventriloquist. No doubt about
it.

Just as his father could have become a murderer had his
wife stayed around long enough to provide a victim. *That's*
what she was really telling him now that she had finally
spoken of *temper,* and *rages,* and *her fear of staying.*

"Chip off the old block," he murmured, hauling a box
of shiny black tacks from the back of the closet. "I'm my
daddy's only boy."

"Son, I'm going to go to the bathroom. You don't have
to come, I can make it myself," his mother called at his
back.

He started, dropping the tacks all over the floor, and
backed quickly from the closet to find her clutching her
robe together with one hand and steadying herself against
the wall with the other. Her head shook and her hands trem-

bled, and she was white as first-driven snow.

The shout welling in his throat died there, the fire that flared was quenched as he swallowed against it. "Mother, you should have called me. Let me help you, please."

He took her arm and let her lean on him as they made their slow, uneven way to the bathroom door.

"I could have done it," she protested.

"That's what I'm here for." He stood guard outside the closed door while she made her water and emptied her bowels.

He didn't notice that he was tapping his thigh with the hammerhead, and that later in the day he'd discover a bruise there that would require an ice pack to bring down the swelling.

Nine

"I wonder where the guy was killed?" Shadow strolled up one side of the circling staircase from the gigantic open living room to the next floor, trailing her fingertips along the wall. Her footsteps on the marble staircase rang out across the open spaces.

Charlene sat cross-legged on the carpet in the living room, leaning back against the sofa. Her eyes were unfocused, staring ahead of her. Her hands lay quietly in her lap. It was evident she was not going to answer the question. She might not have heard it.

Shadow paused at the top of the curving staircase and looked down to where Charlene sat, trancelike. She drew in a breath, wondering what she was going to do. She'd try to get through, keep talking. She hadn't any other plan devised.

"They said he was a monster. He threw the biggest parties along this coast. He had this place built to specification, all these windows barred." She swept her arm before her toward the front of the house where the huge double doors opened onto a portico. Two-story windows blanketed the walls on both sides of the entrance, but ugly black wrought-iron bars set into the brick mortar marred the grace of the scene.

"Did you notice even the middle section of the mansion is barred? Charlene?"

No answer. Not a flicker of an eyelash.

"Can you imagine it? The guy's into young boys. He throws his wild parties with booze and drugs, invites all the kids in here, then he locks the doors and pockets the keys. They're locked in a prison. That's what it looks like when you come down the drive to it, you know, a prison. Or maybe a boy's detention center. Something you'd think you'd see stashed off some forbidden island for the most violent inmates.''

She wished she hadn't said "inmates." Damn.

She moved along the railing overlooking the entrance-way, feeling the smooth mahogany beneath the palm of her right hand. It seemed to have a warmth of its own, a fire inside. Most of the mansion was cold, always cold. Sunlight came in around two in the afternoon and began to warm the marble, heating the spacious rooms, but until then it was a freezer even on the warmest days. Yet this wood that her hand skimmed over felt good to her. It might have come from a sunny wood on a mountain slope; it still contained the summer of a hundred years in the polished grain.

"Okay," Shadow continued, glancing often to see if she was making any headway reaching Charlene. "This nut-case built the mansion, threw his parties, locked the boys inside, and had his way with them. They say he must have locked in the wrong kid that night. He probably paid some of the boys to service him and one another, but that night, hell, he must have offered money to his murderer, and it just didn't set right. Do you think that's how it happened?''

Charlene stared. Stared. Had not moved a muscle.

"Well, the story goes that the cops were called, they were always being called by neighbors because of the noisy wild parties. The cops knew this place like the back of their hands, they'd been out here so much. So they come out again, a couple of squad cars. They park in the circular drive and walk up the steps to those doors, no hurry, they've been here a dozen times, right?''

She pointed to the front, where the police came on a routine complaint.

"A dozen boys are piled up at the door, banging on it. They can't get out, you see, because the owner had the keys in his pocket, and they didn't know that. And the owner was dead by then. They say it was a real bloodbath in here. Blood on the walls, on the stairs. The kid who did him in used a kitchen knife. The cops say, 'Open the door! What's going on here?' The boys are screaming and crashing open the windows with chairs and beer bottles. But they can't squeeze out the bars. Some of them are screaming and some are crying and pleading to get out. The cops look at one another, they think there's a fire inside or something and the kids can't get out. They have to shoot the lock off the door, telling the kids to step back, get outta the way. And what do they find when they get inside?''

Shadow paused, coming down the opposite curving staircase. "Charlene? You heard this story? Isn't it fantastic, like a movie story or something?''

Charlene grunted softly. Shadow jerked a little at the sound. Well, it was better than nothing. She knew about *nothing*. It was a dead place. And lonely. She didn't want Charlene to wander in that place if there was any way she could prevent it. She nodded, moved slowly, step by step, down the stairs.

"It's like a movie, all right. The cops get in here and boys are all over them, scrambling to get outside. Half of them aren't even fully dressed. They're in their underwear and bathing suits, a few are starkers. Some of them have already vomited, others are rushing outdoors to throw up on the lawn and in that circular flower bed you drive around out there. Then the cops see the blood. It was up here somewhere, top of the stairs . . . somewhere here.'' She halted and turned around to look up to the landing where she had just come from. She shivered, wrapped both arms around herself.

"They got the kid who did it. Because of all the witnesses and how the stories matched, they let the kid off on self-defense. He was just fourteen, they said. A big, gangly, redheaded, freckled fourteen-year-old. He wasn't gay. He'd come along with a friend who told him there was a party. He was from Houston somewhere and he didn't know the reputation of the parties in the Shoreville Mansion. When the owner came after him, he panicked, they said. He begged to be released from the house. Everyone laughed at him and he just went beserk. Ran for the kitchen and got a knife. Found the owner at the top of the stairs, threatened to gut him if he wasn't let free. Who knows what happened then? Maybe they laughed at him again or the old guy moved on him. Tragic," she said quietly, suddenly thinking about her children and the one tragedy that changed her own life forever. "An accidental thing."

Charlene turned her head. Shadow saw the movement from the corner of her watering eyes. She came down the rest of the stairs and went to her. She stooped near the sofa and laid a hand on her friend's shoulder. "Are you all right?"

"Do we have to live here?" she asked.

They were making progress now. It was the first time Charlene had spoken since Shadow first found her two hours ago, sitting alone on the floor, staring.

"Nothing here's going to hurt us. What happened here, the guy deserved. He was using the kids and paying them off with drugs and alcohol. He was the scum of the earth. Look at those bars on the windows. He was a sadist to lock those kids up in here. He ruined half the boys in this town. But he's gone, Charlene. He isn't here anymore. You might say this place paid him back. You don't have to be afraid."

"I've seen his ghost. At night. Floating through the rooms."

Shadow sighed and patted Charlene's shoulder. "You were just dreaming."

"I've heard boys laughing."

Shadow brought her head close to Charlene's and touched foreheads. She whispered, "Come on, listen to me now. We're partners, aren't we? We're friends. I wouldn't let anything happen to you, would I?"

"No."

"That's right. I wouldn't. You're safe now. Betty's not here to steal your things. You don't have to hear the women's life stories and remember for them. You don't *have* to lose your mind. You're free, Charlene. I want to keep you that way, but you have to talk to me. You can't let these moods take over where you don't say anything or move. It scares me."

Charlene managed a smile and brought up her arms to

hug Shadow. "You're the best person I ever knew."

"Damn right!" Shadow stood and pulled on Charlene's hand to raise her to her feet. "Now, let's go find out what we have in the fridge. Are you cooking? You're cooking, right? Can we have omelets? We have any mushrooms to put in them? I could eat a basketful of mushroom omelets. And I need a strong pot of coffee, we have any of that chocolate almond coffee we bought in Galveston—what's it called, mocha almondine?"

Charlene let herself be propelled up the stairs, cringed slightly when she passed the wall next to the landing at the top where the blood was supposed to have been splattered, and followed Shadow toward the kitchen. "You'll get fat and then you can't dance," she said.

"Oh, I can dance. After we eat, we'll go run around this place, get all sweaty, and feel glorious. All right? You want to run with me after we have breakfast?"

"It's noon. It's not breakfast time."

Shadow laughed, pushing Charlene toward the stove, taking the egg carton from the commercial-sized refrigerator. "It's *my* breakfast time. I'm a night person, now, remember. I work the night shift at the titty joint. All for you, Charlene. What I do for you, and you're bitching it ain't breakfast and I can't have an omelet."

"I didn't say that."

"Okay then, whip this up and I'll find the mushrooms."

While they busied themselves chopping and whipping and frying, Shadow kept up a stream of conversation until Charlene's frozen demeanor thawed and she became herself again. Soon it was Charlene who was talking nonstop, rattling on about when she was a girl and had to cook for her large family because her mother had died young. By the time the omelets were served at the shiny oak table pushed against one wall of the big kitchen, Shadow wolfing down the fattest, fluffiest mushroom omelet she had ever tasted, Charlene was a changed person. Happy, bubbling, overflowing with enthusiasm, jokes, and talk talk talk.

Shadow grinned while she ate and listened to her friend, but one part of her attention wondered which drawer held the knives, and which knife, if it wasn't taken for evidence, had killed the former owner. Crazy. She shouldn't even be thinking such dark thoughts for they led her to think about violence in general, and her loss in particular.

Trailing Scott to the den.

Pleading for him to put the gun away.

Watching him pull the trigger.

"You're not listening!" Charlene reached over and drew away her plate. "I listened to that whole sick, sick story about the killing in the mansion and you won't even listen to me now. That's not fair, is it? Is that fair?"

Shadow shook herself mentally, blinked, and smiled tentatively. "We both just tend to drift off, don't we? What a pair we make. Isn't it strange and wonderful?"

Charlene grinned uncertainly and started up where she'd left off about what slobs her brothers and sisters were and how much responsibility she had caring for them when she was growing up. It never occurred to her that *drifting off* might not be *wonderful* at all, that the two of them were wounded creatures fighting for survival, and that the odds were against them holding on to reality for any measurable length of time. . . .

Charlene, a tall woman carrying twenty extra pounds around her forty-year-old waist and hips, jogged as easily around the house behind Shadow as any Olympic champion. She didn't even breathe hard or become flushed. Mainly, she thought, it was a trick of the mind, turning off what the body went through. She knew how to close her mind to any event her body experienced so that she wasn't affected greatly by either exercise, heat, cold, even pain.

Especially pain. She had known enough physical and mental pain that she had long ago learned how to escape. Now as she pumped her legs and swung her long arms in the baggy sweater, pacing herself ten feet behind Shadow as they circled the brooding old brick mansion, Charlene went over her thoughts from earlier when she had been sitting on the rug, Shadow's voice coming through to her from the stairway as through veils of thick gauze. She was . . .

Alone. So alone. She *thought* she was alone, anyway, believed it fully. She was ten years old and her father had taken the other children to town. Charlene, the eldest, was supposed to clean house before they returned. Mother was dead. There were always too many chores to do and only Charlene to do them.

Someone was coming to visit, one of Daddy's friends from the chemical plant, his *only* friend, the man he played dominoes with at Joe's Ice House in Houston on Friday nights and bowled with on Saturdays. Charlene was making the beds, the twins' bunks in one of the bedrooms at the back of the house, and she was perfectly content to do the work. She had never whined or pretended it was too much trouble for a ten-year-old to take on so many household duties. She rather liked the mindlessness of housework. She was one of those people destined to find joy where she could, and cleanliness and orderliness gave her a sense of satisfaction that provided her with little gifts of cheer and accomplishments throughout each day.

She tucked the sheet beneath the thin, worn mattress. She squared the corners. She plumped the pillows in their cases and set them just so at the head of the bunks.

She never knew he—that horrible man, that demon man—was coming. She was whistling beneath her breath, "Jesus loves me, this I know, for the Bible tells me so," and he crept up behind her before she ever knew someone was in the house with her. He grabbed her around the waist and pulled her off her feet, the pillow she had in her hands falling to the floor. She shrieked, trying to twist free, heart racing, her song cut off in midtune.

"Hush now," he said gruffly. "You wouldn't want your daddy to find out you lured me in here and took off all your clothes for me."

She recognized the voice as belonging to her father's friend, who wasn't supposed to be there until dinnertime. She had heard it on the telephone when he called and she had met him once at his car when he picked up her father for Saturday-night league bowling.

"Leave me alone!" she screamed, but he clamped a hand over her mouth.

From then on the painful memory blurred around the edges like a partially burned photograph. There was kicking. There were brutal hands searching her little body for all its crevices. There were tears squeezed silently out her lids as he kept her mouth covered. She knew the taste of him. His hand, his penis. She knew the pain of him and his perspiring stench and his weight and his thickness which tore her and made her bleed.

When he was done, he balled the stained sheets from her sister's bed and pulled down the stairs to the attic in the hallway. He climbed up there and left the sheets. He warned her if she told, he'd kill her. And he'd kill her family. He'd kill everyone she knew.

He left by the back door, and she thought she'd heard him chuckling to himself. She sat in the bathtub, the water running until it slopped over the sides, and still she wasn't clean and still she couldn't walk without wincing in pain. She cried until her daddy came home from the store and she told him.

It took some time and buckets of tears, but he believed her. He was her daddy. He knew she didn't lie. He climbed like an old man with aching joints into the attic and found the bloodied sheets. He went with the policemen to his friend's home and watched them cuff and haul him to jail. During the trial, he tried to leap over the table to get at the rapist, to strangle him to death during her testimony, but they restrained him in time.

The man was sentenced to nine years in prison. Just as he left the courtroom he winked at her and shouted, "Wait till I get out, sugar. You just wait."

So for nine years, even though they moved four times and did not install a telephone, she dreamed that her rapist, her worst nightmare, was out of prison and creeping into her room, where he would take her again just to make her suffer before he cut her throat. And the throats of her siblings and her father.

For nine years, until she was nineteen years old, she

woke screaming in the night. Her schoolwork suffered. She was put into the dummy classes and gained a lot of weight. Boys made fun of her, woofing like dogs when she passed them. Girls wouldn't befriend her. She started shuffling and keeping her head down so she wouldn't have to see the world mocking her.

She was alone all the time. Alone.

Just before the rapist's parole date, she had a psychotic episode that scared her father into calling an ambulance. She was completely insane, but she didn't know it until later when she woke up restrained by a straitjacket in Marion State.

From her nineteenth year until her present fortieth one, Charlene Brewster recounted the rape scene in her dreams at least once a month, and sometimes in the day the dreams overtook her and left her paralyzed, unable to function. That was what had happened this morning while Shadow told her about the mansion's history.

She wished she could change everything. Her mother's dying young, leaving her the head of the household. Her father's invitation to his friend for dinner that night. Her staying behind to clean while they left her to go shopping.

But most of all she wished she could have had a weapon, any weapon, when she was attacked, so that she could have defended herself.

Wishing didn't change the past. Wishing didn't keep her safe or provide her with peace. Even Marion State's best psychiatrists over the years couldn't do that.

Her legs pumped and carried her through the sunshine, where the wind blew back her mousy graying hair from wide cheekbones. Ahead of her Shadow pranced, calves rounded and strong in the spandex pants she wore for running. Her black hair had a luster like that of a raven's wings in the burning light.

Shadow didn't know. Charlene had never been able to tell anyone. If they already knew, the way the doctors at Marion did, she couldn't help it, but she never volunteered the facts of her soul's death on that ordinary day when she was ten.

She knew it wasn't any worse a fate she'd suffered than Shadow. Or were there degrees of suffering, she wondered, that demanded some kind of extra payment in this life? Shadow's children, little boys, had had their brains blown out all over the floor. Her husband had stood right there and done something irrevocably evil and made his wife witness to it.

Tears welled up and dripped down Charlene's cheeks. They dried as she ran, her hands clenching and unclenching as she swung them at her sides.

How were they supposed to live? How was she supposed to recover from the death of childhood and innocence? How was Shadow supposed to continue living as if she had never been a devoted mother and wife? Were there really people who were able to go on, unaffected and unmarred by life's ruthlessness? Why weren't every last one of them raving maniacs? That's what she wanted to know. Was there a secret to successful coping that she had been born without?

Shadow ran up the steps and beckoned for her to follow. She said, breathless and hanging over her knees, "I'm pooped. That's enough for today. C'mon, we'll get big glasses of ice water and sit around back by the bay."

Charlene, just as compliant as a child, nodded her head and jogged up the stairs into the mansion's cold interior.

Whatever Shadow said. That's what she would do. She had to listen to someone, trust someone to tell her how to live through one hour after another. It was that or suicide and she wasn't quite ready—not yet—to employ that option.

❧Ten❧

Mitchell stumbled around the kitchen, Pavlov bending his lanky fawn body into half circles barring passage.

"Pavlov! Outta the way, boy." But he stopped going for the coffeepot on the back of the stove and leaned over to rub behind the dog's ears. Pavlov's tail stub wagged like crazy and he made little whiny sounds of pleasure. "I'll feed you in a sec. Let me get some java going here so I can crack open my eyes."

When Mitchell straightened to reach for the pot, Pavlov flipped in a complete circle in the air, all four feet off the floor. His tongue hung out, eyes upturned and pleading, tail wagging like a metronome. Mitchell looked at him again. Holding perfectly still, he said, "You want out?" He knew he did, he just loved seeing the dog flip in the air like a ballet star.

Again Pavlov executed the perfect twirligig, four paws thumping the floor on landing. This meant yes. It might even mean "Yes, are you a moron?" Then he curled again into that odd half circle, butt almost to head, that boxers were known to adopt when they are pleased to have a master's attention.

"You squirrelly mutt. Come on, then, go out and dig some holes so I can make my coffee in peace."

Pavlov ran to the back door, then sat on his haunches as he had been taught, waiting. Mitchell opened the door and the dog vanished out the crack like escaping steam. Holding open the door on the rising sun, Mitchell grinned, watching the dog run in fast circles before pulling up short, turf flying, and scratching with his back paws like a bull. He lifted a leg over a dying rosebush and pissed. All the while he smiled at Mitchell as if to say, "When I tell you I have to go out, I have to go *out,* whatta you think, I'm kiddin'?"

The phone screamed, causing Mitchell to flinch. He left the door partially open so the dog could come in when he wanted, and warily lifted the receiver off the wall hook. "Yeah?"

"Double trouble. Murder-suicide. Need you here, chop-chop."

Mitchell's lieutenant spoke in code language. For some reason it always required a like response. You couldn't hold a decent English conversation with the guy. He wouldn't know a complete sentence if it slugged him in the back. "Just happen?"

"Hour ago. *Looks* like murder-suicide. Could be something else. A hit. Contract. Ain't kosher, maybe."

"I'm on my way. Let me feed my dog." And make my coffee.

He ran water into the dented aluminum percolator, dumped lots of Folgers grounds into the leaning basket, and switched the gas burner on high. On the counter was a bag of powdered sugar doughnuts. He ate half a dozen while waiting for the coffee to perk. He glanced out the window over the sink at Pavlov digging holes to China. The backyard looked like an archaeological dig. But Pavlov loved it so much. You couldn't kill the few delights an animal discovered.

Gulping coffee so hot it scorched his vocal cords, Mitchell carried a cup with him as he dressed in the bedroom. Pavlov had let himself in again so that now he trailed behind every step Mitchell made. He was a pest and ingratiating as hell, licking a hand here, butting a leg there, but he was the best boxer Mitchell thought he'd ever owned. And one helluva watchdog, too. The house had never been burglarized. That said a lot for a house so exposed, empty overgrown lots on each side, crack dealers down on the corner.

In the kitchen again, fully dressed except for his shoes, Mitchell shut and locked the wide-open back door, dumped a couple of coffee cans of dog food into Pavlov's tray, changed his water, and refilled his own cup with coffee from the stove. In the living room he slipped on soft leather Italian loafers, his one outrageous big-ticket vanity, and made for the door.

Pavlov sat in the middle of the room and threw back his thickly muscled neck to let out a howl.

"Hey, you think I don't miss you, too?" Mitchell rushed over to rub the dog's neck once more before breaking from the house, coffee slopping over his hand and burning his knuckles on the way down the walk to his car.

"God, I love that dog," he said, shaking his head in astonishment.

Pavlov came from a litter of twelve, and he was the runt. Long legged, black mask, not much white (which made him far less than show quality, not that Mitchell cared), he had done that flipping in the air trick one time, just two months old then, and stole Mitchell's heart.

"He's kind of skinny," Mitchell said to the professional dog breeder. "And look at those legs. He looks like a race-horse instead of a dog."

"Well, he'll fatten up. And grow into the legs. I can let you have him for four hundred since he's the last one to go. He's smart. He learned that jump trick on his own."

The gangly puppy grinned and butted Mitchell's leg and Mitchell pulled out his checkbook. How often could you find a puppy with a smile? And who was going to buy him, skinny legs and all, if Mitchell didn't?

Life was never the same in the house again. Although Mitchell had owned boxers before, none of them tore up the place like Pavlov. Then again, the dog made a good excuse for the sloppy rooms when company came calling, what company Mitchell allowed. He could always say his dog did it. He's a scoundrel.

Which was the God's honest truth. Pavlov had a thing about pillows. He mangled them when left alone, dragging them through rooms and tossing them into the air until they shredded. He pawed his tray until the dog food splattered all over the kitchen floor. He slopped water everywhere and often drank from the toilet when running low. He hated the mailman so that every time he heard the mailbox slot clanging on the porch, he tried to tear down the front door. There were deep scars in the wood where he'd tried to rake and gnaw his way through. If he ever made it, the mailman was dead meat.

What with buying new pillows all the time, cleaning up behind Pavlov, and having to replace the front door, Mitchell figured having this dog had cost him plenty of money and aggravation, but all Pavlov had to do was twitch his lean muscular body in a flying pirouette and all was forgiven. Mitchell knew he'd grieve forever when this dog died one day. It had occurred to him that God made dogs to teach people how to love and let go. Dogs never lived as long as man; they came, captured your heart, and one day when you least expected catastrophe, they lay down and died, breaking your fucking heart.

Mitchell hurried into the bullpen, slipped past two detectives stuffing themselves with tacos that were going to rot their guts this early in the morning, and confronted Lieutenant Tom Epstein on his way to the john. Epstein reached into a stained jacket pocket and handed over an address written on a yellow Post-it note. "Here," he said, still walking so that Mitchell had to follow. "Cleanup's half through. Hurry so they can finish. I've already sent over Donaldson."

Donaldson. Mitchell wished Epstein had paired him on this new case with one of the other detectives. Donaldson had an attitude. He thought his shit didn't stink. "Why contract?" Mitchell asked, trying to get a handle on this thing so he wouldn't be walking into the situation blind.

"Looks like murder-suicide. Wife, husband. Hubby, though, he's holding the pistol."

"Yeah?"

"In the wrong hand."

"Yeah?" Now it was making sense.

Epstein paused with one palm on the men's room door. "Sister showed up. Got hysterical. Said hubby was right-handed."

"The gun's in his left," Mitchell supplied, way ahead of the story.

"See you. I got gas." Epstein pushed open the door and disappeared.

On the way out, one of the taco-eating detectives offered an extra one to Mitchell, holding it like a cracker smeared with caviar. "Want soma this?"

"You think I care to die? Not on Wednesday." Mitchell moved on past, the scent of fried meat, taco seasoning, and hot sauce in his nostrils. Then what he'd said hit him. *Wednesday.* Christ, he was having lunch downtown with Patty. He almost forgot. How was he going to make it if he got hung up with this murder-suicide?

He'd have to try. He'd stood up Patty once too often lately and she was complaining loud enough to make his balls crawl up his legs.

By twelve-fifteen he had wrapped the scene, had them bag the male victim's hands to check for residue, taken all his notes, and sighed at the work ahead of him. It definitely looked like a setup. The sister insisted her brother wouldn't do this, he loved his wife, he loved life, didn't he pull down a hundred thousand a year selling Houston real estate, and the way he held that gun, he didn't do it, she kept telling him, he wasn't a lefty, didn't she know her own flesh and blood?

He figured she did. The murder scene stunk. It was way too perfect. The bullet entrance angles were correct. But the wife was on the sofa, slumped to the right, and there was no sign of a struggle. Give me a wife, Mitchell thought, who sees hubby boy coming for her with a gun, and tell me she's going to sit still for it. She'd be off that sofa and fighting for her life, not content to let it happen. A magazine she had been leafing through had not even fallen to the floor! Then hubby went to the easy chair facing the TV and put the gun to his left forehead. Him a righty.

Nope. Someone had it in for Mr. Real Estate, that was obvious. He was just too clean with it, though. Made it look too packaged. And he hadn't done his homework if he messed up on hubby's gun hand. Lab results would show if he even pulled the trigger.

Now it might be months of intense investigation before Mitchell ferreted out Mr. Real Estate's enemy, but he'd do it. There were a lot of cases that were so cold when he got to them, he never dredged up the facts. But this one was going to make him happy. It was going to give Epstein cause for applause. He just had to find the motive—women, money, or sour business deals—and he'd find the person who hired the contract killer.

He checked his watch and made for the door. "Wrap it up," he told Donaldson. "I have an appointment." Donaldson lifted one side of his upper lip in resentment. The crime scene men gathered their baggies and equipment.

Mitchell made it to lunch with Patty only half an hour late, but she was there, drumming her nails on the tabletop, drinking white wine, looking like a pissed-off dream.

"I'm sorry—" he began, unbuttoning his coat, pulling out the chair.

"You've already made me late for a meeting."

"I imagine. I said I was sorry. Murder-suicide."

"What?"

He had to start again. He was still talking shorthand like Epstein. "I was out all morning on a murder-suicide case. Except it isn't. Murder-suicide, I mean. It's plain shoot-the-poor-bastards-in-the-head murder."

Patty's upper lip stiffened. He knew what that meant. She didn't like to hear about his cases. Crime insulted her. She said the city was turning into the Bangladesh of villainy. That's how she talked. Her job with the housing authority was "the Cape Canaveral of city politics." *His* job was "the marketplace of lost souls."

Just a quirk she had. If she wasn't so pretty, he'd tell her that silly, pompous, creative mouth of hers should be used for the "sucking of big dicks." But she was pretty.

Mitchell ordered what Patty was having. It turned out to be cold salmon with cream sauce and he hated it. He should have taken the taco at the station. While he poked the flaky fish apart with a fork, she told him how her mother thought it was time to see a printer for the invitation cards. Mitchell hadn't been listening that closely so he asked, "For what? You throwing a party?"

She gave him a squinty look. "For the wedding. Or had you forgotten all about that?"

He shrugged and, to keep from replying, took a big bite of the fish. It sat in his mouth like cold raw hamburger. Why the hell didn't they warm this fish up, for pete's sake?

"Mitchell, I don't know what's wrong with you lately. It's not like I asked you to marry me. Is it? My memory tells me you did the asking. If we're going to do it, it has to be done right. And to do it right, we have to pick out invitations, hire a photographer, make up a guest list, decide on a tux . . ."

He nearly choked. He swallowed noisily and groped for the wineglass. God, what were people doing eating cold creamy fish? The world had collectively lost its mind. And if she thought she was going to get him in a tux . . .

"Well? You want to back out?"

She was tapping her nails again. And that pretty squint wasn't all that pretty now.

"Uh . . . I never said . . . you know, about a tux . . . they . . . uh . . . I don't really—"

"Forget all about it." She stood, folding the napkin from her lap into a rectangle with sharp edges. "Just forget I ever said anything. I knew this was coming, I've known it for months, Mitchell. You never wanted to get married. Cops hate marriage. You even admitted it yourself. Your last marriage didn't last two years. I wasn't going through with it anyway, how do you like that?"

She was into it now, boy was she into it. Her color was high and her shoulders back. Her voice went up another register and he'd probably soon have wine in his face. He stood with her, reached for her arm, hoping to soothe the beast he'd unleashed.

She was right, of course, he didn't want to get married, that had been a mistake when he had asked her. He must have gone round-the-bend la-la romantic, and she *was* terrific in bed, but there was no way he could live with a squinty, nail-tapping woman who preferred cold fish for lunch. And there was no way in this life he was ever going to don a tux and pick out invitations just to please another mother-in-law. Fuck that dull American-made dream shit.

"Patty, it's not like that." He came in close, hoping to head off the big scene in the restaurant, the one that always got out of hand and wound up incredibly messy. Oddly, he couldn't get the dead couple out of his mind, that woman slumped over sideways on the sofa, a fine stream of blackish blood curling down over her brow like a trail of hair dye. Had she insisted on invitations and a tuxedo? Did she ever want children? Had she loved her pudgy husband with his salesman's gift of gab? That was marriage, wasn't it? If you didn't die of murder, you could probably find a way to die of boredom.

"Let me go!" Patty tore off his hand from her arm and turned her back on him. He watched her high heels click across the fashionably tiled floor. He loved how she swung her ass when she was angry.

That bolted him from the spot where he'd been glued. He braced her in the lobby, turning her to face him. She was too good for him, that was the problem. He didn't deserve as good as this. "Patty, I don't want you to hate me. I care a lot for you. I never meant to hurt you. It's just that one bad marriage scared me shitless. I'm so afraid—"

She didn't let him finish. "You are the royal asshole of the universe. Don't bother calling."

As she left him, swinging that great body through the door with enough energy to shatter the glass, he thought he could see his title in all caps. ROYAL ASSHOLE OF THE UNIVERSE. And at that moment he thought he probably was. If he'd been an honest man, he would have straightened out that marriage proposal fiasco long before now. He couldn't think how it had ever happened. Maybe in bed one night she had brought up the subject and he had said sure, fine, anything you want, while his mind wasn't on her words so much as it was on her body.

She had gone so far as thinking of wedding plans; she probably had two hundred and fifty people on a list at home. She might even have rolls of stamps ready to lick, and a dress picked out, and a wedding bouquet. He never should have let this thing slide until she believed it so much.

At home after his shift ended at eleven P.M., Pavlov met him at the door with a pillow in his teeth, grinning. Polyester clumps were stuck in his ears and covered the floor like snowfall. Mitchell dropped his keys on an end table, took out his wallet and badge to add there. He hoisted his coat and gun holster off and let them drop to the floor. Then he knelt, made Pavlov drop his prize, and hugged him around the neck while the dog slobbered kisses on his face.

"A man and his dog," he whispered. "What do we need with women anyway?"

Yet his words were hollow and his stomach did a flop act that not even Pavlov's unconditional love could cure.

﷯Eleven﷯

Son walked slowly around the perimeter of the front
lawn looking for ant beds to poison. He hated red ants
worse than anything, except maybe roaches. Once red ants
took over a lawn, they owned it. They were nearly impossible to eradicate.

He stepped right into the crumbling center of a small
bed, his shoe sinking, and ants surged over the worn Ree-
bok, swarming up his sock. He stomped and brushed at
them, but was bitten half a dozen times before saving himself. "Bastards!" he said. "Little sons of bitches!"

Rather than dipping with the scoop provided with the red
ant poison, he took the round container and poured a pound
of the contents directly onto the teeming pile. The ants were
supposed to take the minute pellets into the nest and kill
off the colony. To make sure, he picked up the shovel and
dug into the bed's center, dumping even more of the poison
inside.

Before moving on around the yard, looking for more of
the beds, he stopped to rub the stings on his ankles and
hands. He peered closely, saw the bites were already swelling redly. "Bastards," he repeated.

It took him all of two hours, but Son managed to find
every new bed in the front and backyard. Outside his mother's bedroom window, he saw her draw back the curtain
and wave to him. He waved back, but a corresponding
smile was too much to ask. When involved in a task he
single-mindedly tackled it, and to request a convivial smile
from him was too demanding.

He had just been out here trying to rid the place of red
ants not more than two weeks before. They were a plague,

one that never disappeared no matter what poison he tried or how diligent he was.

He put away the container of poison and shovel in the metal garden shed. When he was heading for the back door, his neighbor called over the hurricane fence. "Get 'em this time, Son?"

Son caught himself stiffly, hand on the door, and swiveled his head slowly toward the voice. He didn't like people calling him Son. No one had that right except his mother. Did the snoopy neighbors think he was their son, too? Assholes.

"I got most of them," he said.

"They keep coming back like bad pennies, don't they? You know what, you kill 'em over there and they move over here." The neighbor waggled a bald pate and hooked a thumb over his shoulder. "I kill them off, they move back over there. I don't think we're gonna win this war."

Son thought he would, but what was the point in debating it? He pulled the door toward him, hoping to dismiss the neighbor.

"Hey, how's your book coming along?"

Son sighed, turned to look frostily at the man again. "It's fine. Great. In fact, that's what I've got to do now, go write something. Good-bye."

Son might be the only person on the street who ended his conversations with such formality. No one ever said good-bye. The neighbors were always left smiling tentatively, hands raised in farewell to Son's retreating back. They thought this standoffish attitude just came with being a writer. Artistic temperament, they told one another. Those writers, they're eccentric, everyone knows that.

The truth was Son simply didn't want to get involved. People, for the most part, got on his nerves. If he had to speak to them for longer than five minutes, he started sneering at their provincial, bigoted, ignorant comments. The bulk of humanity had individual IQs that left much to be desired. They didn't understand politics, language, religion, current events, where they were headed, or from where they had originated. It was wasteful to spend time with them.

Inside the house, Son set up the ironing board and plugged in the iron. He checked on his mother to see if she wanted anything before beginning the next chore on his list. For three hours he dedicated himself to the pressing of sheets, pillowcases, his mother's gowns, and his own baggy, pleated pants and short-sleeved white shirts he wore around the house.

It was Saturday, and every Saturday he tended the lawn, cleaned the house, and ironed the wash. He worked on his books during the weekdays, reserving weekends for the more difficult, time-consuming chores he had to ignore during the week. On Saturday nights he often visited Sherilee.

At a quarter till eight, after his bath, clothes change, and the preparation of his mother's dinner tray, he stood in the doorway of his mother's room. "I'll be back before midnight," he said. "If you need anything, you've got that number to call me."

"I'll be all right, Son. Enjoy yourself, you hear?"

She thought he visited a married couple he had met while in college. She thought he played pinochle with them and that his partner was Sherilee. She thought his social life was rather restricted and that he should date nice young women, but she hadn't brought that up to him in years.

What she didn't know didn't hurt her.

Sherilee lived four miles from Son's home. He drove there and parked along the street. He hitched his pants as he crossed the curb. This was the one part of his scheduled and patterned life that he most enjoyed. He had read a book or seen a movie where a man very much like himself, a man with an ailing mother and a strict routine to his life, took up visiting a woman no one knew about. Son loved to copy things that made good sound sense to him.

Sherilee was turning into an old, and not very much requested, hooker, having to take her trade from the street, but when Son first began going to her, she had been young, supple, and eager to please him. She did what was asked. She didn't question or show any disgust. Despite her age now, Son was not put off by her. He too was aging, his hairline receding, his jowls sagging a little more each year, the spare tire around his belly going soft and cushiony as a feather mattress. He and Sherilee suited one another. He'd never start over with a young prostitute, one he'd have to teach the ropes. It was Sherilee all the way. They were like an old married couple. He might be a traveling salesman husband, she his devoted and willing wife.

Except that he paid her. And he never spent the entire night in her bed.

She met him at the door of the deteriorating house she had bought with savings ten years before when it looked quite a lot better, just as the two of them had, and stood aside as he strode into the dim hall entrance. She wore a thick quilted pink bathrobe that looked snagged all over the fabric, some of the quilting coming loose, threads hanging. She was freshly bathed—he could smell the Irish Spring soap she used—and her hair, just now showing silver at the crown, hung damply around her shoulders.

She was black. Not brown or cream or mocha, not high yellow, either. She was black as a midnight with no moon or stars, her skin reminiscent of those crude African carvings that were all the rage in the sixties. Her forehead was wide and shiny, her eyes black olives. She had full purple-gray lips that sat in a pout on her face unless he asked her to smile. She never smiled on her own. She said once, "What's to smile about? I got this life, and it ain't got a happy goddamn smile in it."

Son led the way down the hallway to the door that opened into her bedroom. He didn't relax until she had entered behind him and closed the door. There were no other inhabitants in the house, but he didn't like the door standing open, it made him feel vulnerable, as if someone might be spying. He checked the windows, saw the curtains were closed tightly, the shades drawn behind the curtains' sheer lengths.

He turned to her clothes closet, a walk-in one with mirrored sliding doors. He slid one side back and stepped inside the huge space. She already had the overhead light on for him in there. For the shape of the house and the smallness of her bedroom, the closet was out of proportion and

well built. She had a client who built it for her, taking over
a bath and a portion of the hall to enlarge it to her speci-
fications. It was twelve feet wide and twenty deep. Along
each side of the closet hung her costumes. On the floor was
arranged a multitude of shoes from black patent-leather
Mary Janes with straps to white satin spike heels. Above
the clothes ran a shelf down each side, and on these twin
shelves were her hats, wigs, rolled belts that reminded Son
of coiled snakes, corsages, veils, and other accessories that
fit with her various costumes.

It smelled different in here compared to the bedroom and
the rest of Sherilee's house. It smelled of cedar and lace,
of leather and brass. An orange pomander hung from a
ribbon in the center of the closet giving off hints of cin-
namon and clove. The closet was a veritable potpourri of
scent.

Son went to the back left of the hanging clothes and
found the dress first. It was long, to midcalf, and flowered
in an old blue and maroon print you did not see today. It
had a long waist and a high collar of delicate lace. The
bosom was pleated and would balloon over Sherilee's large,
full breasts. It came with a fabric belt of the same print as
the dress. He took it down from the hanger and lay it carefully over his arm.

He searched among the pairs of shoes for a match.

"There," she pointed out, coming to him. "Those will
work."

She was right. They were black and high-topped, button
shoes with a small heel favored in the early part of the
century. He lifted them and set them into her waiting hands.

"Wig?" she asked, raising one plucked eyebrow.

"Yes." He reached overhead to the shelf for a gray wig
cap of curls.

He sat on the side of the bed, hands folded, while she
dressed for him.

She completed the picture by donning the wig, tucking
her still-damp hair beneath. She pointed to her dressing
table where there were myriad cosmetics.

He shook his head no.

She took on an imperial attitude, moving around the room fussing with bottles and jars on the dressing table, closing the closet door, her black old-fashioned shoes *tap-tapping* every step she made. She completely ignored Son.

"Tell me what to do," he said finally, tiring of watching how she moved, though she did it as well as any actress who knew her craft, stiffly, like a woman fighting with arthritis.

"Get up and make that bed." She was in character, her eyes flinty and unyielding. Her hands rode her hips just beneath the belt.

"Don't spare me anything," he instructed, standing to do as she ordered. "If I don't do it right . . ."

"You *will* do it right, my man, you will do it right, or I will strip your hide to the bone, do you hear me? Answer if you hear me, none of that mumbling and lollygagging the way you always do."

"I hear you." He had his back to her, trying to straighten the sheet. His tone had softened considerably. She was in charge now. He was free of responsibility; he need not do anything except what she told him to do. But he understood he must do it with infinite care and always be courteous.

"That's *not* how you make the spread lay. Take it off and do it again. Tuck it beneath the pillows. No! Fluff those pillows first, you stupid idiot!"

He peeled the plain white comforter from the bed and fluffed the pillows. He tucked the spread under them.

"That's better, that's much better."

He turned, head down in submission. "What are you waiting for?" she asked, and his head snapped up. "Go to the kitchen and bring the tea things."

He hustled to the closed door and let himself out. In Sherilee's kitchen he almost lost the illusion. There were roaches here that scuttled across the dirty counter and the tea bags were crumpled in their box where she'd accidentally set a five-pound bag of sugar on top of the container.

He heard her calling imperiously from the middle of the house as the teapot heated. "If you don't hurry, I won't be responsible for my actions. Son? Do you hear me, or are you deaf?'' Sherilee was allowed to call him Son. In her house, that's who he was.

He answered her and hurriedly poured the water over two tea bags in the chipped china teapot. He arranged it all on a Hanna-Barbera cartoon TV tray, the cups, the saucers, the sugar, the cream, the spoons, and he moved like a butler to her door again. "It's done," he reported, elbowing open the door, stomaching the tray before him.

She was at the side of the door, peering down her strong, wide nose at him. She stood a good three inches taller than he and used that superior height during these scenes where she must dominate. "Is it hot?" she asked. "I didn't hear the kettle whistling. Did you even heat the water?"

He ducked his head as he set the tray on the bedside table. "I think it's all right."

She sniffed and arched her neck just a few centimeters. "I'll trust you this one time."

He poured their tea and they drank, Sherilee standing over him, sipping delicately from the cup. When the teapot was empty, she ordered him to take it back to the kitchen.

When he returned to the bedroom he knew what he would find. She was out of the dress, the shoes kicked off her bare feet, and she lay naked, pinned, legs spread, in the center of the made bed.

His lust was overpowering. She had done her part so well, excelled, actually. His erection throbbed and jittered as he flung off his clothes and jumped on top of the compliant woman. She was purple in more places than her lips, and he settled there, suckling her. She did not move or moan or show any response. If she did, it ruined it for him. No matter what he did, how he tried exciting her, she lay wooden, her face a weathered black stone. When he couldn't withhold orgasm any longer, he straddled her body and rode her mercilessly, the covers bunching, the pillows falling to the floor, the headboard of the old wooden bed knocking crazily against the wall.

When he finished, slathered in their sweat, he slid off her and onto the floor, onto his knees. His head was buried in the mattress, his hands clenched over his scalp. He wept while she patted him, smoothing his hair down with her palm, shushing him the way she might a baby.

Exhausted, he stood and left the room for Sherilee's bathroom next to the kitchen where he showered a long time. Tears, sweat, illusion, and sickness all washed down the drain.

Dressed again, hair combed neatly, he met her in the hall by the front door. He handed over a hundred-dollar bill. She opened the door and he vanished down the steps into the night.

On Saturday nights he slept the sleep of the dead and the grateful. He never once woke on a Saturday night wondering if his mother needed him, if she was still breathing, if she might have died while he wasn't watching.

Not until morning did he wake, refreshed, ready to face another predictable week of torment.

❧Twelve❧

Charlene Brewster wandered through the rooms of the Shoreville Mansion, committing the pattern to heart. The house was as large as a dormitory or a detention center, the way Shadow had thought of it, and there were three floors to cover, a host of rooms to invade and memorize on the mental map Charlene drew painstakingly in her mind. She could not feel secure until she knew where every hall led, what every door opened upon.

It was just past dark. A sea fog had drifted from the restless bay over the small, sloping back lawn, and now it shrouded the mansion, sheeting every window with gray gossamer that shifted if you stood and watched it touch and withdraw from the windowpane like a blind phantom. There was a chill on the place that came through the marble floors into Charlene's cornflower blue house slippers as she moved as quietly as possible through the house, opening doors, standing to stare and remember, closing doors, and moving on.

Once, on the ground floor, while glancing around a room with French doors (all barred, every bit of glass in the house was barred), she thought as she turned away to leave that she saw a movement beyond the doors that was human in origin, not a waving aside of the prevailing fog. She paused and looked back over her shoulder as quickly as she could, straining neck muscles. But no one was there, just the curtain of gray that coated all the great exterior of the house. She shook her head, admonishing herself for getting spooked for no good reason, and carried on, coasting along the cold white-and-black-tiled floors to another section of the house.

In the middle section of the mansion there had been built an open area, the windows rising for two stories until the ceiling curved overhead into huge squares of green glass to block the sun. A catwalk twelve feet from the bottom floor cut through this section, connecting the front of the house with the back. On either side of the concrete-floored, railed catwalk that resounded with her footsteps as she crossed were dreams someone must have had (the dead man who had locked in the boys?), dreams an architect might have thought nightmarish to build.

To her left, Charlene glanced down at the brick-lined patio surrounding an Olympic-sized swimming pool shaped like a kidney. It had water in it, but neither she nor Shadow had yet taken a swim. The water was too cold, and they did not know how to operate the heater, or how to clean the pool if it became scummy. She could hear the drone of the water pumps, and a chlorine scent that made her nose wrinkle infiltrated the air along this section of the catwalk. Around the pool sat gaily colored chaise longues and deck chairs.

Charlene suddenly thought she heard the laughter and splashing of young boys, dozens of them, and the brave, reckless yell of a diver cannonballing from the highest of the diving boards. But she knew it was not so, it was her errant imagination, the way the movement she'd caught in the glass of the room with the French doors had been.

To Charlene's right was a maze of brick waist-high planters intended for an atrium garden but empty now, the dead dirt still packed tight in the metal containers that lined the inside of the brick flower boxes. Charlene knew she should descend and walk the mazes, discover their patterns, find her way in and out of them, but that was one part of the house she really disliked. She could not make herself approach it. She tried to see it alive, with plants and flower blooms and hanging vines weeping moisture from the pool on the other side of the catwalk, but all she could see were the zigs and zags of the walkways and the chilling emptiness of the planters.

She moved on, her slippers making dry little pitty-pat

sounds on the catwalk, and beyond the pool, glancing over at the barred windows there, she thought again she saw a figure mistily brushing up against the glass then withdrawing into the cocoon of fog that licked at the house. She stopped. She took a step to the rail and placed both hands on it, holding on tightly, squinting and watching to see a reappearance of the figure. It was a man, she knew that much. A woman would not have such wide shoulders or wear a dark coat and a floppy wide-brimmed hat.

"What do you want?" she called out, and her voice echoed high up to the green panels of roof glass where it left behind an echo in her ears.

The figure did not appear again so she hurried to the other side of the catwalk, but now she was beginning to shake, and she was sure she heard the voices of the children who had attended the parties around the pool area so long ago. They laughed . . .

At her?

. . . at nothing, and their bare feet slapped against wet brick, making sounds like firecrackers popping; they joshed one another and pushed and teased and splashed the water. They lived again, doing what they had done in this house on those nights of revelry that constituted the past.

Oh God, voices were coming back, surrounding her, and Charlene had to cover her ears with the heels of her hands, she had to close her eyes against this invasion, fighting to keep it away.

She had not always heard voices. They had started up in the past ten years or so, tormenting her, breaking down the borders of reality so that she was confused, incapable of understanding where she was and what she was doing. Doctors at Marion State had done nothing to alleviate this torture beyond giving her medications that dulled her senses and made her dream while awake. They said the Thorazine would help, but it hadn't. She wasn't a proper schizophrenic, she supposed, or so they had told her.

"Stop it," she whispered, startling herself, but she must plead with the sounds she could still hear even with her ears sealed shut with the thick flesh of her hands. "Please, stop it."

She turned and ran the rest of the way across the catwalk, rushed down one open side where the pool was at her left. She found a doorway and hurried through it. She found herself in an empty room that might never have been used for anything, by anyone. It had one entrance and exit, and at the end of it windows faced the bay. She couldn't see the water for the fog. Everywhere the fog. And that lurker within it, who had caused the voices to come.

She turned back, flew past the catwalk, to the opening into the big back section of the mansion. Here was another living area, one that provided a view of the bay on sunny days. The furniture here was not as good as that in the formal living room at the front of the house. The long sofa was covered in a brown plaid weave and there were worn spots on the armrests and two of the flattened cushions. There was a wicker rocker facing the windows, its sunflower-patterned seat pad ripped and mildewed. A maple coffee table, legs scarred. Two extra tables too tall for the sofa, one holding a squat aqua-colored lamp with a stained shade the color of smoke.

Charlene shivered, memorizing the dimensions, the placement of the furniture. She rushed through the remaining rooms. Two baths, one full, one a half-bath with toilet and sink, another kitchen, but not nearly as set up or roomy as the one on the other side of the house—the refrigerator was white and old but still running, she could hear the compressor humming; the stove a countertop affair, no oven; a table painted black, two uncomfortable chairs pushed beneath it. There were two more empty rooms like the first she'd entered, meant to be bedrooms, she suspected. One faced the bay, as had the first one, the other was on the side of the house facing the back driveway and the weedy field beyond.

She wanted across the catwalk and away from this empty section of the mansion, but she dreaded the walk across the big open space, and the fog at the windows, and the chance of seeing the coated, hatted figure sliding along the outside again. She drew a deep breath, like a runner readying for the sprint and, gripping the catwalk's railing on each side of her, she took off at a dead run for the other side. "Safe, safe, safe," she repeated to herself as she ran, thinking if she whispered it furiously enough and long enough it would be true, that nothing could harm her. Above her magical incantation the boys' laughter rang out loud and clear as bells in a Sunday village, and she ducked her chin to her chest as she skittered across the vast openness, speaking louder and louder until she was shouting, "SAFE, SAFE, SAFE, SAFE . . . !"

Out of breath, wrapped in her baggy sweater, trembling with relief, she came out onto the marble landing overlooking the front entrance and curving stairway. Ahead of her was a flicker of the man at the front door, trying the door knob. She saw him silhouetted in the panels of pebbled, leaded glass. The hat brim was angled down to obscure his face.

She caught and held her breath, old fears returning to paralyze her where she stood.

She watched the gold burnished knob twist an inch one way and then the other, and she caught the scream in her throat before it escaped. The knob stilled, the man disappeared or never was, she didn't know, she had no way of knowing if she was truly in danger or conjuring it. She had lost the capacity to tell the difference so long ago. It was hell never to know when things might be real or imagined, true hell so much worse than the one preachers talked about from pulpits.

An inner voice—calm and in control—told her to drop to her knees, to crawl beneath the banister railing, to try hiding from view. It would not work, though she obeyed the voice. The chandelier a story above her shone down yellow and bright and revealing.

She crawled this way until she reached her room and did not come to her feet again until she made it to the drapes hanging to one side of her double, ceiling-to-floor windows. She caught at the drawstring, yanking closed the drapes with a rattling *swish*. She stood, watching the drapes sway then hang silently, rebuking her.

She sat on the side of her bed, breathing noisily through her open mouth. Had there been someone outside, peeking in at her? Did she just imagine it? Was he at the door just then, trying the brass knob, skating away into the fog when he found it locked? *Was it the rapist who had stolen half her mind?*

But no one could get inside. This was a fortress, locked and barred and *secure. Safe.* She wouldn't be caught again doing a house chore, taken from behind, astonished to find a hand over her mouth.

Yet the house was too large and empty, full of boys at a party, diving and swimming and involved in horseplay. It was shadowed and dark, lost in a fog so thick it was worse than a somber winter night. That was not safety. That held no security.

Don't think about it.

She wouldn't. She didn't have to. No one could make her afraid if she didn't allow it. Instead, she could go over the map in her head and lay out the rooms, the halls, the closets, the cubbyholes, the exits and entrances, the six-car underground garage that sat empty beneath the back of the house, the immense ballroom, two kitchens, a massive dining room, the men's and women's bathrooms near the pool—with six toilet stalls and six showers in each—the bars, those wonderful bars, all those black wrought-iron bars that covered the entire three stories. The only place she had not investigated—besides the atrium maze, because she couldn't force herself inside—was the dark muggy earthy-smelling passage beneath the brick catwalk. She'd never go in there. It was too much like a tomb, claustrophobic, never ending. It was some kind of passage on that floor connecting the two sections of the mansion the way the catwalk connected it on the upper floor. Who could go in there, though? How could anyone walk down a concrete passageway where spiders and roaches and rats and maybe even snakes might slither?

She glanced at the bedside clock she brought from the hospital, a wind-up Big Ben she carried with her everywhere. It was eight o'clock. Shadow had been gone an hour. She wouldn't be back until the middle of the night, three or four A.M. Until then Charlene had to make do. She had to keep the voices out of her head and the stranger at the windows out of the house. There were—she counted on her fingers—seven or eight hours before she could relax.

She would have to stay busy. When Shadow worked, Charlene worked. It was the sort of arrangement she thought only fair. And she did have to keep herself sane when she was alone, that was the hardest time, and the most difficult thing to do. It was easier in the state hospital. There were other women to keep her company, life stories to listen to and recall, people who needed her to care for them, to talk to them.

On the streets, before knowing Shadow, Charlene suffered the worst of all. No one would listen to her. No one! Not even bums and the street people who seemed to listen to one another, at least. They called her a crazy lady and shooed her away. Her life was in constant peril, ever veering out of control. She imagined every person she saw whispered at her back, every glance her way was one of hatred, every man who came as close as three feet a sexual menace.

She smiled now, thinking of what good fortune she was enjoying. Shadow did listen. Shadow never made fun of her or told her to shut up and go away. She even, on occasion, held conversations with her, just as if she were real and worthy of attention. Shadow brought her take-out food some nights. She let her run with her and exercise with her on the living room rug. She complimented her cooking, though Charlene knew it was really not that good, and she admired how she kept the house so clean, so shining, ''like jewels in a crown,'' that's what Shadow told her, that she made everything sparkly and new the way it once might have been.

Charlene heard a light tapping—*tap tap tap*—at the window covered by the drapes and she started from the bed in wordless fright, the folds of her skirt clutched in both fists. She stood all atremble, listening for it again. When it did not come, after a full fifteen minutes of stiff waiting, she was able to let go her skirt.

She had to stop thinking she was being hounded day and night. Oh, *he* was out there, he followed her and threatened her, that was the truth, no matter what the therapists said about persecution complexes and hallucinations and paranoid delusions, but not all the time. Not every minute.

He probably wasn't there now. The fog cover had made her nervous and hysterical. He wasn't there any more than the boys were here who laughed and played at the poolside. All products of her sensitive and exaggerated imagination, that's all it was.

"I'll make strawberry shortcake," she said aloud. Talking aloud made her feel safer. It was a *real* voice and centered her in her head where she could tell the sounds came from her thoughts.

She went to the kitchen and turned on all the lights. The one over the sink, the fluorescent rectangle overhead, the light in the walk-in pantry. She closed the blinds at the window over the sink. That did away with the slinking figure she kept spying outside the house. She lined up her ingredients on the long counter. There was a package of soft spongy shortcakes she had asked Shadow to buy, the green plastic basket of ripe strawberries, the tub of whipped cream. She cleaned the strawberries, lopping off the green leaves, washing the ripe fruit, slicing them one by one into a bowl. She added a half cup of sugar and stirred and stirred. She let it sit a while to soak in the sweetness while she prepared the round cakes on individual saucers.

Shadow wouldn't eat more than one. She had to watch her figure, after all. But Charlene could eat all the rest, the remaining five. All at once or over a period of a couple of days, anything she liked, because she was free, "white, and over twenty-one," she finished aloud, laughing at herself. Happy now. Doing something. Making things right and real.

Look at the strawberries, she told herself, in the dissolved sugar, how red the juice! Feel the way the cake snaps back if I make an indentation with my finger. Taste how the whipped cream melts on the tongue, sweet and light as a summer cloud. She nearly danced in delight at how sensuous the food made her feel.

Life was glorious with Shadow, it was the way life should be, a friend on your side, a person to care for and watch after, to clean for, to cook for, to be proud of when she brought you money to spend on yourself for *anything*.

"Buy some clothes," Shadow told her. "Buy a hamster or some guppies or a dog. Dye your hair, Charlene, or get a bicycle. Anything you want, you buy. This money's yours." And she did. At the dime store in LaPorte she bought Magic Rocks and put them in a jar of water to watch them grow. She bought a fistful of pale pink roses made from seashells. She bought a cup and saucer that said, TEXAS IS THE PLACE YOU WANT TO BE.

Her room filled with things she had never been able to buy before, things she'd lusted after and hadn't the nerve to steal when Marion State let her out on her sojourns. Shadow never once said she was wasting money or that she should have bought something else. Shadow laughed happily on seeing the purchases, and sometimes drank her coffee from the Texas cup.

While swooping heaping spoonfuls of sweetened strawberries into the cake cups, Charlene halted with the spoon in the air, and thought a black thought that came like the fog from out at sea, quickly, covering everything and blotting out the world. Shadow was crying in the night.

Was that last night, after they had gone to bed? Yes. Wakened from sound sleep, Charlene heard her weeping, inconsolably, the cries muffled. It wasn't a dream. It wasn't her imagination because it had made her come awake, disturbed her sleep. She had tiptoed to the bedroom door and opened it. The crying was louder. She crept down the hall to Shadow's room and stood outside the door to make sure. It was weeping, all right, real and heartbroken.

Now what should she do about that? She dumped the strawberries onto the cake and began filling another one.

What *could* she do about it? Shouldn't people be allowed to cry when they needed to? Didn't it help them to cry, to wash away the pain inside?

But she had never seen or heard Shadow cry before. Not in the hospital. Not in this house. And now that she had found her in that condition, she realized Shadow might not be as strong and dependable as she had thought in the beginning. She might still be sick, the same as Charlene was sick. Sickness might never leave people, she decided, topping the strawberry shortcakes with lumps of cream and placing a half strawberry right in the center for decoration. Mind sickness might go underground and hide but always be there, waiting to come out, like a virus that bided its time, that lingered without symptoms until one day it took over the system and killed you. It was that way with her. It was always there.

What would she do if Shadow got sick enough to go back to the hospital? She couldn't stay in this monstrous place alone. Dear God, no.

Well, she'd return to the hospital with her and she'd care for her there as she had done before. She'd talk her out of it, she'd be at her side until she recovered.

So what if Shadow didn't recover?

Shaking her head, shaking away the very possibility, Charlene took the shortcakes to the refrigerator and aligned them side by side, pretty yellow-red-and-white desserts she couldn't wait to devour one after the other.

Now it was time to clean the kitchen and mop the floor here. Next, she would scrub down the bathroom on the second floor, the one they used most often. It was as large as a normal-sized bedroom, so many tiles to wipe, walls, floor, tub, sink. There was dusting to be done. The banister to polish. The mirrors to clean and make shine. Shadow's bed to make. The halls to sweep. And one night soon she must clean the ballroom, however long it took her, however much effort it entailed.

Humming to herself, Charlene started in, all the while the thought of the strawberry dessert in the back of her mind, making her mouth water.

She did not again see the skulking figure at one of the windows.

Chiefly because she forgot to look for him.

Thirteen

Shadow saw the man come in. He was there to catch her act once, sometimes twice a week. He sat alone, nursing a drink, his face inscrutable. For some reason she knew he was after her. She wondered if all women knew it when men wanted them, wanted some kind of relationship, lusted for them. It didn't have to be something in the eyes. The stare could fool you. Nearly all the men who came to a titty bar stared and lusted. Not all of them really would act, given a chance. But this particular man would, she knew that by picking up the invisible signals coming from him. It was the way he moved across the packed room, trying to keep her in view if he happened to come in when she was already onstage. And in the way his hands clasped around the cup on the table before him, the fingers laced together as if he didn't trust himself to raise the drink to his lips without a firm grasp. The way he homed in on her, like a radar beam, tracking even the subtle moves of her flesh that some of the others missed because they were glued on her breasts or the G-string snaking between her buttocks.

This man. He worried her. Something about him didn't match the regular clientele. The way his sports jacket hung, maybe, or the cut of his hair, or the depth in his eyes, as if he were thinking something unfathomable and not easily put into words.

She finished a dance and walked off the stage to the curtains. Two dancers stood there sharing a joint. One of them was a lush, too, and Shadow thought she was a sloppy, careless dancer, a real slut. The other one, Mad, she called herself, was young, with a pimply ass and cool gray eyes the color of volcanic stone.

Shadow said, "Who's that guy out there, the one in the brown tweed jacket. He comes in a lot."

Mad made a slit in the curtain with long, curved red nails. "That's a cop. Samson. Not Vice, though, Homicide, I think."

"A cop!"

"Oh, sugar, he don't mess with us," the lush said, letting out a rush of thick heavy smoke and handing the roach to Mad. "He's got this thing for the girls. He seems to like watching. There's lotsa guys like that, all walks of life, even cops. They're human too, ain't they?" Then she laughed and choked and reached for the joint. It was Mad's song coming on. She had to hit the stage anyway.

Shadow shrugged, not interested in more conversation with the older woman. She noticed as she moved past her to the dressing room that one of the hag's nipples was puckered, the brown tip bending oddly to the left, like a bent wire. Ought to see about that, she thought. Might be a tumor working. But she would never say that to the old dame. Her nipples were her business.

The girls all dressed in the same long narrow room where a row of scarred wooden benches ran along a counter set into the wall below mirrors that stretched to the low ceiling.

Shadow was finished for the night. She jerked out the bills in her purple G-string, counted them. Ninety-six dollars. She turned the tumblers on the combination lock that secured her locker, pulled out a small black purse, and added the bills to the wad inside. She had made three hundred or so tonight, a good take, *very* good.

The cop in the tweed jacket never tipped her, never came near the stage. Sometimes the barkeep handed the girls tips men left with him, shy men afraid to reach out to dancers onstage, so maybe the cop paid them that way, but she wouldn't bet on it. There was something about him had nothing to do with being a cop that made her leery of his attention.

She stepped out of the G-string. Damn thing had set her back sixty-five bucks. They sold dancer strings and bras and see-through jackets at a booth just outside the dressing room, but the stuff was cheap, gaudy, and too expensive. This purple thing was one of her first purchases, before she knew where to shop for what she needed at a little shop down the street from the club. The G-string was already fraying around the elastic at the waist where the purple sequins were attached.

Shadow laughed and threw it into the gym bag she took home with her. How was she going to become a class act in bits of sequin and elastic that wouldn't last through a week?

Dressed in black slacks, a black silk pullover, and black jacket, she shouldered the bag, her purse, slammed shut the locker door, and twisted the combination. Dancers were notorious thieves. They'd stolen two outfits, a hundred and fifty dollars, her lipstick, and an expensive, waterproof mascara before she remembered to lock everything up tight the minute she hit the dressing room.

In the hall she pushed past Dawn, an eighteen-year-old whose hair was bleached white as snow, and rounded the corner for the back exit door. Outside in the alley, she looked around for lurkers and perverts, saw the cop coming from the front street entrance, and felt her heart catch.

Goddamn it, what did he think he was doing? She talked to no one. Dated no one. Slept with no one. This was business, her dancing, not a leg up to prostitution the way it was for other girls, and she'd be damned if she'd let some cop come messing around.

She turned sharply and hurried to the back parking lane behind the building, unlocked the door of the Toyota, jumped behind the wheel. As she turned the key in the ignition and fired the engine, she glanced in the rearview mirror and saw him rounding the corner, making for her. She slipped the transmission into drive and left just as he raised his hand to flag her down.

Jesus God. What did he want with her? But she knew, deep in her woman's heart, she knew it had nothing to do with police work, it had to do with *want* and *need* and *the illusion,* all the things she was not willing to deal with again, maybe never again in all the rest of her life.

Mitchell stood with his hand raised in the air, feeling foolish. "You damn fool," he said, then grunted in disgust at himself.

He watched the brake lights of her car blink as she turned into the street, vanishing beyond the many-storied buildings on the block. An errant breeze slipped around the corner and licked at his cheeks. It smelled of Chinese food and hamburgers on a grill and burned coffee. It smelled like the city on a lazy, late-spring lonely night.

Whatever had possessed him? He didn't talk to the girls. He had never before followed one outside to the parking lane behind the club, hoping to flag her down.

And if he'd succeeded, what would he have said? "I'm crazy for you. There's something about you that pulls me like a magnet. I can't get through a week without seeing you. Why are you dancing naked this way, demeaning yourself to those scumbags? You've got to stop it!"

He rubbed his chin, feeling the stubble growing there since he'd shaved early in the morning. This was all wrong. He was dropping like a wet sack of cement into a morass. This obsession made no sense in his life. He should have been doing something worthwhile, not hanging out waiting for Shadow to get off work. He had cases—a caseload to kill a workhorse!—that he could have been working. He had people to see, places to go. Didn't he always?

Yet he was acting like some lovesick son of a bitch, some wacko like those stalkers who fixated on girls, complete strangers, hoping to find a way to make a connection. He needed a shrink.

He didn't need a shrink.

He needed . . .

He wanted . . .

To hell with this shit, it was making him crazy. He had a murder to investigate, a gay bashing that went to the dreadful limit, poor guy found in a trash bin with his skull crushed to pulp. Someone on the street would know something, might have seen something. They hadn't found the weapon, but the M.E. had said it was probably a tire iron or length of pipe or wood they took along in the trunk of the car and disposed of later. He didn't have the tissue samples analyzed yet. He'd know if it was metal or wood soon.

The victim didn't go down easy. Bruises laced both his upper forearms, and a half-moon bruise rode one hip, as if he'd been kicked. With that kind of resistance, someone might have heard him fighting for his life.

And *that's* what Samson had to find out.

He had to stop slipping into alleyways at two in the god-damned morning trying to talk with a stripper.

He had a job to perform, bad as it was, depressed as it made him, hopeless as it sometimes seemed.

He turned and moved from the alley to the street, blinking at the lights, the car horns, the giggles of teens breaking curfew who gave him wide berth as he stepped onto the sidewalk. He thought maybe he'd find Big Mac and see if she had something for him.

But before leaving the club behind him, he couldn't help one last quick furtive glance at the framed poster advertising SHADOW, THE NEWEST STAR, and felt his heart leap and settle sick in his chest, lonely for her, sorry she was gone where he could not follow.

She thought she saw someone in her headlights as she drove too fast down the brick circle drive to the mansion, but just as the figure appeared in the heavy fog, it disappeared, and she decided she had been daydreaming, the way she did sometimes when she drove.

She parked underneath in the dark cavernous garage, thinking we need to get lightbulbs down here, and hurried around the big building with the deep thick scent of the garage's packed damp dirt in her nostrils. She ran up the wide marble steps leading to the second-floor front entrance. She had the keys out, the door unlocked, and was smiling before she saw Charlene in her blue slippers and housecoat standing with a dish of something strawberry in her hands. She closed the door.

"Are you hungry?" Charlene asked. "I made short-cake."

"I can go for that." She dropped the gym bag to the floor where she stood and took the saucer. She kicked off her shoes and glided to the leather sofa before the dead fireplace. The first bite was heaven. Strawberries and whipped cream brought a hungry moan to her lips.

"I did the floors," Charlene said, standing over Shadow, hands hanging at her sides.

"They look great. Shiny and all. Why don't you sit down, take a load off? Aren't you eating?"

"I will later. I . . . I already had one. But there's plenty more."

"You're wonderful, Charlene. I could get used to treatment like this. I feel like a princess or something."

Charlene bowed her head at the compliment. She took a seat in one of the big white cushiony chairs and crossed her feet at the ankles, hands in her lap. A content pose. Now that Shadow was here.

"I thought I saw someone outside when I was cleaning house." Charlene's brow wrinkled as she reported this information. Her hands found one another and clasped tightly.

Shadow paused with a spoon of strawberries halfway to her mouth. She frowned. "Where?"

"Oh, at the door. At the windows. But I guess it was the fog playing tricks."

Shadow thought about it. Charlene's nerves were not in the best shape in the world. Easily frightened, easily upset. But hadn't she thought she too had seen someone in the drive?

"When?" she asked.

"Earlier. Hours ago."

"Is the door locked? Did I lock the door?"

Charlene started from the chair immediately, her slippers slapping pitty-pat across the marble to the door where she checked, found it unlocked, and turned the deadbolt, put on the chain. "There," she said softly. "Safe."

Shadow sighed, suddenly tired, the night closing down for those hours before dawn, her inner clock ticking slower and slower, her eyelids drooping even as she finished off the shortcake and licked the spoon clean. "We better hit it," she said. "The dessert was great, thanks for the calories, kid."

Charlene took the saucer and spoon to the kitchen, her sincere and courteous, "You're welcome," trailing behind her.

Together they turned out the lights downstairs, checked the door one last time (Charlene did, just to be sure, she said), and went up the stairs to the bedrooms. Charlene turned to the left of the staircase, Shadow to the right.

"Good night," Shadow called.

"Good night," Charlene echoed.

Soon there was darkness in all the mansion and outside the fog moving conspicuously in waves and eddies against the barred glass.

Charlene swam from the black dungeon of sleep, where nothing disturbed her, to the shoals of wakefulness, just on the brink where reality was whatever she thought it might be.

His hands.

Bringing down the sheet, letting in the cool night to her uncovered arms and legs.

His fingers.

Lightly touching her gown, molding the cotton material against her breasts.

Her legs.

Pushed apart, the gown lifted, the air stirred by the balloon affect so that she shivered and swam closer to the surface where life might or might not be dangerous.

And then the weight!

And his breath staggering her senses, covering her mouth with a rough hand so that she was forced to breathe him in, his sweat and old clothes smell.

Charlene woke completely into terror, frozen on the bed, someone, *someone* on top of her body, pressing at her.

His voice.

Shushing her. "Quiet, quiet," he says, "I can kill you if I want to, if you scream, if you move, I can take your eyes, I can break your neck, I can strangle you in a second, quiet now, still, lie still, I won't be long . . ."

A total frenzy. Charlene coming apart. Flying apart like shattered glass. Splintering with a scream that drove his hand down her cheek to her neck where it tried to hold her fast to the bed, but she was too insane for him, too scared to care if he killed her, too willing to die rather than let him take her as she'd been taken before.

The scream was one long interminable screech from one dying and grateful for it.

His hand slipped, sweaty, from the meat at her throat and plunged down into the pillow behind her head. He tried pinning her down again with his hips, his knees on either side of her, but she was wild with panic, driven to an explosion that made her physical form twisty as a snake, whipping back and forth to dislodge him, to shatter his existence. He lurched forward and down, forehead striking her teeth, blood from the gash spraying out over her face in the dark. His hat flew from his head, was lost, one of his shoes was knocked from his foot and clattered with a bang onto the floor.

She wouldn't stop screaming, the screaming filled the world and set off red blossoms of fear in his head.

But the fire that pierced his back between his shoulder blades caught him by surprise and it was that fire that made him rise up over the woman in the bed, grab awkwardly behind him, then plummet sideways to the hard marble floor, his head cracking, his consciousness spinning through a vortex sparkling with bursts of starlight, fading.

"Stop it!" Shadow slapped Charlene across the face in an effort to bring her from the madness that claimed her.

Charlene's scream died so suddenly that the resulting silence was as loud as crackling from a stadium microphone.

"I think he's dead."

Charlene lifted herself from the bed, her hair all in her

face and standing out like a gray halo. She looked at Shadow in the dim lamplight coming from the bedside and said, "Who's dead?"

Shadow pointed to the body of a man lying in a pool of blood on the floor. He looked like a common middle-class working man, a salesman for an electronics store, perhaps, a librarian, a bookkeeper. But his hair was sparse and blood-flecked, and his head was turned too far back. Much too far.

"What's he doing here?"

"Charlene, are you all right? Listen to me closely now. Remember telling me when I came home that you saw someone skulking around the house?"

"I said that?"

"Well, you were right. I thought I saw someone too, when I drove in, but I wasn't sure. Then I heard you screaming."

"Did he . . . did he . . . ?" Charlene looked down at herself as if just discovering she was a human with a body. Her gown was torn. And bloody near the neckpiece, the lace there a muddy red. And still wet. "Sticky," she said, feeling the material between her fingers.

"He was trying to rape you."

"Did he?"

"No. I ran for the kitchen and found a knife. I need to see if . . ." Shadow dropped to the floor onto her knees and tentatively reached one hand to the man's neck to feel for a pulse. The handle of a knife stuck obscenely from his shoulders, the blade buried to the hilt.

"He's dead."

"Oh God, oh God . . ." Charlene was off the bed in a second, rushing past the body and out the door into the dark hall of the mansion.

"Charlene!"

Shadow raced after her and took a hairpin turn through empty moonlit rooms to where Charlene ended up in the ballroom. Standing in a corner, talking to the wall.

"Aw, Charlene, come on now, it's all over, I didn't let him hurt you."

"... in the twilight of the last day there will be men running swords through the children ..."

"Charlene, honey, don't."

"... when the bugle call sounds the dead will rise up to avenge their murderers ..."

It was babbling. Eerie disjointed talk. Scarier than the man who had attacked them in the night.

"Oh, Charlene, it's all right, you're all right now, nothing's going to hurt you, I promise."

She led the woman from the corner, through the stippling of moonlight, across the wide-open ballroom floor. She shushed her, holding tightly to her arm, whispering close to her face.

Outside the fog had shredded away, washed out to sea or inland, but gone. It was still dark and Shadow said, "I have to call the police." But Charlene began that scream again, the one that was like a siren full blast, and Shadow grabbed her arms and shook her quiet, then said, "All right, no cops. I'll take him out in the motorboat. Before light. And dump him in the bay, the motherfucker."

And that is what she did. No regrets.

Fourteen

Nobody right. Nobody wrong.

As Charlene helped her carry the rapist's body across the catwalk and down the stairs to the back exit of the mansion, Shadow listened as those words circled through her brain. *Nobody right. Nobody wrong.*

They were black vulture words. The kind that scavenged over morals, picking and choosing the tastiest bits.

Shadow had heard them in a song played by the deejay of the club where she danced. She didn't know the song's title or the singer, but the words came back to her when she lifted the rapist, holding him under the armpits, Charlene taking up the legs.

She thought she might have said it out loud to soothe Charlene's hysteria. "Nobody's right here, nobody's wrong. This guy took a chance to do what he wanted to do and he lost. I *had* to kill him, Charlene. He might have strangled you if I didn't."

What she neglected to say was that there was a surprising lift when she'd sunk the blade into the intruder's back.

When Charlene first screamed, Shadow had flung off sleep as if it was a shawl, her mind clicked into fast time, time that ran faster than real time. She dashed to the kitchen, found the knife in the dark, the drawer pulled from the cabinet and dropped with a teeth-rattling clatter to the floor. One reel later and she was at the door to Charlene's room, bursting in, flying effortlessly across the floor to the figure humped over her friend, and it was . . . it was *natural*. It was *easy* to bring the arc of her arm down with all her strength.

Nobody right. Nobody wrong. The rapist should have

died for his sins, therefore he did. Shadow was no more than a conduit of justice. She had served it quickly, thoughtlessly. Execution was not so bad when it was done right.

"Do you want me to go with you?" Charlene had on her gray baggy sweater over the stained and torn nightgown. She stood twisting both ends of the sweater into knots.

Shadow thought it more hazardous to take her. "Stay here. Go back into the house and lock the doors again. I can do this by myself."

"What if he's not dead?"

"He's dead." Shadow untied the boat from the short pier's mooring.

"If he's not dead, he'll drown."

"I don't give a fuck if he drowns. But he won't. He's dead."

"You'll come back?"

Shadow paused before stepping into the bow of the small boat. She looked down at the sack of human excrement she must keep company into the dark waters of the bay.

"Charlene," she said. "I'm your friend. I'll never leave you to fend for yourself. You saved me once. I saved you tonight." She looked from the corpse to the other woman. "We're like sisters. I'll come back, I promise."

Charlene nodded her head, accepting this as truth. Then, as Shadow watched her ravaged face, the tears formed two steady streams that flowed unimpeded down Charlene's cheeks. She cried silently, her gaze locked on the pearl light creeping from the distant horizon of the sea.

Shadow felt the rage she hadn't acknowledged when murdering the intruder. It made her want to kill him all over again, in a slower, more torturous way. To stop those hurt tears from Charlene's eyes at that moment, she thought she would have gladly skinned the rapist inch by inch, even if it took a week to do it.

She stepped away from the boat and put her arms around Charlene. "Don't think about it. Put it out of your mind. Pretend it never happened. It was a nightmare."

"I never know when they're coming," Charlene said in a ragged breath that was hardly above a whisper. "They come out of nowhere and they hurt me. I don't know how to protect myself."

"Hush, hush now. You don't have to. I'll protect you."

Once beyond the breakwater and rolling with the waves of the bay, the distant shoreline a row of lights strung through darkness, Shadow found herself—another surprise—talking to the body.

"You made a big mistake, pal. You picked on the wrong women, you slack-mouthed bastard. Didn't you know there were two of us? If you'd come for me, it might not have ended this way. You might have scared me into submission, but not Charlene, she's damaged so bad, she didn't care what you did, all she wanted was to have it over and done forever."

She shut off the boat's motor and let the waves push them back and forth, flotsam in the Gulf waters.

"You don't weigh so much. You can't overpower any more defenseless women now, can you, you fuck?"

She first lifted his feet and dropped his legs over the side of the boat. Then she moved cautiously down his body to his head and shoulders. That area of his body was soaked. She made a mental note to clean out the boat when the sun came up.

"I get you out of here, I don't want you coming back."

She heaved, her muscles tightening in her arms and her neck tensing as she got his torso onto her outstretched legs. He felt like an unwieldly laundry bag. She realized how much strength she'd gained from all her exercise. But was it enough?

"I fall outta this motherfuckin' boat with you, I hope to God you come back to life and die all over again! Get *out*."

She had one of his arms over the side. The boat shifted perilously. A cold sweat broke out on her face. She smelled his blood, a strong scent she couldn't disregard even when she turned aside her head. She wanted to gag but fought down the urge with pure mental determination.

She pushed and he went over headfirst, the other arm

dragging along behind at his side. His hips rose up and over the boat edge, his body not even producing a splash as he slipped under the water.

"Go, you piece of shit. Go to the bottom and feed the crabs."

She hung over the water, swallowing hard. She washed off her hands, her arms. It was cold this far out. A fish flipped, surfacing near her, and Shadow flinched, for one moment imagining the dead man revived by the sudden shock of the water and coming up for air.

She saw it was a fish. She laughed. Even to her ears the laugh sounded too high, too out of control. Too crazy. She put a hand over her mouth, watching all around for his body. She saw him floating facedown, his big coat billowing out like a dark parachute around him.

She felt the laugh die. She took his floppy hat and threw it out after him.

"There," she said, with finality. "Now you have everything you deserve."

When she returned to the pier, she was relieved to see Charlene had obeyed her and was in the house. She saw a light shining from one of the side front windows. The kitchen?

She secured the boat and climbed out. The pearl light in the sky had changed to a muted yellow the color of the dead lawns of October. No sun yet, but soon.

She saw the front of her knee-length white satin gown was blotched red with his blood. The satin stuck like glue to her breasts, her stomach.

She looked around quickly, but the mansion stood on its own three-acre piece of property. For anyone to see her, he'd have to have binoculars. At five o'clock in the morning. Not likely.

She hurried through the garage, took the wrought-iron spiral stairs to the back section's second floor, ran across the ringing catwalk calling out, "I'm back! I told you I'd always come back. Charlene? I'm here now."

Charlene appeared at the other side of the catwalk still dressed in her bloody nightgown. She did not smile or speak or raise a hand in greeting. But she also was not weeping. Shadow considered that victory enough.

Shadow's thoughts were on the details of the work she had done putting in a new deadbolt lock on the door leading from the garage into the interior of the house. The door with the broken lock where the rapist had entered.

Mad asked, "You don't date men?"

The deejay had the music cranked about ten decibels too high. The dressing room walls vibrated to every bass beat. Shadow adjusted the red-white-and-blue stage outfit and said offhandedly, "Not much." She hoped Mad wasn't making a pass. In some way she needed to get across her sexual preference to the bi's, like Mad. Might as well state it, meet the old red-eyed monster head-on.

"They call you the Ice Queen." Mad leaned over and lifted her tits into the French-cut bra so they stuck out more on top. She rounded them, the way Richard Dreyfuss in *Close Encounters of the Third Kind* rounded the mashed potatoes.

"Do they?"

"You don't go with customers. And we never seen a boyfriend."

Shadow thought of the man in the floppy hat riding Charlene and suddenly the term *boyfriend* made her frown.

"Well?"

"What?" The blade sinking through tough skin and muscle . . .

"Hey, where are you? You on something?"

Shadow looked in the wall of mirrors at the reflection of Mad's inquisitive face. It was a young face, too young to be hardened and aged in this place. "I don't do drugs." She hoped that didn't sound judgmental. She didn't care one way or the other what the other girls were into. Prostitution, drugs, who cared.

"So, you straight or what?"

"Oh. Yeah, I'm straight. I was married." Hell. She never wanted to talk about that. Her husband had killed. Now she had killed. Why didn't this similarity worry her?

"Divorced?"

Shadow blinked back memories. "Dead."

"That's too bad. Sorry I asked."

"No problem. It was a long time ago." Only two years, you liar. Before that you were an ordinary housewife. A living cliché. Look at you now. White thigh-high stockings, blue garter belt and panties, red bra. A looker. A teaser on the professional level.

"What song you doing in that outfit?" Mad asked, her curiosity taking the conversation in a new direction.

" 'American Woman.' "

"Way cool."

"You dance for the money?" Shadow used her pinkie to take off a smudge of eyeliner from the corner of her dark eyes.

"Well, I tried waiting tables, but you get the same hassle from men so I figured why not, right? Now, though, I think I'm hooked on something else besides the money."

"What's that?"

"The excitement. It's like a new adventure every night, isn't it?"

Shadow didn't answer. She thought maybe the girl wasn't looking deep enough. But then how deep did you perceive things when you were eighteen years old? Mad hadn't mentioned how addicting it was to have men adore your flesh. If that was adventure, so be it.

Mad wasn't the only young girl working the club. More than half of them were between eighteen and twenty. The remaining females were women like Shadow, older, although most of them weren't in the excellent physical condition that she was. Some of them had baggy breasts that looked like paper bags with an orange in them, or they were overweight, rolls of cloud-white flesh hanging over their G-strings.

Clubs thrived on variety. There were men who came in especially to see a fat woman, a woman who was not white, or a less-than-model-perfect desirable woman. Men had fetishes and obsessions. None of the clubs featured all young live flesh, not if they were the lower class clubs and they knew the business.

"The girls have noticed our cop's got a thing for you."

Shadow, lost in her thoughts again, was startled to see Mad still in the dressing room with her. The girl was adjusting her stockings and looking over her shoulder in the mirror at her naked ass. Now that ass, Shadow thought uncharitably, is decidedly undesirable. Her pores are clogged. She needs a dermatologist to look at those pimples.

"I'll just ignore him," she said, unconcerned.

"What's so funny," Mad said, "is he never took that kind of interest before. He useta come in here to see one girl, but he never went after her when she got off work. That was Jezebel, but she quit just before you started here."

"How do you know about him trying to see me after work?"

"You forget I was onstage when you left your shift. I saw him leave. He looked like he had a real mission. I knew he was going for the alley and the back where we park."

Shadow shrugged. She was tired of this conversation. What there was of it. She stowed her gear in the locker and turned the tumbler on the lock.

"He catch up with you?"

"Mad, just leave it alone, okay? I don't care about dating customers and I sure won't be in the market for a cop."

"Well, excuse me. I should ask before I take a fucking breath." She lifted her chin and made for the door.

Shadow almost apologized, but decided fuck it, maybe Mad would stop trying to get to know her. She didn't want to know the girls or have them know her. In any way. They didn't know where she lived. They didn't know about Charlene or the state mental hospital. They didn't know . . .

. . . *about the man in the hat.*

. . . about her past or future, and that's just how she wanted to keep it.

She left the empty dressing room carrying a can of Pepsi that had gone lukewarm. She sipped at it while waiting behind the curtain for her turn onstage. She occasionally peeked out at Mad, admiring how she danced. The girl was damn skinny, her breasts no larger than a boy's, and she had that unappetizing ass, but she was young enough that the music surged through her and turned her bones to jelly. She danced energetically, employing all the new dance moves. Men paid her well, as they should have.

Dragging her gaze from Mad, Shadow scoped the room. The cop wasn't there. She sighed in relief. He kept coming around, she'd go to another club. She couldn't afford getting close to a homicide officer.

Because you killed.

He had looked all right. Nice enough face. Good body with strong shoulders, a blocky sort of guy, though not short. But what if he follows you to another club?

She would tell him, then, the way she told Mad. You get out of my face, she'd tell him. You're harassing me. The department know you got the hots for exotic dancers? They know your thing for voyeurism? Don't they have a shrink on the payroll might be interested in having a little talk with a guy like you?

Still, it was interesting, a cop hanging out in titty bars not to bust girls, but to enjoy them.

He might find out you killed the man in the hat.

That was ridiculous. No one would ever know. The rapist was halfway to Cuba by now. Or taken down by sharks. There had been a shark attack the summer before on Galveston's West Beach. Took a teenager's leg in its mouth and shook it like a good supper bone. Boy almost lost his leg. Stitches and miracle drugs saved it. How much better an entire human for lunch?

Mad flounced offstage. She made a wide berth for Shadow, who moved up for her cue.

"Fuckin' Ice Queen," Mad said below her breath.

"Get a life, Mad." Shadow was too sorry for the girls and women she worked with to get really angry with them. They were all sisters under the skin. Bumping and humping their way to glory. Or the bank. Whatever.

The lights rose from punk violet to frosty blue as the first strains of "American Woman" belted from the speaker system.

She was on. She set the Pepsi on the floor. Air caught in her chest, was held there two beats, let out. She drew back the curtain and went into the routine she'd practiced over and over in the mansion ballroom. This was her first time coordinating a song with an outfit.

And the club went wild.

Scaring her for a split second, then rolling over her like . . .

. . . *one of those gentle waves in the bay.* . . .

She fell into the song the way . . .

. . . *the body fell into the water.* . . .

Easy, smooth, she worked out the moves, bending her body around the lyrics, the beats driving fast and solid as . . .

. . . *her hand brought the knife down into his back.* . . .

She never knew how she got through her spots, but even less so this night. Her mind kept slipping off from what she *wanted* to think into alien thoughts coming from somewhere else.

She took off the red sequined jacket for the audience, the panties, revealing a white G-string beneath, and finally the bra just at the end of the song.

The lights went down softer so that a man would have to have X-ray vision to see her well, and she moved onto one of the stage arms leading into the audience. There, in G-string, garter belt, and stockings, her body rocked the men into a lullaby with a slow Billie Holiday blues song backing her up. They stuffed her garter belt with bills. Big bills.

She smiled.

She danced.

She thought of the new lock on the door leading from the garage and of murder most foul.

Fifteen

Son's mother rolled onto her side, swinging her feet to the floor. Son was busy. She could go to the bathroom by herself.

She believed this up to the moment the pains made her grimace and stopped her dead in her tracks, not two feet from the bedside.

The door seemed too far away. Another five or six steps. She couldn't just stand here, her bladder hurting this way.

It was her back, along the spine, and her hips, in the sockets. It was her elbows and her knees. Her ankles. It was everything. Her body had turned on her over the years. If she had any gumption at all, she'd do away with herself, save Son from being burdened with an old invalid mother.

The thought of suicide, even when couched in words like *do away with herself,* left a bitter taste in her mouth. She didn't believe in such things. It was a coward's way. Are you a mouse or a man? Where did that saying come from anyway? It was women who were stronger. Let some man have a baby, see the whole human race die out! She remembered when Son was born. . . .

She turned slowly, like a gear in a machine needing oil, and made it to the bed again. She slumped onto it, leaning over on one arm to support herself.

She didn't want to call Son. He was working.

What a wonderfully devoted man he was, and so brilliant. They had even given him an award for his mysteries, but he wouldn't leave her to go to New York City for the ceremony. They shipped the little ceramic bust of Edgar Allan Poe to him in a carton of Styrofoam wriggles that spilled out all over the floor of her bedroom when he lifted it out for her to see. It was a funny-looking statue, but Son was inordinately proud of it, explaining what an honor this prize was in his genre. *Genre.* A beautiful word that made her think of French silks and Paris nights.

She hadn't seen the award since. She wondered if he put it on the shelf in his office. She never went in there. Son needed his privacy to write. She'd never invade his sanctum or interfere with his creative life.

She drew her legs onto the coverlet and lay back, sighing with pain. She could hold her water a little longer. She'd wait until Son came in to see about her before asking to be taken to the toilet.

She could do it. She had done it before. With only one or two mistakes. Out of how many times? Dozens. Hundreds. She always waited patiently when she could manage it.

She had wanted to be a writer at one time, when she was younger. She had old spiral notebooks somewhere in the attic full of her little stories. She remembered writing them when Son was small. Deep in the night after she had finished the house chores and her child slept, she hauled out a notebook and wrote about an older time, a time that had never existed for her. She thought she might have some writing talent. But of course she had also wanted to be an actress, play opposite Valentino in the silent movies. Have him bend her back and kiss her passionately on the screen.

Dreams. They were lovely things because they caused no harm. It wasn't depressing to her that she had had to work in business and make a living for her and Son. She wasn't unhappy her dreams never came true. They had for Son, and that made up for everything, for every sacrifice and lost opportunity.

She had showed her stories to Son when he first began writing. He was kind (he was her son!), but she could tell her rambling, old-fashioned prose fell short for his tastes. They were soft flowery pieces about girls in gingham dresses picking daisies in the fields outside little rural towns, about families, big families with lots of children and parents who loved one another. They were silly old things and she shouldn't have showed such flawed work to a talented son. What was he supposed to say?

When she read his books—he never let her see them until they were published, their pages smelling crisply of new paper and their jackets splashed with bright, vibrant colors—she was taken by his imagination. When copies of the first novel came in the mail, a box of them, and she read the first chapter, she knew what she called "writing" was a far different thing from what writing really was. Son took you into new places, inside his detective's head, and he made you believe in that world so that time hung suspended.

She, certainly, had never been able to do something like that with her own pitiful scribblings.

Oh, she had led such a charmed life. It was true her husband, Son's father, was temperamental and she never understood him, but once she was out of that situation, everything had been lovely. Even when she had to hold down two jobs and pay for baby-sitters, she thought her life touched by magic to have a child at home waiting for her, looking up to her. Loving her.

She poured all her love into him, every ounce of it she possessed, and when he put his little arms around her neck and kissed her cheek, she nearly swooned with a mother's joy that filled her heart and overflowed to warm every corner of her being.

He was always a good boy. Never once a problem with him. Other mothers confided how their children wet the bed even into their teen years, or how they ran away from home, or took up pot smoking or some other horrible drug. Or they got pregnant or impregnated their teenage girlfriends, became thieves, hustlers, liars, and frauds. But Son made her proud. He brought home top grades. He had a paper route by the time he was nine. He attended the university and found a way to make his mark upon the world.

He *listened* to her.

He loved her back.

A grunt of satisfaction left her lips before she caught it. Why was it as she grew old and weak that she remembered the far past so much better than the near past? She couldn't be making it rosier than it was, could she? Just so she'd have good memories to keep her company? What an odd thought. She wished she didn't have these odd thoughts that set her off balance. Of course she hadn't embroidered the past. She'd had a wonderful life, just like that old Christmas movie said, the one with James Stewart, it was a wonderful life.

She heard Rush Limbaugh squealing from the radio. He must have been tapping the microphone because it snagged her attention. That Rush. She had to smile. He knew how to entertain, that's for sure. She didn't agree with the politics he spouted, but she suspected he didn't mean them anyway. He was playing a little game, though sometimes she thought he might really be a mean-spirited kind of person. But his little game made him famous.

Like her son.

And weren't all the types of entertainment game playing? Books, movies, television, and radio?

Now that was a question that could keep her mind engaged for another thirty minutes or so.

She tightened her legs, hoping to hold her bladder in check a while longer. She felt her tissue-thin skin wrinkle into folds as she did this, but didn't mind it. She was at home in the old body, as useless as it had become to her. After all, it was the only one she had, and she had lived in it for more than eighty years. Eight long decades and more.

If she had learned about playfulness and games, maybe her writing would have blossomed the way Son's had. All she had wanted to set down to paper was an idyllic time and place and family. Wildflowers in fields nodding their heads in the breeze. Mama and Papa in the kitchen bringing the dinner to the table for their many children. And those children! Their ruddy faces, hair the color of new copper, laughing like glass chimes tinkling in the wind.

Ah . . .

To have her body back now. To be able to rule it and make it obey. To have her fingers flexible enough to hold a pencil and a pad of paper. For it was certain she had lost her chance to star in silent films. . . .

She had to pee!

"Son!"

Oh gawd. She hadn't wanted to do that.

"Son! Hurry!"

Or that.

He came into the room with his hair all mussed, a sheaf of typewritten pages in his hand. "What is it?"

"I think I wet myself," she said in a small embarrassed voice.

"You should have called me earlier, Mother."

She turned her face on the pillow to avoid seeing the disappointment and revulsion creeping into his eyes.

He was *not quite* the little boy she remembered. But he was good all the same. And she was a selfish old dolt with hot urine leaking from between her thighs.

She wished she might die.

He helped her take the gown off, pulling it over her head, keeping his stare firmly on the bedclothes behind her so as not to have to witness her shrunken body. He handed her the housecoat, let her stand on her own and close it before leading her by the arm down the hall to the bathroom.

While she attended herself inside, he went back to her room and stripped the wet sheets from the bed, flinging them on the floor around his feet. He had to wipe down the plastic cover on the mattress with Lysol and dry it with a clean towel before putting on clean sheets and arranging the many pillows and the cover.

He grabbed up the soiled sheets in his arms and hurried with them to the laundry room. He started the washing machine and dumped in Tide and a cup of Clorox before throwing in the sheets.

He slammed down the lid of the machine. Stood with both hands flat on it, feeling the agitator swish the water back and forth. The strong bleach smell filled his nose and made his eyes water.

"I'm ready, Son."

He heard her. He deliberately didn't make a move her

way. Not yet. She needed a little punishment for this stunt. "Son?"

Maybe she'd try to get back to the room on her own, fall down, and break a hip. Oh yeah. Then he'd *really* have extra work to do.

He broke from the machine and went to the hall. She stood with her eyes downcast. He took her arm. At the bedside he helped her onto the mattress. He thought he could still smell urine. Did it permeate plastic eventually? Christ. Maybe the room smelled of it, the entire house, and he just didn't know, having gotten used to it. That would be loathsome.

"I won't do it again," she said.

"It was just an accident. You changed my diapers. I don't see why I can't help you out now."

He saw his words had moved her. She was about to cry. "Come on, Mother, it's nothing. How about a glass of iced tea? Would you like that?"

She nodded.

He bent down and kissed her cheek. "I'll just be a minute."

Once he had her settled and happy again, he made for the study where his work waited. The cursor beat like a miniature heart on the screen. He was filching a scene from Lloyd C. Douglas. Douglas had written, "One afternoon in latter August, within a few minutes of the closing hour, a young chap was shown into my cramped cubicle with his left hand bound in a dirty rag."

Son had rewritten it so that it read, "Late August, about to leave the clinic, a boy came into my narrow office, his left hand wrapped in a dirty bandage."

It was tedious to refine and update the old writers he stole from, but he hadn't any alternative. There wasn't a chance in a million that he could think up ideas of his own and write them to completion. It fairly boggled his mind to think no one in publishing or in his audience had caught him yet. If they ever did, he would be disgraced and never published again.

The thought frightened him. How would he live then? Who would pay the bills?

He heard the washing machine change over to a rinse cycle, and it made him think of the sheets, soaking with her old hot piss. Maybe she deserved to have a disgraced son. To know how fraudulent he was. She placed entirely too much stock in his ''creativity.'' She thought he was a rare bird when in truth he was nothing but a raven pecking at the eyes of men who had truly been artists.

Vexed by these thoughts about himself, he turned from the computer to fetch his mother's tea.

In his office again he took the newspaper lying on the center table. He shook it open and took a seat in his desk chair. He carefully combed through the reports, looking for an interesting and unsolved death.

In a two-inch column toward the back of the news section, he found mention of a body washed down the Kemah Channel. Shrimpers coming in from the bay had seen it floating and brought it on board. There was a knife wound in the man's back. Police said the victim had been out on parole for sexual assault. It sounded as if the guy had a rap sheet a yard long.

Well, he wasn't on parole anymore. Someone had yanked it and sent him to hell. It might be something to keep an eye on.

But one body meant nothing.

When was there going to be some excitement in this city? The last serial murders had been two years before, a psychiatrist who had been in on the sadomasochistic scene, taking down wealthy married ladies who led secret lesbian lives. Now *that* had been worthwhile. Three of the older bisexual rich bitches had succumbed in his hands while the psychiatrist lost his innocent plea and wound up on death row in Huntsville Correctional Unit.

Son chuckled to himself, then looked around to make sure his mother had not crept to his doorway and heard him. If she ever did that . . .

He folded the paper carefully and put it away. He twisted around in the chair toward the monitor. He took up the book by Douglas and reread the scene he must update.

Soon he had it clearly in mind and put into modern language on the screen. His editor was going to love it. That Douglas, boy, he sure knew how to write.

❧ Sixteen ❧

Mitchell banged his knee on the corner of his desk as he came from the lieutenant's office. He grunted and swore.

Detective Jerry Dodge, "Dod," glanced up from where he sat at his own desk facing Mitchell's and said, "Bad news?"

"Shit, isn't it always?" He dropped into the chair and rubbed at the knee.

"The contract hit or the gay bashing?"

"You're behind, Dod. We caught the contract hit. He was paid by the son-in-law, old story. Trial will be coming up in a coupla months."

"Then Boss is pushing on the gay bashing." Dod took off his wire-framed spectacles and wiped them clean with a napkin he'd pulled from a bag filled with doughnuts.

"He's got the Gay Rights Committee on his ass. They bite him, he bites me. Another old story."

"That contract hit—I never even knew we solved it. You think I ought to see if we can put up one of those blackboards with the open and closed cases on it, the way they did on 'Homicide'?"

"The way they did on what? What blackboard?" The phone rang. Mitchell grabbed it, said, "Detective Samson." He listened a bit, then he said, exasperated, "I did too fill in the file number. What? Hey, find it yourself then, it can't be that hard, can it?" He paused, listening. "You want me to look it up and call you back? You want me to waste the city taxpayers' time that way for real?" He frowned hard. "All right, damn it, I'll find it. I swear it's on my report, though, you just aren't looking in the right place." He slammed down the receiver.

"I told you your typing stinks."

Mitchell shook his head. "It's not my typing, it's those morons who enter all the data in the computers. They can't read fucking English. Where do they get them, Saudi Arabia?"

Dod shrugged. But he was amused. "About that blackboard . . ."

"Dod, what in the hell are you talking about?"

"You never watch TV?"

"Nature shows on PBS."

"You don't know about that prime time show they tried, David Lynch thought it up?" When Mitchell just stared at him, Dod continued. "Well, it was called 'Homicide' and they kept a list of the cases on a blackboard in the squad room so they would all know what cases were open, what was closed. We could use that."

"We're gonna copy a television show, is that what you're saying, Dod?"

"Well, I mean, then we'd be more organized, we'd know at a glance the case status."

Mitchell shook his head. "You're about nuts, Dod. They ought to call you Edsel." He found a memo pad in his desk drawer and stuck it in his pocket. "I have to get out there, question the street."

"Happy hunting."

"Yeah." Mitchell got out of the building as fast as he could. He was still burning up about getting the old one-two-who're-we-gonna-screw? from Epstein. The gay coalition had a heavy-hitting voting block. Cops didn't look after them, they put on the pressure.

Outside, in the sunlight, Mitchell paused and experienced the heat warming his cold hands. The sun beat down on the top of his head. He wished it could inspire him, but it didn't. He had jackshit on the gay killing. Forensics said the weapon used was probably a wooden baseball bat. There were splinters found in the brain matter. No surprise. No witnesses turned up, but that too was no surprise. People didn't talk unless they had to. He'd go back to the scene, where the Dumpster stood, and check out the surrounding buildings, question the people behind every window on every floor. He could send out someone else to do the legwork, but he had no other leads anyway, he might as well do it himself.

He walked in double time to the precinct parking lot and took the car assigned to him, a two-year-old Buick that had a loose tappet and a front seat that was stuck so he couldn't stretch out his legs. They were always scrunched under the wheel, causing him cramps.

All day long he knocked on doors and stared into the bored, glazed eyes of potential witnesses. Nothing. They weren't home. They were asleep. They had the stereo up loud. They were deaf, dumb, and blind.

That's how most days went. Into the Dumpster.

At five-thirty he was starving. He'd been on shift for two and a half hours, and he was getting nowhere on the case. Now that he didn't have a girlfriend (almost a wife!), he didn't have to worry about working the evening shift. He had tried the morning and late-night shifts, and they hadn't appealed to him. From three until eleven at night proved the best time for the sort of investigative techniques he employed.

He ordered spaghetti at a café in Montrose and drank a Corona with a lime slice. The garlic bread was hard as rock and soaked in enough garlic butter to gag an Italian. Mitchell tried and couldn't eat it. He might break a molar trying. Refusing to pay for inedible food, he made the waiter bring more bread, fresh this time.

A girl in her twenties, blond hair in a ponytail, trendy layered thrift-store clothes, gave him the eye, but he wasn't about to fool with teenyboppers. He figured he was about twenty years past that. He hunched over the spaghetti and ordered another beer.

Around eight-thirty, with the streets alive with tourists from the suburbs and from out of town, Mitchell saw Big Mac sitting on a curb at Alabama Street. He felt for his wallet, found a twenty.

"Hey, Big Mac, how's it going?"

She shivered although she had on two or three T-shirts

and two pairs of running pants. "I feel cold."

Mitchell raised an eyebrow. He hunkered down to her level, balancing on his heels. "It must be eighty degrees tonight. It's June, for chrissakes. Why you cold?"

"Got the flu or some shit. It's going around."

Mitchell reached over and stuffed the twenty in the shopping bag of her supermarket cart. She watched his hand the way a snake watches a rabbit. "You're good to me," she said. "I coulda been younger, we might've had a party."

Mitchell said, "Maybe. What the hell."

"What you need? Jimmy the Head's moving Ecstasy down two streets."

"Drugs, I don't care much about, Mac. It's that dead man they found in the Dumpster out back of the Hungry Lion."

"That was what? Two, three weeks ago?"

"Yeah."

Big Mac rubbed at her nose, sniffled. She looked like a skinny old witch from an illustrated children's book. Her hair was matted. The corners of her eyes ran murky water. He began to feel a worry knot form in his stomach.

She said, " 'Member I told you about them boys from up at the Woodlands? How they cruised through here that time, cussing out the queers?"

"I remember."

"They had bats then. They came back with those bats."

"How'd you know the dead man was hit with a bat?"

"I saw something."

"What'd you see?"

She looked down the street at people filling the sidewalks. "I was sleeping back there when they come in."

"Why didn't you call me?"

She turned her head slowly and squinted at him. He saw there was crust building up in her pale eyelashes. She might have pneumonia. "I knew you'd be around," she said. "And *you* know I don't go courting trouble."

"So who did it?"

"Kids."

"The same ones? The ones from the Woodlands?"

"Not a doubt in my mind."

Samson felt his spirits rise considerably. "If I get year-books from the high school there, you think you could ID them?"

"I could probably do that."

"What'd they do." As if he didn't know. If he hated at all, he hated hate groups. They were irrational and hot-headed. Face it, they were out and out mental defectives.

"They had him by the arms when I woke up. They didn't see me. They must've brought him from the street. He was pretty pissed, so he said some stuff he maybe shouldn't've. There were five or six boys. Big as he was. They all had bats. I never made a move. Nothing I could do about it."

Mitchell hung his head and stared at the sidewalk. His spirits sunk. He might catch the perps now, but the thought of what they'd done and how it had gone down made him feel a thousand years old.

"I wanted to shut my eyes, pretend I was dreaming, but the guy started screaming, then they hit him real hard. I saw that boy, the one who landed the first blow. It knocked the poor man against the Dumpster and put him on his ass. Then it was . . . it was . . . the strangest thing. They were methodical as a gumball machine. Took turns with their bats, hitting him in the head. One of them kicked him, but most of them stepped up like at a batter's plate and let go a good one."

"Shit."

"Ain't it, though? This city can be a turd. Those weren't kids, really." She glanced up at him. "I mean, they *were,* they were high school fluff, but they were old as sin, they knew 'zakly what they were doing. It wasn't loud either. No whooping and hollering, like you'd think. They took him down in silence, just their bats whistling through the air and the thunking sound when they connected. I nearly messed my britches. I knew if they saw me, I'd be next. Bound for heaven's gates."

Mitchell put a hand on her shoulder. He stood up, his knee aching. "Come down to the station tomorrow?"

"What time? I have appointments."

She was joking. Feebly. "Three o'clock. I'll have the yearbooks by then."

She nodded her head. "Sure is cold," she said.

He took a folded, moth-eaten, wool army blanket from the cart and wrapped it around her shoulders.

"God love you," she said. "I'll feel better tomorrow."

He pivoted and left the street for his car parked blocks away. He heard the thunking sounds in his brain. *Thunk. Thunk!* He knew the parents of the boys weren't going to believe it. Their kids had it all, why would they blow it on a gay down in Montrose? Just because, he'd tell them. Because they're vipers. And you taught them to hate. All your money didn't keep that hate from curdling their hearts.

That's what he'd tell them.

He had meant to go home. He even drove in that direction, automatically entering the freeway and watching for the exit sign, but the image of high school kids with so little conscience they could take out a human being by using his head for a baseball kept flooding over into his thoughts.

Jerry Lee Lewis's "Little Queenie" came on the oldies station on the radio, and Mitchell thought of the dark-haired topless dancer. She was one little queenie he'd love to take home with him. And that was an idea almost as crazy as a bunch of kids deliberately killing a man just because of his sex life. You didn't take home topless dancers. Some of them you paid to spend a little time with you in the comfort of a motel that charged by the hour, but you didn't take them home for the night.

He exited the freeway, turned under an overpass, and headed the car back the way he'd come. Back to Montrose. To the club where she danced. To see her again.

And he *would not* follow her out.

He'd just look. Think about her. Try to see into those veiled eyes, if she'd look at him.

He checked the dash clock. Almost midnight. It was too early. He could drink until the best dancers came onstage. He should celebrate the break in his case, shouldn't he?

Wouldn't the lieutenant be happy to get this thing off his desk?

What if Big Mac gets sick and dies?

The thought came unbidden and spooked him. Tomorrow he'd see if she was better. If not, he'd take her to a clinic himself. Dose of penicillin would fix her up. He had to keep Mac healthy—well, *breathing* anyway—to testify. Maybe the department could take up a collection. . . .

Chuck Berry sang, "Nadine, honey, is that you?"

What was his obsession with the dancer? If he could answer that, he should be getting million-dollar grant money from scientific organizations that tried to determine what made people attractive to one another. The curve of her lips, was that it? The way her legs moved? That delicious dip at the base of the spine where her hips began to swell? Her look: tough, hands-off, and yet sometimes vulnerable?

"You're lost, man," he said, twisting the wheel to the right to park the Buick at the curb.

He visited two other clubs before strolling into the one where Shadow danced. He worried he might have scared her off. He was sure the girls had told her he was the heat. What else might they have told her? That he had this . . . quirk? A taste for nearly nude women he never expected to touch?

He wasn't drunk, not even close, but an effervescence bubbled up through his mind the moment he stepped over the threshold into the room where she would perform. He had it bad. It was a real catastrophe, this thing propelling him across the room to the table that afforded the best view, without being too close to the runway where he'd be expected to play with their G-strings.

"Hey, chief," a regular said low over his drink.

Samson recognized Jimmy the Head and stopped, returned to the pusher's table. He leaned down close and said, "Ecstasy, Jimmy? When you gonna learn, man?"

Jimmy never batted an eye. His unusual head was shaped like a spade, wide and square in the chin, pointed toward the top, the crown of his floppy mud brown hair beaten down flat.

"I'm talking to you."

Jimmy raised a drunken pair of brown eyes to stare at the detective he'd called chief. "I hear you already," he said.

"I guess I have to tell Narcotics. Let them put the moves on you. And here you just got outta TDC less than a month ago."

Jimmy said, "Don't. I'll drop the stuff."

"In a toilet?"

"Like that," he said.

Samson nodded and moved on to the table he'd chosen. He heard a blues tune begin to wail, and he knew it was her because that was the music she preferred. It was the Shadow.

It was his heart beating hard enough to choke him.

♭Seventeen♭

First thing she saw was the cop. She almost returned to the curtains and left the club. Only B. B. King and the rhythm of his guitar held her grounded in place.

Screw it. She didn't have to look at him. She didn't have to acknowledge his presence. He followed her outside this time, she'd yell harassment. The club manager didn't care if you were Homicide or the mayor, he didn't allow his girls to be hounded.

She played the opposite side of the club from where the cop sat. She kept her back to him. The place was packed, as it always was lately, and men pushed past one another to get up to the stage to stick money in her elastic wisps of cloth. She smiled. The first time. She had never smiled before. But this was almost like revenge, playing the crowd away from the cop, letting them get close enough to her to stroke the backs of their fingers on her waist as they stuffed the money there.

She moved slow, not with any lewd intent, just working the music, and she could see what it did to the men. They mouthed things to her, the music so loud they couldn't possibly speak over it, and she smiled and smiled.

One man, broader in the shoulders than the others, pushed aside smaller, shorter men and brushed his gut up against the stage edge. She didn't like his face. It was of a brutal cut, all nose and mouth, small ball-bearing eyes beneath beetling brows. He reached out with a bill folded knife-thin along its length. He waved it at her. But his eyes were saying something she didn't like at all. His stare wasn't playful, it wasn't even sexual. It was the look of a starving dog two seconds away from taking off your hand.

She looked from his eyes to the thick moist lips. He might
be saying, "You." Just that. "You." Then: "C'mere."

She used the song's ending as an excuse to move to the
runway and down toward the front of the room. The lights
stayed with her while a rockabilly song by Reba McIntyre
came on and she started taking off the costume a piece at
a time. To the beat. Exactly to the beat. Avoiding eye contact with both the cop and the big scary guy, watching a
spot on the wall behind the crowd where someone might
have thrown a beer bottle one time and cracked the plaster.
It was necessary she pretend she wasn't doing a striptease,
that she was alone, parading her nakedness before a mirror.
That was the only way she'd ever been able to strip in
public, and many of the other girls told her it was the same
for them.

She had the things off her arms, her breasts. She finished
up on the last note, turning to exit in a perfect pirouette in
the scarlet G-string.

The abrupt silence lasted a millisecond before they whistled and hooted and called out suggestions to her retreating
back. In all that cacophony she heard it again. "You."
Then: "Hey, *you.*"

In the dressing room she asked Maybell, the older dancer
with the puckered nipple, what she should do if the cop
was waiting at her car out back.

"Come inside and get Bertram. He'll fix it."

"What if someone else is waiting. Someone . . . dangerous."

Maybell halted in putting lipstick over her stretched-thin
lips and checked Shadow's eyes in the mirrored reflection.
"Freak? Someone out front?"

"Yeah. Big guy. Tried to give me a hundred, I think,
but I moved off. He scared me."

"That case, have Bertram walk out with you."

Bertram said, when Shadow asked him, "I got to do that
shit tonight? The place is full and two girls ain't come in,
and I gotta walk you out?"

"Oh, just fucking forget it, you don't have to fucking
whine about it." She should have been startled at what a

bad mouth she had developed, but everyone in the business talked that way. The word *fuck* meant no more than hello and good-bye. She threw the gym bag over her shoulder and thought about getting a gun. A *big* gun.

She checked both ways at the dancers' exit door into the alley. Empty. Her fist tightened on the bag. Someone came out of the dark, she'd swing the damn thing. She had stiletto heels in there, cans of hairspray and hair gel. She wished she had a brick in it.

She slipped down the alley, sure now she was going to get a gun, and made it to the Toyota's door before the voice stopped her.

"You. Going. Somewhere?"

He was on the other side of the car. Lounging against a tall wood fence that separated the parking area from a residence, a bear waiting to make a run for her. She turned and moved into the alley again, her breath dead in her lungs. It was a long way back to the door.

Too long.

He was very fast, faster than she could have imagined. He pinned both her arms at her sides from behind. Her feet came off the pavement a half inch. He said in a whiskey slur, "I offered you a hundred bucks. You think my money's different from those other geeks'?"

"No."

"How 'bout a date, then?"

"Maybe some other night."

For a half minute he didn't respond. He just held her in place. She thought, I can't swing the bag. If I kick up and back, I might hit his balls, but I might also hit his leg, and that would make him hurt me.

"Soon then," he said. "Here's a down payment." He let go of one arm and she almost rammed her elbow into his fat gut, but something stopped her. His hand came in front of her face with the hundred in it. Still folded stiff along the length. As if he'd had it behind his ear, waiting to hand over. "Take it," he said.

She took it when he let go her other arm. A cold aura spread over her and she was no longer afraid. Her mind had slipped, someway, somewhere, and protected her from fear. She detested this man, but she knew he couldn't get to her, the *real* her, not when she went away into the dark corners of her mind.

He turned her around to face him and before she could stop it, he had mashed his lips into hers, his tongue up hard against her teeth. He broke the clutch and left the alley, away from where she was parked.

She spit twice, getting his saliva out. "God," she muttered, sickened.

On the way home across the city to Seabrook, she never lost that coldness that had siezed her. Instead, she found herself obsessing about the fat man and the way he had treated her, as a commodity, and her fury at this injustice burned harder, colder. Never mind that she was a titty dancer, flaunting her body before the public. Never mind that what she did for a living left an impression open to interpretation. She was a person, wasn't she? She had rights, didn't she? You couldn't buy her off a counter in Woolworth's. The last time she looked, there was no price tag on her back.

The big guy must have hung out at the club every night because no one knew, not even the manager, when Shadow would decide to dance. Some weeks she danced two days, other weeks she danced four or five, depending on how much money she needed. But whenever she danced now, the man was there in the audience with his hundred-dollar bill. She had Bertram walk her to her car. The gorilla didn't accost her again. Until the fourth week after the first time. When her guard was down and Bertram was too busy and too pissed off to walk her out.

This time the fat man hurt her.

"What do you want?" Again she was putty in the vise of his monstrous hands. She had never purchased the gun. She should have.

"I want you, that's what I want. I'm tired of this fucking around. You gonna come across, or am I gonna have to convince you?"

His fingers tightened. The flesh of her arms was crushed

to the bone and then it began to hurt. "Stop it!"

He swung her around to face him and slapped her so hard she saw stars drifting down into the alleyway to lie pulsing on the pavement.

"I paid you a lotta money these last few weeks. I want something in return."

She thought of telling him she'd call the cops, but she knew it wouldn't scare him off. He was like a natural disaster. Was there any way to stop a tornado?

"All right." She still winced from the blow to her face and the pressure on her arms.

"Now?"

"I won't be dancing again until Saturday night. Meet me after work."

Then he released her, and she almost slumped to her knees. She wobbled and ground her teeth to remain upright. She heard his footsteps leaving the alley. She knew what she must do for now she hated him, hated him enough to kill.

She brought her hand to her cheek and felt how hot it was where he'd slapped her.

A series of questions she'd like to ask the jerk began forming in her mind. They took over from the hate and gave her something else to concentrate on. There were so many questions she would like to ask that she couldn't keep them straight. She drove fast and loose on the freeway, lucky not to see a police cruiser.

Once in the mansion on the bay, she strode to the counter in the kitchen where Charlene kept a large yellow legal pad and a cup of pens for taking notes on the phone. She found a black ballpoint. She took it and the pad to her room.

Charlene padded behind her, wringing her hands.

"What's the matter? Something's the matter. You get hurt? Shadow, what's wrong?"

"Nothing," she said, shutting Charlene out.

From behind the door: "Something's wrong. I know it is."

"Nothing," she said again, an edge of anger making her clip the word.

"I'm sorry." Pause. Shuffling of slippers at the closed door. "If it's me, I'm sorry."

Shadow didn't trust herself to explain how the heavy man accosting her in the alley had flashed her back to the night the children were shot to death. How it was men, always fucking men, who ruined every goddamn thing in a woman's life. You had to watch them like fucking hawks or they were right there, in your face, trying to hurt you one way or the other. All they wanted to do was steal away your babies or rape you in the dark of night or proposition you with enough threat so you couldn't refuse.

She needed to be left alone.

To write those questions down. And the plan involving the questions.

Her head came up and she said, "Charlene, you there?"

A small abashed, "Yes."

"Saturday night I'm bringing home company. Man company. When I do that, I'd appreciate it if you stayed in your room when you see us drive up after work."

"Okay." Still smaller, hardly a squeak.

Shadow wrestled suddenly with an impulse to fling open the door and reassure Charlene, but she couldn't, not the way she felt right now, not with this cold ice locking up her heart.

"See you in the morning," she said, trying not to take it out on her friend.

Charlene was gone, evidently. There was a ringing silence in the house.

She stretched out on her stomach in the middle of the bed. She clicked the ballpoint pen a few times while staring at the legal pad. The plan slowly jelled in her mind. Nothing about it seemed wrong, though she understood it was against the law both of God and man. That it was wrong according to law should have set off warning bells that her mind might be sliding into a dark place where madness dwelled, but it did not. She had already killed once. That killing had been done to protect a friend. More might be done to protect herself and other women, and what was wrong with that? It might even protect children, too, for that matter, and how often were they afforded real protection?

She printed out the word: GUN. Then marked it out. She didn't know how to handle a gun. She wrote: KNIFE. Marked it out. There were too many ways a knife might fail her. She wrote: POISON.

Stared at it. Wondered about it. What kind? She knew about household cleaners, bleach, lye, insecticide. She knew about some poison plants, having been warned about them as a child. Belladonna. Lily of the valley. Honeysuckle. Oleander. Even the smoke from burning an oleander bush could kill you. She needed the proper poison, one that worked fast. Fast and hard. Something painful for the victim, oh yes, the more painful the better.

Beneath the word *poison,* she wrote the first question.

If you ever had thoughts about hurting someone you loved, would you go immediately for help or fight those thoughts on your own?

That was the question she wished she'd asked her husband. If she'd ever known he'd had those kinds of thoughts, she could have removed her children from the house and saved them. Blame. There was so much she was to blame for. There must be some way she could make up for it.

If you were sexually excited, but the woman said no, what would you do?

That was a good one. She'd have to decide when they answered if they were telling the truth. She'd *make* them tell the truth. She knew there would be more than one death. More than one poisoning. The world was just too full of men like the one who had hurt her tonight.

She continued writing down the questions she wanted to ask of men until she had ten of them. She went over the questions several times, deciding if they were clear and direct enough. She didn't want any confusion, this was too important, it involved life or death. After a while, she wrote at the top of the pad in bold letters, TRUTH OR PAIN. But it wasn't a game like "Truth or Consequences." She marked it out, going over the big letters again and again until there was a solid black box making them illegible. She could tell the men the name of the game once it was in play. Before then she didn't want them to see the list.

She glanced up from the pad at the bed she lay on. It had no headboard or footboard. It was a plain double mattress set on top of a rolling frame. Wouldn't do. She added below the list of questions:

1) *Iron bedstead.*
2) *Rope or scarves.*
3) *Whiskey. Good Scotch.*

A great sense of satisfaction at a job well done descended upon her and sleep tugged. She set the pad and pen on the floor beside the bed and turned her cheek onto crossed arms. She'd rest a little. She'd get up in a minute and undress, turn out the light.

Before the minute had passed she was fast asleep, fully clothed, sprawled over the bed with her bare feet hanging off the end of the mattress. She didn't wake in nightmare or move until Charlene came knocking, calling to tell her breakfast was ready at noon.

After eating the pancakes Charlene had cooked, Shadow moved to the cupboard beneath the kitchen sink and opened the doors wide. She rummaged beneath, taking up bottles and cartons to inspect before putting them back again.

"What are you doing?" Charlene wanted to know.

"What's this boric acid for?" She held up a quart plastic container.

"Roaches. That's what the state hospital used. Only thing seems to work. Why?"

"Just wondering."

"What are you looking for?"

"We have any rat poison?"

"Rat poison? We got rats?"

Shadow smiled a secret smile, her face turned away from Charlene. They had rats all right. There were rats every goddamn where. "I thought I heard them in the walls last night. In my room."

Charlene shivered where she sat at the table nibbling at

a folded pancake she held in one hand. "I never heard any rats in the house."

"It's a big house. I know we have rats."

"I don't think we have any poison for them."

Shadow swiveled from the sink cupboard. She stood, closing the doors. "Let's go to the feed store."

"What feed store?"

"Well, I don't know where one is, but all these little towns outside Houston have them. I'll look in the phone book."

"You really heard rats in the walls? I don't like rats."

"Don't worry, we'll get rid of them." For all time, she thought.

They had to drive all the way to Channelview, but they found a country feed store. It smelled of hay and chicken feed and chicken shit. In the back was a cage of yellow fluffy chicks for sale. They peeped and chirped their distress. A huge gray cat meandered the aisles, tail held high, king of his domain. Bet that old tom would like to get the little chicks, she thought.

While Charlene played with a barrel of horse hooves that were sold as chew toys for dogs, Shadow searched out the section of wall holding cans of poisons. All of them were wrapped with warning labels or had a skull and crossbones signature on the front. She read the ingredients on the back of one product. Warfarin—45 percent. Anticoagulant.

Made them bleed to death. Inside, she guessed. Down in their black guts.

The other rat poisons had a lesser concentration of warfarin. She chose the 45 percent. On the way to the cash register, she picked up a can of rose-and-flower insecticide spray, a small jeweled cat collar, flea powder, and cat wormer. Just normal stuff people bought from a feed store. She didn't want them remembering her buying just the rat poison.

Charlene pawed through the shopping bag when they were in the car on the way home. She was like a kid that way, looking at new purchases, hoping for a little gift.

Shadow often brought her home things. Ribbons. A lace scarf. Coffee mugs.

"Roses?" she asked. "We don't have any, do we? And what's this cat stuff for? I don't know, hon, it seems like you might've been dreaming in that store or something."

Shadow ignored the question of the rose insecticide. She said, "I think I'll go to the SPCA and adopt a kitten."

"But you're hardly ever home."

"I know. But you are."

"For me? A kitten, really? I can have a pet?" And then she was off, excited as a four-year-old, talking about litter boxes and the best kind of litter to use so it wouldn't smell up the mansion, and how when she was a girl, she'd had cats, what good animals they were, how she loved them, but how she'd never had a home as an adult where she could keep one.

Shadow smiled at this childish enthusiasm, happy her friend was pleased, thinking about anticoagulants and internal hemorrhaging rather than really listening to anything Charlene said.

Their next stop was an antique store in the old part of Seabrook. They had a cast-iron bed with quilts spread over the mattress. "How much?" Shadow asked.

"A hundred-seventy-five," the proprietor said. "If you want the mattress and box spring, that would be another hundred extra."

"I only want the bed frame."

This time Charlene was busy fingering the costume jewelry in a velvet case on the counter.

Shadow took the bills from her purse and paid. "You deliver?"

The owner said they would, for a small fee, and took down the address. "The old Shoreville Mansion?" she asked, raising an appreciative eyebrow.

"The very same. We're house-sitting for the owner."

"There are tales about that place. . . ."

"Yes, we know. Could I have the bed by tomorrow?"

And it was settled. It was all so easy, everything falling into place, clickety-click.

Before they left the store, Shadow bought Charlene a rhinestone-and-paste necklace that was tawdry enough for a Mardi Gras costume. Charlene linked it around her scrawny neck and beamed all the way home. "Now my new kitty and me will have matching neck pieces," she said. "Can I get a black cat? Pure black?"

Shadow agreed to everything. It was a beautiful day, the sun shining full, the water of the bay sparkling, and all the world waiting, holding its breath for someone to come along and set it right. She meant to do just that. At least in her little corner of the world.

He gave her a hundred-dollar bill, that sharply creased bill, when she did her first set. And his mouth said, "It's Saturday, baby." As if she might have forgotten.

She had the bed set up in her bedroom, the old bed stored away. She had a collection of long silk scarves. She had the box of warfarin that she shook each night as if it were a tambourine keeping time to the music in her head. She had cupped her hand and poured about a fourth of a cup of it into a tall glass of whiskey. It dissolved in a day, turning the alcohol slightly cloudy. She poured a small amount into a bowl and set it outdoors, behind the mansion. In two days she found three birds and a mangy old dog dead near the bowl. Blood had dripped from their eye sockets and from the muzzle and ears of the dog. She buried the dog and birds quickly before Charlene saw them. She felt terrible about the dog. She never thought a stray might get into the poison.

Charlene spent more time indoors lately, petting and babying the black kitten. She named it Blackie, the sort of name a kid would choose. She carried it for a while in the pocket of her old gray sweater. She let it sleep with her. She found something to devote herself to besides the housework and cooking for Shadow.

The man told her he was "connected," and he said it in that proud voice people use when speaking of being a member of a respected organization. She didn't care and wasn't impressed. He could be "connected" to the president of

the United States and he'd still be a target for what she had
in mind for him. He was the sleazeball of the earth. He was
the black hole of Calcutta. The ruination of society. The
bringer of fear and humiliation. She knew him without
knowing him. She had known him forever.

But she said, when he told her his little secret, acting
impressed, "Oh, really?"

He sat next to her in the passenger seat of the Toyota,
his body too large for the small cramped seats. He had to
let the seat back as far as it would go and he still looked
like a vulture in a canary's birdcage, craning its neck to
find a way out. He had the window rolled down, one big
elbow sticking out in the wind.

She had him drive his own car, follow her to the parking
lot of a Burger King. When he came over to her window
where she'd parked, she shut off the engine and asked if
he'd get them coffee from inside, then they would sit in
her car to drink it.

She wouldn't go inside with him for fear one of the
night-shift employees might remember them together.
They'd find his car parked in the lot one day. And ask about
his disappearance. She must be very careful. She must be
very smart. She *would not* spend time behind prison bars
for ridding the earth of its evil men.

"Sure, baby, I'll get you coffee," he said, thinking he
was playing the gallant gentleman.

While sipping at the coffee she said, "I'll drive you to
my place. I don't like the neighbors seeing strange cars
parked in the drive at night."

He said that was fine as long as she'd bring him back to
his car.

After she was on the freeway, taking I-45 south, he
wanted to know just where the hell she lived anyway. "We
going to Jersey or something?" He thought he was funny,
a real card.

"It's down in Seabrook."

"Christ, that's a long way from my car. You sure you're
gonna want to drive me all the way back? I could follow
you and park down the block or something."

"This is better. I'll get you back, don't worry." Telling lies was just as easy as dancing them, she thought. You just opened your mouth and said whatever the other person wanted to hear. Easy.

He tried to fondle her on the drive home, but she slapped his hand so hard it stung her palm and then she laughed prettily. "You'll just have to wait," she said. "Tell me more about what you do before we get there."

While he talked, she concentrated on her driving and the good feeling she was getting from the dispassionate mood that held her in thrall. It occurred to her that she had not felt anything in a long time. Other than anger and fury, nothing. Friendship, yes, for Charlene, but she hadn't felt any real joy for more than two years, or even disappointment, sorrow, shame at taking off her clothes in front of men, guilt for killing the rapist, or any real fear she'd be caught. It was as if she had been dropped into another world when Scott killed the children. She had fallen into the world of lonesomeness, of despair and heartache.

She couldn't think of that. She couldn't allow the memories to become too vivid or they'd kill her.

"What am I gonna get for my money?" he asked, breaking into her reverie.

She cleared her throat and took the exit for NASA Road One which would take her into Seabrook. "Whatever you want, sugar."

She could almost hear his mind clicking over. If his thoughts had lips, they'd be smacking right now.

She truly hated him.

"Do you have a wife, a family?" she asked.

"Divorced. No kids. I never liked goddamn brats running around the place."

Perfect, she thought. Besides, who would have him? Who could stand his great ugly hands on her body, his huge flabby lips crawling along her skin? And she was glad for his unborn children who had been spared being saddled with him for a father.

When she drove down the circle drive, the headlights spread over the mansion's wide marble front steps.

"Whoa," he said. "I didn't know you made *that* kind of money dancing."

"I don't. We're housesitting. Rent's free."

"We?" Worried.

"My roommate and me. She keeps house, I work and make the money. Don't worry. She stays in her room. I told her you'd be coming over tonight."

"Oh, well in that case . . . you don't think she'd want to join us?"

Shadow laughed at the thought. "No, I don't think so."

She led him from the underground garage to the front of the house where the porch light shone yellow across the white marble. She did not want to get stuck with him on the dark spiral stairs leading into the back of the house.

She opened the door, then turned and locked it behind her. "Just a precaution," she said.

He looked around and nodded. "Nice. This place must have twenty rooms."

"It has a lot. We don't use them all, of course." She went up the curving staircase and listened for him to follow. She moved down the hall to her bedroom door and opened it. "Here's where it all happens." She held the door open for him to enter first.

He turned abruptly and pushed her against the door, pinning her back against the frame.

She pushed against his chest with both hands. "Hey! This won't cut it, friend. I have ways and I have ways." Her heart pumped hard. She feared he'd hurt her again, hurt her before she could get the game underfoot, before she could protect herself.

He laughed, obviously amused by her secretiveness. "Sure, baby, it's your show."

He sidled into the room. "That old bed gonna hold us?"

She motioned for him to try it while she closed the door. He flopped backward onto the bed, arms flung out at his sides. The mattress bounced, but the heavy cast-iron frame held steady.

"I've been waiting for this a while." He propped himself up onto his side to watch her move about the room, put away her gym bag in the closet, slip out of her shoes. "You sure know how to tease a man."

"You haven't seen anything yet. Do you like games?" She looked at him seductively from below long black lashes. It was a look the men at the club loved. Promises, everything was a promise and a tease, an out-and-out lie, a fraud.

"Sure, who doesn't?"

"Little bondage? Little fun?" She took off her short bolero jacket that left her arms naked. She wore a black bustier, lace cups, low back.

He stood up and began taking off his jacket. "I get to tie you down?"

"No, honey, I get to tie *you* down. But slowly. One thing at a time. You'll see."

He shucked off his clothes like a teenager with a willing date. She avoided looking at him while she slipped off the tight electric blue spandex pants. She lovingly stroked the crystal decanter and two glasses sitting in the tray on her dresser, her finger outlining the rim of one glass to hear it sing. When the bed creaked with his weight she turned to him, smile frozen in place, ready for the game to commence.

⚜Eighteen⚜

"You see a dancer, someone like me, in a club. You like what you see so you try to make a date. If the dancer—she's not me—says she's not interested, what do you do?"

He laughed wildly, spluttering and giggling, having the time of his life. He was already on his way to death. He had failed her test. He had not answered her questions the way he should have. And this was the last one, the trick one, but it didn't matter. For each question he answered the wrong way, she had tied down an arm or a leg until he was fully incapable of moving from the bed. He now lay spread-eagle, naked, vulnerable, arms and legs bound to the heavy iron.

He was a hairy man with a bloated midsection, legs too small for his torso. He looked like a fat trophy brought home from a safari, some wild unknown animal out of a jungle. To her he was an ugly creature, but it was the ugliness inside him, the *evil* there, that needed to be destroyed. He could have looked like Quasimodo and that was no sin. It was his heart which had rotted away inside him that made him worthless.

She could smell him and it made the back of her throat periodically catch so she couldn't swallow. He had a musk scent so strong that he might have been a rutting cat.

"Hell, I go after her anyway, just like I done you."

"What if she really doesn't like you?"

"You don't like me? I gave you lots of money." He moistened his lips, unsure now.

"I didn't say me. I said, what if *she* doesn't like you? And you keep after her. That sound right to you?"

"Hey, this game over yet? I could use some head, you

know? My goddamn pecker is about to fall off from waiting." He laughed again, but this time his mirth was short-lived and forced.

"This is the last question. You've liked it so far, haven't you?" She ran her nails up the inside of his leg, but pulled her hand back before reaching the dark region of his groin.

With her gaze fastened on him, she felt her mind slip. Just a notch. The way a bicycle chain will slip and catch again. Inside her head she felt it: *click.* And found herself thinking about her children. Gabriel and Stevie. Their laughing faces, the way they smelled when she pressed her face into the crevices of their chubby little-boy necks. Then: *click.* Her mind came back to her, the daydream over.

She blinked, knowing she had gone away. That's what happened, she had *gone away.* Only for seconds, but it frightened her nonetheless.

Her victim shivered and closed his eyes. "Yeah, yeah, it's been fun, this erotic shit is great for a while, but let's get the main act on the road, okay? We ain't got all night."

"Oh, but we do. All night long." She glanced at the windows on the far wall, relieved to see it was still dark. "So what if she doesn't like you. You know that. You sense it. What do you do?"

"Oh fuck, I don't know. I pay for something, it ought to be mine. She don't like me, what do I care, I ain't asking her to fucking marry me."

She stood, completely naked now, and glided to the dressing table where the decanter waited. She saw from the corner of her eye that he was straining to keep his head up, keeping her in view. "You asked for a drink before. I'll get you one now."

"Just a few sips. Then you straddle me and ride for the border, whatta you say?"

She brought the glass to the bedside. She sat beside him and slipped one hand beneath his neck to raise his head. He had been tied down for most of an hour. He was thirsty, his lust driving him wild, while she teased and played her game.

He drank down the entire highball glass of whiskey and

warfarin before he started coughing. She moved away from him with the empty glass. Then she returned, bringing the chair from her dressing table. She positioned it beside the bed, but at a little distance, sat down, crossed her legs. She smiled beatifically.

"Goddamn! That whiskey tasted like shit. You need to pay more and get better booze."

She nodded. Smiled.

"I can't get this awful taste outta my mouth. Christ." His throat worked while he swallowed and swallowed. "You don't have something in the house better than that stuff, something to chase it with?"

"No." She waited.

"Why you sitting there looking at me? Look now what you've done. My hard-on is dying, and if you want to know, these scarves are cutting off the blood in my hands and feet. How 'bout you untie me so we can fuck for real? I'm not all that hot into this bondage stuff."

"You treat women like slaves. That's bondage."

A flicker crossed his eyes. He winced and tried to pull his legs free. "Look, I'm getting pissed, okay? Enough's enough. Now let me loose. I don't think this is funny any-more."

An involuntary moan escaped him. He tried to jerk his hands from the bed. The scarves held fast, tightening more around his wrists. "I feel sick. My stomach . . . my stomach's . . ."

"Hurting?" she asked. She leaned forward a little to look him in the eyes. "Is there pain yet? I'd be interested to know what it feels like."

"Listen, you bitch, I don't know what kind of game you're up to, but I don't like it! I ought to get up from here and beat the living hell outta you."

"You're dying," she said coolly. She was surprised how complacent she sounded, how detached she felt.

"What are you talking about?"

"You won't beat the hell out of me or any other woman again. You won't hound them, use them, abuse them, or screw them. Not anymore."

"You know who I am? You know who my friends are?"

"I couldn't care less."

He pulled his head to his chest. He blanched. He began to gag. White rings of flesh stole around his eyes and sweat seemed to magically appear on his forehead.

"You'll probably vomit some of it up."

His eyes were popping from their fleshy shells. He was sweating profusely now so that the musky smell of him filled the room. He murmured, "You're not lying. That whiskey ... poison ... you've poisoned me. . . ."

"Absolutely," she said, "a pretty nasty poison, too. The dog it killed, it made bleed from the eyes. I don't know if that was before or after it killed him, but either way, it's not pretty. I felt real regret for the dog. I hated that it happened."

He started to scream, but she had an extra scarf ready. She stuffed it in his mouth and sat in the chair again to wait for the end of the show.

It was not pretty. It was sickening. She suspected his stomach hemorrhaged first, filling his abdomen with blood. She had made a special effort to consult a book on poisons in the local library. She knew more of what to expect than she had let him know.

He vomited some of it up. Then as he thrashed about, his nose bled, his ears, next his eyes bled, and finally, while he still breathed, the frothy blood bubbling in his nostrils, he bled from the penis and rectum. It made a mess on her sheets. Luckily she had known, thanks to the library research, to cover the mattress with a plastic liner.

Funny, but she hadn't thought out the emotional ramifications of murder. What it would feel like to sit idly by while someone died. It didn't surprise her, though, that she was not moved. Even the stray dog she'd accidentally poisoned deserved life more than the man thrashing and gagging and bleeding on her bed. The dog had been innocent. This man was not.

Several times during his death throes her mind slipped again. In and out of a groove. She didn't know when she'd "go away" or when she'd return. *Click. Click.* The bicycle chain ratcheting round and round the teeth of the gear, clicking in, clicking out.

Flashes of the past came and went, some so fast she couldn't catch them. Right before her eyes raced various visions, or perhaps they were hallucinations, she didn't know exactly what they were or what was happening. First she saw her children, who she mourned deeply each time they appeared. And then her dead husband with his perplexed look, standing before her, arms at his sides, the gun in one of his hands. He was whole again, his brain not yet splattered across the room from the gun blast. "I have to do this," he said plaintively. "It's the only way."

"Do what?" she cried, stricken with a fear so deep it paralyzed her.

He stood over the boys in the den, the gun in his hand. Stevie thought it a toy and reached for it. She thought Gabe said something, but she didn't hear what it was. "Daddy . . ." something. Daddy don't?

"It's the only way out," he repeated. Then she came unglued and reached toward him, her body taking her across the room to stop him, dear God, let her reach him before he did it.

But he pointed the gun at Stevie and he pulled the trigger. She didn't see . . . it was so fast . . . but she saw him . . . pointing the gun at Gabe, who screamed . . . and she was at him, on him, in fact, clawing at him with insanity replacing all normal thoughts, but he had the gun, smoking still and hot, in his mouth, and she leaned away, hoping he would, hoping he wouldn't, hoping she was dreaming a nightmare, that it wasn't real, it couldn't possibly be . . . real.

Faster and faster the images came, wavered, disappeared. *Click, click, clickclickclick.*

After the poison had done its job and the man on the bed stopped breathing, she came back to herself. She blinked and came to know how rigid she'd been holding herself in the chair. The muscles of her shoulders hurt, her buttocks were numb, and it felt as if her hands had turned to slabs of frosty meat.

She worked her arms and stood, feeling behind her to massage the globes of flesh she had been sitting upon. It dawned on her she had not thought out the plan beyond her victim's death. She had arranged every detail from the decanter to the scarves, but she had not thought about how to remove from her bed a man who must weigh quite a bit over two hundred pounds.

As she stood looking out the window contemplating the problem, the sky lightened to old unpolished silver. The smell in the room, of his sweat, his blood, his agony, made her move from the window to pace the floor.

Finally she had to wake Charlene.

"I need your help," she said, tiptoeing into the other woman's bedroom.

Charlene came awake suddenly, sitting up in the bed. She wore another old-fashioned nightgown, long and flowered, with a lace collar. "What is it? Who's here?"

"You saw the man I brought home?"

"Shadow? What's the matter? I stayed in my room, just as you said."

Shadow was nodding in the dark. Charlene had the blinds closed. She reached out and turned on the bed lamp. Blackie hissed where he lay at the foot of the bed. "Well, he's dead," she said.

"What?"

"I killed him."

"You what?"

"Murdered him. Poison. Rat poison."

"Oh, hon, tell me it ain't so. You're just kidding, right? It's some kind of awful joke." Charlene hurried from the bed and went to the doorway, peeking around the corner into the hall. "You didn't really do nothing, did you? You're just playing a trick on me, huh?"

Shadow led her by the hand down the dim early morning hallway. They stood together staring at the inert body lying on the bed, staining the white sheets red.

Charlene bolted. She rushed down the winding stair to

the living room. She was at the front door, trying to undo the deadbolt, very much like the boys had done when imprisoned with the murdered former owner. But Shadow caught and stopped her.

"Hush, Charlene, it's just like before only this one didn't break into the house. He broke into my life. At the club. He wouldn't go away. He wanted to use me, he caught me outside and hit me in the face. I couldn't make him leave me alone. And if I didn't let him come to the house, he would have hurt me again. A lot worse.

"Don't you see? They shouldn't go on living. They keep doing these things to women. They never stop. And no one else can stop them. Police can't and jail can't and shrinks can't. They keep on doing it, hurting people and forcing them to do things until someone has to end it. . . ." She talked fast, her voice hardly above a whisper, the words tumbling and rushing as out of control as a raging river.

Charlene shook her head and squeezed shut her eyes. "You're sick as I am, Shadow . . . Kay . . . remember? Your name? What it was like in that place?" Charlene turned in Shadow's hands to confront her. "We're both sick, we ain't right in the head, honey, we're way over the deep end. We're living in a nightmare. I see ghosts and hear voices. I was counting on you to keep me sane. I needed you. But you can't *kill* people!"

"I'm not Kay anymore. I'm someone else. Kay Mandel had a home and a family, she had a life. She had little boys. Babies. Who ruined that for me, Charlene? Who?" Again that odd clicking sounded in her mind and she saw the boys, mutilated beyond repair, beyond identification. She shook herself, denying the memory a chance to linger.

"A man destroyed all that. And men keep after me, Charlene, they just keep after me." Shadow turned away and crossed her arms over her chest. She had dressed again, after his last death rattle. She wore black slacks and a black turtleneck pullover. Working clothes. Night clothes. She didn't know how to make Charlene understand. She had to enlist her help. Without it she didn't know how she'd remove the body.

Charlene sighed. She touched Shadow's arm tentatively. "I'll help you," she said. "Maybe I can help you, I don't know. I don't know anything anymore. I guess we have to stick together no matter what."

Together they rolled him into the sheet and liner, then hauled him onto the floor. They dragged him across the catwalk and down the back stairs, across the moon-splashed lawn, to the short pier. The entire time Charlene talked, but Shadow didn't listen. There was no dialogue in the world that was going to change what had been done.

"You can't do this," Charlene said, wheezing from the exertion of getting the big naked man into the boat. "This ain't right. This is *murder*."

Shadow still wasn't listening. She was hearing the man talk to her, answering those questions in all the wrong ways, answering with bravado and vulgarity and sometimes with cruelty.

He would lie at the bottom of the sea. And the world was a safer place because of it.

Son might have missed the report of the dead man had he not had the late television news on while he read over and edited the pages he had written earlier in the day.

". . . man found floating . . . Kemah Channel . . . cause of death unknown at this time. . . ."

Another body dumped in the bay? The second one in a few weeks. He could feel his pulse rate increase because his heart fluttered in his chest.

He put away his manuscript and switched the channel to another local station to see if there were any further details. All the channels were into the weather report now.

Man. Dead in the water. Floating into land.

Serial murder? It could be a trend, a pattern building. He must watch this very closely. Perhaps a game was underfoot. He couldn't let it happen without becoming a player.

The next morning he was up early, waiting for the paperboy to throw the paper onto the front lawn. As soon as he saw him cycling by, he opened the door and made his way down the front walk. He had the paper in his hands seconds after it hit the dew-wet grass.

Inside, he stripped off the clear plastic bag and opened up the pages to the overnight crime report section. Autopsy pending, it said. Cause of death unknown. But the man did not appear to be a fisherman. He was naked as the day he was born. He had not yet been identified. It was definitely murder.

It was not until two days later that Son found out the cause of death. In a small column the dead man was identified as Gregory Corgi, twice-convicted felon, on parole for extortion. He had been murdered with an anticoagulant generally found in retail rat poison products.

Son could hardly control his elation. There wasn't a real pattern yet, but he had a feeling in his gut that this was the work of a serial killer. He couldn't be certain, any more than the police could, not with two similar murders, and it was true one man had been stabbed to death and the next poisoned, which wouldn't usually point to serial murder, not with two MO's, but Son had a feeling about it anyway. The victims were both male. Both found floating around the Kemah/Seabrook area of the bay.

Something was going on. The cops wouldn't pick up on it yet, but there was definitely the possibility of a killer working the area. *Some* kind of killer. It might just be a few kill-offs of the Mafia persuasion, but for some reason Son doubted that. They didn't much like their handiwork showing up so easily. The mob got rid of a guy, the guy disappeared. Unless the death was meant as a warning to someone or some group. And this just didn't smell like mob work. Why dump them in the bay, for instance? Why not on the doorstep of the party to be warned?

"Just one more," Son whispered. "Come on, one more, and we've got a ball game."

He sat back in his desk chair and contemplated the ceiling. Male victims almost always indicated some aspect of homosexuality in the killer. John Wayne Gacy and his young men. Dean Correl and his young men. But these two victims so far weren't young. They were in their forties.

It was a true puzzle. And why stab one, poison the other?

He shrugged. Maybe he was wrong. Maybe they weren't serial killings. Just a coincidence, two murders washing up the channel.

It would take three victims to make this worth his investigation.

Son prayed for that one more victim. That he be dispatched soon. And that his remains be found in the waters off the coast of the Seabrook area.

He had been too long idle. His skills unused. His taste for violent action too long postponed.

There *must* be one more death. He knew it would happen because he wanted it so.

❧Nineteen❧

Mitchell found himself in an emotional bottleneck, his head stuck up above the rim, arms pressed tight to his sides, feet dangling.

Big Mac might die of pneumonia and, for worried moments while she tried in a dry raspy voice to answer the questions put to her about the murder in Montrose, Mitchell mentally reasoned with himself over that fact.

"Face it," he told himself. "She's old, she's undernourished, she's depleted." And did that mean she should die in the county hospital? No. No one deserved an end in a charity ward without a soul to care.

She's just an old homeless hag, what's wrong with you? What was wrong with him had nothing to do with Big Mac's economic status. It had to do with how much he'd invested in the gaunt, liver-spotted woman, an investment he didn't know, until now, had been so significant.

She had looked through the yearbooks from Woodlands High School and picked out, without hesitation, the five boys responsible for the bashing and murder of the gay banker killed in the alleyway. While doing so, Mitchell caught his lieutenant's eye watching him with a sad she's-not-gonna-make-it-to-testify look.

Anyone could get a glimpse of Mac and know she was on her last legs. Her color was high, the blush in her cheeks not the charm of roses but the searing scald of scarlet banners. Mitchell thought she must have a high fever that was burning her up. While checking the yearbook she had slowly removed two outer layers of jackets as sweat beaded and slipped from her brow into gray-ringed sunken eyes.

Only one other time in his life had Mitchell seen someone as deathly ill as Mac. His own mother on her deathbed, dying of cancer rampaging through her body, had looked this way. Death stamped a footprint on fatally ill people nearing the chasm, and it was apparently crushing the life force from Mac even as she sat, scarecrow thin and trembly, in Epstein's office.

She's not your mother.

Hell no, she wasn't his mother, she probably wasn't anyone's mother, but she was his friend. And he cared about her. She was a goddamn decent human being. She had to survive.

"You want a glass of water, Mac?" He moved toward the door thinking he had to leave the room before he did something really stupid like call 911, swoop her up into his arms, and rush her through the bullpen, the outer offices, and down to a waiting ambulance.

She looked up at him, eyes faded and rheumy. Why was it when people got old the color of their eyes washed out? he wondered. Did age drain the color, leaving watery husks behind? Noticing how the elderly's eyes faded was sadder to him than any number of wrinkles or the whitest of hair.

She gazed at him a full ten seconds as if she were having trouble placing his name, and then a spark lit within the depths of her eyes, and she smiled a little, licked dry lips, nodded. "That would be nice, Samson."

He hurried away, breathing easy again. At the water cooler he drank two paper cups of water before getting a fresh cup and filling it for her. He shook his head, worrying, worrying.

All right. As soon as she had identified the teenage killers, he'd whisk her to the emergency room. He'd make them save her, by God. They had fucking miracle drugs, didn't they? *Not for cancer sometimes.* They could save anybody from anything. *Except your mother.* Let them work some magic on this one old woman, and he'd forgive the medical community anything from now on.

Back in Epstein's office, he handed over the water cup. Again Mac smiled at him, but it was a slow, sad, sick thing playing on her lips, threatening to disappear into a painful grimace at any second. She'd been coughing, hacking, belly-shaking, body-rending coughs that turned her blushing cheeks blue, the pain of the ordeal crinkling her eyes shut. She had the cough under control now, but it could come back, it *would* come back, he knew that.

"Thanks." She took the water gratefully and sipped the way a connoisseur might sip expensive cognac.

"Well . . ." The lieutenant cleared his throat and shifted in his chair behind the desk. "I think that'll do it, Mac. We'll have you sign a few forms and a statement against these particular boys, then you're free to . . . uh . . . go."

Mitchell said, "I'll be unavailable a couple of hours. I'll call in."

Epstein lifted his eyebrows in question and Mitchell shifted his gaze toward Mac to indicate he had to take care of this. Right now. Before it was too late.

"Uh, sure, that's fine. You want me to send out a car to pick these kids up or wait for you?"

"Wait on it. They're not going anywhere. I want to bring 'em in."

Mac rose, gathering her frayed and weathered garments into her arms. "Put the boys away, gents," she said in a hoarse whisper. "They're stone killers if I ever saw any."

Mitchell took her arm and led her into the squad room where the stenographer's notes had been typed up. Mac signed everything she was supposed to sign, then turned to go. "Wait," Mitchell said. "I'm taking you someplace."

"What place?" Her voice was a croak. Cocking her head that way, she resembled a crane on long skinny legs watching the skies for a sign to fly away.

Mitchell hustled her from the room with as much gentleness as he could muster. He had her down the hall before he answered. "To a hospital."

"Look, that ain't necessary—"

"It sure as hell *is* necessary! You won't make it through the night without some penicillin in you."

"Crock of shit."

"I'm not arguing about this, Mac, we're going to find you a doctor and that's that."

She relented, mostly he figured because she couldn't fight him over this or anything else. She could hardly walk, how was she going to stop him? And it was then the wracking cough came back and he had to support her, standing there on the steps of the station, until she could draw a breath again.

"Okay." She sounded exhausted. "Okay, if you say so. If you'll stay with me."

"I wouldn't think of leaving you alone, don't worry." He got her to his car and drove like some kind of Hollywood stuntman maniac through the clogged city streets to Ben Taub's emergency entrance. They thought they'd make him wait, have the old woman sit in the waiting room for her turn, but he took out his shield, brandishing it like a sword, and his voice dropped a register and grew hard. They took Mac straight into the back to an examining room. Mitchell trailed behind, hands in his pockets so he could keep them still.

A nurse came in, made a moue of disgust upon seeing Mac in her old layers of cheap torn clothes sitting upon the examining table. Ben Taub had to take the indigent and those without insurance, but most of the poor who came in through the waiting room wore clean clothes. And not so many of them layered thick as a quilt.

"You'll have to get out of those things. Sir, would you mind stepping out?"

Mitchell stood just outside the closed door, chewing the inside of his cheek. The hallway was strangely empty. He could hear a child whimpering somewhere, a hydraulic door hissing shut, a telephone ringing, and the intercom voice calling for a "Dr. Hajune," but there wasn't a soul in sight. Where was the doctor? Where were all the goddamn doctors when you needed them?

Then he laughed to himself. It was what they said about cops. And for both professions it was true. You needed help, you couldn't find it to save your life. The more you needed it, the longer it took to reach you.

He saw a man in a lab coat swinging down the hall, head lowered, scanning a medical record.

Maybe that was the doctor. It *better* be the doctor.

The man came right up to Mitchell before taking his eyes from the clipboard. Then he looked him in the eye. "What have we got here?"

Mitchell jerked his head at the closed door. "My friend's got the flu or pneumonia, I think. Something with her lungs. It's pretty bad."

The doctor nodded and pushed through the door. Mitchell followed. The nurse glanced over her shoulder at them. She took a thermometer from Mac's mouth, read the digital numbers, and jotted them on a pink sheet attached to a clipboard before handing it to the doctor. He set it atop the other he carried, reading over Mac's vital signs.

"So! Feeling sickly, are we?"

Mac rolled her eyes at Mitchell. "*You* may not feel sick, but I feel like hell came to visit and decided to stay." Saying this much threw her into a paroxysm of coughing. The doctor patiently waited for it to end before pressing his stethoscope to her scrawny chest.

"How long you had this cough?"

Mac shrugged her shoulders.

"Week? Two weeks?" He prodded her diaphragm, tapping at it with two fingers.

"Three maybe four," she said. "It's been getting worse."

The doctor moved behind her and listened again with the stethoscope. Lifting it, settling it in a new spot, lifting again, listening.

"We need to do some blood work, but I think I can tell you right now this is a serious case of pneumonia. Double pneumonia, actually. Both your lungs are involved. Your temperature is elevated—"

"How high?" Mitchell interrupted, stepping forward, his heart a regular trip-hammer. He knew she was sick, knew she was in really bad shape, but it was one thing to think it and another to hear a doctor say it.

"Hundred and three."

Jesus, Mitchell thought. It goes much higher her brain will boil.

"We'll have to keep you—"

"I don't want to stay." Mac looked made of sterner stuff than she had when they first entered the room. "I don't like hospitals."

"Well, ma'am, if you don't stay, this thing might kill you. Just giving you a shot of antibiotics isn't going to make this go away, you know."

"She's staying." Mitchell took her elbow and looked into her old watercolor-washed eyes. "Aren't you?"

"Samson, I don't like—"

"I don't care if you don't like it here, you're staying. *Aren't you?*"

She tried, with her steady fierce gaze, to fight him, but finally she glanced down at her hands lying in her lap on the hospital-issue gown and she said, "I guess I will."

Mitchell hung around the hospital until they'd done the preliminary blood work-up, taken a chest X-ray, and assigned Mac to a bed in a ward. He saw her tucked in, given a shot in the butt, an intravenous situated in her left arm, and then he knew he must go.

"I have to leave for a little while, Mac, but I'll be back later tonight to check on you."

"You don't gotta do that. I was just kidding about you staying with me. I ain't no kid."

"I don't *gotta* do nothing, but I'll be here. I said I would and I will. Now you do what they tell you and when they're not around jabbing or poking, try to rest. Okay?"

"Mitchell?" She wrapped long bony fingers around his wrist. "I don't get well, you shouldn't worry about it."

"What the hell you talking about, not getting well? God-damn it, you're in a hospital getting shot full of miracle drugs, of course you'll get well."

"If I *don't,*" she insisted, "if I don't, then you ought to know I've had a good run. Not a great one, but a good one. Even on the street life ain't so bad sometimes. And . . . ," she paused, out of breath, swallowing hard and frowning as if it hurt to swallow, ". . . and at least I did a good thing telling you about those boys. I want you to do something about them, Samson, make them hurt a little for that killing.

It was a cold-blooded thing they done.''

"Don't worry on that score. They'll be put away." He knew the chances of putting kids under eighteen years of age in jail for any length of time, any *hard* time, was a possible, but not a probable, outcome. Yet he wouldn't tell Mac that.

Outside in the sunshine, Mitchell ground his teeth. Even the light summer breeze blowing gently across his face as he retraced his steps to where he'd parked his car didn't relieve the pent-up tension he had been holding in his gut ever since Mac walked into the station that day.

He should have found a place for Mac to stay and she wouldn't have gotten pneumonia from living out in the elements. He should have forced a shelter or halfway house to take her in. He should have taken her himself if he couldn't find a place.

He should have *done something*.

"Hell," he mumbled, screeching tires leaving the parking lot. "Hell and damnation and cat shit on a stick."

It was Mrs. Darnell who answered the door, inviting him into her spacious, country-decor den. Mr. Darnell wasn't home yet from work at one of the many ultrachic laboratories huddled in the woods of the Woodlands. Ricky Darnell, a boy Mac had identified, was in his room "doing his homework," Mrs. Darnell said. "What's this about, Officer Samson?"

"Could you have Ricky come in here?"

The woman, heavy from the hips down but slim from the waist up, rather like a badly put together stuffed doll, stood her ground. "First," she said, opening her eyes a little wider with the first tinges of alarm, "why don't you tell me what this is about, please?"

Mitchell sighed and took a breath. "Mrs. Darnell, I have a warrant for Ricky's arrest. He's a suspect for murder. We want to question him about the night of May twenty-eighth. Five boys were seen beating to death a man named George Calloway in an alley in Montrose, and your son was identified by our eyewitness as one of those boys. If you'll call

Ricky in here, I'll read him his rights."

The woman simply stared at him, incredulous, her lips parting and letting out a sibilant hissing sound. "Beating to death?"

"Yes. Calloway died of his injuries. He was beaten with baseball bats." This wasn't the easiest way to tell a parent the news, but she had forced him.

"Ric-key!" She screeched his name and now she was fumbling behind her with one hand to feel for the edge of the sofa where she immediately sat, slumping forward. "Rickeeeey!"

A tall gangly teen, blond hair cut short, piercing blue eyes, a boy who would look at home on a surfboard on a Venice, California, beach, came striding into the room. He halted seeing a stranger with his mother. "What is it, Mom?" His mother did not answer. She pointed a shaky finger at their guest.

Mitchell turned to the boy. "Son, I'm Detective Mitch Samson, HPD Homicide Division. I have a warrant for your arrest for the murder of George Calloway."

"Huh?" The youth stepped back, his face twisting with a look of alarm identical to the one that had taken over his mother's face. "Whadda ya mean?"

Mitchell read him his rights, stepped forward, and took his arm. "Turn around and put your hands behind you."

He had the cuffs out when he heard the first horrible high-pitched scream from Mrs. Darnell. He turned instantly, the hair rising on the back of his neck. She was coming for him, her eyes wild and crazy, both hands held up and made into claws. He ducked to the side, put out an arm to keep the woman from falling. "Wait a minute . . ."

"Nonononono," the woman moaned. "He didn't do it!"

She made another pass, and Mitchell knew she was out of her mind at this point, her little sterile world crumbling before her eyes, her son being taken from her for a heinous crime he was sure she knew about from the coverage it had gotten on the television news.

"Look," he said in a loud voice to get her attention, "the boy's under arrest, and if you don't get hold of yourself, you may occupy a cell next to him. Now calm down and *think about it*. You might want to call your lawyer. Ricky doesn't have to talk to us without representation. I suggest you stop wasting my time and do something that might actually help your boy.''

Ricky stood, penitent, hands behind his back, waiting for the cuffs. He stared at the floor, saying nothing.

Mrs. Darnell paused and lowered her crabbed hands. The shock still commandeered her features, but a semblance of sanity had already come back into her eyes. ''Lawyer,'' she said, repeating after him.

Mitchell cuffed the boy and led him toward the door.

''Mom?''

Mrs. Darnell was crying, silently, tears streaming down her cheeks. ''Ricky . . .''

''Mom, call Dad!''

Mitchell had to get the boy to the car before the woman lost it again and caused some real trouble. He stopped in the entrance hall long enough to slip a card from his shirt pocket and drop it into a brass tray on the hall table. ''Here's a number you can call. We'll need both you and your husband to come into the station to take care of the boy's things.''

Ricky Darnell was the one Mac had identified as leading the band of boys on their killing rampage. He was the one who took the first swing. Mitchell didn't even like touching the kid. It made him itch to hurt him, and he couldn't do that, he *never* did that. Hardly ever, he amended.

Hurting this kid would have felt good, but it could ruin the case against him too if his attorney found any marks on him. That would never do. This one wasn't getting away so easily, not on stupid technicalities and fumbled procedure.

On the way to the station for booking, he talked to the kid in the backseat. ''Big strong heterosexual boy like you, big smart rich boy got everything you ever need, and what do you do? Go on some fucking crazy joyride with your friends and a trunkful of baseball bats, man, that's about the stupidest fucking thing I ever heard of happening. You like cracking open that guy's head? You don't have night-mares about it, you stupid little bigoted asshole?''

The boy didn't protest. He didn't say anything, in fact, for the entire forty minutes it took for Mitchell to drive him from the Woodlands area, north of the city, to the down-town station.

Mitchell gave him an earful and he liked doing it, and if the kid *had* said anything back to him, he would have been hard pressed not to turn in his seat and swat him in the mouth, attorney or no attorney, just for the general principle of the thing.

After booking, Mitchell volunteered two more detectives from Homicide and the three of them, in separate cars, went out to the Woodlands again, this time to round up the other four suspects. None of their parents gave them grief, not physical grief anyway. All of them were like Mrs. Darnell in that they were stupified with shock and disbelief. *Their* little boys? Murderers?

No one made a move because it was a lot harder to come on tough against three cops than it was against one, and Mitchell, a man without a suicidal bone in his body, didn't want to chance a replay of Mrs. Darnell, her of the clawed hands.

It wouldn't be nice to have to shoot down some rich housewife mommy or respectable scientist daddy on a Monday afternoon.

❦Twenty❦

Big Mac lay on her side, making it easier to breathe. Mitchell sat in a vinyl chair pulled up close to the bedside. He watched Mac sleep.

Her face was pasty white and he could hear her rattling breath from where he sat, hands in his lap. She did not wake while he was there and at ten P.M. a nurse came by to whisper that visiting hours were over, he'd have to leave.

Outside the hospital, he looked at the night sky peppered with stars. His stomach felt queasy and he realized he had not eaten any dinner. Too busy booking the kids from the Woodlands. Too busy worrying about Mac.

He drove down Elgin toward the Montrose section of the city. Knowing it was not just to find something to eat. He needed a few hours of drinking Irish coffees and watching the girls dance. Would Shadow be onstage?

He ate two bean-and-red-chili burritos from a Mexican street cart, washed them down with a Corona beer with a slice of lime floating in it. Probably give him indigestion on an empty stomach, but the spicy food followed by the tart cooling quench of the Corona made him feel better all the same.

He sat alone in the club where Shadow danced, waiting for her to perform. Finally, when it was after midnight, he asked the waitress, "Shadow on tonight?"

"She quit."

"What?"

"I hear she's dancing at one of the places down the street, if you want to find her."

Mitchell immediately stood, depositing a larger tip than he usually left on the table, and walked out into the cool night. Where could she have gone?

He had to find her.

He couldn't find Shadow. He discovered what club she was dancing in, the Blue Boa, by asking club managers all up and down the street, but the cadaverous man with the pockmarked face running the Boa said she wasn't scheduled tonight.

Mitchell thought it just as well. He had had one or two too many whiskey and coffees. His stomach boiled like a pot of water left on the burner too long.

At home, Pavlov jumped him from behind the door when he got it opened, covering him with slobbery kisses and planting huge front paws on his chest. "Down, boy. Whoa, slow down."

The house smelled closed up. Doggy. And something else, like the inside of an empty can of liver dog food. What the hell. It was home. It wasn't much, but it was home.

He dropped his keys on the end table and locked the front door. He hadn't yet turned on a lamp and thought he wouldn't. It would hurt his tired eyes. They felt like sandpaper.

Pavlov couldn't be quieted. He kept butting his master with his back end swinging around in that silly semicircle dance.

Mitchell let his right hand drift down and trail along the dog's broad head as he made his way through the dark to the bedroom. When he had his clothes off and stripped to his shorts, he climbed wearily into the unmade bed. Pavlov bounded onto the mattress, circled once, and lay down next to him. Mitchell was too tired to give a damn, though he never let the dog sleep with him. The old saying came to mind, just as he was reaching out for sleep: Lie down with dogs, get up with fleas.

But then that was fine with him. Fleas being better than some things a body could take on after a night in bed with certain kinds of beasts.

*   *   *

Shadow killed the third man at about the time Mitchell fell into deep sleep next to his dog.

His name was Wilson. Chap Wilson, he said, moved recently to Houston from Peoria. Shadow had picked him up at the back entrance of the Blue Boa since it was her night off and she never met the men far from where she worked.

"Is this a man-hating thing?" he had asked in the moments before his death.

By the time she had pondered out a reply, it was too late. "It might be," she admitted to the open glazed eyes. Certainly it was her hatred of this man that led to his death. He might be the most perverse man in America, though how she could know for sure was something else that would take some steady, uninterrupted thinking.

When she asked him one of her listed questions: "Have you ever hurt a woman or a child?" he had answered, "Lots of them."

She raised her gaze from the yellow legal pad lying on the dresser and turned to him. "Who?" she asked. "And why?"

He smiled at her and wriggled in his bonds, flexing his fingers. He was slightly built, not much larger than Shadow. He had a dark growth of beard that grew to a point on his chin, making him appear more sinister than he would have looked without it. "Where do you want me to start?"

"Anywhere."

"They asked for it," he said in a morally superior tone.

"Did they? Children asked to be hurt?"

"Even them."

She returned to the chair and sat close to the bed. Her mind tried to slip away to remember Scott, but she would not let it. "Tell me."

"If you'd like." He spoke of his exploits the way a mountain climber might tell cronies of his journeys around the world to scale the highest peaks.

Her face never betrayed her. The club nightlife and the dancing had taught her how to camouflage her thoughts. She sat quietly, listening without commenting until he was done. It took more than two hours and her thoughts did not wander from him even once.

Depravity. He reveled in it. If he told the truth—and she knew he had; who would admit to oral sex with a six-month-old if it was not the truth?—then he was lower than a slug, lower than the demons stoking the fires of hell.

She gave him the highball glass of doctored whiskey.

A man-hating thing? Was that what this was all about? Just that and nothing else? Did she need to be back in the state hospital, blissed out on drugs, for thinking she should clean the city of its brutal men?

Or did this man, and the other two she had killed, need to continue walking the earth and getting away with their crimes against women? Was she going insane or was she simply growing *more* sane? She thought of Charles Bronson in the *Death Wish* films and felt a kinship with the vigilante character he had portrayed. At one time she had thought his movie character oversimplified and his motives too elementary. Now she thought just the opposite. Revenge was perfectly suitable and ridding the world of evil perfectably acceptable by her lights.

But this was no movie.

This was blood and vomit and the most deadly poison.

It still bothered her to play the game. It took nerves of steel, a clear mind, true courage. Murder took the most courage of all, even more than coming back to herself had taken when she was lost in the fog that year in the hospital. If she made a mistake . . . if she killed someone who didn't deserve to die . . .

But that wouldn't happen. She shook her head now, slowly, and reached out to untie Chap Wilson from her bed.

This man could never have left the Shoreville Mansion alive or she would have been responsible for loosing a monster back into the world to commit more crimes against children. Babies. Little innocent—

Her mind slipped a gear, and her hands paused in the untying of a scarf. A memory floated to the foreground of her thoughts. She saw her mother, tall as the ceiling, it seemed, which meant Kay must have been less than five years old. Her mother was being struck by her daddy. He knocked her to the floor with one backhand blow to the face. Kay ran to her and went to her knees on the kitchen linoleum. She could feel the cold come through her knees. She could smell Mama's sweat and the background scent of garbage in the pail, dishes unwashed in the sink. She brushed back Mama's curtain of black hair and touched her hands covering her face. "Mama? Mama!"

The hands fell away and there was a red welt rising, closing off her mother's left eye. Kay looked up at her father, his raised voice booming like thunder above them.

"She ain't hurt. Get away from her, girl."

His hand clamped around her forearm and lifted her aside as if she were a sack of potatoes. Then his hand closed over her mother's arm in the same place and lifted her, too, into a standing position.

Kay struggled to wedge herself between them when he raised his hand again to hit her mother. Kay pushed his legs. They were hairy legs sticking out of big white boxer shorts, the firm, muscled legs of a young man. Rock beneath her small hands.

Then the vision faded away and Shadow understood something she had never known about herself. She had not consciously known the recalled scene from her childhood existed. It was a revelation since her father was gone before she was really old enough to remember him well, and her mother had never mentioned those times when he must have beaten her.

"Oh, Mama."

Why didn't she miss her mother now? Why hadn't she called her since her release from the hospital?

She thought she might know the answers. She just hadn't thought of them before. Her mother had never been strong or dependable. She wasn't good in a crisis, she had never been a fighter, she let men and life and disaster roll over her and wear her down smooth as a stone in a creek bed. That's why Shadow left home early and married. Her mother by that time was . . . a shadow.

True! She had lost substance as Kay grew, moving into

the background of life like a ghost seeking corners. She hardly spoke. She didn't have a hobby or care about herself, about her daughter, about anything enough to make a fuss or an effort.

Why *would* Kay think to call her for help or to even let her know she was free from the hospital?

But wait . . .

Shadow leaned over, feeling a cramp in her chest like a fist wadding her lungs into crumpled balls. She sucked in little sips of air until the cramp passed.

Her mother was dead.

She had died during her daughter's first marriage and before the divorce. Kay had been at the funeral, paid for by her husband, and saw her mother put into the ground.

How could she have forgotten such an event as the death of her own mother? Was she truly losing her mind? Or just her memory? And why?

She heard the door opening and turned from the dead man on the bed. Charlene stood in the doorway, light from the hall showing through her long gown.

"Shadow, you can't do this. I told you before, you can't do this."

Shadow glanced at the dead man and back at her friend. "He hurt a baby." Her voice cracked. "He admitted it. He sexually abused *children,* Charlene. What should I have done?"

Charlene sighed and stepped into the room. "I don't know," she said. "I don't know nothing anymore. I don't know if I ever did know anything."

She came to the bed and helped Shadow finish untying the limp body from the iron rails. "At least he's not fat," she said, rolling the bloody sheets over him and taking the man's torso into her arms to help carry him through the darkened mansion and down to the pier where the boat was moored.

The phosphorous light from the computer screen bathed Son's face in a pale blue glow. He was not working on a detective novel. He was thinking.

Earlier in the evening the local television news reported a man found out in the Gulf between the island of Galveston and the mainland. It did not appear he had drowned and no one had reported a man missing from a boat. Cause of death unknown at this time.

Son knew it was victim number three. He was sure the man had not drowned. He had been murdered.

It was time for Son to make a visit to his old friend who worked in the morgue. He needed more information than he was able to glean from the papers and the TV news. What, for instance, did the victims have in common? Where did they come from? How were they murdered?

He turned off the computer and went to his bedroom. His mother had been asleep for hours.

He lay in the dark with his hands behind his head, thinking.

The next morning after breakfast he told his mother he had to go to the library to do research. He left her with a pitcher of iced water and made sure she did her business in the bathroom before he left.

Once downtown, he parked and walked two blocks to the entrance to the hospital. The city morgue was housed underground. He took an elevator down, wrinkling his nose at the smell of antiseptic filtering through even into the elevator's carpeted floor and walls.

Stanley worked days as a morgue attendant. He logged them in, and after he acquired his degree, he would assist in autopsies. Son found him idle in a little back office eating pastries and drinking coffee. "Hey, there, how the hell are you?" he said as Son poked his head around the door. "Come on in and have a bear claw."

Son ambled in, hands in his pockets. He sat down on a metal folding chair facing the desk. "I haven't seen you in a while, and I'm working on a new book, thought I'd come down for a chat."

"Sure, anytime. I was wondering how you were getting on. I *loved* your last book, man. That was a good one. I didn't know the killer until the very last page."

Son smiled. "That's kind of you to say, Stanley. A writer

never can tell if he's really getting it right without his readers."

"When's the new one due out?" Stanley held out the tray of pastries to Son, then set it down again when Son shook his head.

"Not until the middle of next year. I haven't quite finished it yet."

"God, I wish you wrote faster! I need a good book to read."

"I just can't crank them out fast enough, huh? I'll try to do better. Listen, what I'm here for is to see if you might help me with an idea for my next proposal."

Stanley grew animated, his hands moving in the air as he talked. "Whadda ya want to know? We have plenty of stiffs to pick from."

"I keep hearing on the news about bodies brought in from out of the bay. You get them?"

"Yeah, we got 'em. New one just today, fact is. They're kind of chewed up. Fish, man, they seem to love man meat." He stared at a raspberry jelly doughnut and grunted.

"What do you think killed them?"

"M.E. says the first one was stabbed. These last two, though, they've been poisoned. Just like the papers reported."

"Now that's a tasty method." He knew Stanley would never release specific information to the press guys. He trusted Son to use it in a novel and that didn't matter. Fiction never mattered. And since Stanley's boss never found out, who could it hurt? He would grill him about the poison.

"What kind of poison, you know yet?"

"Rat poison probably. Victims have a high concentration of warfarin in their organs. You know how bad that shit tastes? I don't know how someone got these guys to swallow it, but there's traces of it in the membranes of their mouths and plenty of it in the stomach lining. They drank it, all right. Real weird."

"Can't be suicides, I guess," Son said.

"No way, man. There's lots better ways to check out

than drinking rat fucking poison. Might as well be drinking shit. And two men poisoned isn't a coincidence, it's premeditated. Nah, somebody killed them, that's for sure.''

"Any leads who might be doing it?"

"Nope. Any fingerprints forensic might have wanted to lift off their skin got rubbed off in the salt water. Or eaten off by the fish. They float in butt naked, now there's a detail you could use, huh?'' He laughed. "Won't be any stained clothes to check on these dudes. Whoever's doing it is taking 'em out in a boat, we guess, and dropping 'em over the side. Might be killing them on land. It's gonna be tough for the cops to crack this one.''

"You expect there will be more?"

Stanley contemplated his coffee cup. "I'm no expert, but since we have three, two of them poisoned, I'd say we'll get more.''

"Serial killer then,'' Son said.

"Looks to be.''

"These guys, the victims, they have anything in common?''

Stanley held out his hands in a helpless gesture. "Now this is completely confidential, you know? Ah, hell, I guess I don't have to tell you that. But if the press boys got it, hoo doggie!''

Son scooted forward on the metal chair. "What is it? C'mon, this is great stuff for a book, Stan, absolutely great.''

Stan's voice dropped to a whisper. "Well, see, I overheard a Homicide dick say this newbie, this new floater, he's the *second* one that had been hanging out in the titty clubs. Down there in Montrose, you know, those places, nekkid girls and all?''

"Wow.''

"Maybe it's a woman doing it. Feature that for a minute if you want your balls to go into hiding. Some bull dyke hates men or something. Or some chick got a grudge against the whole male gender, you know what I mean? Gives me the fucking creeps. I always knew women would make good killers. Now I'm sure of it.''

"The cop say it was a woman doing it?"

Stan shook his head. "He didn't say it, I just worked it out." He laughed, slapping his hand down on the desktop. "I'm starting to do plots like a writer, ain't I? Kee-rist."

Son stood. "Well, it sounds promising."

"Think you can use it?"

"It might work out. I haven't used poison in a book yet. And the literature does say poison is the favored method of murder for women. I think you may be onto something. Maybe you ought to tell that cop what you suspect when he comes back."

"You think I should?" He stared off into the middle distance. "Yeah, I should do that, shouldn't I? Meanwhile I'll keep an eye on this one for you. You come back if we get another one, and I might know more to help you out."

Son put out his hand to shake. Stanley stood and took it. "I appreciate the hell out of this, Stan."

"Hey, my pleasure. I feel like a real consultant, you know?"

"I'll have to put you in one of my dedications soon."

"You'd do that? God, that'd be terrific. My mom would love it."

Son left the building thinking about the nakedness of the victims found in the waters off the coast. Somebody was stripping them before dumping them in the bay. Why? It sure as hell cut down on the clues. Just making indentification was a bitch. And he wondered if Stan was right, that it could be a female killer. That would be a real switch for him to copy a female. A challenge. A perfect game.

How many female serial killers had there been in history? Precious few. The latest was the woman down in Florida, let men pick her up hitchhiking, then offed them in payment. Geraldo had interviewed her from prison. Spooky woman. Cold hard eyes.

This killer wouldn't be caught anytime soon, even he could tell the police that if they didn't know it already. This was one smart killer. One thing Son hated worse than anything was coming along behind a stupid killer and trying to imitate his crimes. It took real intelligence to do it, but it was time-consuming, too. And not nearly as much fun.

He drove home whistling an old Doris Day tune, "Que Será Será." Whatever will be, will be.

Twenty-one

Shadow sat alone at a table in the Blue Boa sipping a Coke. Her set was ended and she wasn't ready yet to leave for the long drive home. Besides, she needed a little more money to make the night profitable and worth her long drive in from Seabrook.

The way most of the girls made money was table dancing, dancing one dance on a customer's table, or sitting at a table between sets of dances just talking to the customer, letting him buy drinks. He was supposed to pay for a dancer's time whether she table danced or whether he simply sat at the table with her, making conversation.

Sometimes a man peeled off bills as the girl talked with him, handing them over every five minutes or so. The girl accepted the money, stuffing it in her bra without missing a beat. Often talking at the table with a customer escalated into the man touching the girl while they talked. And during a table dance, though the man wasn't supposed to touch the girl, he often did, leaning in close as she danced, smothering his face in her crotch or touching her breasts when she leaned over him.

For these reasons, Shadow never table danced. She did, however, agree to sit at a table and talk with customers as long as they paid for her time and as long as they did not touch her. When men tried touching, she always stood from the table and said, "I'm not what you're looking for. I'll call another girl for you." She rather liked talking to the customers; how else could she decide if a man deserved to continue living or not?

She had a mission. Without that mission, she thought she might disappear, vanish, her personality desert her.

None of the girls ever gave out true information about themselves. They gave false names, false addresses or parts of town where they lived. The truth wasn't what the man was buying, and if he thought he was, he didn't have brains. The whole situation was a fraud, a manipulation, an illusion. Just a game played between men and women, one not that much removed from the games they played in office settings, at singles' bars, or apartment parties.

Regular customers learned which girls allowed flesh pressing and which didn't. In the Blue Boa, Shadow was the only dancer who kept herself so pristine. Most of the girls needed the extra money and didn't mind a little grabbing now and then.

Just as at the former club, at the Blue Boa Shadow was known among the dancers as the "Ice Queen." All up and down the street at the strip clubs, the girls were beginning to hear about her. She wasn't really into the game, they said. She made nearly the same amount as the other girls, but she did it without allowing her person to be manhandled. It did not make her popular, but Shadow let it be known she didn't give a rat's ass about popularity.

"Familiarity breeds contempt," she told the girls. "Why don't we just keep it businesslike, what do you say? I'm not interested in finding a girlfriend. I'm here to make a living, okay?"

As she drank her Coke this night, she saw a man angling across the room toward her. She sat up straighter and self-consciously adjusted the lace jacket she wore over the black French-cut bra. The jacket hid very little, but it made her feel less naked nevertheless.

The man looked respectable enough. He wasn't dressed expensively, but his clothes were pressed and clean. He wore Wrangler jeans and a plain vanilla white shirt. He was a little overweight, but he had a nice, clean-shaven face. And he did not look drunk.

"Hello," she said, smiling as he hesitated next to her table. "Would you like to sit down?"

"Yes, thank you." He sat across from her. Some of them tried to sit *next* to her and she didn't like that. Usually she left. "I'm sorry." He looked around at the other tables. "I'm new to the club scene. Do I . . . uh . . . pay you to sit with me?"

"That would be nice," she said. "Whatever you think you can afford. And we just talk, nothing else, okay? Save the hanky-panky for the other girls. What's your name?"

"My name's Frank. And listen, I wouldn't think of . . . you know . . ." He let the sentence go unfinished. She thought he might have blushed and she felt a kindling in her heart for him. He wasn't much older than she, but he seemed younger and certainly less experienced. He was the first man she'd met in the clubs who didn't put her on guard and make her want to ask him the list of questions she now had memorized. Though she probably would. If he came back to sit with her more than this one time. A man should never push his luck with her.

She gestured to the waitress. "I'm drinking Cokes," she said to him. "It'll cost you the same as a mixed drink, but I don't drink the hard stuff. I never saw the point in lying to a customer."

"I don't mind the money." He drew out his wallet. "I'll have a Coors Light," he told the waitress. "Another Coke for the lady."

He withdrew a twenty and handed it to Shadow, then when the drinks came, he paid for those rather than running a tab.

"How long have you been dancing?" he asked.

"Almost a year now."

"I haven't seen you before. You look . . ."

"Like I don't belong here?" She laughed. "I'm sorry, I hear that line so often it just makes me laugh every time I hear it now. The thing is, I *do* belong here. If I didn't, I'd be in an office somewhere typing insurance forms."

He looked down shyly at his hands clasped around the bottle of beer. "I'm sorry. I said I was new at this."

"You might want to put your wallet on the table. Or at least some money stacked to the side. The going rate for 'talk' is about a dollar a minute." She wondered if that would scare him away and realized that for the first time since doing this job, she hoped that it wouldn't. It wasn't that she was attracted to him physically. He was a bland-looking sort of man and not at all interesting in a sexual way, but he seemed so fresh, so . . . vulnerable. She hadn't realized she was that tired of the old hands with their lines of bullshit.

He dutifully withdrew his wallet again and took money out, a few twenties, she saw, and laid them in the middle of the table. "That should cover an hour or more."

She smiled. "Looks about right to me." She took the money and put it into the left cup of her bra. He didn't watch as she did this. God, he *was* a shy one. The men usually leered when the girls did that.

As they talked, he had to keep leaning in toward her to hear what she said as the music volume was turned up for one of the dancers onstage. She saw he never looked at the girl. He seemed to drink her words instead. He had three Coors Lights, they discussed the Astros and why they never won the championship, the Oilers and why *they* never won the Super Bowl, the cost of air-conditioning in the summer in Houston, other clubs in Montrose, how some dancers were good enough to be onstage in Vegas if they wanted, and just any subject that seemed to fall between them.

She found out he liked to read Travis McGee novels and she had him explain to her what they were. He liked sports, of course, rooted for the local teams. He liked music, all kinds of music, and even listened to the lyrics. When the deejay played a song by Queen, he knew all the words and offered the opinion that the lyrics were more poetic than one would expect from a rock group.

When the hour was over, he put out his hand for her to shake. "It's been real nice talking with you," he said. "You wouldn't mind if I came back and did it again some-time?"

She said she wouldn't mind at all and told him he was a gentleman. Then she watched him leave and sighed after him. If only that kind of man would come into the clubs, she wouldn't mind her work so much. She had begun to think the only sort of men left in the world were ones on the make or ones whose agendas were so deceptive and cruel she had to take them home and administer the drink of poison whiskey. It was a real surprise a nice man found his way into a club such as this and was willing to pay to talk with a dancer.

Of course, she didn't really *know* him. For all she knew he was another pervert who was better than the others at wearing a mask. But for some reason she thought not. He couldn't be that accomplished an actor, she didn't think. How many people were? Then again, who would ever guess the truth behind *her* mask?

She smiled thinking how his name, Frank, seemed to fit his demeanor. And how Shadow fit her own.

She was just about ready to head for home when she saw the cop. He came through the door, his gaze fastened on her, and before she could move to leave, he was sitting across from her in the same chair Frank had just vacated.

"I want to apologize for waiting out back that night for you," he said. "It was a stupid move. I had no right to do that."

She had tensed, seeing him. Now she tried to relax. Maybe she could get some things straight with this guy. "It costs to sit at my table," she said.

He dug in his shirt pocket and put a fifty-dollar bill on the table. She waved over the waitress, then tucked the fifty away.

"Irish coffee," he said.

"Why don't you tell me what you're up to hanging out in the clubs?" She decided she'd needle him.

He leaned back in the chair, looking her over. "It's sort of a hobby of mine, a stress reliever, if you like. I enjoy watching the girls dance."

"Ever try the ballet?"

He laughed and maybe she was in a mellow mood or maybe talking with Frank had eased her feelings toward men, but when the cop laughed she caught herself smiling in return, pleased she had caused that reaction. She was so serious most of the time that humor seemed hardly to play a part in her life. She couldn't remember making anyone laugh except Charlene.

"I don't care for the tights," he said. "Or the music."

She nodded. The waitress brought the coffee and left. "What do you want with me?"

"Nothing really . . ."

"You want something. You keep following me around and coming to my sets. What's the deal?" Best to get the shit into the fan right away, let it fly.

He took a swallow of the coffee. "If I answer that I'll just be saying what a dozen men have probably already told you."

"Like what? I'd like to hear your explanation."

He looked into her eyes and she saw truth residing there, waited for it to issue from his lips. If he lied to her, she'd recognize it. "No, really," she prompted. "I'd like to know what it is with you."

"You're beautiful." His voice had changed, dropping into a lower register, and his eyes remained steady on her face. "You mesmerize me. I don't talk with the girls, ask around. Until now I only came in to watch. With you, it was different from the first time I saw you. I wanted . . . to get to know you a little."

When she opened her eyes wider to indicate he might be entering the territory of the lie now, he said, "I mean it. I don't expect . . . well . . . hey, I'm just wasting time, it's nothing to get alarmed about. I'm not going to stalk you or anything. I'm not one of those fucking freaks you get in these places. That's why I'm apologizing for waiting out by your car that night."

"Then you aren't interested in arresting me." Maybe she could tease, rather than needle him. He didn't seem a bad sort, but his adulation made her uncomfortable. Who needed a cop fan? Jesus.

"Not tonight," he said, surprising her.

"But I guess you want to know what a nice girl like me . . . blah-blah-blah."

"Actually," he said, "I don't need that question answered. I pretty much know all the reasons women dance in the clubs.''

"We're exhibitionists.''

"If you say so.'' He looked at her solemnly over the rim of the coffee cup as he drank. "Is that why you never get friendly with the customers? The whole dance thing is to show off, get attention?''

"I didn't know you were a psychiatrist, too.'' She tried to change the direction of the conversation. "So if you're not Vice, what kind of cop are you?''

"Homicide.''

She remembered now one of the girls telling her that. "Solve any good murder cases lately?''

"One or two.''

"Any I might have heard about on the news?'' This was easy money. Get them talking about themselves and their jobs. Easy way to make the time pass. She figured she owed him another thirty or so minutes. If she felt like it. And he didn't threaten her.

"You know about the gay banker who was killed down here a few weeks ago? Found in an alley with his head bashed in?''

She faintly recalled the word on the street about it. Montrose was a haven for the gay population. The killing had caused gay rights leaders to demand the police do something and do something *now*. "I heard of it,'' she said.

"I picked up the kids who did it.''

"I thought people were considered innocent until trial by jury.''

"That's the way the law states it. I know these kids did it, though. I have an eyewitness saw it go down. They're guilty all right.''

"Kids? Like teenagers?''

"Privileged little pricks out for a joyride.''

Shadow sipped at her Coke. She heard the steel enter his voice and it gave her pause. This cop wasn't as easy to talk to as she thought he might be. Nevertheless, it gave her a secret little thrill to know she was talking to a Homicide detective about murder without him knowing she had committed more crimes than his joyriding little pricks. Of course, there was a world of difference between what she and the teens had done. They killed an innocent man for nothing. She killed for better reasons, not that the cop would agree with her on that score. "Will they go to jail?"

"For a while. Unless mommy and daddy bring in F. Lee Bailey or old Racehorse Haynes to get them off. Which wouldn't surprise me in the goddamn least."

"Ever read about a guy called Travis McGee?" she asked. "I think he was kind of a detective."

"The novel series? John D. MacDonald? Yeah, I've read them. Travis wasn't a cop, though. He was a 'salvage consultant.' People came to him to get something back that belonged to them. One time a guy came to him to get back his lost reputation. They made it into a movie, but it didn't work. Travis doesn't translate well to film. Have you read them?"

She shook her head. "Someone else told me. I hardly ever have time to read."

"Yeah, well, when I'm not on the job or in these places, time's all I've got." He didn't appear happy to admit it.

"You married?" She knew it was the next question in the queue expected of her.

"I was once. No more. Cop's life, old story, nothing new, blah-blah-blah." He smiled winningly and she liked that smile. "You?"

Now it was her turn to laugh at the absurdity of a question. "No," she said.

"Divorced?"

She narrowed her eyes. "Widow," she said. "My husband killed himself." It had simply popped out. She felt like biting her tongue in half.

"Hell, that's a damn shame."

"I think it was exactly what he should have done." She sounded colder than a block of ice. She might as well stick to the truth as long as it never really told him anything *specific* about her past or her life now.

"Oh? Was he an asshole? Beat you, that sort of thing?"

She searched her brain for yet another subject to aim him

toward and came up blank. Finally she said, "I don't want to talk about him. He's dead. He's good and dead."

The cop drank his coffee and sat watching her a while. She let him, unconcerned with his scrutiny. He ordered another drink. She asked for coffee too, straight, black.

"Any kids?" he asked, breaking the silence.

She frowned at him. "Look, you don't pay me to divulge my personal life history here. We can talk about books or dancing or the hole in the ozone layer, but not about my life. I'm afraid I have to leave now."

She stood, leaving the coffee, and went to gather her things from the locker in the dressing room. She hadn't looked back at him. She didn't care what he thought of her. She should have known a cop was going to pry, ask questions she didn't want to answer. That was the job they did. Next time he came to her table, she'd leave right away. So what if he was good-looking, with soft brown eyes and a football quarterback's kind of body? So what if he had a crush on her?

She had no time for romantic involvements. She hadn't wanted a man for a long time. The bottom had dropped out of her sex drive. If her ovaries were still producing hormones, they just weren't moving through her bloodstream in enough quantity to make a damn bit of difference. She might as well be a nun as far as sex was concerned. And it wasn't that she was moving toward any lesbian relationship with Charlene either. Charlene was like a sister. She loved her, wished to protect her and keep her on track, but she sure as hell didn't want to get in bed with her.

Why was she making all these excuses to herself anyway? Why had she thought the cop's eyes were nice?

Christ. Maybe her hormones *were* working. Edging her toward the first tantalizing steps that would lead to normal sexual activity again.

Now wouldn't that be something? Goddamn it. But not with a cop! Especially one who asked so many piercing and potentially dangerous questions.

When she saw a drunken fool wending his way down the sidewalk and turning toward the parking lot where she was unlocking the driver's side door of her Toyota, she was suddenly very tired. So tired she wanted to just curl up on the backseat of the Toyota, cover her head, and go to sleep.

She wondered if Charlene was still up waiting for her and if she had made anything good to eat. She needed to tell her she had a fondness for lemon meringue pie. She was positively lusting for lemon pie, all of a sudden. She could almost taste the lemon bite on her tongue. Pie and sleep. That's all she wanted. Nothing more. Except some peace from men, men, goddamn boring-ass men. . . .

" 'Scuse me, baby, you goin somewhere?" The drunk had her by the upper arm.

She wrenched away. "Get lost."

She shut and locked the car door before she heard what he replied. She knew all the curses. They did not bother her in the least. Fuck him and his need for her. That's what it was, too, *need*. Except for Frank . . . and maybe the cop . . . the men she had run into in the clubs were just eaten up with the need for a woman, any make or model of woman. A woman to bed down with, not just to talk to. It was as if all the males over the age of fifteen had been stranded on a dry desert island for twenty years without female companionship. Or locked up in the penitentiary. Which is where most of them belonged.

Either there or the deep blue sea.

❧ Twenty-two ❧

While Charlene worked she thought about Shadow. It had been a rough night. Every creak in the mansion set her blood pressure soaring. She had developed a headache that no amount of aspirin could touch.

She bent over to wring out the mop in the bucket of Clorox and Pine-Sol. She had put off cleaning the ballroom for too long. Now it must be done. She kept the lights blazing the whole time so there would be no shadowy corners calling to her overactive imagination. She brought a portable radio with her and turned on 102.9 FM, the easy-listening station, so as to drown out the voices in her head. With Bette Midler, Streisand, Michael Bolton, and occasionally Doris Day and Frank Sinatra singing at her back, she handily completed the chore, stood at the entrance door to the ballroom when she was finished, and beamed at how the floor shone clean and spacious. A sea of white marble.

Though the music kept the voices overpowered, they still talked to her as she worked, therefore the headache. It was like listening to FM with static bleeding through.

"Go away," she whispered wearily, standing in the ballroom doorway holding the bucket of wash water in one hand, the mop in the other. "Please leave me alone."

She remembered chanting this same plea in her head all the time. At home, out shopping, on the bus, at the park, watching television, wandering the hospital wards. *Go away. Please leave me alone!*

The voices had increased in both volume and frequency ever since she discovered Shadow was killing the men she brought home. Murder was something she never would have thought her friend capable of. But after stabbing the rapist, it appeared murder was the one thing Shadow did exceptionally well. Not only was she capable, she was *expert* at it.

The voices that dogged Charlene throughout the day and night now were new to her. They belonged to the three men Shadow dropped into the bay. They said things to her that drove her crazy.

Why did you let her kill us? they said.

What did we do that was so horrible we should die?

It's cold here, in the waters, in the deep waters. It's lonely here and cold.

Shadow is insane, they said, surely you know that. Surely you can stop her. You're not so crazy yourself that you can't stop her.

Watch her, they said. She'll kill you next. She'll poison you the way she poisoned us. Do you want to bleed to death? Internally? Do you know what that's like, to die that way?

She's evil, they said. She's monstrous.

Charlene sometimes argued back with the voices. She's not evil. She is my friend. She can't help it. She thinks she's doing right. And anyway, you were all horrible people. Shadow was right about that. . . .

Not so horrible, they chorused. Not so horrible as you think.

But they were. Charlene came to know just how horrible they were the more they tromped around inside her head, giving her no peace and quiet. They invaded her sleep and created nightmares, forcing her to live through them until she woke screaming into her pillow. They badgered her endlessly to *do something*.

But what could she do? She loved Shadow and she loved living in the mansion, even if sometimes when she was alone here, she feared the big open spaces and the dark rooms and the many barred windows.

She didn't want to go back to the state hospital. She didn't want to go back there ever. Nor did she want Shadow to have to return. This time either or both of them could die there, never to be free again.

The price of freedom might just be learning to live with the new voices. If she couldn't persuade Shadow to stop.

She saw the car lights turn into the long drive before she heard the engine noise. She glanced at her wristwatch. Three thirty-five A.M. Please, God, she begged silently. Don't let her bring anyone home tonight.

She sat on the top step just above the entrance, waiting. She could still smell the Clorox and pine scent on her hands, though she'd washed them with a bar of soap. She brought her hands down from where she'd had them propping up her chin and lay them in her lap. She straightened her aching back.

She wondered if there was anything stronger in the medicine cabinet than aspirin for the raging headache.

Shadow glanced up at her as she unlocked the front door and came into the foyer. "Hi there. What's the matter?"

"I have a headache."

"You look terrible. Have you taken anything for it?"

Charlene watched her climb the staircase, put down the gym bag at her feet, and take a seat on a lower step so that she was looking up at her.

"I took aspirin. Hasn't helped."

"Oh, poor baby. Want me to massage the back of your neck?"

Charlene shook her head and it made the headache shift from over her right eye to her left. She winced and held her head stiffly. "It'll go away soon. I wanted to talk."

"Shoot. But first, tell me, do we have any lemon pie filling or lemon pudding in the kitchen?"

"No. Butterscotch. Chocolate. No lemon."

"Damn."

"We have fresh lemons. I could make a glass of lemonade, if you want it."

Shadow shook her head now, her silky black hair lifting from her neck and moving back and forth before lying still again. "I had a craving for lemon pie. Lemonade just doesn't sound the same." She smiled.

"I'll make one tomorrow. I make pretty good pies."

"So what did you want to talk about? Aren't you sleepy? I'm pretty beat, myself."

"I won't keep you long. I just wanted to tell you . . ." She touched her temple where the headache throbbed, lowered her hand again. "It's the voices," she blurted. "They want me to turn against you."

Shadow went perfectly still. "Turn against me how?"

"I don't know how, exactly. They yammer at me all the time, hon. They tell me it's . . . cold in the water. They say it's . . . lonely."

Shadow blinked and then some sense of understanding glowed in her eyes. "The men I dumped in the bay? They talk to you?"

"Yes. All the time. Even in my sleep. They call you evil and they say we're both insane and they tell me I shouldn't let you do it anymore."

"I see."

"No, you don't see! If you could see what I suffer, you wouldn't let this happen. I'm your *friend,* Shadow. I wouldn't do anything that made you stop talking again. I wouldn't *ever* remind you of . . . of . . . things that bother you."

"I know that, Charlene. That's why I love you the way I'd love a sister."

"But what can I do about these voices? What do I tell them when they say we're both crazier than loons? How do I stop thinking about them down in the water, cold and lonely? They say they weren't horrible like you said they were. They say you're just a . . . an . . . evil killer. A murderer." Charlene started crying. The tears fell down her face and her eyes pleaded with Shadow to make things right again, the way they were before she began this deadly game of death.

Shadow let go her gym bag and now moved up the steps quickly to sit next to Charlene. She put an arm around her shoulder and leaned her head against Charlene's head, speaking softly.

"That first one, you know the really big guy? Not the man who was in your bed that night, but the first one I brought home, remember him?''

Charlene nodded carefully so her headache wouldn't shift again. She didn't bother to wipe her eyes, though now the tears had stopped. The tear tracks cooled her face and cooling her face might help the headache.

''I think he was involved in maybe the Mafia or something. I think he was a sort of hit man. He told me things I don't even want to tell you, Charlene. Awful things. He was like some kind of creepy-crawly bug, he was so low and despicable. And the second guy? The one we just took out a few days ago? I told you he had molested kids. Even a little baby girl. A *baby,* Charlene. What do you think that baby girl will grow up to become? What kind of nightmares will she have because of him? Will she remember a big grown man going down on her? Spreading her little chubby baby legs and—''

''Don't!'' Charlene covered her eyes with her hands. Tears started again and she didn't want them. The voices, too, were screaming for her attention, refuting every word Shadow said. Did not! they screamed. She's lying! Don't believe her.

''All right, all right, now, hush. Don't cry, Charlene. I just want you to understand how *bad* they were. There's so many of them, you wouldn't believe how many there are. They hang out in the club I dance in. They come over to my table and talk to me. I begin asking them questions, sometimes pretending I'm curious or I'm playing a game, and they start telling me things. Things you couldn't believe unless you were there and you saw their faces, saw their eyes, how they glitter, and then you know they mean it, they're telling you the truth and they don't care if you know, if it disgusts you, if it makes you sick to your stomach.''

''We'll have to go back to the hospital, Shadow. If this keeps on, they'll catch us, and they'll put us away forever. We won't get out ever again.''

''I don't think so. I don't think anyone will ever miss these putrid shits, if you want to know the truth. I'm doing the world a fucking favor.''

"They're missed already. At least they were *found*." Charlene removed her hands from her face and turned to Shadow. "I've seen it on the TV news and heard it on the radio. They found the bodies."

Shadow caught her breath audibly. Then she said, "You're sure? It's the men I took out in the bay?"

Charlene nodded. "They know about all of them. Two washed into the channel and the other was snagged by a shrimp boat."

Shadow looked down the stairs toward the door. "They won't find anything on them. Two were naked. They'll never know it was me."

"But what if they find out?"

"They won't." She said this emphatically. She stood then and took up the gym bag. "Listen, I want you to stop worrying. That makes the voices come to torture you, you know that. They aren't *real* voices, you know that, too. They're like your conscience talking to you. And you have nothing to feel guilty about. You didn't do anything but help me carry them to the boat. You've never hurt anyone in your life. So ignore the voices. They're trying to make you sick, that's all, and they will too, if you let them."

"I can't make them stop. I don't know how."

"Would you like me to get you some tranquilizers? I could get some from the girls if I ask. They carry around whole damn bags of pharmaceuticals."

Charlene came to her feet very slowly, holding her head as still as possible so the headache wouldn't thump so hard at her eye socket, half blinding her. "That might help," she admitted. "Maybe I could sleep then. Without nightmares."

Shadow came up the stairs to her and they walked together down the hall to Charlene's room. "Try to think of other things. Think of something pleasant. Leave what I'm doing to me. I know I'm right."

Are you? Charlene wanted to ask, but didn't.

Are you sure?

*   *   *

Samson wasn't sure his take on Shadow was right. He could usually compartmentalize people and know what they were about, what motivated them, what made them tick, it was part of his trade. But he wasn't quite sure about the dancer. All he really knew was what he felt about her. And it had to do with sex, primarily, what else could it have to do with, he didn't know her. And sexual attraction tended to fog the perceptions, he had to admit.

"She's a real puzzle," he said out loud to Pavlov.

The dog pranced around the kitchen floor as if he'd been complimented. If dogs really knew what words meant, Samson thought, they'd kill their masters. How many times had he called Pavlov a shit-eating dead-brain mutt?

Samson swallowed three coated aspirin tablets down with a glass of water from the tap. There was a very slight pounding in his head that he knew would turn into a hangover headache if he didn't nip it in the bud. He moved to the wall to turn out the light. In the hallway to the bedroom he said to the dog, "She bristled when I asked about kids. I think she has kids. I never messed with a woman who was a mother before. It gets overly complicated, you know? There's a lot of responsibilities go along with kids. You'd think Shadow would have stretch marks and shit, but this woman, she's got the smoothest belly . . ."

He moved into the bedroom without turning on the overhead light. Pavlov jumped on the bed and began circling and pawing at the covers to make a spot for sleeping.

"Get outta the bed, boy. That's where *I* sleep. Since when do you think you're so privileged?"

The dog halted his fretful bed making and stared at Samson with big sad eyes.

"Down!"

Pavlov jumped to the floor, ran to Samson's side to be petted and forgiven. He thrust his broad head beneath his master's hand and pushed up. Samson scratched between his amber-brown eyes. "Good boy. Good, Pavlov."

In the adjoining bathroom, in the dark, Samson found one of his toothbrushes and the Colgate. As he brushed his teeth, he grinned. Pavlov was butting his legs from behind.

Damn dog was like a cat, rubbing up against him.

He threw water on his face, soaped it, rinsed. While he took off his clothes and dropped them to the floor, Pavlov stood back, tail wagging, and making deep, throaty, happy growls.

"This girl . . . ," Samson began. "Woman, I mean. She *must* have children. When I brought up kids, she left the table, didn't even give me a backward glance. Now I figure, hey, I put a fifty on the goddamn table, that entitled me to longer than I got to talk to her, but what the hell, something I said offended her, I have to chalk the money up to a loss.

"And see, this is really a change for me, Pavlov, because I don't hand out money to dancers. You know me. El Cheapo. El Ultimo Cheapo when it comes to the titty bars. Which I'm not particularly proud of, by the way, being a cheap bastard. I just don't see handing out dough for talk, talk that costs can't be worth a plugged nickel. It's like paying for a fuck—how much can it be worth? Until now that was my policy, tight-assed as it may sound."

He went to the bed and tried straightening the sheets. He heard the dog circling at the end of the bed, making a nest in the pile of discarded clothes there.

"So if she's got kids, and her husband's dead—did I mention he was a suicide? Now that's interesting, even the way she told me he was a suicide was intriguing. Now if she's got kids, then she's dancing to support them. So what I want to know, what mother proud of her kids, dancing to send them to school, doesn't want to talk about them? What's the problem with her anyway? She acted like I'd asked her if she ever used strawberry douche or something. Definitely weird."

He crawled beneath the sheet and reached out to click the button on his alarm radio. He had to get up before noon. He ought to wash the clothes Pavlov used for a bed before he had to go to his shift. Going to get more doggy smelling in here soon if he didn't.

"Did I also mention she's got great lips? And eyes so dark they look like black coal. And when she talks, her eyes are serious—dead-on, drop-dead serious—but her mouth keeps trying to smile. That sort of betrays her, doesn't it? Damn mystifying if you ask me."

The dog must have fallen asleep. He had stopped pawing at the clothes and Samson couldn't hear anything from him.

But the boxer didn't care about his master's women.

After all, he was just a pesty dog.

As soon as Samson walked into the squad room for his shift, he was called into the lieutenant's office.

"We think there might be a connection between the three guys found floating in the bay."

Samson took a chair and waited. He had heard about the floaters, but hadn't known they were homicides. He hadn't seen the news on television for days. "Out of our jurisdiction, aren't they? Wouldn't that be something for the Harris County sheriff's office?"

"Would be," Epstein said, "but they're getting nervous. Unidentified floaters turn out to have records, all three of them. Two of them found naked, the last two, also *poisoned,* the last two."

"You're saying it's serial? But you said two. We need three to make it serial. Was the first one connected?" Samson felt a buzzing in his head at this news. Whenever serial killers worked Houston, he was the one they used to head the task force. He had spent most of his career studying these killers. He was the one they sent to Quantico for the FBI's annual training and updates on serial killers. He knew when the sheriff's office thought they'd stumbled on these kinds of murders, they didn't have the trained personnel to handle them.

"We're not totally sure on the first kill. It was a stabbing and that one had his clothes on when he was found. But he had a record, too. Was wanted for parole violation for sexual assault. So it still could be serial, if the latest is the third one. Looks like it's turning into that. Here're the files on the victims." He handed over three manila folders. "You know what to do. No one's linked them yet, the papers aren't onto it, and we'll want to keep it that way as long as possible."

"A task force?" Samson thumbed through the folders, casually looking for the autopsy reports.

"Not yet. If there's another one . . ."

"Gotcha." Samson stood and headed out to his desk. He spent the next hour studying the files, lost in thought so deep he didn't hear the noise of typewriters, computer printers, telephones, and conversation in the room. There was a yellow Post-it note attached to the third victim's file. "This one and the one before frequented bars in Montrose nights before their murders. The second victim's car was found in a Burger King parking lot."

It was unsigned. One of the county cops had done the legwork and found this bit of information. Why hadn't he noted *which* bars. Jesus, Montrose had back-to-back bars, pubs, cafés, strip joints, clubs. Which bars had the victims been in? And was this the only connection between them besides their rap sheets? Since Montrose was known as a predominantly gay hangout in the city, were the victims gays? What was it about gays got them killed, anyway? This sure wasn't connected to the kids from the Woodlands. By the time the third victim had died, the boys were in custody.

That was something he'd have to find out. The car in the Burger King, what was that about? Was the victim transported somewhere? That and about a thousand other questions had to be answered before he could even get involved in the investigation. He picked up the phone and dialed the county sheriff's office. He had to track down the nameless Post-it noter.

❦Twenty-three❦

It was a Saturday night when he came into the Blue Boa. It was crowded, peak hour, near midnight. He hadn't yet reached an open table when he saw the cop talking to the woman.

He turned and threaded his way through men and to the entrance door, to the sidewalk. Narrow call. He knew Samson. Had even interviewed him once, briefly, a long time ago—three years? five years?

He had visited the downtown police station and announced that he was a mystery novelist. He took along a few of his jacket covers to prove it. They let him talk to some of the detectives who weren't all that busy right then. Samson was one of them. Someone had told him Detective Mitchell Samson was unofficially the serial killer specialist. He was called in to head those cases. At the time, Son thought he shouldn't talk to him, but he couldn't help being curious.

He was especially careful what questions he asked. He said he didn't do crime suspense novels anyway, he wasn't into serial killers, so he didn't want to waste the detective's time. He asked a few innocuous questions involving procedure and office politics and how things were set up in the event of an arrest, and then he moved on to a patrolman who offered to let him ride in a squad car that night, get a feel for the "real thing," as the young cop had put it.

But Son would never forget Samson's face. That hard intelligent stare. The loose movements that belied the strength of the big-muscled body beneath the casual attire. The slight twist to the mouth when he paused to think before answering a question.

He had just seen him in the Blue Boa from the back and, for a brief moment, in profile when he turned his head, but he had recognized him.

Now what was the cop doing with the dancers? Did he visit the dives often and take out the prostititues? It wouldn't surprise Son, not a bit. Cops were screwy to begin with, else they wouldn't be cops, so hanging out in low-class nightclubs seemed right up their alley.

He wouldn't be onto the same idea Son was, would he? Ever since Stan had told him the victims found in the bay had a connection to the club scene in Montrose, Son had been prowling the area, looking for signs. He was like a jungle cat, hunting spoor. He talked to the girls, he talked to the managers, the customers, the street people. He did it, of course, in the most unobtrusive way possible, so no one would think him overly interested in things he shouldn't be interested in.

Mostly he let people talk. They got around to what he wanted to know sooner or later, though usually it was later. He didn't mind. He had plenty of time late in the night while Mother slept.

And he *was* a novelist. Maybe not much of one, but he picked up on things about people others didn't. Tones of voice, a shifting of the glance, the words behind the words, the story inside the story. Lies people tried to hide. Lies they believed to be true. Lies they used to make themselves look better. It was strange not everyone noticed these tell-tale clues. Were they just stupid or unconcerned or were they so locked inside their own skins they couldn't see out the other guy's eyes?

Son had long known people were, on the whole, incredibly ignorant. Like cattle. Feed them, give them water, lead them around by the nose. They liked that. Ask them to *think,* analyze, question, collect information—forget about it. It was just too much trouble for your average Joe.

Maybe Samson was doing the same thing as Son, casing the area, looking for leads. Sniffing spoor.

Son would have to do something now he really hated doing. He'd have to watch his back. No more lounging easily, fearlessly, making himself at home in the area, making friends. Every moment he spent here from now on would entail his being on guard, checking where the cop was before he chose a club. He could always say this was research, but if he was caught too many times by the cop, and if the cop noticed he was asking too many questions, he'd fall into the category of a suspect.

That hard intelligent stare would turn on him and dissect him like a frog, flay him open to prod at his brain.

Detective Samson was not one of the cattle herd.

Shadow was distracted as the cop talked. She heard maybe every other sentence he spoke. She couldn't concentrate because something boiled and writhed inside her mind. She had made another date. The kind that might or might not lead to a poisoning. The man calling himself John—and that was a crock—had sat at her table earlier, before the cop came in. She listened to him a while, saying barely enough to keep him talking, and her mind started working. She wanted to wait to ask her list of questions until she had him in Seabrook. She suggested he meet her after work outside Wendy's. She suggested he might like to go home with her. He agreed that he wanted whatever she wanted.

"I'm sorry?" She tried to catch up on the conversation. The cop had asked her something, but she didn't know what.

"Where are you? You're certainly not here talking with me."

He didn't sound peeved, just curious. If he'd sounded peeved, as if she *owed* him her complete attention, that wouldn't have set well. "I guess I was daydreaming. It's rude, I know. I'm sorry. What were you saying?"

They had talked about nothing, nothing at all of any import. He had not again asked her anything personal, not since days before when she had walked out on him.

"Nothing that needs repeating," he said, and then smiled.

She did like his smile. He didn't do it often so that when

he did smile, it meant something. "I'm really sorry. I'm afraid I have to leave a little early tonight, you don't mind, do you? I can give some of the money back."

He waved his hand expansively. "Wouldn't think of a refund. Maybe we'll apply it toward the next time."

She cocked her head. "You really like sitting here and talking to me, don't you?"

"I wouldn't do it otherwise."

"You don't feel it's demeaning to pay a woman to talk to you?"

"Why should I? Do you feel demeaned by taking money to talk to me?"

She smiled. "Not to you. Maybe to some other people. *Most* other people."

"Men, you mean."

"Yes, men. If you can call them that."

Samson drank the last of his coffee and rose from the table. She watched how lithe and smooth were his movements. He must not have a clumsy bone in his body.

"I have to go anyway. I've got some work to catch up on."

Shadow also stood. She impulsively held out her hand. He paused, looking confused, and then he took it in his own big palm, gently, and shook it.

"I really like you," he said softly. "I don't think I've shaken hands with a woman in a social situation in . . . oh . . . a while."

She pulled closed her jacket, feeling modest suddenly. It was pretty stupid to shake a guy's hand when she was almost totally undressed. She would have blushed if her skin tone had not been so dark. She looked away, unable to meet his eyes.

Just as she did, he moved, she felt him move the small step separating them, but it was so quickly done that she hadn't a chance to retreat. He leaned over and kissed her on her turned cheek. "So beautiful," he whispered, then he was moving through the tables for the door while she stood staring after him, surprised. And something else. Pleased?

She raised a hand to her cheek to touch where his lips had left a warm impression. A man at another table behind her said, "Hey, c'mere and I'll give you a *real* kiss!"

She tossed her head and walked past him without a glance.

Silly kid stuff. Shaking hands. Kissing someone on the cheek. Saying you liked them. Christ. She didn't have time for this. Didn't have *time*. Why did he have to be a cop, damn it?

At Wendy's she had John get into her car. While she drove to Seabrook and the mansion, she let him talk. It seemed all she did lately was listen. Her head should be full of words, full of secrets. It should be overflowing, bursting . . .

As she unlocked the door of the house, she saw Charlene scurrying down the hall at the top of the stairway. She had seen them coming and was going to make herself scarce. Until later. What a good friend she had turned out to be.

Shadow led the man to her room. He sat on the bed next to her, and when he tried to make a provocative move, she carefully pried his hands off and asked one of the required questions.

"Hit a woman? Or a kid? Me? Hell no, that's sick," he said. "Only reason I'd ever hit a woman was if she was about to kill me or something."

Shadow heard the truth in his voice and thought she must have made a mistake with John. She asked another question. She explained first that this was a game, sort of, and during the game, she would tie him to the bed, *then* they would have some fun.

He looked nervously at the iron bedstead, then back to her. "I'm . . . uh . . . not much into that kind of thing."

"That's all right. I am. It won't be for long, don't worry." And it wouldn't be if he continued answering her the way he should.

Which he did. He had been in prison, yes, but it was for stealing a portable TV from an old geezer who lived next door to him when he was a kid of seventeen. They sent him off to Huntsville for a couple of years, and he came out unable to find work. She understood that. Look what she had done to survive when Scott died.

He had finally wandered into construction work and now he was a foreman, he made pretty good money, he didn't have to steal. He didn't have a lot of ambition and the foreman job suited him fine.

He had had a wife who left him when he couldn't buy her a new car.

He had no children. He liked kids, though, and was a Big Brother to a little fatherless Mexican boy. He talked about taking the child to the zoo and the movies.

She came to like John pretty well, after all, and whatever he had said at the Blue Boa that got her to thinking he might be a prime candidate for poison vanished from her thoughts. There was just one thing left to test him over.

"Listen," she said. "I think I've changed my mind about the game. And about going to bed with you. I like you just fine, but I made a mistake. I'll drive you back to your car now."

If he protested too vehemently or if he tried to take her against her will, she'd kill him. She would. Because no man had the right to force her to do anything. Never again.

John looked disappointed, but he said with a sigh, "Oh, that's all right. I'm not really sure we know each other enough anyway. I just thought you were a real knockout and maybe I got carried away at the club, you know how it is in those places. I'm ready to go, if you are." And he stood, a fly who was free of her web, a man who would walk out the same way he walked in, on his own two feet, the first man to pass her test.

She gave him a brief hug then opened the door, caught Charlene standing outside her door, just standing there staring down the hall toward Shadow's bedroom door. She smiled at her. Saw Charlene's eyes widen when the man stepped out behind her. Saw her hurry inside her room again to hide from view.

It was after four in the morning when she returned home after dropping John at his parked car in the Wendy's parking lot. She didn't see Charlene when she came up the stairs.

Good thing. She was too tired to talk, to explain.

Sleep sounded good to her.

Letting them live was more troublesome than killing them, it seemed. It sure took more time.

After visiting Big Mac in the hospital ward, Samson dropped off to see if Shadow was working. He was depressed. Big Mac was getting better. A *little* better, but she still needed the hospital. He knew she was better because she argued with great vigor that she was perfectly all right and she hated staying in bed and the damn IV's were such a bitch when she tried to sleep. Samson assured her she would be well enough soon to leave, but she pretended not to believe him.

"I'm going to die in this place," she said. "How would *you* like it if a nurse had to help you to the bathroom to take a piss? How would *you* like eating Jell-O and pudding every meal? I bet *you* wouldn't let them come stick you for blood samples every few hours!"

He tried to laugh and jolly her out of the extremely bad mood she was in, but she was touchy, and his laughter only made her worse.

"Sadists work in this place, Samson. Did you know that? They must have recruited them from somewhere where torture is expected of a hospital staff."

"Now, Big Mac, now now."

"Don't you '*now*' me! I'm a grown woman here. I am an independent and free woman! I don't have to take this shit."

Samson got tough then. "If you try to leave, it might kill you, Mac. You're still running a fever. Your lungs aren't so hot, either. They're still infected and there's still drainage. You want to bellyache over a few pinpricks and go out in this summer heat and die? That what you want? It's a hundred and two in the shade out there. The heat might climb today to a hundred and five. It'll kill you."

She sulked. She turned over on her side, groaning while

trying to pull the IV lines with her across the bed.

Samson sat still, waiting for a long time without talking again. When she wouldn't speak, he finally touched her on the shoulder and said, "I'm leaving now. I'm sorry I raised my voice."

She said nothing.

"I'll be back tomorrow. Aren't you even glad we got those kids in the slammer? Doesn't that cheer you right the hell up?"

Nothing.

Samson sighed and left. Mac was worth saving, but damn if she wasn't a handful the minute she started getting better. He hoped she wouldn't try to leave the hospital when he wasn't there. He'd kick her old sagging ass all the way to Puerto Rico and back if she did.

He found Shadow, alone at a table, sipping a Coke. He sat down, took out his wallet, slipped two twenties across to her.

"You look tired," she said, taking the money.

"Got this friend in the hospital. She's giving me fits."

"Lady friend?"

"She's an old bag lady. Supplies me with info from the street. She was down with double pneumonia, dying, when I talked her into the emergency room. She's crazy as hell, but I like her."

"How's she giving you fits?"

"She wants to leave the hospital. She does, she'll get sicker and probably die."

"If she's on the street, she will. It's hotter than blazes now."

Then he talked about Mac and the street, about the boys who killed the gay banker and how Mac witnessed it. He talked about police work and old cases he'd solved, old cases he hadn't. He talked about living alone with a boxer he called Pavlov. He talked and talked and she listened. Then he saw her attention had wandered and he realized how long he'd been going on about himself. His life. His problems. He was abashed.

She apologized for daydreaming and he would have

given his next paycheck to know what her "daydreaming" involved, but he couldn't ask her that. He'd made up his mind that he couldn't really ask her anything, not anything personal anyway, and what was left? Wasn't everything personal?

What was that word that meant people believed the whole world revolved around them? *Concentric? Egocentric?* He couldn't think. *Damn.* It was a word that had a pejorative meaning, but he couldn't think of it. He could think of *pejorative,* but that was as far as his vocabulary would take him tonight. He figured everyone thought like that, though, believing the world revolved around him. Only natural.

So while he was hung up on Big Mac and his cases and his work and his life, Shadow was probably lost in thoughts of her own, about her life. He did not blame her. Maybe she was thinking about her husband's suicide. Or about buying a new dance outfit. Or sleep. Whatever it was, he finally noticed he'd lost her, and she readily admitted that he had.

He had to go anyway. He had the three murder files to read over for about the hundredth time. He carried them around with him in the car. He read over them while having lunch, while at home scratching Pavlov's head, while sitting on the john. He read them until the three men ran together, became one. He was losing perspective.

The Post-it note had been written by Deputy Joe Dappo. Samson took him out for burgers the night before at a little twenty-four-hour café that made the best burgers in the southeast side of Houston. He asked Joe about the note and how he had come to his conclusion. Joe was a nineteen-year-old, green from the academy, but he was bright, brighter than many an old detective Samson had known. It was Joe who had tracked the men's movements in the days before their death.

The first one, stabbed, the one on parole for sexual assault—rape—was the hardest to find out about. He had wandered around Pasadena, staying first with this ex-con, then with that one. It seemed the con had *not* been in Montrose before his death. But the other two, the poisoned ones, they *had* been. Friends and relatives informed Joe Dappo the men hung out down in Montrose when they could afford it. Both were into the strip clubs, or rather, the girls in their G-strings, and that answered for Samson what *kind* of bars they frequented. And didn't *that* obsession ring a bell?

No one knew exactly which clubs they went to, but all agreed it was the strippers they liked best.

Samson now had more than one reason to hang around Shadow and the Blue Boa. Not to mention all the other strip clubs. His stomping ground. His home away from home. Same as for the dead men, which gave him no small pause.

It wasn't certain, of course, that the two victims who liked Montrose clubs had died because of anything to do with their whereabouts beforehand. That was just Samson's wild supposition. Unsupported, no wait, there was the victim's car found in the Burger King lot. That *did* support the theory. But Montrose was the only connection between them. And it might take him weeks, months, to even find out where they were the night before their deaths. But eventually, he would. Someone knew something.

He just had to find that someone.

Not that he'd done such a good job of it tonight. He'd spent his entire time at the Blue Boa getting things off his chest, thanks to Mac and her frame of mind. That wasn't going to help his investigation.

When he kissed Shadow, he had smelled her scent, the one coming off her skin, not one put there by perfume. He didn't think she wore perfume. If she did, he hadn't detected it. As he kissed her lightly on the cheek, he was reminded of the region of west Texas around Abilene. There was a sunbaked cactus flower scent about her that he found both unusual and attractive. He had never thought a woman could smell like a place before. An open sunny windy place.

Boy, he had it bad. He knew that. The more he was with Shadow, the more he wanted to be with her. It wasn't a good thing. There were good things and bad things, and she might not be so bad for him, at least as a temporary obsession, but she definitely wasn't good either. What was he going to do getting involved with a stripper?

He didn't know anything. Not about his feelings that were leading him back again and again to this dancer, not about the files he carried around, worrying over them.

With the murders, all he could do was wait for another victim. This left him helpless and stirred a well of anger that lay festering in his gut.

With Shadow, all he could do was wonder about her and see how close he could get before she either bit him or ran. That also left him helpless and angry. Because at this point he was afraid he cared just as much about what happened to the budding relationship with the dancer as he did about solving his caseload.

What a dangerous combination that was. It was inexplicable, he couldn't change it, but it was definitely a hazardous mix.

ᨠTwenty-fourᨠ

It had been two weeks since Samson had been able to slow down. Big Mac had recovered enough to be released from the hospital, provided she take antibiotics and take care of herself, meaning not letting herself get rained on or cold and damp in the open elements.

"I never been so happy to see the back end of a place." She spit on the sidewalk just before rising from the wheelchair to enter Samson's car.

"I have a proposition for you, Mac." Mitchell shut the car door and circled to get into the driver's seat.

"Like what?" she asked suspiciously.

"I think you ought to move in with me." He had both hands on the wheel with the motor idling. He looked directly into Big Mac's eyes so she'd know he meant it, this was no joke, cruel or otherwise. He had thought about it for a long time, ever since she fell ill.

"Move in with you? You gotta be nuts."

"No, I'm serious. Look, I'm a bachelor, I don't get time at home much, so the place needs somebody to take a broom to it now and then. And I have a dog, a big dog, who needs company."

"You *know* I don't take handouts of that sort, Samson."

"It's not a handout. It might be a hand up. Or a hand to steady me. I think I might be getting a little squirrelly, living alone. I talk to myself."

"So who doesn't?" Mac's eyes twinkled merriment. She was in a good mood, but she really wasn't buying his offer, he knew that.

"I think it would be an all-around good thing, Mac. You need a place to stay, I need a housekeeper and a companion.

What do you say? I could pay you.''

Mac looked out the window at the rows of cars in the parking lot's hot sunshine. "I don't need a place to stay. I needed a place to stay, I'd get my own place.''

Samson sighed and sagged as he did so, his hands loosening on the steering wheel. "I wish you wouldn't be so goddamn stubborn. I'm asking you politely to help me out here.''

Mac turned on him. "Like hell you are! You got Pity City written all over your face. You think I could take that? You think I need your charity? I don't need nothing! Now will you drive me down to where you kept my stuff or do I have to walk all the way through town?''

Samson gave it up. He drove her to the station and told her to wait in the car while he got her shopping cart and personal possessions. "You kept it in the police station?''

Samson grinned mischievously. "It's logged in with the stolen property. They had the room, they didn't mind.''

He came out a side door from the building pushing the cart before him. It teetered, piled high with bags and clothes. He popped the trunk and stored it all there. The lid wouldn't close over the shopping cart, so he tied it securely with a rope. Back inside the car, with the air-conditioning running full blast, he wiped his face of sweat. "That shit's heavy.''

"That shit's my shit, and I'll thank you not to call it shit.''

He drove according to her directions down into the Montrose area and let her out on a corner. He had to double park to unload her things. "You sure you won't change your mind?''

"I got no reason to sit in some man's house all day playing with no dog.''

"If you change your mind, you know where to call me.''

He drove away, keeping her in his rearview mirror, watching while she stood in the gutter, pawing through her things jumbled in the cart. He didn't understand the world, he realized. He thought he did, he pretended he did, but he didn't know spit about what made people turn down a home, what made a woman want to live on the street instead. She was a little off in the brain department, sure, but she wasn't a basket case. Why couldn't she just come home with him and latch on to a *real* life, with a roof over her head. It wasn't like he was going to imprison her, for christ's sake.

Three days later Lieutenant Epstein called him into the office. Jerry Dodge, hunched over his desk across from Samson, swigged from a paper cup of coffee and said, "I already know what he wants with you."

"That so? Clue me in, Dod."

Dod reached out and tapped the file folders holding the floaters. "Got another one."

"I guess I expected as much." Samson stood and straightened his tie. He reached for his sports jacket from the chair back and shrugged into it.

"You gonna form a task force?"

"I don't know yet, depends on what the boss says."

"I could run legwork for you if you do."

"Don't you have a full caseload already?"

"Doesn't everybody? I'd still like to learn a little bit about how you track down serials."

"Oh, you mean the glamour of the job, yeah, it's real uptown, Dod. The guys in Quantico call me up all the time, fly me by private jet into Virginia, ask my opinion on where I think the Zodiac disappeared to and if the Green River Killer's dead, in prison, or hanging out at the Vegas roulette tables."

"You don't have to be sarcastic. I just offered."

Samson paused. He leaned over toward Dod. "It's shit work, just like what you've got on your own desk. You wouldn't like it. It's more tedious than the Parole Violation Squad."

"But there might be a promotion in it." A knowing glint had come into Dod's eyes.

"I don't think so," Samson said, heading for Epstein's office. "You've been misinformed."

In the lieutenant's office he studied the new file folder while the boss talked.

"We have a definite pattern now. This one cinches it. Guy's naked, poisoned, floating up the channel. Not much left of this one. As you can see . . ."

Samson stared at the photo of the dead man. Both eyes were eaten from the sockets, his nose was gone, as were his lips. Although Caucasian, he was black from the water, and bloated so much he looked like someone had pumped him full of helium. Samson flipped the photo facedown and looked at the next one. This was a close-up showing striations on the victim's heels.

"How'd he get these, the M.E. say?"

"It's in his report in the top folder. He thinks someone dragged the corpse over rough ground after death. There were still bits of gravel imbedded in the skin."

Samson closed the folder. He'd study it later. "I wonder if this one hung out around Montrose."

Epstein shook his head. "I don't know. That's something you'll have to find out. What do you think so far? What's going on?"

Samson was careful. "I don't have anything solid yet. The other two were in clubs all up and down the streets. I have a feeling it has something to do with dancers. Maybe a crazy boyfriend, someone jealous of his ole lady."

"Fucking poison, though, seems a boyfriend would just shoot the bastards. Well, get on it. The broadcast news tonight's going to do a five-minute report. They know about the poison. They might nickname the killer any day now."

"Do you want me to gather some people, get some help?"

"Up to you. At this point you may not need it. Draft someone if you do. I don't want to get anything official looking started yet, gives the case too much attention, makes it too easy for the reporters to camp on our doorstep."

Samson took the folder to his desk. Picked up the phone. Needed to find out if the victim had been identified yet through his fingerprints.

"They already got it," Dod said, swiveling in his chair to the portable TV sitting on a sideboard against the wall.

Samson put down the phone again. He looked up to see the midday newsman on Channel 2 speaking from the scene in Kemah. It was a videotape taken earlier when the body was found. "Turn it up."

Dod rolled across the room in his chair and turned up the volume.

Mitchell watched the news spot while his stomach started to roil. The heat was on, the media was all over it. When that happened, it was always a real mess. The boss was right. The second he formed a task force, reporters would crawl over him, ants on a carcass, breathing down his neck, asking for updates, trying to follow him around, and getting in the way.

"Fuck," he swore softly. Picked up the phone again and made his call.

That night, with the moon in full regalia and the stars more plentiful than other nights of recent recall, Son slipped out Sherilee's door and down the steps to the street. If he turned he knew he'd see her standing, watching him go, and if he turned, she would give him a little wave good-bye.

Most of the time that kind of domestic scene would have warmed him. Tonight it just made him more nervous. These *connections* with people dragged him down. Sherilee. His mother. Women, fucking women. Even though you paid them for something, they started thinking they owned you.

He stopped at his car door, key in his hand. He *didn't like* women. Funny how he could miss a thing like that for so many years. Oh, he knew he would never marry one. He'd never have a regular honest relationship. But he hadn't thought about it beyond that. Until now, with Sherilee standing on the porch in the moonlight watching him go, and that uneasiness creeping up from his back to his neck making him feel spied upon.

He didn't like women at all. He used Sherilee for sex, he needed *that,* but look at her. She was black. She was old—at least for her line of work. She was without any principle whatsoever. She'd do anything for money, anything he asked of her, do anything with anybody anytime.

Fucking whore dog.

And he didn't like his mother, either. He loved her, had to, he was her son, but he didn't *like* her. She was too rich in spirit, too accepting of what life handed her, too . . . good for him, oh, wasn't she now, too good. . . .

He unlocked the car door and slid inside. Hot. Suffocating. Humidity, even at this time of night, in the nineties. He started the car and got the AC going. Angled the vents on his face and shut his eyes. He hoped Sherilee had gone inside now. He'd hate to think she was still looking after him.

A lake of moonlight lay over the interior of the car, almost blinding in its brilliance. Son put the car into gear and screeched the tires leaving the curb.

He couldn't go home yet. Too bent out of shape. *Pretzelized.* That was a good word for how he felt. Bent into figure eights, baked hard and lightly salted.

He drove slowly down the inner-city streets. A patrol car passed him. A cab. Two cars empty except for lone drivers. Both men. Women didn't drive down through Houston late at night, alone. Wasn't done except during an emergency of some sort. There were too many ''bump and robs'' where guys bumped into the rear of a woman driver's car, waited until she got out to check for damage, then took her car or took her *and* the car. Too many drive-by shootings. Too many dope dealers high on their own products and crazy enough to jerk a woman out of the driver's seat at a stoplight and beat her face in just for kicks.

Too many of everything!

Son pounded at the dash. Damned AC didn't blow cool enough. Needed to get it fixed. You couldn't buy your own cans of freon anymore and fill up a leaking compressor. EPA outlawed the stuff because of the damaged ozone layer. Now you had to go in to a repair shop and pay hundreds of dollars to get the fucker fixed. What would they think of next to persecute honest, hard-working citizens?

An entrance ramp came up for the Loop. Son took it, aimlessly driving. He circled around the city until he came to the I-45 south exit, took it. Maybe it would be cooler down by the ocean.

He wanted to get a look at the channel anyway, the one that separated Kemah and Seabrook, the one where they brought in the bodies.

None of the restaurants were open this late. He parked on a spit of land outside the little town of Seabrook where the channel flowed on the right and ahead lay the bay. He got out of the car and walked over to the bulkhead. A dozing gull flew off with a squawk.

The wind was blowing here, smelling briny. It ruffled his hair back from his forehead and caressed his cheeks. He saw a freighter out in the bay, its lights outlining the ship's body. A moon path stretched wide from the horizon to the bulkhead, like a silver highway.

Four dead men had walked it lately. From somewhere *out there* where they slipped beneath the waves, they rolled and tumbled and were nudged by currents and fish back toward land.

It would soon be morning and the moon hidden.

Son turned abruptly and hurried to the car. He had to get home, he'd forgotten. His mother shouldn't be alone, not all night this way. What if she needed to go to the bathroom? What if she tried it by herself and fell? Or stayed in bed and wet herself? What if her heart gave out and she'd called for him?

Jesus God, all he thought about was himself. Having sex, finding a cool breeze, driving all the fuck the way down 45 to SeaForsakenBrook just to look at the water.

He had to get home. Now.

''Mother? Mother?'' He came into the house calling her name. He got her bedroom door open, panicking, still calling for her. ''Mother?''

''Son! What is it?''

She turned on the bed lamp and the room exploded into light. She was up on one elbow, squinting at him, frowning at him.

He was shaking all over, trembling so badly his teeth

chattered uncontrollably. All the way home across the city he had let his imagination run wild until he was sure, *sure* she had died while he was gone.

"Oh, Mother, I'm sorry, I . . . I didn't mean to wake you . . . I was . . ."

"Son, what's the matter? You're shaking. Sit down right this minute. You look awful."

She tried to rise from bed. Her color was bad. She looked yellow in the lamplight. Her eyes were watery and there were blue hollows underneath them. He put out his hands. "Don't move, just stay there. I'm all right. I'll sit down." He collapsed in the chair and put his hands over his face.

"Son? Honey, what's wrong?"

"I'm sorry, I'm really sorry. I was out, we played cards too late, and I didn't notice the time. I got scared, that's all. It was silly."

"Sweetheart. You were worried about me. You needn't do that. I sleep all night, you know that. I never call for you on your card nights. You always make sure I have everything I need."

I'm a good son, he thought. I really am.

"Do you want me to sit up with you a while? Would you like to talk?"

He lowered his hands from his face. "We need to get you to that appointment," he said. "We've put it off too long already."

"I'm going to be fine." She adjusted the covers over her chest.

"You haven't been doing so well lately. You need a checkup. They should see about your medications, maybe they aren't strong enough."

"You can't fix this old heart, Son. No one can. Worrying about things you can't change will only waste your time."

"You don't want to die, do you?" He hadn't meant to raise his voice. He was out of control and hated that, hated it.

"Please don't shout, Son. I'll go to the doctor if that's what you want. Just don't get worked up so."

"I'm sorry. I told you I was scared. I'll call for an appointment tomorrow, or rather *today*, after I get a nap." He stood shakily. "I'll let you rest now. I really didn't mean to disturb you."

"Get some sleep, darling. Tomorrow things will look brighter, mark my words." She reached and turned out the lamp.

Son shut the door quietly. He moved through the dark hall to his own room, her scent in his nostrils. Baby powder, cotton gowns ironed and crisp, old paper skin, old denture breath.

His mother was dying. This time she was going to die.

But what would he do without her, what would he do if he didn't have her to care for?

What would he do if he was left alone, all alone, in the world?

Twenty-five

Shadow knew she was taking him home with her.

"I'd like to see where you live. Not many people know, do they?" Samson looked around the club as if someone might have overheard him.

"I don't talk about my personal life at work. Most of us lie, anyway, to the customers."

"I've always wondered about that. It makes you work at being fraudulent, doesn't it? I don't mean to imply there's anything wrong with lying to customers about where you live or your name. Hell, it would be a big mistake to let most of these guys know where you live. But it just seems lying all the time could make you . . . well, forget what the truth is."

Shadow thought it over. She didn't like the word *fraudulent* applied to her and that must have shown on her face. "Everyone's a fraud anyway, what's the big deal?"

"I said I didn't mean it was so bad." He sipped at the Irish coffee. "Everyone's a fraud when you come right down to it. For instance, I'm a cop so I'm supposed to be brave, upright, and civic minded."

"It sounds like the Boy Scout oath. But I suppose you're right. Tell lies long enough and the truth fades out." She paused. "Which one of those things are wrong? You're not brave? Upright? Civic minded?"

"Rarely any of the above," he said, smiling that smile she liked so much. "Will you tell me your real name then?"

She hesitated. "Kay. But I'm not the same person I was when that was my name. Shadow suits me better now."

"Kay." He stared into his coffee, mulling over the sound

of it. "Katherine?" She nodded slightly. "Kay what?"

"Mandel. My married name. Mandel." He was the first person in over a year, outside of Charlene, she'd told her real name. Why was there such power in a person's name? Under the name of Shadow she was free to be anyone and act in any way she pleased. As Kay Mandel she was held responsible for her actions. *That* was the magic of a nickname.

"Why don't you call me Mitch?"

She nodded her head. "Well, Mitch, how would you like to take a ride with me?"

"Now? Where to?"

"To where I live."

He looked startled. She smiled, enjoying surprising him. "It's a long drive. We can go in my car."

"Why don't I follow you in mine instead?"

She hadn't done that before. Because she meant to kill them. But she knew she didn't mean to kill the cop. In the first place he wasn't the type of man who needed to be destroyed, wiped from the face of the earth. He fell in the category of wipee. He did the same thing she did, which was to clean the streets of its scum layer. They had this in common. In the second place—what the hell was she doing, did she even know?

Her heart rate went into warp speed. She knew what she was doing. She wanted him. In bed. As a lover. She must have known that the first time she saw him, but she couldn't admit it then. Now since she had met with him and talked a lot, she knew it was inevitable. She actually *did* have hormones. She *really* was still a normal woman with some kind of sex drive left. It was astounding but true.

"Okay," she said. "I'm ready to leave now. How about you?"

He stood and came to her chair, pulling it back as she rose. The way gentlemen used to do for ladies. The way Scott used to—

She broke off that thought and turned to Mitch. "I have to change and get my things. I'll be in the parking lot in a minute if you want to wait there."

She felt his eyes tracking her as she moved to the dressing rooms. For the first time in ages she felt embarrassed at how little she had on. The lace jacket covered nothing. The G-string covered less. What had possessed her to get into this business?

Oh yes. Survival. Vastly overrated as it was.

She walked as unself-consciously as possible through the curtains to the back. Taking home a cop. Seducing a policeman.

She *must* be out of her mind.

They lay separated by inches, breathing heavily, sweat drying on their bodies. The air-conditioning vent over the bed blew cold air and chilled her flesh, but she did not move to cover herself.

"I might be down this way more often," he said. "I'm taking over a case. You hear about the bodies washing in?"

Her breath caught. "Oh . . . yeah, I did."

Funny how a man's mind went straight back to business the moment after intercourse. It had been difficult for Shadow. They made love in her bed, the same bed where men had died. Men had bled. She could even feel the plastic sheeting deep under the sheets, two blankets, and bedspread they lay atop. She wondered if he noticed. He might think she was incontinent. She almost laughed aloud.

Then she thought about his heading the case of the poisoned men. It sobered her. Her sweat dried in the chilly air and she shivered. This meant he was the one who was her greatest enemy. Lover. Enemy. Which was he?

He turned to her, wrapping her in his arms. Her face fit into the crook of his neck. She loved his scent. She could drink it in all night. He was her lover. He could never be an enemy to her. She would never let him find out what she had done. And meant to do. Never.

"If I'm down here more often, that means I might be able to see you here, rather than at the club."

"Um-hmm." She snuggled deeper into the crevice of his body. Her breasts pressed flat against his chest. She looped one leg over his hip. "It's been a long time since . . ."

"I thought so," he said, and said no more.

She didn't want to explain. He spoke again finally, telling one of those truths they had kept from one another. "For me, too." She believed him.

"I was engaged a few months ago. It didn't work out," he said. "She was class. I was a gutter crawler. She wanted invitations to the wedding printed in gold. I wanted to hand out my business card to friends."

Though he was trying to make light of it, Shadow understood some of the things he was leaving out. She knew what it meant to be on the outside, out on the edge, not flowing in the mainstream of society. Unless you had been there, you couldn't know how different it was, how alien the rest of the world appeared, how awful those *others* sometimes treated you.

"Did you love her?"

"I thought I did. But I guess I didn't."

More truth. She was glad he had not truly loved the other woman. She was jealous of her without knowing any more than that he had asked her to marry him.

She let her hand rove up and down his back, feeling his muscles there, powerful, strong, the little bumps of his spine, the swell of his buttocks. He was cool to her touch. Dry now, his skin like the marble floors of the mansion, hard and flat.

She felt him growing excited again. As long as he thought of her and kept his mind away from the murders, she was safe. Safe in his arms, safe to let herself go. He moved a bit and she knew what he wanted to find. If he had to get up to get another condom, she would feel too naked and abandoned.

"Wait," she whispered. "Wait." She leaned back in his arms a little, reaching behind her to feel blindly along the bed-table top in the dark. Her fingers danced over a little square package. She drew it closer and palmed it. She snuggled again, tearing it open with her teeth. She looked into his shadowed face. Thought he smiled.

"I thought you might want me to leave," he said softly next to her ear. He nibbled at her earlobe, and a delicious thrill went down her body. Her nipples hardened against his chest.

"Not yet," she said. "Oh no, not yet . . ."

As he fiddled with the condom, getting it on, she turned in his arms, her back to him so they were together like spoons. He slipped in her from behind, his hands seeking and finding her breasts. She bent her head until her eyes were hidden in the bend of his arm. She lifted one leg again, draping it over his hip. She opened to him and let his measured thrusts wash her toward orgasm.

The fourth floater was identified as Ossie Cherkovania, an escapee from Huntsville Correctional Unit where he had been incarcerated for four years and three months after being found guilty of murder in the second degree. He had been on the loose for six months. He had a sheet going back to his teens, everything from hot-wiring and stealing cars to assault with a deadly weapon.

Samson sat at his desk chewing the eraser on a pencil. He pulled a yellow notepad over and wrote:

1) Victims frequented nightclubs in Montrose area.

2) Victims all have records.

Dod interrupted his thoughts. "ID the guy?"

"Yeah. Escaped TDC six months ago."

"Good riddance, then. Saved the taxpayers money putting him up."

Samson moved his gaze from the notepad to Dod. He stared at him, thinking about what he'd said.

"What is it? My breath stink?"

"It might. That's not what I was thinking. What you said. About good riddance this guy got offed."

"Yeah?"

"The others were known perps, too. Some on parole."

"Somebody's cleaning up the city."

Samson pointed the pencil at Dod. Then he bent to the notepad and added:

3) Killer is vigilante?

"We got us a Charles Fucking Bronson," Dod said. "But why poison? And how'd he get them to drink the stuff?"

"How do you know they drank it?"

"I can read autopsy reports, too. I have a genuine high school diploma." He grinned to soften the admission that he had been snooping in Samson's files.

Samson shrugged. He didn't really care just as long as Dod didn't get in his way. The news stories said the men were poisoned. It never said how. You could just as well overdose someone with a needle full of something as get them to drink it. In the case of warfarin, getting someone to drink it had to be a real iffy proposition. How *did* the killer get them to drink it?

Samson tore off his note and stuffed it in the new folder on Cherkovania. He bundled the files together and stood, grabbing his jacket.

"Need help?" Dod asked.

"Dod, give it a rest, okay? I need you, I'll send a fucking marine marching band past your house with a printed invitation." That reminded him of what he'd told Shadow about his engagement. And *that* reminded him of being in bed with the most desirable woman he had made love with in years. Maybe ever. He shook his head as he left the bullpen.

"You don't have to be a bear!" Dod yelled at his back. "I was only trying to help."

But I do have to be a bear, Samson thought, pushing through the glass doors to the hall. I have to be a big brown roaring-ass grizzly to get your nose out of my cases, you sneaky ladder-climbing dick.

On the street the heat slapped him in the face. After the air-conditioned building, he could hardly draw a good breath. It was like breathing in plastic wrap. It felt as if his lungs were going in and out and nothing was happening. He hurried to his car, threw the folders on the front seat. When he got in, the enclosed heat made drops of sweat pop out on his face and under his arms. Rivulets set up a stream down his back. The vinyl scorched his legs through the material of his slacks. He got the car started and the AC blowing full blast.

"If I was a polar bear, I'd be on an ice floe in Alaska right now."

He heard himself and grinned. It was five o'clock in the afternoon and it felt like noon in the Sahara. Houston was experiencing a heat wave that had produced a mini drought. It had been a month since Samson had seen a drop of rain. Trees in the park drooped sick, wilted limbs. Grass was a shade of green rapidly fading to brown.

It wouldn't be cool enough to tackle the street and ask questions until the sun was down and that wouldn't happen for another two hours.

He thought he'd go to the dark bar section of the Blue Boa and get a Corona. Hell yeah. It was too goddamn hot for *any kind* of coffee. He'd watch for Big Mac through the window. She'd need another twenty spot by now.

For the next two hours Samson sat on a stool drinking Coronas, although he was on duty, and trying to study over the file folders. Most of that time, however, was spent thinking about sex. Sex with a capital S. Sex with Shadow. Sex backward, forward, sideways. Kay Mandel. The one the other girls called the Ice Queen.

A nickname he found appropriate only if a person didn't know her intimately. And he hoped no one knew her as intimately as he did. He'd be tempted to take out his six-gun and meet the crud at high noon, blasting away, a regular Rory Calhoun.

At six-thirty, he slipped out a prison photo of Cherkovania he had faxed from TDC. He held it out to the barkeep. "You seen this guy around?"

The slender young man wore a starched white shirt that did not seem to jibe with the scraggly two-day beard he sported. He looked like a man who needed a few good home-cooked meals, pasta maybe.

"Nope."

"You're sure?"

"I said."

"You said?"

"I said nope. But I don't pay attention to the people come in here. 'Cept for you. I know you." He gave the impression of smiling, but who could tell when his eyes were dead?

"You're the night bartender?"

"Six nights a week. I'm off Saturdays."

"Who subs for you?"

"Day man. That'd be Charlie."

Samson put the photo back into the folder. "Thanks."

"You hunting that fella?"

"Already found him. Just wondered if he'd been around." Samson didn't elaborate. No point in getting the street clamming up if they discovered he was showing about pictures of dead people, murdered people. They admitted they'd seen a murder victim, they knew there would be more questions. Down at the station maybe. No one wanted a hassle.

"Give me another Corona, will you?"

When the keep leaned over in a cooler, Samson saw Mac stroll past the window outside. "I'll be right back." He snatched the files and hit the door, walking fast. "Mac!"

She turned, "My hero."

"Stuff it, Mac. Here, got something for you." He pulled the twenty out of his shirt pocket and pushed it into a white vinyl pocketbook open in the cart. Where in the hell did she get all these strange old purses? She pretended not to see what he'd done. "How're you feeling?" he asked.

"Half-dead."

He peered closer, concerned.

"Oh, stop it. I feel great. Wonderful. Top of the world, ma!"

"You look feverish." He reached out to press the back of his hand to her forehead.

"I look nothing of the kind."

She felt all right. Maybe even too cool to his touch for such a hot evening. "You been taking the prescription? All of it? On time?"

Mac turned her back and started pushing the cart forward. He walked with her. "Well? Have you?"

"I am. I am. Such a nag. You need to apply for motherhood status."

"That's my Mac. See ya around then. I left a beer warming."

"Beer, hell," she muttered, but he heard her as he walked away. "Women," she said. "He's going back to look at the nekkid women. The pervert."

Though she said it in a friendly, joking tone, and she knew he'd hear her, the observation bothered him just the same. Was he? A pervert?

But Big Mac was a bag lady who wouldn't take the offer of a free home. What the fuck did she know?

So he smiled, glad to be alive and drinking Coronas and puzzling over floaters found in the bay. Perverts never spent their time doing something useful, did they?

Besides, naked women were God's gift to the men of the world. You could dress them up and take them out, but au naturel was absolutely the best way to deal with a woman, say, under the age of fifty.

Twenty-six

The night after Son saw the cop talking to the dance girl, he returned to the Blue Boa and hung out drinking draft beer. He didn't much like beer, but in a joint like this you had to drink to be able to abide the place. The girls onstage were sluts in G-strings, teasing strangers with their sex. Son watched them with a critical eye. A text of their offenses ran through his thoughts. Working in this kind of business. Drug addicts. Alcoholics. Prostitutes. Lesbians. AIDS carriers.

The girl who had been with the cop didn't dance. It might have been her night off. He signaled one of the waitresses over and asked, "Where's that girl, the dancer with black hair, the pretty one . . . ?" He hadn't forgotten her name. He just didn't want everyone knowing what he knew.

"Shadow? Oh, the Ice Queen's not coming in tonight. She comes in when she feels like it. If she's coming, she's here by ten or earlier. So she's not coming."

"Ice Queen? Why do you call her that?"

The waitress turned down her mouth and shrugged. "That's what the other girls call her. Forget I said it, okay?"

"They call her that because . . . ?"

"She don't like screwing around with the customers, you know, that's all."

"Ah, I see." He put a couple of bucks on the waitress's tray.

He stayed just a few minutes longer, then left for home.

The following night he was back again. He hugged the bar, watching the girls. Shadow danced her first number around ten-thirty. Son left as soon as he recognized her. He drove around for a while, ate a steak at a Luther's restaurant, then drove to the club again. He waited in his parked car, a half block down the street from the Blue Boa's parking lot behind the building. At one-thirty Shadow appeared. He slouched down in his seat so as not to be seen. When she drove from the lot, he started the car and followed.

He wondered, all the way across town, where she might be headed. She was the one he'd noticed parked in her Toyota two streets over from the Blue Boa the night a man parked behind her and left his car, getting into her car on the passenger's side. Then that man, the one who had been spotlighted in his headlights as he passed by, turned up as a floater. Cherkovania. An escaped con.

Son wasn't sure Shadow had anything to do with it until he had seen on the news the man's car was found on the same street, in the same place he'd seen him park it.

His hunt had turned up the killer. Being in the right place at the right time and *noticing* things made all the difference. He had been rejoicing his good luck and powers of observation for days. Of course, she might not be actually doing it. She might be leading the men somewhere and someone else did the nasty work. But she was involved. She was definitely a part of it.

She lived this far from work? Fifty, sixty miles? Where the hell . . . ?

When she took a side street in the small seaside town of Seabrook, he waited in a convenience store lot until she was far enough ahead of him so she wouldn't know he was behind her. When she turned onto the road close to the water and then drove through massive wrought-iron gates and brick entrance columns, he slowly passed by, killed his lights, and coasted to a stop along the roadway. He got out of the car. Looked around. The few houses along this street were dark. Everyone sleeping. No dogs barking. They weren't going to see him.

He peered down the long drive that circled in front of a looming silhouette of a large house set back on a few empty acres right at the water's edge. She lived here? In a place that looked like a boy's reformatory? Would anyone actu-

ally live here if he didn't have to? There were bars on the
windows and doors of the three-story structure. How did
she even afford the upkeep on a place like this? He didn't
think strip dancing paid this well. It couldn't possibly.
Could she be a rich girl, dancing for kicks? Did she have
a sugar daddy? It just didn't compute.

He hiked down the drive, keeping off to the edge and
out of the line of view from the front windows on the
house. When he reached the steps, he saw lights going out
inside. She was going to bed. He crept to the front door,
listening for the sound of a guard dog somewhere. He
cupped his hands around his face and looked through the
grill on the double glass door. Shadows intermingled and
effectively hid everything from his scrutiny except the wide
winding stairway leading to a landing on the second floor.
Moonlight washed over marble floors like pale watery
strokes from an artist's brush.

He'd have to come back. The dancer lived near the water,
the same water where men had been found dead. She was
called the Ice Queen; she didn't like men coming home
with her or she didn't go home with them, he guessed.
Some kind of hang-up about sex?

Could she be the one?

Son crept back down the stairs and walked the long walk
of the drive to his parked car. He had his hands in his
pockets. He didn't smell the ocean breeze or hear the click-
rustling of wind in the dry limbs of the tall palms. He didn't
hear the crickets chorus or the bullfrogs croaking in the
roadside ditch or the plaintive call of a night bird. He didn't
notice the moon, halved and hung in a clear starry sky.

He heard, saw, felt, and smelled nothing that interfered
with his thoughts as he drove across the city again and
home.

He didn't even hear his mother call weakly from her
room as he went to his own room down the hall from her.
He did not know, until morning, that she had needed him
to help her to the toilet, and even if he had, he might not
have gone to her.

He had too many important things to do to be side-tracked.

Charlene thought the cat helped keep the voices muted so she could think straight. She tried to stay in whatever room the cat was in so she wouldn't go insane.

But she'd lost track of the cat. Couldn't find it. Hadn't seen it for hours.

"Kitty, kitty, kitty, kitty." She called for it everywhere. "Kitty, kitty, kitty, kitty." She looked for it in the usual hiding places. It liked to play with the floor-length curtains on the French doors in the side room facing the front porch. She looked there. *Kittykittykittykitty.*

She hunted for it in the kitchen, put out fresh Nine Lives food for it, but it didn't come. She went down into the forbidden (forbidden because she forbade herself to go into it) maze opposite the pool and walked in circles calling, "Kitty, kitty, kitty."

Where was her cat? Shadow bought her a cat. Where was it? Who had taken her cat?

The voices echoed back all her words, mirrored them back inside her brain so that they doubled, so that reality shimmered, doubling, and still she hunted and she called and she began to cry, silently, wondering what might have happened to her little cat, her Blackie.

How she needed it!

It was a while before she heard the knocking at the door. When finally she did—a steady *rap-rap*—she hurried through the house to the sound. Someone might have found her cat and brought it home. Oh please let it be that.

When she reached the bottom of the stair landing and faced the front door, she could see through the beveled and clear glass and iron bars that a man stood there. She rushed to the doorknob and turned it, opening the door wide, and said breathlessly, "You brought my kitty?"

The man stood with his arm still raised as if about to knock again. His eyes opened wide and his arm lowered slowly, as if to move faster would frighten her.

"Well, did you? Where is she? Where is my cat?" In

her brain the words echoed endlessly. *Where is. My. Cat. Whereismycat. Whereismycat.*

"I'm sorry, I don't have your cat, ma'am. I just came to see the property for sale. Have I come at a bad time?"

"Bad time? You don't have my cat?" Charlene spun, slamming the door in his face. She ran up the stairs again, hurrying down the hall to the bedrooms. ". . . bad time?" echoed. *Badtime. Badtime. Whereismycat? Kittykittykitty.*

She found the cat in Shadow's room. Lying on the dresser near the silver tray with the two crystal highball glasses and the decanter of whiskey. The cat must have batted it during play and the decanter tipped over, spilling the contents. A puddle of the poisoned liquor lay in the base of the silver tray like a still lake, amber in sunshine.

Charlene slumped onto her knees, clutching the dresser edge with her fingers. "Kitty, kitty?"

A new word echoed in her head. *Dead. Dead. Dead.*

She could not bear to touch it. She crawled from the bedroom on her hands and knees, found a closet door in the hall, and crept inside, shutting the door firmly behind her.

Maybe in the closet, in the stuffy darkness, the voices would stop.

Maybe they would.

Maybe.

Son drove away down the circle drive from the mansion. The woman was completely out of her mind. Stone-cold crazy. Where was her cat?

She was crazy, that's all there was to it. It was a pitiful thing to see. Hair all bedraggled and hanging in her face, those eyes wild with despair and skittish, just waiting for terrible news, her hands trembling. Why, she hadn't even dressed properly. She had on wrinkled baggy shorts and a T-shirt half in and half out of the waist of the shorts, a ratty gray sweater—in the middle of a heat wave—buttoned up all wrong so the sweater hung askew.

Who was she? What was she doing there? He had seen Shadow leave for work and he had wanted to find out if anyone else lived with her. He wanted to know what the situation was in the house. He never expected to be met at the door by a raving lunatic.

He shook his head, perplexed. He leaned down and beat at the front dash, hoping he'd rattle something inside so the AC would work better. He was sweating like a pig. The whole front of his shirt dripped wetly.

At least the crazy woman hadn't attacked him. He would have had to do something to her if she had tried. She *needed* something done to her. Something permanent. A person had no right walking around raving mad. It was like happening upon a mad dog, you put it out of its misery, that's what you had to do.

He had had a cat once. Pretty tabby. Sweet and loving, rubbing his legs all the time when he came home from school, lying across his books when he did his homework. Everything was fine until the cat grew up. When it was an adult, it hardly ever came near him. He'd try to pick it up to pet and it would hiss.

One time he was lying on the floor in the living room doing a page of math and the cat came over, curled itself in a ball near his arm. He thoughtlessly reached out to stroke its fur. The cat leapt straight into the air screeching, and when it landed, it had its sharp teeth imbedded in his arm. He jumped to his feet and flung his arm down to rid himself of the terrible burning pain there. The cat maintained the tenacious grip. He screamed for Mother and again flung his arm as hard as he could. The cat was thrown across the room, hit the wall, and landed on its feet, scampering away.

After Mother doctored his wounds, and they were deep ugly gashes, Son went in search of the cat. He had a knife and meant to make short work of it.

He found it cowering in his room behind the bed. He stabbed it five times before it stopped trying to bite him. He didn't even bother to bury it. He walked out into the yard and heaved its carcass over the fence into an empty overgrown lot.

Son hated cats after that. And hated people who loved

them. Like the crazy babbling woman in the seashore mansion.

How could Shadow stand it? What was the deal between those two anyway? Was the woman her sister? A relative of some kind? You couldn't put up with a crazy person unless you loved her and you had to. Even then it was bad.

Son took an exit that led to downtown. It was after ten at night now. She would be onstage, dancing her first dance.

He wanted to see again the face of the pretty woman who lived in a big rambling monstrosity of a house with a nutty fool. It was obvious the lunatic wasn't killing the men. Lunatics couldn't think straight enough to button their sweaters properly, much less commit murder without being immediately detected. He really had to see the dancer and try to understand.

Living with a burden made him think of his mother. She had not said a word about his being gone so much from the house lately. She had such forbearance. Such grace under duress. She would be all right, she would be fine, she said, go on, go ahead. And he went, guilt trailing out the door, hanging onto his coattail like a string attached to a kite.

Well fuck. Maybe everyone had a burden. Shadow did. He did. Everyone had someone who weighed him down and anchored him to earth so he couldn't fly, he couldn't breathe, he couldn't live.

He parked and sat looking across the street at the neon sign of the Blue Boa. He had to go in easy and check for the cop first. He prayed he wasn't there. He really wanted to see the woman who *might* be the city's next big serial murderer. There was something special about her, he knew that, felt some kinship with whatever it was that was special, but he couldn't put a name to it. Except that they both carried someone else on their backs, he didn't know what the connection was.

Unless it was murder. He hoped it was murder. He couldn't wait to try his hand at poison. Stan said the victims had warfarin in their stomachs. Luckily Son had a box of it at home for the disposal of rats.

How convenient.

Shadow discovered Charlene after frantically searching the house, calling for her. It was early morning and she was tired, and at first she thought Charlene had wandered from the house or she had been abducted or something, but then she found the cat dead on the dresser, and she knew her friend had freaked.

Shadow opened the closet door and there Charlene sat, eyes wide, staring. "C'mon, come out of there, Charlene. Let me help you." She reached down and took the other woman's hand to lift her from the floor. She pulled and Charlene came to her feet.

"I couldn't find my cat," Charlene said in a small voice.

"I'm sorry about the cat. I should have closed the door to my room when I left."

She guided Charlene down the hall to her bedroom and had her sit on the bed. She went to her knees and removed her friend's cotton slippers. "Aren't you hot in that sweater? Let me take it off you." She removed the garment and dropped it on the floor. Charlene smelled of fear sweat. How long had she been hiding in the closet? "No need to get into a gown tonight. Just lie back on the bed, get under the sheet."

"Voices," Charlene said. "Repeating stuff in my head." She touched her forehead and closed her eyes.

Shadow looked down at her, sad, tired, worried that things were getting worse and there was nothing she could do about it. "Try to rest," she said.

"I can't. The voices won't let me."

Shadow sighed. She sat on the bed and took Charlene's hand. "Look, I'll get another kitten. It's going to be all right."

Charlene's eyes opened and her gaze fastened on Shadow. "I don't want another kitty," she said. "They die. They just die."

"Why don't I call the hospital tomorrow and see if the doctor will prescribe something for you?"

Charlene turned her head aside on the pillow. She stared at the wall. "I don't care."

"You're alone too much. Maybe I'll stop working so many nights. We don't need the money. I'll stay with you more, would you like that?"

"I don't care."

"Oh, Charlene. Please try to fight off these spells. Please? I'm doing my best to take care of us. I don't know what else to do to help you."

"I used to hear everyone's story," Charlene said, veering into the landscape inside her mind. "I used to remember everything so if a woman had shock treatment, I could tell her about her life. Now I can't remember things. I can't *remember* things."

"Did you take those Valium I got for you from work?"

Charlene nodded. "I can't remember."

Did she or didn't she? Shadow wondered. "If you'd take those, they'd help you."

"Those men . . ."

Shadow waited, holding her breath. She didn't really want to talk about the men. She didn't know how to stop her friend from thinking about them. As for herself, all thoughts of them left when they slipped beneath the bay water.

". . . they talk to me . . ."

Shadow shut her eyes now. She heard that *click-click-click* of the bicycle chain slipping, slipping gears, slipping her away.

". . . they are very angry with you . . ."

There was a time when I was happy.

". . . they talk all the time and say how wrong it is they had to die. . . ."

There was a time when my children were babies. Snuggly, warm, held close to my chest while I rocked them. There were times . . .

". . . I wish they hadn't died, too. If they were alive . . ."

. . . when life was sane and real and average. When I shopped at the supermarket for the week's groceries, when I sat on the floor and read from books to the boys . . .

". . . I wouldn't hear them in my head now . . ."

. . . and their laughter, when I bathed them, the two of them splashing the bathwater above their heads, holding a washcloth in little hands, wetting it and then slapping it on their hair, pretending to wash. . . .

Charlene was asleep. Her hand limp, fingers splayed, in Shadow's hand. The moonlight snaked a path across the foot of her bed, to lie across bare feet. A water pipe gurgled somewhere in the house, in the walls.

Shadow slipped back and found herself sitting still on Charlene's bed in the dark of the night. She stood, feeling disoriented, and left the room. She needed to sleep. She needed to forget about Charlene's troubles and forget about . . . about . . . everything. It would all look brighter in the morning. It always did.

❧ Twenty-seven ❧

Samson worked the streets after the sun set. He showed the photos of the victims around, but no one remembered seeing them. Or if they did, they wouldn't say.

Samson knew there had to be a connection between the killings and the Montrose area. He found Big Mac in McDonald's and sat in the booth opposite her. He ordered a large coffee, wishing there was some whiskey in it.

"I'm hitting dead ends," he said.

"New case?" She bit into a Big Mac, squirting the special sauce all over her hands.

"Yeah, what might be some serial killings."

"Down here?" She spoke around a mouthful of hamburger.

"They didn't happen down here, at least we don't think so. The bodies were dumped in Galveston Bay and they keep coming in around Seabrook and Kemah, the channel down there, or shrimpers haul them in."

"But you're looking here, in Montrose, for something?"

"The victims, all men, were known to habituate this part of town. Some of them liked the club scene."

"Habituate? Is that college-boy talk for 'hang around'?"

Samson grinned. "Yeah. They hung around down here. But no one remembers seeing them."

"Show me the pictures." She took the last bite of the hamburger and fastidiously wiped the fingers of both hands on a napkin.

Samson pulled the photos from inside his sports jacket pocket. He tossed them on the table. They spread out across the varnished wood. Mac pulled them with a forefinger one at a time toward her, checking the faces. "I don't remember them either. You sure they hung here?''

"Relatives and acquaintances said they were last heard of when they headed this way.''

"That don't mean they hung out. Means they *visited,* maybe just that one time. Sounds funny, though.''

Samson thought it over. ''You may be right. Maybe they didn't make a big habit of coming to the clubs. Maybe each one of them happened to come here the night they died. That would explain why the street doesn't remember them.''

"Now *this* one . . .'' Mac stabbed her finger at one of the pictures. She had casually perused all the photos and then drew one off by itself.

"Yeah?'' Samson leaned over the table to see which victim she meant. It was the first poison victim. ''You saw him?''

"Can't be sure. This guy's fat? Hefty, big in the shoulders?''

"Yeah, he was.''

"Was. Right. Food for worms now. Anyway, I'm not real sure, but something about how big he is, I remember. It's been a while.''

"Think, Mac. Where were you when you think you might have seen him?''

"Hell, it was during the time I was coming down hard with that pneumonia. I was feverish. But still . . .'' She studied the picture. ''He sure looks familiar. I might've just seen him walking along the sidewalk . . .''

"Where, Mac? Near what club?''

Mac grabbed her drink and sucked on the straw. Samson didn't want to push her, the memory might retreat. He waited, sipping his coffee.

A gay couple took a table next to them. They held hands across the table and stared dreamily into one another's eyes. Samson thought one of them was downright pretty—thick black lashes, dark eyes, smooth jaw. The thought didn't disturb him. Some men's attractiveness crossed gender and could be appealing to male and female alike, not that he ever talked about things like that to the guys at the station.

He brought his attention back to Mac, who slurped the drink down to the ice.

"Chez Tigress?" she said.

"You're not sure."

"I can't be sure. It was a while ago, I told you, and I was sick."

Samson noted the victim's name and the club name next to it on his notepad. "What about now, how are you feeling? Looks like your appetite is back."

She smiled a little, showing a missing incisor. "I took *all* my medicine. I feel like a hundred bucks."

Samson smiled. "I'm glad to hear that. Think any more about my offer?"

"What, move in with you? I'm old enough to be your mother. Our sex life would be dull donkey droppings."

Now he laughed and the gay couple looked over. "The offer was for housing, not for a love affair, Mac."

She methodically picked up all the litter from the table and arranged it on the tray. "I'm okay," she said. "I'm fine now."

"But this heat . . ."

"I wander round the Kroger's when I get too hot. They got the best air-conditioning in town. And they also got cheese and cracker samples sometimes. Great snacks for a light lunch." She stood with the tray. Samson pocketed the photographs and stood with her, coffee in hand.

"If you change your mind . . ."

"I know how to reach you, yeah, I know. Now get outta my way, I'm a busy woman." She shouldered past him, dumped the tray, and put the empty in a stack. He followed her out the door and onto the street. The heat, even in the night, was oppressive. It enclosed the body like a sheet directly from the clothes dryer. Mac went around back of the restaurant, heading for the Dumpster where she had left the shopping cart.

Samson strolled down the sidewalk to the Chez Tigress. He had to show the photos around some more. Then later he might catch Shadow at the Blue Boa. If he didn't stop thinking about her, he'd never get this case on its feet. She dominated his thoughts too much. Or else he was too god-damn horny. Or both.

Probably both.

Son befriended the bum during the time Samson and Mac shared a table at McDonald's no more than five blocks away.

"What's your angle, mister?" the bum wanted to know. Son had offered to give him a bottle of wine he had stashed in his car.

"Since when would you want to be suspicious of free booze? I just thought since you answered some of my research questions for my book, I'd repay you. It's good wine. Not that cheap shit you've been drinking." Actually, it really wasn't bad wine. He found some strong red wine from the California vineyards, took it home from the liquor store, carefully removed the cork, and added enough rat poison to gag a maggot. It meant he had had to pour some of the good wine out down the kitchen drain, but it was all for a good cause.

He had been nervous, though, at home with Mother, trying to add poison to the wine. He kept thinking she had made her way from the bedroom to the kitchen and might be watching him. He couldn't stop looking over his shoulder to catch her there, spying. When he was busy being a copycat, paranoia was his best friend.

"I guess I'll take it then," the bum said from the side of his mouth. "I ain't too good to turn down a free drink."

Son thought the man must have had a stroke recently. Or some kind of nerve damage to the left side of his face. When he talked, the words formed with half his lips in motion, half his facial muscles. He was ready for the undertaker, no one would miss him.

He wore mismatched pants and a jacket, a shirt with holes in it, and his shoes had seen much better days. Son found him in an alley, sitting on a blue upturned milk carton crate. Drinking. Swaying. Ripe for the picking.

"I'll go get it," Son said. "Don't go anywhere."

"Where'd I wanna go, the Ritz-Carlton?"

Son found his car and drove it to the alley. He doused the lights as soon as he saw the bum on the crate. He exited the car with the bottle of wine, holding it by the neck aloft and before him, a gift for a friend.

"See you been sipping on this one," the bum said, holding the bottle up to measure its contents level. "You ain't got no disease, do ya?"

"What do you care?" As soon as he'd said it, Son wished he hadn't. His disgust had gotten the better of him. He wanted this human piece of repellent garbage dead. He wanted him to hurry and drink the wine so he could watch how he died.

"Hey, I'm human, ain't I? I got worries, too. There's all kinda shit people got today. I don't wanna catch none of it."

"No, I don't have a disease. I didn't drink from the bottle anyway. I poured out a half glass at home, that's all. Of course, if you don't want it . . ." He moved to take the bottle back.

The bum jerked the bottle near his chest. "I want it, I just don't wanna drink no slobber in my wine, that's all. Why doncha sit down? You make me nervous standing over me like that."

Son relaxed. He looked around, found a cardboard box that was empty and clean, flattened it, and sat next to the man. With his knees up in front of him, he didn't know what to do with his hands. He wrapped his arms around his knees, hugging them. In his eyes anticipation danced like fairy elves on All Hallow's Eve. This was going to be interesting. They shouldn't be interrupted. The alley was dark, unlit by streetlights, unappetizing for anyone but the bum. Moonshine hit one side of the alleyway, the side they sat on. Democratic, it lay a strip of silver over wall and garbage cans alike. In the moonlight Son could see pretty well, now that his vision had adjusted.

"You want the first slug?"

Son looked at the poisoned wine and shook his head. "It's yours. I don't even drink much."

The man pulled the cork by placing the bottle between

his knees and struggling with it. The unplugging sound was a soft, delicate *pop.* "Much obliged," the man said, saluting Son with the bottle before putting it to his lips and throwing back his head to drink deeply.

Suddenly the bottle came down, wine spilling out over the bum's hands and shirtfront. Son watched the other man's rheumy drunken eyes. Good thing he'd chugged a good bit or the poison might not have worked.

"You call this shit wine? Kee-rist, it tastes worse than Thunderbird. I thought it was gonna be *good* wine."

"It cost enough. What's wrong with it, I thought it was fine."

"Then you didn't get a good goddamn taste of it. Tastes worse than licking old whore cunt, *goddamn.*" He spit to the side.

"Well, if you don't want it . . ." Son sighed dramatically and reached for the bottle again.

"Wait! I ain't giving it back to ya. Maybe I can get used to what it tastes like or something. You wouldn't wanna go round the corner and pick me up another bottle of something else, though, would you?"

"I'm fresh out of cash. Sorry."

The bum grunted and lifted the bottle again to his lips. This time Son knew he was holding his breath. How did the killer get anyone to drink poison? If this didn't work, he'd have to figure out something else. Or maybe the bum was so drunk and so stupid and so *thirsty,* he'd drink enough anyway.

Again the man swore and spit after swallowing. This time he did hand the bottle back to Son. "Hey man, I'd go get my money back on that, I wuz you. It's some rotten-ass shit, I'm here to testify."

Son checked the contents level much the same way the bum had. In two swigs a quarter of the bottle was emptied. Son corked it and slipped it next to him.

The dying started within seconds of the second swallow. The bum grabbed his throat, but he was having trouble talking now. He leaned over away from Son and tried to heave it up. Nothing came.

Then he curled into a ball, hugging his stomach. Crying. Like a damn baby. "That stuff . . . ," he mumbled, ". . . it's hurting me. . . ."

Bet it is, Son thought. Just bet it is.

Son watched closely as the man died. There were convulsions, legs kicking out; there was some vomiting, some bleeding from the nose. And then the eyes. But by that time the man was dead, staring into eternity while first capillaries burst, then veins, and blood seeped down the bottom lids of his dry cooling eyes.

Son had not experienced such a thrill in a long time. Two years, to be exact. He had never used poison before. It wasn't a favorite method of serial killers. In fact, it might be the first, unless that crazy old bitch out in California used it when she killed her elderly boarders for their Social Security checks. He couldn't keep up with all the killers, there were so many now.

The excitement that had risen as he worked the old guy into drinking the wine now rose a notch more, just this side of crescendo. He didn't think of this excitement as sexual, he couldn't think that clinically about it. It was a feeling of fluttering butterflies in his stomach. Then it changed to a piercing wing-flap thundering on an Armageddon plain. If he had touched himself, he would have felt his engorged penis, and it would have shocked him. He *never* touched himself, never masturbated, even as a boy. And though his erection grew while a victim died, he was never conscious of it at all, and would have denied it ever happened.

He turned the bum on his back. Ugh. Messy as hell. Heavy fucker, too. And stinking. Of wine, vomit, blood, old sweat-soaked clothes, rank body odor.

Son had to hold his breath and suck in snatches of air as he pulled the body up by the arms and dragged it to the trunk of the car. He unlocked the trunk lid, stowed the man inside.

He went back for the wine bottle. He saw there were vomit and bloodstains on the tarmac of the alley. He drew the flat cardboard box over to cover the place where the body had lain. Who would look? Who would care? Bums threw up back here all the time. And the blood could have come from anywhere, even a cut finger or an animal or rodent, or from some wino with perforated ulcers. There wasn't that much of it to worry about.

The trip to Seabrook was uneventful. Son drove back to the spit of land next to the channel. He sat in the car a while, waiting to see if there was any life over at the closed bayside restaurants or any boats coming through for night trolling.

After a few minutes without movement, he went to the trunk. He got the man's clothes off him—after much cursing and sweating labor—and threw those back in the trunk for disposal later. He'd stuff them in with the trash for the weekly pickup.

He carried the man over his shoulder, head and arms dangling down behind him. Son was careful not to touch the man's bare buttocks. He might have bugs on him, body lice, crabs, something creepy-crawly that would leap off onto Son to plague him. He held him by the back of his grubby knees.

He knew the police could pick up fingerprints from flesh, but his would be gone after the body was in the water a while. Besides, he had never been fingerprinted. They wouldn't have his prints on record to find anyway.

He walked to the bulkhead to stand between two thigh-high creosote-treated posts. He carefully tipped the body's weight toward the water. It fell with a loud splash that sent cold saltwater spray up and onto Son's clothes.

This body would be found soon. By morning, maybe. Would they notice how soon after death it was found floating?

It didn't matter. What really mattered was that he had done it. He had carried it off without a hitch. He had been able to watch the dying of the light in the eyes. He had felt the thunder in his brain after so long a time without it. And the other one, the *real* one, the murderer he copied, would know.

She would know.

And wonder.

Son clapped his hands as if applauding the sea. The white body below him bobbed, floating facedown out from the bulkhead. The audience of one watched the curtain call of the flabby human body as it sank without a sound of protest beneath the dark brine.

The next day a child visiting the land spit across from Kemah's restaurants pointed out to his mother something strange bobbing in the water near the bulkhead.

That night the TV and radio news carried the story, with the television carrying pictures of a body bag being lifted into a waiting ambulance.

"Spooky how many men are being found down near the bay."

"Yeah, me, I'm not going swimming in Galveston for a long time. And I am *not* eating seafood at the Kemah restaurants. Can you imagine finding one of those guys all bloated up?"

The dancers were discussing the news as Shadow exchanged her street clothes for a green G-string and matching bra. She heard them and froze. Her eyes unfocused.

Body? Found in the bay? That wasn't possible.

She came back to herself, turned to the other women. "Maybe this one was a drowning off a fishing boat."

"You didn't see the news? Guy was naked as a jaybird. The police haven't confirmed he was poisoned, but of course he was. No one's reported a man overboard on any of the fishing boats. Not no naked man, anyway."

Shadow moved toward her locker to finish dressing. She wouldn't talk about this. They were mistaken. It had to be a fisherman, or maybe someone went swimming in the nude and drowned.

Her fingers slipped as she tried fastening the bra's complicated front closure. She kept trying. Could she dance tonight, thinking about this?

She glanced at herself in the long mirror along the counter. No. She wouldn't dance. She would get into one of her hostess dresses and work the tables.

The two girls who had been in conversation left the

room. Mom came in. She was big, black, and motherly to the dancers. Hence her name. She had not been working the Blue Boa long. She supplied them with any kind of cosmetics they needed, eye shadows in every color, eyeliners, blemish covers, body paint, lipsticks, blushes, mascaras. And costume jewelry. She even did hair if she was tipped well. The club paid her a pittance. She made her living off the girls' tips.

Mom moved to the counter and straightened everything. She kept it neat, all the items in little open Tupperware containers. She *tsk-tsked* as she worked. "Messy girls, bad messy girls."

"Hi, Mom."

The black woman turned. "Didn't know any of you was left in here. You want Mom to fix up your hair for you tonight?"

"No thanks." Shadow slipped a tight, short black dress over her head and pulled it down over bust and hips. It fit her curves beautifully. It paid to buy good clothes.

"Why's they call you that name, girl? You don't seem like no cold person."

"Ice Queen? You heard them call me that?" Shadow sat down before the mirror. "I guess they think I'm a prude. I don't sleep with the clientele." Not for money, she thought, remembering Mitch and the stolen time they had spent in her bed. She touched a lipstick to her lips. Remembered his lips on hers. Put the lipstick down again and stared at her reflection.

Mom shook her head. She picked up some of the eye shadow containers and closed their lids, depositing them into the proper Tupperware bowls. "These girls are real slobs, you know that?"

Shadow held her silence, thinking of the man floating in the channel.

"You a different one, all right."

Shadow brought her attention back to the present. "I am?" She glanced at Mom reflected in the mirror.

"Got some age on most these girls. How old'r you, twenty-four, twenty-five?"

"Thirty."

"Goodness! Thirty. You don't look that old."

"You're doing a helluva job on my self-esteem, Mom."

"Aw, honey, I ain't putting you down none. You look good as any these girls here. Bet you make just as much, too. I just don't see too many *women* working this job. They get old, they find another line of work."

"This is the only line I could find. You really think I don't look thirty?" She shouldn't have asked that. Who the fuck cared what Mom thought? It was what the men thought that counted.

Mom put a big hand on her shoulder. "You a pretty woman. *Real* pretty. And sweet, too, I can tell."

The thought of the new body in the bay made her frown. "Not so sweet."

"You coulda fooled me. I think you just fine."

I did fool you, she thought. I fool everyone. I'm a regular fool when it comes to deception.

Mom moved down the counter to pick through the jewelry, probably to make sure it hadn't been borrowed without her permission. Shadow took up the lipstick again and carefully finished applying it. She fluffed her hair with her fingers, feathering it around her face. Should she line the bottom lids of her eyes with black kohl pencil?

"Think I need to underline my eyes?" she asked Mom.

The woman came closer. "Uh-uh. Those eyes are dark enough without liner. *Real* pretty."

Dark, deadly dark, calculating, lying eyes. Maybe pretty, but definitely not sweet, Shadow thought, eyeing herself in the mirror once more. There was no point in lying to herself.

She left Mom to clean and tinker with the beauty supplies. The smoky club wrapped its ambiance around her as she entered it. The music was loud, the girls young, ripe, sexy. *Fraudulent,* wasn't that the word Mitch had used?

She noticed Frank sitting at a table alone and moved toward him.

Frank. The nice respectable guy with money. She might as well make the night pay.

"Hi, can I join you?"

He had been watching her cross the room to him. He stood now and said, "Please do. I was hoping you were working tonight."

She sat and watched him place bills in the center of the table. She took them and began to fold the money. She told the waitress to bring her a Coke.

"I don't really see you hanging out in places like this," she said.

Frank looked away from her. "You either."

She waved that away. "I belong here, I definitely belong, but you, you're not the type I see around."

They talked about Nolan Ryan pitching for the Rangers and him in his late forties before retiring. They talked about movies. Frank liked comedies. He even liked the old Abbott and Costello films, and the few Laurel and Hardy ones he had seen. His favorite present-day actor was Steve Martin. He had a fondness for the Chevy Chase *Vacation* films and did a fair imitation of Chevy bobbing his head when his wife in the movie asked him to look at the Grand Canyon.

They talked about Shadow's roommate, Charlene, and about cats, and about the dancers, comparing the good with the bad ones.

Shadow realized, only after Frank had left and she sat alone at the table, that not once during the hour they talked did she think about the naked body found floating in the bay.

Before she could worry about it, another man came over and asked to sit with her. She said, "Have a seat. What are you drinking?"

The night wore on this way until she had the amount of money she required, and sighing because she had not seen Mitch for a few days—had he dumped her?—she left for home. On the drive she turned on the radio to a talk station and waited for the news recap.

It was not good.

Twenty-eight

Mitchell stood on the catwalk overlooking the swimming pool, his hands on the rail. "Do you ever swim in it?"

Shadow stood next to him, nervous as a schoolgirl on her first real date. She had not been with him in over a week and now it seemed that one night together was a dream she vaguely recalled. "Once in a while. I like running to keep in shape over swimming, but with this terrible heat . . ."

From the corner of her eye, Shadow saw a movement and turned her head. She saw Charlene appear and disappear from the hallway in the main body of the house. Watching us, she thought. How do I explain Charlene to him?

"Why doesn't she come out so I can meet her?"

Shadow flinched. He had seen her, too. "Charlene's . . . she's . . . well, she's been sick."

"Is she sick now?" He still faced the pool, still studied the big blue bowl of water below them. Yet he never missed anything. He even probably noticed her nervousness around him and wondered about it. He had not asked again about whether she had children or not. She knew he wondered about that, too. But there was a difference between sleeping with a man and getting deeply, intimately involved with him. A difference as wide as the world.

Shadow nodded her head slightly. "She's still sick," she admitted. "We were together in the state mental facility in Austin." She had said it and she was glad. If he wanted to leave now, that was perfectly fine with her.

He drew his gaze away from the pool and stared at her. She couldn't look him in the eye. No matter how many people tried to argue that having mental problems carried no stigma, it was a damn lie. It was still shameful. It still hurt to confess to weakness.

"When did you get out?" he asked, quietly.

Charlene took that moment to magically appear and disappear again. Shadow shut her eyes and tried to relax in the darkness behind her lids. "Almost a year ago. Charlene's been having more and more trouble lately. I hardly know what to do anymore. She hears voices, she tunes out the world, she's hard to reach."

"How about you?"

Yes, how about her? How was she doing, that's what he wanted to know. Was she insane now? Slipping toward insanity again? Had the disease spread from Charlene to infect her, too? If only he knew . . .

"I'm fine," she lied, remembering the fugue states where her mind clicked off like a parking meter throwing up the red violation sign.

She opened her eyes. Turned to face him. "I told you my husband killed himself." And my children, she thought, but did not say. "I couldn't handle that. They say I didn't talk for months. If it hadn't been for Charlene I might never have talked again. She was always there, Mitchell, watching out for me, protecting me from other women there, talking to me as if I could hear her."

"She's a good friend then."

"The best. Now, though, she's been slipping, and it's hard to know how to help her."

"Should she return to the hospital?"

"Maybe. But I couldn't do that to her. She never abandoned *me*."

Mitchell looked down at the pool again. "I have someone like that in my life, too."

"Oh?"

"Remember the bag lady I told you about? I've been watching out for her for years. I recently asked her to come live in my house and I'd support her, but she's too independent. Or too crazy. She won't leave the street."

"It was good that you offered, though. Not many people would."

He kept silent. She reached out along the rail and covered one of his hands with her own. He turned to her then and drew her to him. She let herself be folded into his arms. How long had it been since she trusted a man this way? It seemed like a lifetime. She lay her head against his chest, heard his heartbeat, felt the pulse in his throat, smelled the sunshine smell emanating from the cloth of his shirt.

If only she could stay like this forever, held close and secure. If only she didn't fear betrayal and disaster waiting just around the next corner, ready to pounce.

"Let's go find your friend." He let her go but took her hand. "I think she's curious about me."

Curious to know why you're still alive. Shadow reluctantly stepped away and led him into the house calling, "Charlene? C'mere a minute, I want you to meet someone."

They found her sitting on the sofa in the big formal living room. She sat with her ankles crossed and her hands lying quietly in her lap, a schoolgirl on her best behavior. She contemplated the cold marble fireplace until Shadow said, "Charlene, this is Mitchell Samson. Mitch, meet Charlene Brewster, the woman who saved my life."

"Hi, how are you?" Mitch stepped forward and held out his hand.

Charlene looked at him a moment and then she gave him her hand to shake. "Uh . . . hi . . ."

Shadow watched, amused and relieved, while Mitchell put Charlene at her ease and even enticed her to talk a little. Soon Charlene was rattling along, calling Mitchell "honey" and inviting him into the kitchen for a dish of pecan pie with vanilla ice cream on top. The three of them ate the dessert at the kitchen table. Charlene and Mitchell hit it off and were like two old friends before a half hour had passed.

When Shadow walked Mitchell to the door on his leave-taking, she said, "She really likes you."

"It's mutual. Anyone who saved you for me is going to

be my best friend, too.'' He leaned forward and kissed her. ''Meet me after your work tomorrow night at the Blue Boa?''

''Um-hmm.''

''Go with me to my house, spend the night?''

''We'll talk about it.''

He smiled. ''God, I love a tease.''

''I never would have guessed,'' she said.

He laughed and she wanted to kiss him again, kiss him passionately. Instead she reached up and gave him a peck on the cheek. She watched as he skipped down the steps to his car in the circle drive. His car stirred dust into the air as he drove down the lane to the road. Then she heard someone breathing behind her, the hair on the nape of her neck rose, and she turned straight into Charlene's face. ''Oh! You scared me.''

Charlene moved back to arm's length. ''You're not going to kill him, are you?''

''No!''

Charlene released air from her lungs. ''I'm so glad to hear that. I like him a lot. He tells funny stories.''

''He's a cop, Charlene. In Homicide with the Houston police.''

''Isn't that . . . dangerous? Having him around, I mean?''

Shadow shrugged. ''It might be. But I'm not worried. No one will ever find out anything.''

Charlene looked unconvinced, but she didn't protest. She must have known it wouldn't do any good.

Charlene was cleaning the closet in her bedroom, bent over from the waist straightening shoes, when she heard on the radio news of another floater found near the channel. She stiffened, listening. A man, naked, washed up near the bulkhead on the Seabrook side of the channel. Authorities suspected another murder.

She backed from the closet like a crab, on her heels, moving so fast she fell backward to land on her bottom. She hurriedly came to her feet and ran to the door, swinging herself around the door frame and into the hallway.

"Shadow! Shadow!"

Shadow came from her own room. She was nearly ready to leave for the club when she heard Charlene calling her. "What is it?"

"Who did you kill? When did you do it? Why didn't you tell me?"

"Hey, slow down."

Charlene let Shadow take her by the arms and hold her still even though she felt like running around the mansion, pitching a fit. How could Shadow do this? How could she keep it a secret from her?

"They found another man . . ." She was breathless. ". . . in the bay down near the bulkhead. You did it and didn't tell me!"

"Now, listen, Charlene, I didn't do it. Do you hear me? That was reported on the news yesterday and it upset me, too. I didn't do it. Do you understand? It wasn't *me*."

Charlene furrowed her brows. "But how could . . . ? What does that . . . ?"

"I don't know what it means. They say he was found nude and they suspected he'd been poisoned, like the others. But I *swear* to you, it wasn't me."

"Not you," Charlene repeated.

"No. I didn't do it. Someone else did. It's like—what do you call it?—a copycat thing, I think. I know it's crazy, but that's the only explanation I can think of."

"Why didn't you tell me?"

"I was going to, really, I would have told you about it. I heard the girls at the club talking about it, then I listened to the news on the way home last night. I've been trying to puzzle it out ever since."

"It's on the radio. What does it mean? There's a copycat killer now? Oh, Shadow, we have to stop. This has to end. You need to tell someone, you need to tell Mitchell."

Shadow shushed her and put an arm around her shoulder and said soothing things to her, but Charlene was suddenly beset with a barrage of voices, all of them male, all of them dead, all of them begging her to save them from drowning in the sea.

✥Twenty-nine✥

Son stood in the doctor's office, his face devoid of emotion. Inside he seethed with hatred for the doctor. It tore at him, like claws scrabbling through his innards, swiping pieces and gobbling them up.

"How long?" he asked.

"Six months. A year if she's lucky. Or she could go tomorrow. I'm sorry."

It was his mother's heart. It was too old and ragged to keep her alive much longer. And doctors couldn't do anything about it. Oh, they could try to find her a heart for a transplant, but by then she might be dead, and anyway, there were much younger patients waiting for a donor heart. Nope. Nothing to do but let nature carry her away.

Son turned and left the doctor's private office. He met his mother in the waiting room and escorted her to the car.

"It's not so terrible, Son," she said, once he had the car started and on the street heading for home. "I have to die sometime."

"Please. Let's not discuss it."

"But that's exactly what we should do. I'm afraid this news is more upsetting to you than it is to me. I expected I didn't have long left. It's not a big surprise."

"You want to die?" He glared at her and then was sorry. "I didn't mean to raise my voice, Mother. I'm just . . . it's terrible they can't bother to help you."

"I've had a long life. A pretty good life, on balance. I believe we live on after death. I don't know how or in what manner, but I don't think the light goes out forever."

"Can we not discuss it?" He had the wheel in a death grip. His hands were sweaty. Beads of perspiration formed on his forehead. He reached out and banged the heel of his hand on the dash. "This goddamn air-conditioning!"

"Son!"

He bit his lip. He hardly ever spoke a swear word in her presence. "I'm sorry."

"I'm serious about talking, Son. You'll be alone soon and I think you'd be happier without me to drag you down. It's never been fair and I know that. I've always been sorry that you haven't made a life for yourself, with a wife, children of your own—"

"Please." He said the word so sharply she stopped talking in midsentence. Couldn't she see he hated to think about her dying? That he would miss her? That his life would be empty without her?

As much as he dreamed about her demise, her leaving him to enjoy a measure of freedom without having to care for her, the pain at the thought of it really happening astounded him. She would never know about the things he had done, the depravity and sickness that pervaded his every cell. She would never understand him and could never forgive him if she knew. He hadn't been able to tell her, and once she was gone, he would have no more chances to confess. That's what it was. She wouldn't be there when he *might* confess, when he might *need* to confess.

He knew he couldn't do it now, or six months from now, but one day he thought he could, one day he could go to her, sink to his knees, and say, "Mama, I've done terrible things. I'm not sorry I did them, but you need to know you gave birth to something demented and twisted."

He could only tell this to his mother. He would never admit it to anyone else, ever. But if she died before he could find the nerve, the courage, then what would he do? How could he live with the thought he'd never share it with anyone?

He banged the dash again, agitated beyond description, hot and hurt and worried. Scared.

"Son . . . do you blame *me?* You know people die. Wanting me to live forever isn't reasonable. I've come to accept dying. Or as much as a person can.''

''Mother, I . . .''

''What is it, Son? Tell me. What is it you want to say?''

He gnawed at his lower lip, causing it to bleed into his mouth. He couldn't tell her, not now. If he had a few months maybe he could. Maybe before her heart gave out, maybe before death swallowed her into the void, maybe . . .

''I'm just sad,'' he said. ''I love you so much.''

He felt her reach across the seat and touch his arm with her old gnarled fingers. He wanted to cry. His eyes stung and he blinked hard.

He realized the tears were not for her, but for himself and how fucked up he was and how fucked up the whole goddamn world was and how fucked up he would be without her, without the *possibility* of forgiveness. It wasn't Christ he wanted to redeem him. Nothing supernatural could save him. Only Mother. Only the person he loved most.

Once at home and with his mother comfortable in her bed, Son went into his office to turn on the computer. He had the old novel from which he was copying lying on his desk. It was an antique tattered and yellowed paperback titled *The Call of the Corpse*. The cover showed a leggy woman in a red dress sprawled dead on a carpet. The pages were flaking on their edges, little coconut scales flying off at the slightest disturbance of air, and the glue had vanished from the binding. It had been published in 1934 by someone who never became a big name in the mystery genre. Although Son had to update the language and he changed some of the locales and names of the characters, he was essentially typing the book into his computer directly from the page.

He sat looking at the paperback and thinking about doing the copy work today to take his mind off his mother's deteriorating condition. Next to the paperback, however, lay a stack of correspondence he should attend to first. There was a renewal contract from his literary agent that he had to sign and return. There was an invitation from an anthologist for him to submit a mystery short story. He needed to write a short "thanks, but I'm not interested" kind of note. He had never cared for short stories and felt copying them for submission was a waste of time since the form paid so little. Indeed, what was he doing all this for if not for money and the freedom not to have to work in the everyday world?

There was a letter from a mystery writers' conference organizer who wanted to know if he would head a panel. He would not. He never attended conferences and he had never been to New York to meet his agent and editors or to rub shoulders with the authors of the Mystery Writers of America who held the Edgar Allan Poe Award banquet every year. Five years ago his novel had won the Best Novel prize, so he had them ship him the statue. He just did not socialize on any level with other writers or publishing people. Part of it had to do with being too busy churning out books to have the time for frivolous activities, but the chief reason was because he didn't want to answer questions. Would a real writer discover his subterfuge?

One of those writers at a conference might actually be well-read enough to someday notice one of his books was plagiarized from an old out-of-print novel. And then where would he be? Without work of any sort. Without an income. He'd owe all the money back he'd taken from publishers. They might prosecute . . .

How could he go to work like other people? He couldn't. His rage against the human race boiled too close to the surface to permit him to interact with other people on a daily basis. He'd lose his mind. He'd take up an assault rifle and mow down everyone in an office building. And that's where he would have to work if he could not sell his books. In an office typing reports or entering data on a computer like the numb, brainless horde of white collar workers.

No, he had to refuse the panel invitation, send the note to the anthologist, sign the agency renewal contract, and perhaps then he could return to work on this new book he had under contract. All of these petty duties would help keep his mind occupied.

As long as Mother did not call out for him. Or die while he was looking the other way.

The night was as muggy as only the semitropical summer climate in Houston could be. Late night drivers wove slowly through the streets, semitrailer trucks hauling produce into market from the valley in South Texas lumbered restlessly down the avenues. Overhead a pale gray three-quarter moon ducked in and out through scudding cloud cover.

"Lookit the scandalous, man. We ought to bust her. Hey, Ray-Man, get the breakdown."

Big Mac heard the Spanish-accented voice intrude on her dream. She was lying beneath a big blooming apple tree in the dream, watching bees pollinate the blossoms. She could smell the sweet scent of spring flowers, the crushed fragrant grass beneath her head.

"Wake you, bitch!"

Big Mac struggled up from the dream into the humid night alleyway. She opened her eyes, blinked, saw figures surrounding her, spears of darkness darker than the night. She rolled over and stumbled to her feet. She found herself cornered in the alley by a Hispanic gang. Sleep still owned her vision and made it blurry, but her mind came suddenly alert. She felt the siren of danger wailing through her veins.

"You boys get on outta here. Leave me 'lone." She stood shakily behind her shopping cart, holding tightly to the handle. All thought of the pleasant dream was gone. Fear of the present situation displaced apple blossoms, grass, sunny days, and comfort.

"She sho is a lizard-butt. Might be fun taking her down."

The one called Ray-Man came from the Chevy low rider with a shotgun. "I got the breakdown," he said.

Mac realized he meant the weapon, what looked like a sawed-off shotgun. Idiot-ass kids and their instruments of death. "I don't have no money, y'all know that, now get on away from here."

"Man, she is one eastly mother, she so eastly she need her face mashed down."

There were five of them grouped in a semicircle around her. She had her back to the brick wall of a building and her cart in front of her. Could she shove through them? Could she talk them out of whatever they had in mind?

"I say we get in the bucket and leave her here."

Mac turned to the one who had said that. She tried appealing to him with her eyes. "That's right," she said. "This boy's right. I didn't do nothing to you. Why don't you go off and pester somebody else?"

"Whassa matter you, Shank? You boned out? You think we oughta do a ghost?"

Mac had no idea what they were saying. It was like a foreign language the gangs spoke. She just hoped she'd see it coming if they rushed her or if they lifted the "breakdown" to kill her. She needed at least two seconds to prepare herself for heaven. The inside of her mouth had dried into a desert floor, and her heart thumped like an agitated Gila monster trapped against her breastbone.

"What you say, old eastly mama? Think we ought to bust you?"

Mac thought the speaker was the leader. He talked more than the others and looked the most menacing. There was a hardness in his eyes that she had seen before. They were killer eyes. Stone and ice. Merciless.

"I . . . I just wish you'd go away. I don't want no trouble. I was just . . . just sleeping here." She didn't want to stutter, but couldn't help herself.

The leader rattled off something in Spanish to his companions and they laughed. She tried to smile, but expected it came out more of a grimace. She could feel her tongue sticking to the roof of her mouth. She was trembling, but hoping they wouldn't notice. She held onto the bar of the shopping cart to keep her arms steady.

"My friend . . . my friend's a cop. Anything happens to me, he'll find out who did it."

"Hey, essey, this bitch must drop a dime on the pigs for her living. 'Nother good reason to bust her."

Ray-Man cocked the shotgun.

Mac felt her heart lurch. "Wha . . . what's dropping a dime? I don't mess with no dope."

The boys laughed and slapped one another on the back. Suddenly the leader said, sober and serious now, "That's a snitch, eastly. You snitch to the cops, that what you do?"

Mac pondered her answer. Decided the truth would serve her best. "Yeah, I'm a snitch, I drop a dime. And my cop's in Homicide and he's a hard man. He'd track you punks down and step in your faces if you mess with me. I seen him do it before. I don't think you want him on your case."

The leader looked over to Ray-Man, thinking it over. The boy to Mac's left, the one who wanted to leave, said, "Let's bail. This eastly ain't worth it, man. She's just an old sop-with camel, and she don't need jacking up."

The leader spat toward her. Mac turned her head aside and watched from the corner of her eye.

"Okay, Shank's prolly right, we do what he says this time. She's just scuz, not worth our time. Let's bail." He waved the gang toward the car and then backed away slowly himself, keeping his steady gaze on her.

"You tell your friend and we find you again, eastly. Next time I don't let *nobody* talk me outta busting you." He nodded and left then. The Chevy roared to life, tires squeal-ing and trailing smoke as it raced from the alley into the night.

Mac stood a long time with her hands locked on the metal bar, leaning into it for support while her heart slowed. She knew her escape this time had been narrow, merely a spit and a whistle between her and the grave. Things on the street were getting worse than they ever used to be. Once you could depend on people leaving you alone when they could see you had nothing, when you slept on card-board and dressed in rags. No more. It was people like her who were the easy victims, the ones taken out just for kicks or for initiation into a gang. The news on the street was that the latest floater in the bay had been a homeless man.

She had to find Samson, tell him she'd changed her mind.

She wanted to see what a roof over her head and a safe haven at night might feel like. She was entirely too old for this shit. And too scared.

The time was closing on noon when Mac saw Samson at a hot dog stand. She trundled the shopping cart up to him and bumped his backside.

"Hey . . . ! Oh, it's you. How's it going, Mac?"

"I needta talk to you about that offer you made."

Samson squinted down at her over the hot dog in his mouth. He took a bite, chewed, spoke with his mouth full. "Let's go sit over here."

She followed him to a low brick wall beneath the shade of blooming crape myrtle trees unruffled and still in the hot air. They sat next to one another.

"There was a gang of boys woke me up last night," she said. "Might have killed me with a shotgun. Just dumb luck they decided not to."

Samson frowned. "Fucking gangs. There's more and more of them."

"Anyway, it scared me like I ain't been scared in a long time. It seems living out here just ain't what it used to be."

"Will you move into my house then? I'd be less anxious about you if you would."

Mac waited a beat and then nodded. "I'd like to try it. Maybe part of the day I can stay out on the street and still feel . . . free. And at night I can stay there. Would that be all right?" She looked at him, asking for his permission and hating having to ask anyone for anything.

"However you want to work it is all right with me, Mac. I'm hardly ever home, you might not see me much. I sleep there. But sometimes I don't come in at night either. We'll live our separate lives, how's that?"

"I don't have to cook your dinner and shit?"

Samson laughed and that made her grin, too. She realized, after she'd said it, that it sounded like she was saying she might cook his dinner and then go shit.

"I'd rather you *not* cook my dinner. I don't eat there much. My hours are just as erratic as yours are. But at least you'll have your own room and there will be food in the fridge when you want it.''

''I ain't giving up Big Macs.'' The very idea of doing without a daily Big Mac made her queasy. What was she going to eat in Samson's house? Macaroni and cheese? Frozen pizza?

''You do what suits you. C'mon, I'll take you there now so you can get settled in. I don't have to be at work for another couple of hours.''

She rode in his car without talking too much. He asked about the gang, what they were like, had she seen them around the area before, did she think they were really dangerous types, and she answered with monosyllables. He decided they might be *Mexikanemi*.

''In nineteen-eighty-four,'' Samson said, ''Huerta, while in prison, founded the *Mexikanemi*. Or *'La Eme,'* as they call themselves. He went to war with the 'Texas Syndicate', and there was a bloodbath. Forty-seven inmate murders and more than four hundred stabbings in one year. We've been trying to get them on the RICO laws, but it's tough sledding. They get together in prison and grow stronger. Now they're not only in the prison system, they've moved out into the cities. We have a big problem here in Houston.''

''They sure were a problem, all right,'' Mac agreed. ''Only way they let me go was I told them I had a cop friend.'' She grinned at him. ''You come in handy sometimes.''

At his house, a fair distance from the Montrose area where she had lived on the street, he took all her things from the cart into the house and deposited them in one of the bedrooms. She stood looking around at the twin-size bed covered with a quilt, a small chest of drawers, and a bedside table with a reading lamp. It looked cramped to her. The walls felt as if they were closing in.

Then she thought of the gang leader's eyes looking at her as if he were a cobra and she a rabbit and she knew it was either accept the enclosure of walls or die badly at the hands of a snake.

''Thanks,'' she said to Samson when he had made a

few trips and brought everything inside. "This is just fine. It's . . . nice."

He showed her the kitchen and opened cabinet doors so she would know where the dishes and food were shelved. His dog, Pavlov, followed her around grinning and hopping and butting her legs with his backside. She never much liked animals. Could she abide this place, really? It had been so long since she lived indoors. A lifetime ago.

"I have to leave for the station now, but you'll be fine, won't you?"

She said she would, she knew she would just as soon as she got used to things.

Then he was gone, the front door closing, and she was alone with the dog standing in the kitchen. Feeling lost. Wondering why the world had to be so relentlessly unforgiving to people like her who never really fit in anywhere.

"It's a funny thing about falling in love. You never expect it to happen and then it happens. It's like finding a goldfish in your bathtub."

Shadow thought about what Frank was saying to her. He sat at her table having a beer and she had talked about feeling something for Mitchell. She didn't name him, of course, she just said he was a male acquaintance who was turning into more than that.

"I'm not sure I'm 'falling in love,' " she said, shaking her head in denial. "I mean, I don't know him well enough for that yet. I don't even like the idea of love. The last time I 'loved' someone, he destroyed . . . everything."

"I knew a woman once for approximately three hours and I was in love with her."

"Oh, really? When did this happen?"

He looked down at his bottle of beer. "It was a long time ago. I was a lot younger. I met her at a roller skating rink, of all places. I watched her for a while out on the floor and then I skated out and put my arm around her waist. We talked while we skated and then we sat down and talked some more. Pretty soon I thought: I'm in love with her. And I was."

"How did it work out?"

"Not very good, actually. She had another steady boy-friend and they were both going off to the same college that fall. I think they were married in their senior year."

"Oh. That's kind of sad."

He shrugged. "It happens. But now I know falling in love can be something instantaneous. It doesn't have to grow over a period of time."

"Well, I didn't say I was in love with this man I was talking about. I . . . like him a lot. He's . . . well, he seems to be a good man."

"Are there any good men?" Frank laughed. "Besides me, of course."

She smiled at him. "Not that many, take my word for it."

"But you run into some pretty skaggy men in this place, that's all it is, it's warped your view of men."

"They're everywhere, Frank. Not just in here. There are bad men everywhere."

When Frank left her, she sat thinking about what love was and if she would ever feel it for a man again. It was hard enough to find a man she might trust, much less *love*. And she could not say why she trusted Mitchell Samson but knew it had nothing to do with his being a cop. She should have distrusted a cop above all people considering the things she had done. It was the way Frank said. Some people just inspire you to confide in them or to love them, some attract you in a way that has no rhyme or reason. They appear in your life, goldfish in the bathtub.

She smiled.

Then darkness spread over her thoughts and she remembered the people who so easily tempt you and convince you they'd be better off dead.

"Hey, honey, mind if I join you for a minute? I don't go on for a few minutes."

Shadow was so lost in thought she hadn't seen the other woman near the table. She gestured for her to take a seat. She noticed her dress. It was a breakaway red spangled number held together in appropriate places by Velcro strips.

When she reached beneath the sleeveless arm she could rip the dress straight down to the hem and pull it forward to reveal her body beneath. The straps were also held together with Velcro, so she could detach it from her pale white shoulders and drop the entire garment to the floor of the stage.

"You're not dancing tonight?"

Shadow was trying to remember the woman's name. What did she call herself? "No," she said, "not tonight."

"I've been watching you, you know. I think you move like an angel up there when you're dancing. You don't even work at making the men get hard-ons. It comes as naturally to you as snapping my fingers to a good beat comes to me. You wouldn't happen to be bi, would you? I sure think you and me would make a good couple. We'd light up the night sky, you better believe it."

Shadow felt herself harden inside. As much as she had learned about the club scene and the women in it, she was always startled when one of them came on to her.

"No, I'm not bisexual."

"Hetero, I guess, huh?" She sighed and glanced up at the stage to the dancer there. "What a fucking shame. I heard them saying you didn't go with the guys, so I just thought maybe . . ."

"Sorry, no." Shadow was ready to leave the table and the conversation, but the other woman spoke again.

"Know where I pick up the best-looking guys?"

"Wouldn't have a clue."

"The gay bars. Bi guys cruise there and they're all dolls, some of them the most handsome men you've ever laid eyes on. God in his heaven would fuck one of those beauties. You ever want a date—"

"No thanks."

"Well, Jesus, hey, I was just trying to give a little friendly advice. I guess you don't do drugs or even smoke cigarettes, either. I guess maybe you're slumming here with the rest of us just for the kicks or something."

"Listen, don't start getting hostile," Shadow said. "I don't care what you or anyone else in here does in private.

It's not my business. But it's not *your* business what I do or what I think or what I had for dinner last night. Okay? Now if you'll excuse me . . .''

"You're excused. Bitch," she added.

Shadow made a hasty exit for the dressing room. Most of the girls were tolerant about lifestyles given they had unusual ones of their own, but once in a while a girl came along who was a militant lesbian or had a chip on her shoulder or was just plain jealous, and those women were the ones who could spell trouble big-time. The manager had just fired a lesbian who mocked the girls who prostituted with men and showed no interest in her.

It seemed to Shadow that the more she learned about how women handled themselves in the world, the less respect she had for them. They went to such extremes. They were puritans living and working in the suburbs, raising families and looking down on their sisters who happened to have to work as strip dancers for their living. There were those women who hated men and loved women exclusively. There were women so confused about their sexuality they had turned to sex toys for gratification over any relationship with another human being. Women who were punching bags for their violent husbands, women who let themselves turn into baby factories, women who wanted to be men, by God, and rule the world for a change.

Mom came out of a toilet stall. "Shadow girl! How's it shakin' tonight out there on the floor?"

"Oh, about the same as usual, Mom. I think I'm going to call it a night, though."

"Make your money already?"

Shadow considered the bills stuffed in the cup of her bra. "Not as much as I'd like, but it doesn't matter."

''I hears how you and that cop got a thing going."

Shadow turned to her. "Who told you that?"

"This ain't no secret, girl. People's seen you with him at the table. Even I know something's happening when *that* man sits at a girl's table."

"Why is that?"

"He got a rep. He never before come on to a girl in the

clubs. He's been hanging in these places for lotsa years and not once before any of us seen him get hisself attached. He *got* to be in love, child. Maybe I ought to be congratulating you. I 'spect he soon want to take you outta all this.'' She laughed at the idea of it.

Shadow turned away to find her street clothes in the gym bag. ''Hold off on the congratulations for a while. I don't know what to think about him yet.''

''He a fine-looking man. Yes, ma'am, fine looking. Most lawmen got a real hard face, but his ain't so hard. Not no more'n yours is.''

''And he's never hurt a woman or a child.''

''Say huh?''

''Nothing, I was talking to myself, Mom.''

Mom, whose hips were so large she had to turn sideways to move through a normal doorway, brushed past Shadow to the cosmetics counter. Shadow smelled her scent and liked it. It was a mixture of a cheap flowery perfume and sweat that, combined, smelled rich and opulent. She had known this scent from somewhere before, maybe from childhood or just in passing on a street or in an elevator or in a crowded mall. Few people managed to have a strong personal scent that did not confront and confound the nostrils. Mom was one of them, and it made Shadow like her better than she might have just from their brief and shallow conversations.

She must hurry now. She stripped off the tight black dress and withdrew the folded bills from her bra to stash in her purse. Soon Mitchell would meet her in the parking lot and she would go to his house.

She would, wouldn't she? Or would she back out of it? It came to her that she was afraid of having to walk through rooms of a real home, feel the presence of a man stamped on his choice of furniture, his offering of drinks to her, his expectations when he came to take her into his arms.

Oh, to hell with it, goddamn it, son of a bitch. She was going, that's all there was to it. She needed to have his heat near her, feel his hands on her body, make love to him. She didn't care what demons she had to wrestle from the past, demons who came carrying remembrances of a home lived in, a home where people lived decent, prudent, innocent, and secure lives.

She paused in dressing, deep in thought. Might this affair cure her of the madness of murder? Might it really? Could he take away her compulsion to poison the lowlifes? She hadn't felt compelled to look for a victim in some time.

She did not know that Mom paused in her tidying and turned from the mirror to watch her curiously. She also did not hear her say, softly, as if to the walls of the room, "He gonna be a fine man for you, I predict. Lord knows, he better."

Thirty

"She's not here." Mitchell looked through into the kitchen, stepped into the hall, and checked out the spare bedroom. "She must be on the street."

Shadow stood in the center of the living room rubbing Pavlov's big square head. Mitchell looked like a man who would own a dog like this. "Should she be out this time of night? That's a little dangerous, isn't it?"

"No, she shouldn't, but at least I've got her staying here part of the time. I can't chain her to a chair. She's about the most obstinate person I've ever known. Her old habits are going to die hard if they die at all. You might call this an experiment that just might turn into my worst nightmare."

"Why do you call her Big Mac?"

"She practically lives at McDonald's. She'd rather eat a Big Mac than T-bone steak." He pulled Pavlov away by the collar and stashed him in the spare room. When he returned, he said, "You want a drink?"

Shadow shook her head. Pouring drinks made her think of the decanter on her dressing table in the Shoreville Mansion. Sometimes at the Blue Boa when she lifted a glass to her mouth, she imagined she could smell the poisoned whiskey, and she couldn't drink a swallow. "I don't want anything, thanks."

He didn't seem to know what to do next. He brushed his hands together, looked around the room as if inspecting it with her opinion of it in mind. "Well . . . I guess I'll get a glass of water. I'm a little thirsty."

Shadow sat on the sofa. She patted the cushions. She wished she hadn't come.

As she turned her head, feeling someone nearby, she found Mitchell down on his knees next to her, his face inches from her own. She flinched. "I thought . . ." She thought he was getting water, but he had changed his mind, he had come to her, and in his eyes she saw the longing. She lifted her hands to his face and looked into his eyes. "What are we doing, Mitchell? What's happening to us?"

"Hell if I know."

He put his arms under her legs and behind her back, lifted her from the sofa, and stood there in the living room, holding her weight, breathing slow and easy.

She almost asked him to kiss her, but before she could, he was kissing her. She locked her hands around his neck. He moved his lips over her cheek to her ear and down to her throat. She lay her head back and sighed. She wanted this, needed this. She loved it. Loved how he made her feel, loved the heat he created.

In the bedroom he put her gently onto the unmade bed and sat down beside her. She reached out to unbutton his shirt. In minutes they had their clothes discarded on the floor, and Mitchell lay beside her, clutching her tightly to him. She ran her nails down his back and felt his muscles tighten and his pelvis push closer to her.

"I don't know what I'm doing," she whispered. "I shouldn't . . ."

"Shhh."

He made love to her slowly, in total silence. The room was dark and smelled of damp towels and dog. Shadow thought she would not climax, that she would not be able to lose herself, that she would think of where she was and what she was doing, her mind would be a million miles away, but his hands caressed her so, his body brought her into rhythm with him, his lips sought her breasts in the darkness, and soon all she could think of were the sensations of her body collapsing into his, buckling up to his, and she moved with him, beneath him, and there in the strange, odor-filled dark room she reached for release, with all her might, and came with a shudder that shook them both.

He lay beside her, kissing her face, murmuring love talk while her breathing slowed and her skin cooled from sweat evaporating.

"Now we know what we're doing," he said.

"And we do it so well," she said.

They lay awhile side by side, luxuriating in the peace, holding hands. Then he led her to the bathroom saying, "Come with me." They showered together, soaping one another, and again grew aroused so that they had to make love even more passionately than before. He had her against the shower wall with the water trumpeting on his shoulders and streaming down over her breasts to run between them in a soapy river.

He finally had her wishing she never had to leave.

As she toweled dry he said from behind her, "Why don't you move in with me?"

Her hands froze.

"I didn't mean to leave you speechless. I know it's too soon, and a bathroom isn't the most romantic place in the world to propose a living arrangement, and I can't explain this, but I do know I'm in love with you."

She covered her face with the towel to buy time.

"You don't have to answer now. Maybe you need to think about it."

"Mitchell . . . I . . ."

"All right, I know it's nuts, I know I surprised you, but I wish you'd do it. Move in with me."

"You don't know me." She turned to him, lowering the towel so she could see his face. He could never really know her, not the person she had become.

"I know what I need to know."

She was almost in tears. He meant it, she could see that in his eyes. He loved her, he wanted to live with her, one day he'd probably ask her to marry him. And it was the craziest thing she had ever heard of. Maybe crazier than her, a murderer, sleeping with a homicide cop. Doing what he asked would be the ultimate joke on the criminal justice system.

She couldn't do that. "I can't do that," she said, voicing

her thoughts, which spilled willy-nilly all through her brain.

"Can't or won't?"

"I . . . just can't."

"You could bring Charlene, I don't care. This is a big house, there's enough room for everyone." He moved to her and took her into his arms. He was so tall compared to her that her head barely reached to the top of his shoulder.

She lay her cheek against his damp soapy-smelling skin and fought back tears. It really wasn't fair, was it? Things never worked out as they should. She would have been better off having never met him.

"Think it over, will you? Just think about it."

She thought about it. Could think of nothing else. When she was at the mansion again with Charlene tagging behind her as she nervously paced through the house, the thought dominated her mind.

"He asked me to live with him," she said to Charlene.

"The cop?"

"Yeah, the cop."

The silence lasted and began to gnaw at Shadow. She stopped pacing and faced her friend. "What do you think?"

"I think maybe it would be a good thing."

"Oh, hell!" Shadow turned from the ballroom's floor-length windows and crossed the room for the hall. She heard Charlene behind her, pitty-patting in her loose cloth house slippers.

"Did he want me to move in, too?" Charlene asked. "I don't want to go back to Austin."

"Yes, he invited you, too. He already has a bag lady living there. I feel like one more stray animal he's taking in."

"Oh, don't say that."

"You're right, I shouldn't say that, that's not the way it is. He feels sorry for the bag lady. He says he loves me. I suppose there's a difference."

"I'd say."

Shadow wrestled with the idea until she felt herself going in circles. Finally she said she had to dress for work.

"Aren't you off tonight?"

"I'm on because I choose to be on. Maybe it'll take my mind off this other business."

Charlene was standing outside the bedroom door when Shadow appeared with her gear and the car keys in her hand.

"He's a nice man," Charlene said, taking up the dropped conversation as if there had been no interruption of time. "This . . . this *thing* could stop if we move in with him. Maybe the *voices* would stop then."

"I don't want to talk about it anymore. I have to leave or I'll be late."

"Shadow?"

"*What?*"

"This may be God's way of saving us."

Shadow began to laugh sarcastically and then she stopped abruptly. Charlene needed something from her, something from life she had never found. If there wasn't enough there—and there wasn't—then she needed God, and so be it. "Maybe," she mumbled, moving into the hall and for the front stairs.

"Won't you think about it?" Charlene called after her.

And what do you think I've been doing? Shadow wanted to say. I am, I am, she wanted to shout. Why is everyone pressuring me? she wanted to scream. But she said nothing and pulled the door closed softly behind her as she left the house.

Son watched from a distance. He was there, parked on the street, when she came to work. He was there hours later when she came from the Blue Boa's exit door at the back of the building and walked to her car.

His belly tightened and he sat straighter in the driver's seat. His buttocks were numb and he was terminally bored from sitting, waiting, but now that his sacrifices might pay off, he didn't care.

She drove a few blocks away and turned into a Kroger's parking lot. He drove past, then around the block, and cruising by again, saw she had parked. There was a man at her driver's side window. He was bent over at the waist, talking to her.

Son saw a dark house with a gravel driveway next to the grocery store parking area. He pulled into it and killed the headlights. He could see Shadow's car from where he sat. He brought his thumb to his mouth and gnawed at a hangnail. What did this mean that she had met someone again at a place away from the club? This time he'd tail her. He'd find out for sure if she was the killer or if it was the crazy woman she lived with or someone else she worked with as a team player.

Maybe it was where she made arrangements for prostitution. He wouldn't be surprised. Most of the dancers in those clubs were for sale when the price was right. But he suspected this was something else, he could feel it in his bones.

He saw the man circle Shadow's car and get in the passenger's side. He reached over and placed his fingers on the ignition key. Shadow backed from the parking spot, drove around the lot and out the exit drive. When she reached the stoplight at the corner, Son started his car and followed her.

"Hotel California" by the Eagles was playing on the radio. Shadow listened to the lyrics rather than the inane babblings from her passenger. At the Hotel California you could check out any time you wanted, but you could never leave. Hadn't she created a Hotel Texas in the Shoreville Mansion?

Her passenger would never leave.

He had come to her table around one A.M., an hour before closing. He was overweight and sweating. He kept mopping his doughy, red face with a white linen handkerchief. She saw the tattoos that ended just before the cuffs of his white long-sleeved shirt. She reached out and took his wrist. She said, "These are interesting. How far up do they go?"

"They're all over my body."

"Didn't that hurt?"

"Not too bad."

She inclined her head to peer closer. It appeared the tail of a snake was woven around his wrist. Then, turning his hand a little, she saw a swastika tattooed between his thumb and forefinger. "What's this? You a Nazi?"

She had said it as a joke, but his eyes changed to a troubled gray. "No," he said.

"Then what does this mean?" She rubbed her thumb over the swastika.

"I'm a white supremacist. I don't like anyone who isn't white. You don't have any nigger blood in you, do you?"

She felt her heart grow leaden. It was a sudden sensation that was suffocating, as if an elephant sat on her chest. She thought of Mom in the dressing room and what this man might do to her if her caught her alone in an alley. "No," she said. "I'm mostly German."

That pleased him, as she had calculated it would. He began shoveling money into her palm. The more he gave her, the more she hated him. She wanted to tell him that he wasn't white, who was? He was filthy muddy no-true-color, and his blood was a gray-water pollution; his ancestors were fucking apes who didn't have the sense to come down from the trees. His kind made her want to gnash nails between her teeth and spit them out crumpled as foil paper.

"Are you in the local KKK?" She asked this just to needle at his self-image.

"I don't talk about things like that," he said.

"What do you do for a living?"

"I run a landscape service company."

She knew he employed only whites, trashy uneducated whites who cut grass for him and raked leaves. Whites who hated colored skin as much as he did.

"You're awful dark or maybe it's these lights in here," he said. "Germans are blond. You sure you don't have some spick or wop in you? With that black hair and all . . ."

Shadow shrugged. "I can leave if you want me to." She made to stand from the table. He grabbed *her* wrist.

"No, wait," he said. "You're the best-looking gal in

here. You say you're German, that's all right with me. Even the führer had dark hair.''

She sat again. She listened to his hate-mongering babble. She weaseled out of him admissions of violence against other men, admissions he might not have made had she not threatened to leave him alone at the table. He came from a long line of white supremacists. He had lived most of his life in Vidor, Texas, where they had kept blacks completely out of the town until only recently when by court order a housing development had been made to abide by the law. His grandfather formed the first KKK branch in the area. His great-grandfather had owned slaves and died fighting the Yankee carpetbaggers, who not only took his landholdings but courted away his wife and daughters, too.

He had killed his first nigger when he was seventeen, he said, not bragging but stating it as a simple fact. At nineteen he beat a Mexican-American to within an inch of his life and left him crippled and in a wheelchair.

Had he ever had relations with someone other than a white woman? she asked of him.

''Not once. I wouldn't dirty my hands. I'd vomit if I tried to do something like that,'' he said vehemently. ''But I've cut enough of the bitches so they won't be making anymore of those fucking nappy-headed brats, I've done that, by God.''

He told her all these things in a low, conspiratorial voice. He truly thought he had found in her a sympathizer. He had so easily bought her lie that she was of German ancestry. Which just went to show how much intelligence he had at his disposal.

He was stupid, though racists, in her book, could be nothing other than stupid.

And this man was more.

He was incredibly, utterly evil, and although he had no suspicion, he was not long meant for this world.

Son parked where he had before, the night he came to the mansion. He left the car and sneaked up to the house until he was on the wide front porch watching through the windows. He couldn't see anyone. Not Shadow, the man she had brought home, or the crazy woman who had met him at the door asking about her cat.

He sat down with his back to the wall and waited. Again He let his mind wander and entertained himself by trying to roll a quarter over his knuckles without dropping it into his lap.

It might have been an hour later, it could not have been longer because he had not managed to get the quarter to roll smoothly over two of his knuckles, when he heard voices and turned to peek through the window. He saw the two women trying to carry . . .

a body

. . . something big and heavy, wrapped in a sheet and plastic liner. Shadow was cursing and the crazy woman was weeping. They both kept dropping the end of . . .

the body

. . . the burdensome cargo. He pressed closer to the glass to be able to hear the conversation inside. He clutched the quarter tightly in the palm of his hand. Dizzy excitement caused him to breath rapidly, shallowly.

"You said this wouldn't happen again. . . ." That was the crazy woman and she sounded heartbroken. He could see her face was wet with tears and splotched red from crying. She looked as insane as the woman in that old movie—what was it? *Snake Pit.* Was that Rita Hayworth? Or maybe it was . . .

Shadow shouted, "Lift his feet. I'm going to drop the son of a bitch right here if you don't try to help me."

"We could have moved out of here if you hadn't—"

"I'm never gonna get this bastard out of the house."

"I think we need to call the doctor for *you,* not me. You have to stop—"

"He's a fucking *monster!*" Shadow screamed.

"I hear him and he says he is not a monster, he never did nothing."

"He did, too. You didn't hear him, Charlene, you don't know. And you don't hear him now."

"But I *do* hear him—"

"Shut up and lift him, goddamn it, lift his *feet*. Damn!"

Son saw them make the corner on the landing and move through an opening into darkness. He immediately stood and raced down the stairs to the yard. He moved around the right side of the house. He fought his way through chest-high weeds to the green glass that rose two stories to a curving glass roof.

Was this a conservatory? An indoor greenhouse or arboretum? His feet sunk in soft loam. A spider, a daddy longlegs, walked up his forearm, and he swatted it off. He pushed onto tiptoe and peered through the glass. He smelled mildew on the brick siding. Light spilled from both ends of the glassed-in section inside. Star- and moonlight shone in from overhead. He saw nearest him a brick maze, a marvelously strange configuration of paths weaving through brick formations that would have been higher than his waist if he had been inside. On the other side he saw a glittering blue-green swimming pool. Between the two and high up he could see the metal catwalk connecting the front and back of the building. There he saw the two women struggling to transport the . . .

body

. . . heavy burden.

He watched with shining eyes, startled but thrilled. The dancer killed the floaters they kept finding in the bay. He had proof. He knew now for certain.

Was that why the cop hung around her? Did he suspect, too? Oh God, he hoped not. The game was just beginning. He didn't want her caught yet. He had only had one turn, and if she were caught soon, he would have no time to commit another murder. The thought seized and held him, carrying away his breath.

They were at the far end of the catwalk, having dropped . . .

the body

. . . what they were carrying several times before getting it across. When they disappeared into the far end of the house, he pushed from the side and started toward the back to see where they exited into the moonlight.

It took them a long time to get the body down the steps and across the short lawn to the dock, then down the dock and into a small boat with an outboard motor. Shadow continued cursing and the crazy woman cried, while Son sat in the shadows, hidden by weeds, contemplating and relishing the scene of the crime.

A peace descended on him unlike anything he had experienced in many years. He felt a kinship with the woman called Shadow, and suddenly it occurred to him how perfectly matched were their nicknames, how *fateful* it was she was the shadow and he the sun (Son!). They were two elements that ruled the world, the light and the dark, the yin and the yang, the day and the night. They performed the duties others were too afraid and too weak to perform. They *owned* the lives of others and took them at will. She led him and he followed, sun chasing shadow.

He smiled at the coincidence but sobered when he thought that perhaps there was no such thing as coincidence in the world. It was destined, perhaps preordained that they meet and become partners, dancing together, leading the band at Death's cotillion ball.

He had to stop this. Stop thinking in metaphors, like a stupid novelist. This was deadly serious business, his *main* business. To wrap it in literary gauze and bury it deep in flowery language was to separate it from the real world where he knew what he was about and what the world really needed. He could not afford to pretend this was anything other than willful and premeditated murder, death of the first order, and he needed all his wits to deal with it.

He stayed, growing damp with dew and bitten by mosquitoes, while the crazy woman reentered the house and Shadow took the small boat out into the waters. He waited until Shadow returned, her great burden discarded. Watched while she wearily, head hanging, arms limp at her sides, made her way up the pier and into the house.

He left, tired but replete, just as dawn broke with slow stealth, golden and rosy, over southeast Texas.

❧ Thirty-one ❧

On the day his mother died, Son killed his second victim. He met the man in a bar across from the Blue Boa. He was as unlike the bum in the alley as the man in the moon. Young, clean-cut, earnest, and sober, he presented the ultimate challenge.

They sat at a back booth together talking football. Son faced the entrance to watch for the patrolling detective who worked the dives.

The young man, Clive Winnows by name, proved to be obsessive about the Dallas Cowboys. Son didn't give a shit about NFL teams, didn't really care about sports at all, but to keep the conversation lively, he pretended to be a rabid Houston Oilers fan. In Texas, Cowboy fans disagreed vehemently with Oiler fans, and vice versa. The subject was always good grist for a heated debate.

"Moon should be replaced, man, he loses all the games for you." Clive was not without intelligence. Son knew enough about football to know that the Oilers' quarterback, Warren Moon, was one of the best players in the league, but it appeared his age was telling on him. Maybe they'd trade him soon.

"I suppose some would say when Moon's hot, he's unbeatable, but like any other quarterback, when he's off his feed, there goes the ball game." Son, working to get Clive's trust, would not deliberately alienate him, especially not about something as frivolous as sports.

They talked late into the night, the conversation spinning on first this sports subject and then that one. The bar was just a bar, a neighborhood place to hang out, not a strip club. They were not disturbed by loud music or agitated by naked women parading on a stage. The draft beer was cheap and cold.

Son sized Clive up as sexually straight, but kinky as all hell about football. He could not get his fill of showing off what esoteric knowledge he possessed on the sport. He must have made a study of it for a number of years, judging by the way he wouldn't let it go. He even professed to have decorated his house in Cowboy trinkets, from Cowboy mugs and glasses in his cupboard to Cowboy clocks, rugs, and throws. The man was certifiable.

Son wore a disguise. He wasn't about to be seen spending hours in a bar with a man who would turn up in Gulf waters tomorrow or the next day. On his head he wore a black gimme cap with a tractor dealer insignia. Baggy clothes stuffed in strategic places so that he seemed to weigh a good fifty pounds more than he actually weighed made him look older and more vulnerable. He wore lifts in his shoes. He had even brought out an old mustache from his collection in the bedroom closet, one left over from use in encounters with other victims, and, using theater glue, attached it to his face. He looked undistinguished and as ordinary as mud.

When Clive left with him, an hour before the bar closed, accepting Son's offer to walk down the street for hamburgers before heading home, Son led him first to his car. It was parked in the shadows on a side street.

During their hours of conversation, Clive had offered the information that he was an automobile repair technician, an expert, if you will, with any electrical problem on nearly any make or model of car.

Son sadly reported that his car lights had kept blinking out on the way downtown. He didn't know if he could drive home.

Clive good-naturedly offered to check it out.

Once inside the car, with Clive in the driver's seat bent down under the wheel feeling for the wiring harness, Son tapped him hard just once behind the ear with the business end of a hammer. He pulled the body toward him until it was on the passenger side of the car, got out, and circled to the driver's side so that he might drive them from the area.

It was not until he had the unconscious Clive at Seabrook that Son parked, propped the man against the window, and poured a can of Coke laced with rat poison down his throat. Clive coughed and woke. He fought, but he was much smaller than Son, much weaker from the wound to his head, and he succumbed without too much trouble.

Son had to hurry to get him from the car before he vomited the blood.

After undressing the body and disposing of it in the bay, Son wondered what he should do about the mess on the rocky ground. He found the short-handled camping shovel in the trunk and made fast work of lifting the offensive and incriminating dirt, shovelful by shovelful, and carrying it over to the bulkhead to drop into the water. When he was sure he had gotten it all, he scuffed the area with his shoes so it would not draw notice as a place where soil had been extracted.

On the way home he sang with the Beatles on the radio about yellow submarines. We all want one, he thought. That's what we want, a yellow submarine.

The moment he walked into the house, he knew something was wrong. The silence was as vast and as deep as it is in an empty midnight cathederal. No radio from his mother's room. No sounds at all, nothing.

He let out a strangled groan and rushed down the hall without turning on the lights. He slipped on the hall rug that had worked loose from the carpet tacks, caught himself on the wall, and kept going, calling, "Mother, Mother . . ."

She lay on the bed as he had left her earlier. She lay perfectly at peace, her hands crossed on her chest.

He knew she was dead. Even in the dark, without seeing her up close, without feeling for a pulse, he knew. She would have heard him enter the front door, heard him call her, awakened long before he slammed open her closed bedroom door.

She was dead and the paralyzation would not let him go to her across the room. He stood immobile until the grief rose up like a great beast from her bed, stalked the distance to where he stood, and smote him between the eyes.

He cried out.

He fell to his knees and covered his face with his hands.

Bruce, the manager of the Blue Boa, told her there was a phone call and she should know personal phone calls were verboten while at work, but go answer it, damn it, and get off quick, this was no kind of place to gab on the phone.

Shadow raised the receiver to her ear, perplexed, wondering if something might be wrong at home with Charlene. She drew in her breath and said, "Hello?"

"You're all I have left," he said.

His voice was unfamiliar and hushed and something else that she did not readily identify. Was it a little British?

"Who is this?"

"There are just the two of us now," he said, "and I have to tell you something."

"You obviously have the wrong party. I don't know what you're talking about." It must be a freak calling her. Who else knew her stage name and could ask for her at the Blue Boa besides Charlene, Mitch, and the clientele?

"No, no." Breathy. "You're the one, Shadow. My other side."

"Listen, I have to go—"

"I killed another one tonight for you," he said, rapidly now, tripping over the confession before she hung up on him.

She gripped the phone until her hand hurt. She pressed it closer to her ear. "Who are you?" she whispered, turning her back to the hallway where other girls came and went behind the curtains.

"I'm Son," he said.

"Sun?"

"Male child of Darkness and Death. Also sun, bright as an avenging angel. And you are my Shadow."

"I'm hanging up now."

"That's all right. I'll be in touch."

The dial tone buzzed in her ear and she stood listening to it another few seconds to buy time to think, to rearrange her features before she turned to face anyone in the club.

Sun? The opposite of shadow? The copycat killer? He knew about her, that she . . .

He had called her!

A trembling bout overtook her limbs so that she had some difficulty fitting the black pay phone receiver into the hanging metal slot. Her legs threatened to wobble out from beneath her and give up her weight to the floor. She held on to the wall, then turned.

No one looked at her. No one knew she was alive.

She stumbled down the hall to the dressing room and made it to her locker. She couldn't turn the tumblers on the lock. She pressed her forehead against the cool metal and shut her eyes.

A toilet flushed, the stall door opened with a squeak from the hinges, and Mom said, "Whassa matter, girl, you feel faint?"

Arms came around her and led her to the bench before the long mirror. She was lowered and steadied by big soft hands. "Want I should call Bruce or maybe a doctor?"

She managed to shake her head. "No." Small protest. Her control over everything—walking, talking, coping with this new world—had deserted her.

Sun? Child of . . . *Son!* Did he fancy himself the son of Satan or something with that "child of Darkness" remark? How did he know about her? Had he followed her, watched while . . . ?

"I killed another one tonight for you."

Her mind clicked over and went far away. When she returned, Mom was on her knees staring up into her face. Mom's eyes were distressed. Deeply etched lines described the flesh around her mouth. "I think you ought to go on home, if you can drive yourself," she said.

"I'll be all right in a minute. I'm . . . sorry. I must be getting a . . . bug or something. I'll be able to drive. Will you tell Bruce for me?"

All the way across the city the man's voice haunted and

tormented her. She had to do something, but what?

When she arrived home, Charlene was in the kitchen scrambling eggs. Shadow made her put the pan aside and sit with her at the kitchen table.

"You look white as a sheet. What happened?"

"He called me at the club tonight. That man."

"Who called you? What man?"

Shadow raised her gaze until she stared into Charlene's frightened eyes. She debated telling her, but she had to, this would affect them both, Charlene couldn't stay ignorant of the situation. "The copycat killer. He said he killed another one tonight."

"Oh God. Oh God!"

"He knows I can't tell anyone, I can't ask for help. I don't know what he wants, Charlene. He talked to me like . . . a lover or something. Or like we're partners."

Charlene balled her fists on the tabletop. She began hitting the table with them, one at a time, taking turns with each fist. Shadow tried to reach out and stop the nerve-wracking noise, but Charlene jerked away and continued using her fists, now on her own knees.

"We will go to jail forever or they'll put us to death," Charlene said.

"No we won't. I'll do something, I'll think of something. . . ."

"He knows who you are. He knows where you are. He probably even knows this place."

"We don't know what he knows yet."

"He probably watches us through the windows, sees everything we do."

She continued pounding at her knees to punctuate her words. Shadow scooted her chair closer and grabbed the other woman's wrists, held them rigid. "Look at me."

Charlene looked and grew calmer. She stopped trying to free her hands.

"I don't know yet what this means. I'll find a way out. You believe me, don't you?"

Charlene began to nod her head, halted.

"You have to believe in me or everything falls apart. I

don't want to go to prison or back to a mental hospital. Neither do you. We wouldn't survive it. Not again. You know that, don't you?''

Charlene nodded this time, tentatively.

''He's like one of those men I killed. A sick pervert, a diseased sick crazy bastard with . . .''

Charlene tore her gaze away and hung her head in a posture of one dropped into a great depression.

''Charlene? You have to be strong to help me out of this.''

''Will you stop?'' Charlene asked. ''*Now,* will you stop?''

She knew she must. That what she'd done was insane, that it jeopardized not only her freedom, her life, but her friend's life and freedom as well. She didn't have the right to bring Charlene into her mad zealous project when it meant possible incarceration or the death sentence. What had she done? Had her own unthinking madness been jolted from her by the madness of Son?

''What have I done?'' she asked.

''Terrible things,'' Charlene said, her voice as soft as a dove cooing. ''Crazy things.''

''Yes,'' Shadow said, though not sure she believed it, any of it. She had been so sure, so strong in her resolve, so pure in her motives. Hadn't those despicable men *needed* to die? Hadn't they virtually *asked* for it? She remembered the rapist, the pedophile, the murderous racist . . .

''I'm going to lie down now,'' Charlene said, gently shaking loose her wrists from her friend's firm grasp.

''Yes. All right. Of course. Get some rest.''

Shadow sat in the kitchen all alone, listening to the air-conditioning's low uniform growl venting from overhead, breathing the scent of the forgotten scrambled eggs cooling on the stove, and thought: I have to find him.

I have to find him before he leads the police here.

❧ Thirty-two ❧

Samson let a handful of dirt and pea-sized gravel sift through his fingers. He looked up at one of the members of the crime scene team and said, "There was blood here."

He twisted around on his haunches to look toward the bulkhead. "He must have dumped the stained dirt in the water, trying to get rid of it. He used something to scoop it up."

They had found the body, the tire tracks, and striations in the dirt near those tire tracks. The removal of the dirt could mean the killer didn't want them to know the murder had taken place here. None of the others had as far as they knew.

"Check this and I think you'll find some drops of blood he missed. It'll most likely belong to the victim, but we have to make sure." He stood, scuffed his hands together to clean them, and ambled toward where the body lay in an open black body bag on a gurney ready for conveyance to the morgue. A cordon of police kept the media types at bay behind a crime scene rope. They wanted pictures of this.

Samson gazed at the face of the dead man. It was obvious to anyone familiar with the case that this death was an aberration from the normal MO. This man was young, in his twenties, where the other victims were older. He didn't look like an ex-con or a wino, and Samson would lay even money that he had nothing criminal on his record. He would bet the victim had been murdered elsewhere and dumped here.

He thought he knew the victim's identity. The desk at the downtown station had been getting calls for two days from a hysterical woman reporting her missing husband. Until now it had been treated as an abandonment—so many men walked out on their wives. But Samson felt in his gut this was the woman's missing spouse. She'd be called in to identify the body, *if* this was the body.

Ignoring the racket of the crowd at the perimeter of the scene and the Crime Unit photographer and investigators, the local deputy who had sent word to HPD, the fisherman who had found the floater, Samson leaned closer and noticed bruises on the man's neck just to the side of his windpipe. He must have been half-strangled. But that wouldn't be the cause of death. Poison would. Had the killer held this man down by the throat to make him drink? If so, it threw out the theory that this time they might be looking for a female serial killer. There were not too many women strong enough to force a man weighing approximately one hundred fifty-five pounds into imbibing a poisoned liquid.

Samson stood again and turned for his car. He waded past the inquisitive onlookers and media types. Some reporters tried to get him to make a statement, but he waved them off like annoying flies. He started the car and switched on the air, hoping to get the stink of death out of his nostrils. The briny deep was not kind to a corpse.

At the station again, Dod broached him in the walkway between desks, blocking him in the bullpen from reaching his own desk. "Tell me about it," Dod implored.

"Another floater, what do you want to know?"

"Will you start a task force now?"

"Dod, you'll be the first I tell if I do." He brushed past, but knew Dod followed right on his heels. Sudden anger surfaced and before Samson knew it, he had whipped around to face the other detective. "Don't you have your own cases? Can't you stay off my back even one goddamn minute?"

Dod flinched and his face reddened. "I have plenty of cases," he said. "It's just that my homicides are never quite as full of potential . . . media glory . . . as yours are."

"Well, now isn't that a fucking shame? Why didn't you try out for anchoring the news on Channel Eleven if you wanted to get your mug on television?''

Dod did not retreat, but neither did he pursue the conversation. He stared hard at Samson, unmoving.

Samson shrugged, swore again at the state of police work and the world in general, made it to his desk, and snatched up the phone. Someone had to call that woman with the missing husband. The sooner the floater was identified, the sooner Samson could find out his whereabouts two nights ago, the night the M.E. estimated he had died.

If the woman had any information that could help him, he'd be hard-pressed not to leap around the bullpen like a lunatic high on PCP.

Dod passed by the desk just as the woman answered the phone. From the corner of his eye Samson saw him wink.

Now what the hell was that about?

On his first foray into the hot, glimmering sexual milieu of the Montrose clubs, Detective Dodge took with him his girlfriend, Mona. It was a big mistake.

''You really think I'm going to accompany you into stripper joints?'' Mona's eyebrows rose so high they were lost beneath her shaggy bangs. ''I'm *not going* in places where women dance naked and that's that.''

So it was. He tried leading her into another club that didn't advertise women performers, and it turned out to be a leather bar. Mona's eyebrows ran for the border of her hairline again. ''Out!'' she hissed. ''Take me *out* of here.''

They tried a couple more places, but each one had something about it Mona found morally offensive, and finally she put down her feet on the sidewalk and would not move. ''Take me home, Dod. I don't want to go on any more of your undercover assignments ever again.''

He had not realized what a prude Mona was, but his worst mistake was not knowing the area and stumbling into all the wrong places with her hanging from his arm.

The second time he went fishing in Montrose, he went alone. He knew Samson's serial murder cases down to the minutest detail. He knew this was where Samson was hunting for clues. He knew if he, Detective Dodge, found a lead

and worked it and came close to solving the crimes before
Samson, a promotion was almost certain. Brass wouldn't
like the idea that he'd gone out in the lone cowboy mode,
or that he had stepped over the line to intrude on another
detective's investigation, but if he solved it, if he actually
caught the killer, they'd forgive all that. His star would rise
straight into the stratosphere.

It was tricky. If he was caught prowling—interfering,
they'd call it—in Samson's territory, he'd be reprimanded,
and it would *hurt* his career. He had to stay out of Samson's
way. He had to be very clever, more than a little manipu-
lative, and as deceptive as a timber rattler lying among
wood chips.

He found that he rather liked the clubs. There was always
talk about Detective Samson, how he hung out down here
even before there was ever a connection with the floaters.
Most of the men shrugged and said what the hell, he's
single, let the guy alone. Dod was one of those few who,
though he kept it to himself, thought Samson was just two
shades over into the blue world. He didn't know what it
was that was kinked about him, though he certainly did
speculate, but there was *something*.

He might have any kind of secret life. He might even be
a frigging closet faggot for all Dod knew, though he pretty
much doubted that. Or Samson might be into the S-and-M
scene, which was a distinct possibility. Or he could even
like to cross-dress or have the hots for transsexuals.

It had to be *something*. And if Dod happened to ferret
out the secret while hunting for the Gulf Water Killer (the
unofficial nickname for Samson's case), wouldn't the police
psychiatrist be interested in hearing that little bit of information?

Dod smiled over his drink. He was doing Seven and
Sevens while watching the women dance. He didn't drink
all that often, and he was feeling slightly woozy. Fuzzy
around the old brain stem, he thought, better watch it.

The place was called the Chez Tigress, and the girls
weren't really girls, they were women, and not particularly
pretty women. A dancer calling herself Babycakes was on-

stage, gyrating to a song by Extreme, but Dod wasn't too interested. He swung his head around to scan the crowd. It was late, closing in on midnight, and the hours, God, they were hell on him, but if he wanted a promotion . . .

He caught a man looking at him from across the room and his gaze stopped in its track. He weighed the possibilities. Was this a come-on or was this something else that might help him? He gave a half grin and glanced over the rest of the room. By the time his gaze had wandered again to the man, he saw he was on the way across the floor to the table.

Dod stood, wobbly, catching himself on the table edge and swearing below his breath. He had to lay off the booze or he was going to be shitfaced drunk any minute now. No good, no good.

"Hey," Dod said.

"Hello. You're a detective, right? Homicide, HPD?"

Dod frowned and lowered his backside into the chair. He motioned to the man to take the chair opposite. "Who said? And what of it?"

The man made himself comfortable, spreading his legs out from the table, leaning back in the chair. "The bartender knows when he's got a cop in the house. He told me."

"Which leads me to repeat: what of it?" Dod would not usually be so abrasive, not since he was down here to talk to the street and the regulars to glean information, but there was something goddamn cocky about the man across from him that he didn't like. At all.

"I hear you've got some photos you've been showing around. I frequent Chez Tigress about three times a week. Maybe I can help."

Dod narrowed his eyes. "Yeah, maybe you can." He pulled the photos from his jacket pocket and handed them over. They were copies from Samson's files. He had a friend at a photo shop copy them in one hour so he could slip them back in the files before they were missing. Samson ever found out he'd done that . . .

The man slowly riffled through the photos. While he did

so, Dod tried to size him up. What was his angle? How many people volunteered to help a cop? Precious goddamn few.

The guy looked innocuous enough. Brown hair mostly covered by a black gimme cap. An untrimmed, droopy mustache. Fat. He might sell insurance. Or real estate.

"Well, see anyone you know?"

The photos were handed back. Dod inspected them, then unconsciously grunted. He never liked looking at those morgue shots. Gave him the creeps.

"I don't recognize anyone."

"Well . . . thanks for trying anyway." Dod held out his hand to shake so he could dismiss the stranger, but the other man leaned forward abruptly. Dod let his hand drift to the table.

The man said in a low voice, "I know some people . . ."

"Yeah?"

". . . who might be able to help you."

"What people would that be?"

"They hang out at the Blue Boa, you been there?"

Dod tried to remember. Shit if he could keep the club names straight, especially after four Seven and Sevens. He slowly shook his head. "I don't know, I might have."

"Well, we could head over there now before the joint closes and I could introduce you. It's a girl. She has sharp eyes and a great memory, knows just about everyone comes down here."

Dod felt a tiny thrill of excitement needling through the Seagram's fog. This was what he had been hoping for. A break. Someone in the know. Someone who knew the regulars and might remember the faces. "You sure this is worth my time?" He wanted to be convinced, but there was still that indefinable something about the guy he hadn't quite latched on to yet, and it nagged at him.

Although Dod's record as a detective wasn't anywhere near as successful as Mitchell Samson's (he thought maybe that was the lieutenant's fault for not giving him the really difficult to crack cases), he had spent some time on the street as a patrolman. He didn't have the great hound dog instincts of a top-grade investigator, that's why he was always paired with better men, more experienced men, or he was put on the paperwork detail, but he still had his years on the force, and even without possessing finely honed instincts, there was something off about this whole deal with the man at his table. He wanted to follow up any leads, but he must be very careful while doing so.

"Okay," he said, pushing up from the table. "Let's go see your friend at the Blue Boa."

The stranger smiled behind his mustache and just for one single second an internal alarm sounded, making Detective Dodge wish he hadn't agreed to go with him.

Now it was too late.

"She's not here, damn."

Dod looked around nervously, relieved Samson wasn't in the room. "Well, maybe another night. Give me her name, I'll check it out."

"Tell you what, I'll take you to her house. She doesn't live far from here. She's . . . well, she's sort of my girlfriend."

"Oh, I don't know . . ." Dod had turned for the door. He thought he'd call it a night. The Seagram's was making his stomach burn. Could he be developing ulcers from this job?

"I'm telling you, she remembers every face she's ever seen. What do you call it? A photogenic memory?"

"Photographic." Dod stood fingering the photos in his jacket pocket and wondering if this was a wild-goose chase or maybe worth his time. What the hell. It was the first break he'd gotten. He'd kick himself tomorrow if he let this one slide past and it turned out to be the one witness that could break the case wide open.

"Okay, take me there."

"Just leave your car here, why don't you? I can bring you back. It's only a few blocks."

Dod nodded and followed the fat man down the sidewalk. He secretly slid his hand over his side arm just to make sure it was there.

*   *   *

Sherilee opened the door to two men at twelve forty-five. She peered into the yellow light from her porch bulb and said, "Son, is that you?"

"Yeah, can we come in? This is a homicide cop wants to talk to you about something."

Sherilee visibly recoiled at the news. She saw now the other man did indeed look like a cop. She had been off the street too long. She should have made him the second she laid eyes on him.

She stepped back into the hall and let them enter. Whatever Son was up to, it was his business. He wouldn't be bringing a cop to her house to get her in any trouble. It was something else he had planned and, knowing Son, it probably wasn't going to be a good scene.

Son hustled the cop in front of him, Sherilee trailing behind after closing the front door. The hallway was dimly lit from light filtering in from the living room, where she had been watching the late show on TV. She didn't know anything was wrong until she stumbled into Son's back. He'd halted and then she heard the cop falling to the floor with a loud *thunk*.

"Son?"

He turned to her and took her by the arms. "You don't know anything about this. I'm taking him out to my car and you won't be involved."

"A cop? What're you gonna do to a cop?" She could see past Son now to the man facedown on the floor. Blood seeped from the back of his head, staining his thinning hair red.

"It doesn't matter what I'm doing with him. He's a threat to me. Do you understand? I have to get him out of the way. Now go on in the bedroom and shut the door. Forget you ever saw me. Or him."

She did as he said. She had no love for the pigs anyway, what the hell did she care what happened to him? What worried her, though, was that she had just seen evidence of Son's capacity for violence. She had always suspected he was capable of more than brutal sex and then weeping afterward at her bedside. There was a deeper river of abnormality running through him than his sexual preferences might lead a less experienced woman to imagine. And tonight, there was a new frigidity in his eyes she had never seen before.

She closed the bedroom door and stood leaning against it, listening.

She thought it wise to be afraid of Son after this incident. Very afraid.

Maybe she'd put her house on the market and move to Tucson where her sister lived. Houston was getting too weird for a working woman.

❧ Thirty-three ❧

"Your boyfriend is head of the murder case," he said.

Shadow sucked in her breath and held it. "What do you want with me?"

She was home, she had not been in to work for three days. When she answered the phone at a little past three in the morning, dragging herself up from sleep, she had no idea who might be calling, but she recognized his voice immediately. There was a hint of British accent in it.

"He told you already? Baby, he'll put you away."

"Then maybe he should. You have to stop this," she said, switching on the table lamp to dispel the darkness in the room. She felt sick all over. Should she hang up? Should she listen? What was she to do?

"I can't stop," he said in a sibilant hiss so that she almost missed the words. Was he speaking through cloth? He sounded muffled.

"You have to!" She heard her voice nearing the screaming point and tried to gather herself. "You have to stop," she repeated. "I'll stop if you will." Now she sounded like a child making pacts, but she couldn't help it.

"You already have," he said, disapprovingly. "You weren't supposed to do that. We're partners now. I'm doing all the work and you've quit."

"You killed another one?" She didn't really want to hear his answer. She had to make him understand that he was going to bring them both down.

"Yes, he makes my third."

She closed her eyes. "Tonight?"

"Yes. He was a cop, not your boyfriend, take it easy, it was another cop. They're getting closer. This guy was sniffing around the clubs. The only reason I've left your boy-friend is because I care about you."

"Oh Jesus."

"I'm doing it for you, making you look good, making sure your name will go down in the annals of crime."

"You're a maniac."

"And you aren't? You think you can really stop? You can't. You're just like me. It's in your blood now. You'll never stop."

"Liar!" She slammed the phone into the cradle so hard she hurt her fingers. She put her fingertips into her mouth and only then realized there were tears on her face. She tasted them, salty, on her tongue.

Mitch was looking for the killer, he was heading the case. He had mentioned the murders, but he had never said he was leading the investigation. She couldn't see him again.

That thought hurt so much she shook her head against it. But she couldn't see him. He'd figure it out and hate her forever, that was part of his job, hate the criminals, wasn't it? He would have to take her in, testify in court against her. She should leave town, take Charlene and flee.

To where?

And what was she going to do with the man who called himself Son? Her partner. Her alter self. The one who was going to destroy them both before he was finished.

She slipped down under the sheet and drew it close to her chin. She felt the depression sweep in like the tide, covering over her mind with dark, disjointed thoughts.

I should kill myself, she thought.

I started this.

I've created a monster who calls me on the phone to report his murders. He's taken over and is carrying on my plan, but he's made all those mistakes.

Three people dead because of her, and Son wasn't doing it right. The first victim was a homeless man. The second was a family man with three children at home. He was young and the news reported that unlike the other victims of the Gulf Water Killer, this man had never committed

any crime or been involved with any illegal organization.
Now Son had murdered a policeman.

Son was killing randomly, killing anyone, killing people
who didn't deserve it. And if they caught her, she would
be blamed for all the crimes. She could tell them all day
long there was a copycat and that he was the one who was
doing it now, and they would have no reason to believe
her. The victims were poisoned. Dropped into the bay naked. That they differed from the slugs and slimeballs she
killed would be noticed, but that didn't provide her any
protection. They would just think she had decided on random victims now.

She had to stop him. Had to.

So how would she find him? When he called next she'd
ask for a meeting. Would he do it? And if he didn't?

She lay staring at the ceiling, sinking deeper and deeper
into self-pity and such profound sadness that she didn't
even want to breathe anymore. If she could make herself
crawl from bed and take the decanter from the vanity table,
she could end it all.

It was such a shame she could not be like Scott and do
away with herself. Sometimes, wasn't the world better off
when the cowardly act of suicide became the only alternative? But no. She wouldn't. Never.

She thought of her children and the tears returned. The
maternal pain residing in her heart pushed the depression
down into the pit of her brain, and there it took up permanent residence, coiling and twisting like gray smoke
from a banked fire.

Son sat brooding, looking at the telephone on his desk
for a few moments. The room was dark, his computer
wasn't turned on, nothing moved in the house.

Earlier he had sat on the toilet in the bathroom with the
light on, taking care of his natural functions while studying
the victim's photographs he had taken off the detective.
What if he'd never seen the dancer with one of these victims just nights before he was found floating in the bay?
He might never have connected her to the crimes. He might

still be casting around blindly, the way Samson was, merely mimicking an unknown killer as he had all the other times. This was so much better.

He turned the photographs this way and that in the light. He counted up her kills and his. They weren't even yet, four for three. But if she stopped, his number would surpass hers. That had never happened before. Before he was more cautious than he had been this time. It wasn't that he was getting sloppy. More *efficient*, that's what was happening to him.

He glanced at the dead monitor screen. Already his work had suffered. He was behind his schedule, had missed his deadline to turn in the next book. His editor would be calling soon, wondering where the manuscript was.

Who cared? That wasn't his *real* work. His real work was the acting out of crimes he copied from serial killers. He always knew that there would come a day when his routine life—his *fake* life—would be interrupted forever by the mission. That time had come.

It was because of Shadow. She was his turning point, his pivotal experience that lured him down deeper into the dark side of his nature. Before he had been able to govern his urges. Now that they governed him, he felt so free, so alive! Hallelujah and amen, brothers. Praise Jesus.

He smiled into the dark, the cherub smile that mothers loved.

His thoughts tumbled over, returning to Shadow. He loved talking to her. He realized this was the first time in his life he had ever contacted the other killer. He also knew it had something to do with his mother dying. *What* it had to do with her passing, he didn't know. Was he lonely, so lonely he had to create a relationship with Shadow? That was part of it, but not everything. He had never come along behind a woman killer before to copy her murders. Houston had never had a female serial killer, how could he have?

She was so beautiful. Not a man to be swayed by feminine beauty before, he didn't understand this new response, but it was undeniable. That she killed and got away with it (so far) added to her attractiveness. He did not fantasize about relations with her, but was nevertheless drawn close and closer still into her sphere.

He had to make her understand she must give up Samson. Samson threatened them both. If Shadow fell, so would he. Not that they would believe her about a copycat doing the killings. That made him laugh. But if she were caught, he would have to stop killing, and if he stopped killing now, he could very well explode into a million splintery pieces, an event that would wreck his mind.

He was that close to walking the edge and he knew it.

He stood and went down the hall in the darkness to his mother's room.

She was beginning to smell terrible. He felt along the bed table in the moonlit room for the paper mask he had bought for use when painting. He donned it. He didn't want to breathe any germs.

He took up the bottle of rubbing alcohol and the clean, neatly folded washcloth from her bedside table.

Mother was naked, lying with her arms at her side.

He must wash her with the astringent and keep her clean. It did not help the smell or halt the decaying process, but it insured she would not become infested with the larvae of flies.

If maggots ever began to wriggle . . .

He squelched the thought and set to his task.

Samson hurried to dress and gulp his coffee. He had slept most of the day and was due on his shift at the station in less than an hour.

Pavlov whined pitifully until he stopped what he was doing—trying to get down a bite of buttered toast—and petted him behind the ears.

"I'm going out," Big Mac said from the hallway.

He nodded.

"You hear me? I'll be back inside before too late."

"All right, Mac." He was preoccupied and didn't have time for conversation. He didn't see her shake her head as she tottered across the living room to the front door. She was weighed down with a garbage sack containing her things. He had asked why she didn't leave them in her room, forget about the grocery cart. She was emphatic in her stand that where she went, so did her things. They were important to her, he could never understand how important. And by moving in with him she had not relinquished her lifestyle, he should get that through his head.

He finished off the slice of toast and wiped crumbs from his shirtfront. Pavlov was crazy, hopping and whining. "You want out?"

Samson cracked the door just an inch. "Sit!" Pavlov sat, ears pricked stiffly, big eyes fastened on his master. "Go!" Samson opened the door wide and grinned when the dog leaped straight into the air, clearing half the patio before landing and taking off for his normally hyperactive run that circled the backyard.

Mitchell watched, sipping coffee. He thought of Shadow and how he had not had time to see her in days, how he missed her. He hadn't even been in the Blue Boa in a long while. She might think he'd forgotten her. As if he could even if he wanted to. He hoped she'd move in with him and Mac. Then he'd see her more often. He'd sleep with her. He'd win over her confidence and her love. He'd get her out of the strip club and back into the normal world.

Or he might not. She was nothing if not unpredictable. She might never change.

He could deal with that, too. Given no alternatives, he would gratefully accept her just as she was, strip club and all. That's how crazy he had become. He was willing to share her time with the scumbellies who crawled through the doors of the Boa.

Maybe the manager at her club would give him her home phone number. He hadn't thought to ask her for it.

He reached for the phone to make the inquiry just as it rang, startling him. He lifted the receiver. "Samson here."

"Mitch? Get down to the Kemah Channel. Now."

Epstein's voice was shaky and hollow. He didn't sound like himself.

Samson sighed audibly. "Not another one so soon. The killer must be experiencing delirium." When a serial killer stepped up his killing pattern, it was often because he was losing control.

"Mitch? Do it now!"

"Hey, I'm on my way. Jesus. What's the matter, is the victim the mayor or something?"

There was a pause and Mitch felt a coldness start in his belly and move up.

"It's Dod."

Samson was left speechless. Dod?

"Dod?"

"Yeah. Get down there, will ya?"

Samson held the phone to his ear while the dial tone burped. He turned in a daze and opened the back door to Pavlov's scratching to be let in. He set the coffee cup on the counter and put a hand through his hair, leaving it spiked and messy.

Dod? Why had the killer targeted Dodge? Dodge didn't have the sense he was born with, but how did he fall into the hands of the murderer?

This was . . . it was . . . it made no . . .

He grabbed the car keys and slammed out the front door and down the walk to his car. He drove all the way to Kemah during rush-hour traffic with his siren blowing full blast.

Dod had floated right into the stilts beneath the outdoor restaurant on the Kemah side of the channel. A waitress saw him first, bobbing down there, white as a billowed parachute.

One section of the restaurant parking lot was cordoned off. By the time Samson arrived, they were putting Dod into the ambulance. He was heading for the morgue.

Samson was more confused by the time he got to the scene than he had been when Epstein called.

"He was in his cuffs," Detective Holly said, closing her notebook.

"His cuffs?" Samson felt his head was full of muddy water.

"Behind his back. He must have put up a helluva fight.

There are contusions and abrasions all over him. The M.E. thinks one of his arms is broken."

"Fuck."

"I hope you'll let me be one of the team going after this psycho," Holly said. "I'll work with you twenty-four hours a day if you want me."

Samson acknowledged the offer with a nod of his head. He had never liked Detective Dodge, but he by no means wanted him dead. He had to form the task force now. Maybe he shouldn't have waited. But he thought he could work better alone, and it took Dod's death to prove to him how wrong he'd been, how fatally wrong. "Show me where he was found."

Holly took the lead. Overhead, gulls swooped and cried, mistaking the gathered crowd of onlookers for diners who would throw them bread. The sun hung insistent and low over the western horizon, cooking southeast Texas. White gravel crunched beneath their shoes, the trees seemed to exhale dry breaths as a breeze moved through their slack limbs. Heat waves rose shimmering from the hoods, roofs, and trunks of parked cars.

In the relative coolness of the shade beneath the pilings supporting the dining porch, Holly pointed out where the body had been discovered.

"I guess there aren't any witnesses," Samson said.

"No break yet. He must dump them during the middle of the night when everyone sleeps."

"What about the surveillance team we had across the channel where we found the blood on the ground?"

Holly shook her head. "Nothing. They never saw a thing out of order. He must have driven into the lot with his headlights off, if he dumped him here."

"He might have dumped him somewhere along the coast besides here. I don't think he'd have taken that much of a chance, just across the shipping lane from a cop car."

"Yeah, but where else could he have done it? There must be a million secluded places all along the shore he could use."

"Fuck." Samson turned from the gently lapping, fishy-smelling water and moved out again into the sunshine. "I want the shoreline searched from Texas City all the way up to La Porte. You want on my team, that's my orders. Get some men and get on it."

Holly said, "You got it, sir. We'll start right away."

"Scour the goddamn place. Check the yards of private homes and public businesses fronting on the water. Don't miss anything."

"Right." Holly veered away from him, making for her car and the radio there to call in help.

Sometimes he hated this job with a passion that really surprised him. No cop, even one as blatantly ambitious and hard-assed in-your-face as Dod, should have bought it with his hands cuffed behind him, someone pouring poison down his throat. When Samson caught the murdering son of a bitch, he'd show him what a drastic mistake he'd made to fuck around with the HPD.

❧ Thirty-four ❧

Shadow forced Charlene to take two Valium and go to bed. The woman had been hysterical ever since she saw the news of the dead detective on television.

They needed money. The refrigerator was nearly empty and the electric bill long overdue. Shadow reached down deep inside and drew on her strong survival instinct. She packed the gym bag with a dance outfit and headed out the door.

While she danced or talked to men at tables, she'd also work on the problem of dealing with the copycat. Only now she thought of him as the Copycat, with a capital C. Maybe he would call her at the club. She must talk him into meeting her face-to-face.

She felt in the bottom of the gym bag for the stubby stainless-steel Smith & Wesson .38 revolver, a gun she had bought off one of the girls at work. Shadow knew little about guns other than what Scott had taught her when deer season hit east Texas, but she listened carefully when the dancer who sold her the gun said, "This is a Chief's Special, two-inch barrel, with a shrouded hammer so it won't snag on your clothes. It's an 'airweight,' weighing just fourteen ounces. That's a few ounces heavier than what cops carry, but not by much. I've found it to be a perfect weapon for protection."

"But will it stop a man?" Shadow wanted to know.

"Stop 'em? Honey, it'll kill the sons of bitches dead. But one thing you gotta watch—"

"What's that?"

"Gun like this has no safety. Anytime that trigger gets

pulled, there's going to be a helluva blast. So handle it careful.''

It was unregistered, and although it might take more than one shot to bring down a determined man, if she aimed at the head, there wouldn't be any problem in dropping him where he stood. Son needed a bullet to the brain.

The new resolve and the fourteen ounces of metal in her gym bag made her feel made of reinforced concrete. She was invincible. She was smart. She wasn't crazy like him.

Now to find the freak and end all this before he brought down not only her, but Charlene, too.

Bruce had called complaining that the men wanted to see her. She was one of his headliners, she couldn't just take off for days this way, damn it. And the cop had called, he added. ''You ought to get your head examined, hanging around with that guy,'' he warned. ''You can't trust the heat.''

She bit her tongue to keep from telling him what an asshole he was and that she'd prefer he stay out of her personal business, thank you very much. But it was no time to argue with the boss. She needed the job to pay the bills and buy food and gas. She needed the job as camouflage while she hunted down Son.

At the Blue Boa after she was dressed for a set onstage, she peeked between the curtains and saw Bruce had put in strobe lights. It made the dancers look like puppets on strings, flickering in and out of light and dark. God. It would give her a migraine.

The strobe lights also completely ruined a dancer's chances of seeing who was in the club at the bar and tables. Shadow suspected Bruce wanted it that way. Some of the girls had been giving blow and hand jobs in the back booths. Vice caught them doing it, they'd close down the club.

Was Mitch out there? She had to deal with him sooner or later, but she did not yet know what she would say.

''Phone call!'' Bruce yelled from the pay phone.

Shadow flinched and looked to see if he meant it was for her. He gestured, his mouth set in hard lines. It was either Son or Mitchell. She hurried to take the call.

"Will you fucking please tell your boyfriends not to fucking call you here?" Bruce dropped the receiver so that it banged the wall. He stomped off, cursing women who got involved with his customers.

"Yes," she said into the phone.

"Will you take the next one?"

It was Son. That hushed, muffled, slightly British voice that sent chills scuttling like long-legged spiders up her spine.

"I gotta use the phone." Mad tapped Shadow on the shoulder. "Okay? I really gotta have it."

"Wait . . ."

Son said, "I don't think we should wait. Don't you enjoy running the cops in circles? We should keep them guessing."

"Not you," she said into the phone. "I wasn't saying wait to you, I was talking to someone here."

"Oh, you're busy, aren't you?"

"Lookit, I got an important call to make. You mind?" Mad moved over so she was in Shadow's line of sight. She didn't look as if she was going to leave until she got what she wanted.

"Meet me," Shadow said quickly.

"I don't think so." He sounded amused.

"Please. We have to talk."

"No, that's quite impossible."

"But . . ."

"This is *important*, I said!" Mad's voice bordered on a screech. Her face was foxlike, feral and pointed, eyes squinted. Shadow wanted to slap her.

"It's your turn," Son said. "If you don't do it, I will." Then he hung up and Shadow took the receiver and knocked it once, hard, against the wall.

Mad said, "Well, shit, don't get pissed, I have to call my baby-sitter. She called while I was onstage and told Bruce my baby's running a fever."

Shadow glared at her before stalking away. This fucking

lace, she thought. These fucking people.

That fucking lunatic calling her, ordering her around. . . .

After her set with the drowning tune of an AC/DC song echoing in her ears and the strobe lights blinding her, Shadow received word in the dressing room that Mitch wanted to see her out front at his table. So he was here, all right.

The lingering flicking of the strobe lights, the thundering music, the roomful of smoke, the tension that came into her belly when Son called, had not gone away—now all of it conspired to bring on the headache. She swallowed three aspirin, chased them with Coke, before dressing and going to him. She had to say something, but she wasn't yet sure what.

It felt as if she were on a merry-go-round and it was spinning out of control faster and faster. The world blurred by, unreal, intangible. She couldn't get a firm grip on anything, most especially her thoughts. They twirled and eddied so that she was talking to herself in her head, talking in snatches about Son first and then Charlene and, next, she was preparing a speech for Mitchell, something to make him give up on her, but then she'd argue with herself, not wanting him to give up at all. It was like having multiple personalities, she guessed, where a dozen conversations at once went on in her head. It was all mind-numbing static in the end, none of the internal dialogue helpful to her.

She stepped from the wings of the stage and took the two steps down to the club floor. She couldn't see a damn thing. Lightning lit up the club, plunged it into darkness, over and over again. She stood frozen, realizing she couldn't even move through the tables because she couldn't see them long enough to navigate her way. She had no idea where Mitch was sitting. She'd trip and break her neck trying to find him. She briefly considered turning around and leaving the club by the alley door. Couldn't she just ignore some of the problems that plagued her?

A male hand came around the tender flesh of her forearm and she suddenly jerked away, afraid it was one of the drunken customers manhandling her.

"Shadow, it's me."

It was him. She let him lead her past tables to his ow~
She felt for the chair back with both her hands outstretche
in front of her, blinded each time the strobe flashed. H~
helped her be seated. She thought: I can't work here
Bruce keeps those lights. I'll have to go somewhere else.

"I tried calling you," Mitch said. "You were never he~
and the manager wouldn't give out your number. It's u~
listed, isn't it?"

"Yeah, it is."

"What's wrong?"

His hands came around hers where she had them ov~
her face. "I can't see you anymore, go out with you, be
come involved with you," she said.

He laughed and she wanted to jump up and move aroun~
the table into his arms, tell him, yes, it's just a joke, I'~
testing you. But she said, "I mean it."

His hands fell away from hers. "I don't see how yo~
can really mean that."

"But, I do. It's just not . . . it won't work out."

"Why the hell not? What's changed your mind?"

"I can't talk now. I have to leave. My head's killin~
me." She came to her feet, avoiding looking at him, an~
was not more than two feet away from the table when sh~
ran into an occupied chair. Someone said, "Hey, baby, ho~
you doin'?" and she moved on, bumping into tables, chairs
people, until she stumbled her way into the dressing room

"That funny light's making everybody blind," Mo~
said, coming to guide her. "How you been, girl? Haven'~
seen you in the place for days on end."

Shadow sat down and closed her eyes. "I have a head~
ache."

"Want some aspirin? I think I have a bottle of Baye~
around here somewhere. I might even have some Extra
Strength Excedrin."

"No, I already took something. Just let me . . . I have t~
be quiet."

Mom made reassuring sounds and went back to arrang~

ng the cosmetics in their Tupperware bowls while Shadow
dealt with a headache that was nothing compared to the
throbbing that rampaged through her heart.

Son had called her from the St. John, a club that was
new, up-and-coming, featuring some of the most talented
girls in the business. It was going to give the Blue Boa a
run for its money.

He sat at a booth in disguise, almost hoping the cop
would come in. The cop wouldn't recognize him at all in
the mustache and extra weight padded around his midsection. He might not have remembered him at all, even without the disguise, since it had been years since he
interviewed him at the station.

Son wasn't on the hunt or hoping to pick up a victim
tonight. He just didn't want to spend time at home. With
Mother. It broke his heart every time he moved past her
closed door. He couldn't stand it.

Could. Not. Stand it.

He should call a funeral home, he knew that. He would
do it presently, really, just as soon as this other problem
was out of his way. He was too busy right now to handle
all the tedious details of burying his mother. He'd have to
pick out a coffin, find a dress for her to be buried in, select
a monument. Wood coffin or steel? Her pale pink dress
with the rounded collar at the neck or the robin's-egg blue
she favored for sunny spring days? An angel atop a square
granite stone or a nice, restrained plaque with just her name
and the date of birth and death? He didn't know, he
couldn't decide, he wondered *when* he could ever decide
all those details. . . .

Oh, he couldn't handle those thoughts. If he did. If he
took care of those things, she would . . .

haunt him

. . . be gone forever.

He expected she would be angry if she knew . . .

she knew she knew

. . . he had left her lying in her deathbed, but what could

he do, he was too busy, there were so many noises in h
head begging to be . . .

heard

. . . silenced.

Lost in these jingle-jangle thoughts, Son didn't know th
man was sitting at the table with him until he spoke.

"You got a light?"

Son came from reverie and saw the speaker. A fag, crui
ing for a one-night stand. The lifestyle screamed from th
stranger's tone of voice, the look, the posture. He was slig
in body, about thirty, had a receding hairline that created
sharp widow's peak. He was dressed well in pressed slack
and a cream silk shirt underneath a good quality spor
jacket. Son almost said something rude and insulting lik
"Do I look gay to you?" but thought better of it. He shoul
not turn away a true victim when he presented himself,
gift from the gods.

"Sure, I have a pack of matches here somewhere." So
felt around in his pants pocket until he brought up th
matchbook with BLUE BOA inscribed in blue gothic letter
across the front. He handed it over.

The other man made a production of lighting a cigarett
a Virginia Slims, for chrissakes, one of those mile-lon
sticks of tobacco for neurotic women. The stranger sucke
hard on the filter until he had it going. He handed th
matchbook back, but Son shook his head. "Keep it. I don
smoke."

The fag sighed. "There's so many of you nowadays. W
smokers have become second-class citizens, highly discrim
inated against. So is it all right if I smoke at your table?"

Son said he didn't mind. He almost smiled thinking ho
a homosexual should be used to being treated in a second
class way since the minority he belonged to had alway
gotten the same raw deal from society. But he didn't. H
commiserated and helped start the conversation.

It was not long before Son had conned the victim int
following him to his car where they could be afforded
little privacy for the sexual act and resultant fee mutuall
agreed upon.

* * *

Son had never indulged in a homosexual experience. On the way to the car, he wondered what it might be like. No one would know, what was the difference? If he didn't like it, he could always call a stop at any point during the transaction, couldn't he?

In slang terms, they called it the "kneel and bob," but in this instance it could have been called the "bend and knock your head—*bang, bang*—on the steering wheel." It was horribly uncomfortable and a distinct turnoff. Son's member was as wilted and shrunken as a dead peony. An idea came into his head before things were under way too seriously.

"Let's get out of here and go to my place."

The other man, going by the improbable name of Cato, rose from where he had his head buried in Son's lap and said, "Oh God, am I glad you said that. This furtive shit in cars gives me a real pain in the neck. Literally."

Son grinned, zipped his pants, and started the car. On the way to the house, he talked about being a writer just to pass the time.

"Really? I never met a real published writer before. One of my friends, well, actually he was my former lover, but anyway, he's been working on a book . . ."

Son tuned out. He had heard that a million times. My friend, lover, ex-wife, parent, cousin, grandfather, child is writing a book. Yeah, right. Half the world was writing a book, to hear tell it. The sad thing was, they really were. The whole goddamn nation had turned into a land of scribblers. Tell-all books, histories, memoirs, confessions, and a plethora of imaginative novels penned by those who thought they actually knew something to write about. Not that he was any better. Cribbing from the dead didn't exactly make him into a Nobel winner for literature.

What would Cato say if he told him he plagiarized everything?

"So what do you write, Westerns, or horror maybe, like Stephen King?"

"More like John D. MacDonald," Son said, slowing for a light.

"Who?"

Son sighed. "I write mystery. Have you seen the movie *Cape Fear*? That came from a book by MacDonald called *The Executioners.*"

"Oh, right! DeNiro, man, he's ace, isn't he? I love movies. I've always been a film buff. Any of your books been made into movies?"

Son shook his head. "Hollywood's not that interested in whodunits. They like more gore and sex than you can find in a mystery, *The Executioners* notwithstanding."

They discussed movies, good, bad, indifferent, until Son turned into his driveway. He had never brought a victim to his house. His neighbors were abed and asleep by this time of night, but still, it was risky to walk in someone and then carry him back out again.

What the hell.

He wanted Cato to meet his mother.

After Cato had finished going down on him, Son decided that the old kneel and bob wasn't as great as banging away at Sherilee, but it would do in a pinch. Now he could see why homosexuality had its adherents. Not that he would switch over permanently, but it wasn't as disgusting as he had thought before he tried it.

Lying back on the sofa, Cato between his knees panting, Son said, "Want to see where I work?"

Cato rose to his feet. "You got anything to drink first?" He took a handkerchief from his back pocket and wiped his moist lips.

"Sure. Have a seat, I'll go find something." In the kitchen he pulled out another bottle of the California wine, poured half a glass into a water tumbler. He found the rat poison in the pantry and put an even teaspoon of it into the glass, then stirred the concoction vigorously. He sniffed the wine. Didn't smell too bad. There wasn't enough poison in it to kill Cato, but it would certainly serve to debilitate him so that Son could pour some stronger stuff down him later.

"Here," he said, offering the glass to his guest. "I'm sorry it's not chilled."

"Burgundy? You don't have any white wine, do you?"

"No, sorry." White wine. Of course. How stereotypical.

"You're not drinking?"

"I don't drink. Go ahead without me. When you're done, I'll show you my office."

"Great!" Cato lifted the glass to his lips, tipped forward the blood-red liquid, took a big, lusty swallow. He grimaced, rubbed the back of his hand across his mouth.

"What's the matter? The liquor store told me this was the best wine they had from California vineyards."

"Well, hey, you won't catch me disputing a liquor clerk." He smiled at the weak joke.

Son shrugged. "I don't know a thing about wines."

Cato tried another swallow, obviously out of courtesy. He then set the glass on the coffee table. "You know, maybe the clerk was pulling your leg. I'm afraid what we have here is some bad-tasting fermentation. No offense, of course."

"None taken. C'mon, my office is down this way."

Cato made appreciative sounds while looking at Son's computer, the stack of typed pages neatly piled to the right of the machine, the walls of books, the odd looking little bust of Edgar Allan Poe. "Nice," he said. "It must be wonderful to work at home and not have to put up with a boss."

"Listen, my mother's usually awake most of the night. How would you like to meet her?"

"Your mother! You live here with your mother? Jesus, she could have walked in on us."

"No chance. She's an invalid. I should have told you she was here, I guess. I just take it for granted and didn't think about it. She's a swell old lady, you'll like her." Son moved from the office into the hallway. Behind him, Cato followed, protesting.

"I really think we ought not disturb her. I should be getting back to the club, you know, find my friends, be getting home . . ."

"This won't take long. Mother would never forgive me if I didn't introduce my company."

Son didn't know quite what he was doing taking the stranger down the hall to the closed bedroom door. He wanted him to be shocked, yes, he wanted to note his reaction to a dead woman lying on a bed, and the man would never have the chance to report it, but was it wise? It meant more things could go wrong.

Son acknowledged he was taking all kinds of new risks he had never chanced before. A pinnacle of excitement, though, climbed so high inside him he thought he might burst out into song. This was better than any kind of sex, any day.

He opened the door, crossed to his mother's night table, and did not hesitate to flip on the lamp switch. The body emerged into view, bathed in a soft pink glow. She looked so peaceful. Even naked, she was the most beautiful woman he had ever laid eyes on. If it wasn't for the smell emanating from her decaying flesh, she might be an aged goddess, an elderly Sleeping Beauty awaiting the kiss from her prince while reclining against the hand-crocheted pillows.

He turned to watch Cato's face. "Cato, meet my mother. Mother, this is Cato, a little friend of mine."

"Oh, good Christ." The man was frozen in place, a rictus of horror holding his features in thrall.

"I'll tell you something else about me, Cato. A secret even Mother didn't know. I love to copy, to mimic, duplicate, reproduce, imitate. I've been doing it for years. Maybe since I was a kid. I copy books, movie scenes and plots.

"For instance, this scene you now witness is very similar to the one in the movie *Psycho,* don't you think? Did you ever see *Psycho*? You said you were a movie buff. That famous movie came from a Robert Bloch book, you know, *not* from the scriptwriter and *not* from the mind of Alfred Hitchcock. The best movies come from books, from *authors.*

"Remember Norman Bates in the movie? Anthony Perkins? How he had his mother stuffed and sitting in the rocking chair in the cellar? Don't you think I've done a good job with the materials I had to work with? I don't have a cellar, you understand.

"But I do have a dead mother, the poor old dear."

Cato went from frozen terror during Son's recital to sudden frenzied action. He swiveled, knocking a doily from the back of the easy chair, bumped into the door facing, staggered into the hall, gained control of his feet, and like a sprinter in a race, hunkered down to dash for the side door leading to the outside where Son had parked the car.

Son took his time in pursuit. No hurry. The door was locked. By the time Cato discovered how to unlock it, he would be restrained.

Son walked right up to him, wrapped an arm around his neck, hauled him off his feet, and dragged him, his scream a mangled gurgle, to the living room. He threw him onto the sofa, onto his back. He climbed on top, to straddle him with his knees, effectively pinning him to the cushions.

There he proceeded to choke him unconscious while murmuring into his horrified face, "There, there . . . shhhh . . . hush now . . . there . . . isn't that better?"

❧ Thirty-five ❧

It was a feeding frenzy. Mitchell Samson presided over a room where eight detectives sat talking nonstop. Outside the door marked PRIVATE waited a gang from the press corps, including three reporters from the local television stations with all their gear and cameramen. Samson hoped the lieutenant was giving them the promised statement right now, otherwise they'd still be out there waiting to descend on him and his team once the meeting was over.

Finding nothing else at hand to use for rapping the table, Samson balled his fist and hit the scarred wood with his knuckles. "Quiet down," he said. "Quiet!"

The room fell into uneasy silence. They shuffled their butts, most of which were broadened from sitting in chairs at desks for too many hours a day, and shoe leather scraped at the tile floor. Samson cleared his throat, looked down at his notes, realized they weren't going to be of much use, and glanced up again.

"The time periods between the crimes has escalated. We're getting a new stiff every other day, at least for the last four days. If that continues we can expect another victim tomorrow."

Samson turned to the man at his left. "John here is going to put you into two-man units. I'll let him and you decide who works with who."

"Whom."

Samson shifted his gaze to Detective Gonzalez in the back of the room, where he stood leaning against the wall, his arms folded. "Whom, then. That's what we need right now, a grammar professor on this fucking case. Or should that be grammarian?"

The men chuckled and Gonzalez dipped his head to accept the slight reprimand.

"Now, no use going into what trouble we have on our hands. You all know the ropes when we have to make up a task force. So far, thanks to Detective Holly and some volunteers from this division, canvassing the bay area all the way from La Porte to Texas City has turned up nothing. No suspicious characters. No witnesses. No physical evidence. *Nada.* I've been working the street people down in Montrose and I didn't come up with much from that either.

"I want one unit backing me up down there. Twist arms if you have to. Call in all your IOU's from the snitches. Put them to work sniffing out the word on the street.

"I want another unit here in the station doing background checks on the victims, *in-depth* checks. Making calls to family and friends, trying to find more connections. I want to know where these guys worked, and if they didn't work, where they got their money, what they ate for supper, who they screwed, how much they loved their women, and who those women were.

"A third unit goes downtown to question the M.E. I want some names of commercial products that have the poison in them . . ." He looked down now at the notes. "Warfarin. We know it's used in rat poison. See if it's in anything else easily available on the market. That same unit then starts checking outlets that sell it. Start with ones in Montrose, go on to ones around the bay area."

Again Gonzalez interrupted. "You mean Clear Lake and Channelview and everything?"

"That's right. Every conceivable outlet."

Groans rose and fell into silence again. Samson raised his eyebrows; no one wanted that detail. "We want Dod's killer, don't we? Or do we? It's up to you."

He stared his detectives down, then went on, clicking off how he wanted the teams split up to deal with every aspect of the series of crimes. He ended the meeting with, "I'll talk to our psychologist again, see if he can add anything to the profile the FBI sent us. Also, you want me, you can see me down in Montrose. I do my best work on the street."

When the task force was dismissed, John shook his hand. "I'll put them to work within an hour."

Samson ran his fingers through his hair in an unconscious gesture of fatigue. He had been up most of the night going over the papers in Dod's case file. "Good, the faster we—"

"I'll see to it," John said, breaking for the door. Samson gave a bemused smile. John was a workaholic with three bad marriages behind him and four kids to support. He moved like a coon dog when he was off the leash.

Outside Samson heard the fading voices of the detectives discussing what detail they'd like to be included on. Some of them were querulous, others sounded resigned. Most of them had been called onto serial-killer task forces before. They had no illusions. These were not the happy-bullshit throwers aching for a promotion the way Dod had been. They were neither young nor old, but all were tried and true veterans of the hunt, some with specific talents helpful on a task force. Gonzalez, with the mouth, had been instrumental in cracking the last round of serial killings that petrified the city. He might speak up more than he should, but there wasn't a better Hispanic detective in HPD, and Samson was lucky to have him.

It was rumored Gonzalez was making noises about quitting the force and entering politics. Try for a city council seat representing the Hispanic block struggling in the brown ghettos ringing Houston. Samson sighed thinking of how he kept losing his best minds to the political wheel of fortune.

He sat down heavily and drank cold coffee from a mug that had written on it LUV YA BLUE. Only the dedicated and the crazy stayed a detective for a bum's salary when they could do security work for Standard Oil or Texas Eastern or try for the political brass ring at triple the money. What did the city expect the good minds to do, rot here in the bullpen on cases that half the time couldn't be solved?

But right now he had Gonzalez. He had John Borden. He had the finest people the precinct could spare.

Who could predict if it would be enough?

Wearily Samson rose to his feet. A flash of recall made him pause. Shadow, in the club, holding her head and saying it was over. That was . . . Well, that was not only startling, but more painful than he could deal with right this minute. He wanted her to . . . fuck it.

He left the station for Montrose wondering if he'd left out enough dog food for Pavlov. Because Big Mac sure as hell wouldn't think to feed him. She still spent her free hours out on the street, habit being the mother of obsession, and obsession being the inventor of bag ladies, serial killers, and, possibly, Homicide detectives.

Shadow and Charlene sat at the kitchen table desultorily eating whatever their fingers groped blindly to find. There were potato chip and tortilla chip bags, an opened package of thawed chicken tenders slightly heated from the microwave, a jar of Hellmann's Dijonnaise mustard with a butter knife sticking out of it, Sociable crackers, a chunk of cheddar cheese, and a small jar of sweet pickles. Charlene didn't want to cook. She had not cooked a single meal in three days.

They both waited for the evening television news. The TV that had been in Charlene's room, a nineteen-inch color with remote, sat on the kitchen counter. Dirty dishes circled it and sat precariously on top like a small army camped and awaiting a marauding enemy from over a rugged hill.

Charlene had the remote and kept flicking through the channels. Shadow tired of the blitz of voice and picture. She reached out wordlessly and took the remote from her friend's hand. Charlene grunted. ''I don't care,'' she said.

And that was the problem. Charlene had stopped caring more than forty-eight hours ago when the detective had been fished from the bay channel, naked and dead and bloated as big as a whale.

Shadow changed the channel to one of the stations where the five o'clock news would begin in just a few seconds. She eyed the clock on the wall. Hurry up, she thought. Tell me the bad news now so I don't have to keep waiting for it.

"He said he'd do another one if you didn't, so we know he did." Charlene said this around a small scalloped cracker between her square, off-white teeth.

Shadow sighed and shrugged. What was she supposed to do about it? She had been hunting for some sign, some . . . signal . . . in the clubs for two nights running. What else could she do? And what good was her search? Was the Copycat another woman disguising her voice on the phone some way? Was it a man, mad as a hatter, with wall eyes and a sardonic sneer to his lips? If the cops couldn't catch him, how was she supposed to do the miraculous?

But then they hadn't found her out, either.

Because she was careful.

Which meant so was the Copycat.

So how was she to . . . ?

The lead news item was the murder.

"I told you so," Charlene whispered.

The videocam on the scene took a far-off shot of the restaurants hugging the channel two miles from where Shadow and Charlene sat at the kitchen table. In the distance was the navy blue bay leading to the Gulf of Mexico. As the camera scanned, viewers could see the outline of Galveston Island dozing in a golden haze of noon sun. Then the camera shot tightened and zoomed until the viewer could see the body bag and the men lifting it onto a gurney.

Shadow sat rigidly, holding her breath. Son did not lie. He had waited for her no more than one day and then he struck again.

The crime scene shot dissolved and the female anchor was saying something about the police asking for civilian help in identifying the victim. As the anchor listed the specifics, a grainy police sketch filled the television screen.

"The man was five feet seven inches tall and weighed approximately one hundred and forty pounds. Brown thinning hair, brown eyes. He wore contacts. There was a distinguishing mole on the right collarbone. If anyone has any information about this man . . ."

Shadow gasped and knocked over the Dijonnaise bottle with a clatter. Charlene turned to her silently, watching.

Shadow *knew* the victim. She didn't really *know* him, but she'd seen him in the clubs, seen him in the Blue Boa, for that matter. He was . . . wait! She had seen him somewhere else. And it was recently. It was . . . She closed her eyes to concentrate. Remember, she admonished, you've got to remember, this is important.

It was at the . . . St. John club. She had gone there after her set at the Boa, just poking around, wondering what she was going to do. She—*wait* . . . she had walked in . . . and . . . she had seen a man she knew, but he was in some kind of disguise, that or else he had a twin brother who was older, heavier, mustached. But that only entered her mind for a moment because she knew it was him, not a brother, not a cousin. It was him, *disguised.*

Frank.

She had seen this latest victim with Frank. Was it Frank whose voice spoke to her on the phone, who called himself "Son," who was the Copycat? Could it be? The man who read Travis McGee novels and watched comedic movies? One of the few customers she had felt at ease talking to, a nondescript, nonthreatening, asexual *friend?*

"Jesus," she whispered.

"What is it?" Charlene asked. "You know the dead man, don't you?"

Shadow rooted herself in the present. She gazed vacantly at Charlene, the pit of her stomach sinking. "Yes, I know him," she murmured. "And I know who killed him, too."

He crouched in a tangle of vines that hugged the brick wall. For minutes at a time he sat this way, knees creaking and aching, feet going to sleep, numb as rock, and then he would rise, slowly, thinking of soap bubbles drifting skyward, how pure and clear and silent they were, and turn, again slowly, twisting from the waist.

Inside the window he could see them at the far end of the kitchen where they sat at a table eating and watching TV. The crazy woman in the gray sweater, that sweater she wore despite the killing summer heat, and Shadow, dear, lovely Shadow of the black midnight hair and bronzed skin.

He knew her name was Katherine, but sorry, she was no Katherine, or Kate, Kitty, Kathy, Kat. She was Shadow, it was as pure and clear to him as the thought of soap bubbles rising. She had taken the name and wasn't there something grand, something original in the act of choosing one's own name that made it real and meaningful? Katherine was a name parents choose for a girl child, a baby they hope will grow up straight, strong, and completely diligent. Shadow was the name of things that slipped along the earth, covering it, protecting it from the fury of the sun. The Son.

He had *not* chosen his name. He had adopted it, however, and made it as fully his own as if he had made the choice himself. He was not Frank, that was a pretend name, a made-up-on-the-spur-of-the-moment name. He was also not the name his parents gave him, that name on the spines of his books, the name he used to sign checks, to pay his taxes to the government.

He was the son of his mother. The son of his father. The son of the world. He was kin to everyman and named for the savior, that King of kings.

His lips curved, a smile splitting his face in two like a knife blade. He should have been a writer, his thoughts were so marvelous, melodic, and poetic. It was true that's what he should have been had things been different and he had been willing to sacrifice his ideals.

So what was he besides a mimic? Really?

The one free man, unencumbered and light and airy as a soap bubble.

His attention drifted from the thoughts playing through his mind to the women inside at the table. Shadow stiffened and knocked over a jar on the table. He heard the clatter from where he stood. The crazy woman said something. Shadow closed her eyes as if to think. When she opened them she spoke. He couldn't hear anything they said. How he hated that!

An itching along both arms caused him to look at the vines he had his hands looped through. Probably sumac or poison ivy. Poison, yes, he rather liked poison, especially how it made them bleed from all their orifices as if they were bags of blood leaking. That's all any of us are, he thought, carcasses hauling around so many pints of blood.

When next he looked through the window the kitchen was empty, the table deserted, the television mute.

He slithered down into the vine-covered earth, his back to the wall, and he waited, breathing regularly and evenly, psyching himself to leave his hiding place and return once again across the city to the darkened house where his mother waited.

Always so patiently.

❧ Thirty-six ❧

"We have to move out of here." Shadow moved irritably around the bedroom pulling out drawers and lifting out stacks of folded clothes. These she put on the bed. She went to the closet and found her old suitcase she had brought from the hospital.

"Why? What's going on?" Charlene hung in the doorway, a scarecrow of a woman, her hair in disarray, baggy sweater hanging almost to her knees.

"I *know* who the Copycat is. He knows *me*. He knows where we live because I told him. Don't you get it?" She paused in the packing and turned to face Charlene. "I told him things about us because I liked him. Can you believe it? I liked him! He didn't seem like the other guys. He's just this . . . average, normal kind of guy. That's what I thought, anyway. I told him where we live, in a huge house called the Shoreville Mansion. I told him it's in Seabrook. He's probably been dumping the bodies from here, right off our pier, for all I know."

"We have to tell somebody," Charlene said pensively, her gaze shifting erratically from Shadow to the suitcase to the windows on the far wall.

"We *can't* tell anyone. Christ! Am I supposed to go to Mitch and tell him I killed four men and now there's this psycho who's been killing the others for me? Do you think anyone would believe me? If I'm ever caught, there won't be any excuses that will hold up. I'm as guilty for four murders as I would be for eight. If the cops catch one of us, that's all they'll want, they won't need *two* killers to pin it on. There's no way they'll believe I didn't kill the others."

"Where are we going to go?"

Shadow sank onto the bed. "I don't have enough saved to get us an apartment and pay all the utility deposits."

"What will we do?" Charlene's voice was on the edge of hysteria.

"Now just hold on, let me work it out. We just can't stay here any longer. We have to get as far away from here as we can."

"Mitch said we could move in with him."

Shadow looked at her. After some seconds she said, "I guess that's our only alternative. We move into the camp of the enemy. At least Son won't try to contact us there."

"Sun?"

"That's what he calls himself."

"Sun and Shadow . . . it's like a poem. Black and white, cold and hot, sun and shadow."

"No, I don't think he means *sun* like the sun in the sky. I think he means *son*, what a mother calls her little boy."

Charlene gave her a puzzled look. "It's awful funny, isn't it, how it's gotten so complicated . . . and strange."

"It's not funny at all," Shadow replied. "It's a nightmare and we can't wake up." She failed to add that it was a nightmare she had first created and one she was now solely responsible for sending back to hell where it came from.

Samson was floating on air. He had been in the middle of a shower when Big Mac called through the bathroom door that he had a phone call. He took it on the bedroom extension while water dripped and puddled around his bare feet.

Kay and Charlene were going to move in with him. Could they? Of course they could! It's what he wanted more than anything. He wondered, however, what had changed her mind. She had dumped him, couldn't see him anymore, she said, and now she wanted to move in. She was like a Rubik's Cube. He couldn't get the colors to match all in a row.

Dressed and ready to go to the station, he explained the

situation to Big Mac. He needed her cooperation, he said.

"So you're pretty crazy about this woman, huh?" Mac seemed leery.

"I think that's a fair assessment," he said. "So if you wouldn't mind hanging around this afternoon until they get here . . ."

"I'm the welcoming committee?"

"If you don't mind, of course. I have to get to work and she said they'd be over today. Someone needs to be here to let them in."

"I'm supposed to make cheese trays and serve coffee?"

"C'mon, Mac, don't give me grief, all right? This is important to me."

"Seems like you're running a halfway house, all these strangers you keep taking in."

"That's not fair and you know it. You'll like Shadow. I mean Kay. Shadow's her stage name. I call her that most of the time though. I think everybody does."

"Oh, that sounds promising. Guess it's better than Big Bad Mama or Miss Melon Titties."

"Mac . . ."

"Okay, okay, I'll be good. Who's this other character coming with her? And where do you want me to put them?"

"Her friend's name is Charlene Brewster. She's an older woman, a friend of hers who helped her out of a bad situation once. She's kinda nice, cooks a good meal. Put her in the empty bedroom next to yours."

"And Shadow? She goes in your room, right?"

"I have to spell these things out for you, Mac? You're being a pain in the ass, if you don't mind me saying so. I'm going to be late for my shift, this keeps up."

"Oh, go on, get outta here." Mac waved him off. "I'll handle everything."

"You'll be good, you said."

"I will. I never seen a man so damned ready to take in strays, but I'll be good, I'll be nice and polite, but I am *not* hanging around after they get here, you understand? I have things I wanted to do."

Samson tried not to smile or he'd insult her. They both knew she had nothing to do at all, nothing but tramp the streets saying hello to all her old street-bum friends, collect empty aluminum cans, and stay out of the confinement of four walls as many hours of the day as possible. He shook his head, stooped to pet Pavlov. "I'll call later, see how you're getting on."

"You do that. I probably won't be here. Not after they're settled in."

"Fine. Thanks, Mac." Samson touched her on the shoulder as he made for the door. He turned, snapping his fingers before he got there. "You need any cash?"

She shook her head and strands of hair from the bun at the back of her head fell loose around her face. "I'm fine, don't worry about me. Now get out of here. You make me nervous."

Now he did grin. "I think I love you, Mac. See you later."

Mac stood in the kitchen frowning for all she was worth. "I'm mighty worried about him," she said to the dog. "He don't act like he's got the sense of a turnip."

Pavlov flipped, then looked up at her expectantly, his tongue hanging out.

Son felt a prickle of uneasiness begin as he walked up the driveway. The house was dark. Usually there was a light shining in at least one of the rooms.

He went directly up the front steps to the door. He couldn't see anything beyond the darkness inside. He circled the house warily, like a cat after prey, wondering why it felt so deserted. He came to the underground garage and saw Shadow's Toyota was missing.

He would break into the house. If the crazy woman appeared or turned on a light, he'd stop, retreat. But something told him no one would hear him because no one was inside. It was empty. This would give him the opportunity to see how they lived.

He tried the wooden door, turning the old metal doorknob. It was locked, of course. He turned, searched around the shelves in the garage, and found a crowbar leaning in a cobwebby corner. He took it up and placed the wedge end between the door frame and the door near where the lock was located. He heaved outward and the door gave with a splintering crack. It swung open on noisy unoiled hinges. He paused, waiting for a light or a voice. When none came, he entered, the crowbar in his hand.

Just inside the door he was confronted by a spiral iron staircase. He took it to the second floor, paused again, listening, letting his vision adjust to the interior gloom. He could hear the tiny *tick-tick* of feet scampering away somewhere in the darkness and imagined it was a mouse. He could smell the scent of chlorine from the swimming pool.

An inner jitter forced him to call out, "Anybody here? Hey, anyone home?"

No response. He was alone in the house. He crossed the catwalk, free to make as much noise as he wanted. He glanced down at the pool water. It was as serene and black as a satin sheet stretched tightly over a bed. He looked at the maze on the other side. Shook his head. From above it was just as strange and confusing as it appeared from outside the windows.

He came to the landing above the curving staircase that led to the white-tiled front entrance and the living room off to the right. It looked too neat and clean to have been a place humans inhabited. He turned on the landing for Shadow's room. He had seen her take this hallway. He wanted to see where she kept the poison and where she slept. He wanted to touch the clothes hanging in her closet.

He opened a door on an empty room where a cast-iron bed stood. There were no sheets or covers or pillows. What could it mean now? He looked quickly around. The dressing table and end tables were bare. He jerked open the closet door. Empty. The vacuum he had created by throwing open the door caused the hangers to dance together, rattling and tingling, wire against wire.

He turned now, thinking he had made a mistake, this wasn't her room, after all. He went down the hall opening doors to empty rooms. He entered a great ballroom, turned on his heels, and trudged down the hall where he had just come, crossed the landing, searched the other bedrooms on the other side.

They were gone. They had moved out. He reached to the wall and flicked a light switch, uncaring now if anyone saw the lights in the mansion. Nothing happened. He flipped the switch twice, nearly ripping it off the wall. They had turned off the electricity.

They had left him. Shadow knew who he was. She had discovered his identity. He knew it. Why else would she move them out?

He hurried across the clanging catwalk, down the spiral staircase, the noise of his steps thunder in his head, and to the garage door. He closed it carefully. The wood of the door was old and warped from the dampness. It stayed closed, though now unlocked. No one would discover the broken lock for a while. He flung the tire iron across the packed dirt and hurried away from the house.

Shadow saw him coming through the door. He did not wear the disguise.

Her breath caught in her throat. She had left the gun in her purse in the dressing room locker. She felt paralyzed in the chair, unable to move fast enough to leave the table.

He watched her face as he came. He took the chair opposite and sat down casually. "You moved out," he stated. "Why did you do that? You don't think I'd hurt you, do you?"

Shadow tried to swallow down the fine skim of fear that rose up her throat, stealing away her voice.

He stared at her levelly, never blinking. She tried to look him in the eye, but involuntarily her gaze fell to the table and her hands lying there motionless. "What do you want from me? I thought you were a nice man. I thought you liked to read and watch comedy movies. I thought you were . . ."

His voice dropped to a small whisper. The girls weren't onstage yet, and the deejay was playing a soft reggae tune by UB-40. "Were what? Another dumb guy you could get money from for nothing? A stupid, backward, lovesick Mr. Lonelyhearts? I'll tell you what I want. I want you to *participate* with me. It's your turn. Don't you see how you're ruining everything?''

"I never meant to—"

"To turn into a killer? You were doing it for your own personal satisfaction, is that it? You think murder was something you could get away with and then quit, without anyone knowing or finding out? If I found out, how far behind me do you think your boyfriend is? Finding people like you and me is what he does for a living, for crying out loud. I'm the only friend you have left.''

She still could not look at him.

His tone changed from nagging and scornful to friendly, cajoling, as if he were trying to convince a buddy to go out on a fishing trip with him. "Shadow, you started it. I *never* start these things. You can't quit when you think the game gets rough. It's only now turning into something worth your time. I don't have to know why you started, that's not important.'' He gestured with his hand, waving it away. "But you can't just stop now that you have me involved.''

"I didn't ask you to kill anyone,'' she hissed, leaning forward, suddenly furious. "This was none of your business. You're going to get me caught.''

He smiled and she had to look away again, afraid of that smile, afraid of him and what he was and what he might do. "It's my only true business, Shadow. And I won't get you caught. Not if you do as I say.''

"Do as you say? Who do you think you are? You must be insane.''

"And you're not?''

She pushed the chair away from the table, but before she stood she said, "You have to stop. You *have* to.''

"Why did you move out of the Shoreville place? Where are you staying now? I can find out, you know.''

"You're not listening to me, I said it's over, I don't even know how it began.''

He peered at her. "Yes, you do. It began as it always

does. You work it out very carefully, you lay all the plans, you think about it all the time, then you follow your plans to the letter. You clean up after yourself and you don't leave any clues behind. That was a stroke of genius to dump them naked in the bay. It does away nicely with fingerprints and hair and fiber samples that get left on the bodies by careless killers.''

"You *will* stop," she said.

"No, I won't. I can't, not yet, it isn't time yet, but you wouldn't understand that, would you? *Would* you? If you don't continue, I'll do it for you.''

"No." She said it harshly and with all the command at her disposal.

"Yes," he said, standing from the table and turning his back to her to leave the club.

She sat dumbfounded and shaking. Even if she'd had the gun with her, she couldn't have done anything differently. Son was not to be threatened, she understood that. Not in public. Not unless she knew exactly what she was doing and had the advantage. How long would it take him to discover she and Charlene had moved in with Mitch? How long would it take him to get her caught for murder?

❧ Thirty-seven ❧

Shadow had slept very little. Every time she dozed off on Mitch's living room sofa, she jerked awake, alert to every creak in the house. Finally the sun rose and she woke again to the boxer licking her in the face. She pushed away his warm muzzle and sat up. Someone had put a cover over her as she tried to sleep. It might have been Charlene. Or even Mitch. He was asleep in the bedroom when she came from work last night. She hadn't wanted to disturb him so she had stretched out on the sofa.

She found coffee in the kitchen and an old dented percolator. She made coffee and sat at the table drinking it while watching Pavlov race around Mitch's backyard. When Mitch finally woke and joined her, he noticed her uncharacteristic silence. She told him she did not feel well. It might be a touch of the flu or a cold virus. He tried to make her feel at home, taking her around to show her where things were, bringing coffee in a mug to the table for Charlene when she stumbled into the kitchen.

Shadow was moved by how gentle he was with them, how accommodating. He probably loved her very much. It was too bad she had no time for his love, too bad it was doomed to a bad end just as soon as he discovered she was the murderer they called the Gulf Water Killer. She had formed a psychic distance, a barrier beyond which she could not move toward him. She wondered if he knew yet, if he sensed her withdrawal even though she had moved into his house. She wondered if she would ever sleep with him again, ever hold him in her arms.

She left for work early, soon after Mitch left for his shift at the precinct. Big Mac had also left the house, being al-

most as uncommunicative as Shadow. Charlene moped and
complained. This wasn't the same as being on their own.
When could they move out again? Would anything ever be
the way it was?

Shadow couldn't tell her. Events were spinning out of
control, escalating into madness.

As soon as she reached the Blue Boa, one of the girls
told her there was a phone call. She went to the pay phone,
wearily, feeling a thousand years old.

"Will you do it?" he asked. "Have you thought over
what I said and will you make the next move?"

She shut her eyes. "No. I told you I wouldn't. I told you
it was over."

"It may never be over," he said. "If you want to see
how it really should be done, meet me down at the pier of
the house you just moved out of. I'll be there around midnight."

He hung up. She replaced the receiver and stood immobile, staring into the distance. Then she dropped a quarter into the slot and dialed Mitch's house. Charlene
answered.

"I'm meeting him at the Shoreville Mansion."

"Who?"

"Son. He just called. He wants me to be there."

"What are you going to do? Shadow? I don't want you
to go."

"Don't be upset. I'm going to be all right. I have a gun."
She heard Charlene's intake of breath. "I have to stop him.
I don't know any other way to free us."

In the dressing room she took her things out of the locker
again. Mom said, "I thought you just got here."

"I did. But something came up, an emergency. I have to
leave."

Once in the Toyota, she sat a minute before starting the
car. Her hands were trembling. She waited for the bout to
pass. She felt in her gym bag for the shape of the Smith &
Wesson. Its hard contours comforted her. How difficult
could it be to pull a trigger?

Of the men she had killed, none had been as deserving

of death as the Copycat. He had stepped into her life and
made of it a madhouse. He wanted her to stop him. If he
didn't, he would never have told her where he would be
and when he would be there. He knew she'd try to stop
him and counted on it. It was a form of suicide and he had
to know it.

He didn't want to kill anymore.

He wanted to die. He wanted her to do it for him. She
felt happy to oblige. It might end then. She might wipe the
slate clean and start over.

She sighed and turned the key in the ignition. It was a
long drive back to where she had left behind the acts of
judge, jury, and execution. If she were lucky, it would be
her last trip.

It was almost midnight when Samson thought to check
the wall clock. He was off duty but still working. He
wanted to get home to Shadow, but this was the first break
in the case since he had started working on it.

Forensics had found a thumbprint on the handcuffs holding Dodge's hands behind his back. It was a partial, but
enough to indict the killer when they caught him. So far
the check Samson had run hadn't turned up the print in the
computer banks. It might belong to a killer who had never
been caught for anything, never been fingerprinted. That
was the kind of bad luck they kept running into on the case.
Small clues led to dead ends. It didn't exactly put Samson
into a good mood.

He was tired, his back ached, and from the reports he
had been scanning on his desk, the reports turned in by his
task force unit, nothing much was going right. The thumbprint was all they had. And that wasn't going to be of any
help until they had a suspect in custody. Most days this is
how police work went. He ran into blind alleys and turned
in circles, helpless. Meanwhile the bodies kept washing into
land.

He glanced up and across his desk at Dod's old empty
desk area. They had taken away his personal things. His
father had come for the articles, hefting the cardboard box

close to his chest, tears shining bright in his eyes. Samson wanted to say something to him, but he couldn't get it out of his mouth.

The desk was clear now, waiting for another detective to claim it. They wouldn't do that, in respect for the dead, for a few months. Until then it would sit empty and forlorn across from Samson's desk in the bullpen, a reminder that this job could turn into a piece of shit right before your eyes.

This job could get you killed.

Samson heaved a great big tired-sounding sigh as he closed the folders and turned off the power to his computer. Computers were rare, not all the men in the precinct had them. Samson had requested one for the case and it was sitting there one afternoon when he came to work. A note taped to the monitor read, "We need this back when you're finished. So are you finished yet?"

Yeah, he thought. I *know* I don't get to keep the damned thing, you fucking jerks, think you're so funny. I keep it, everyone in here's going to clamor for one. The taxpayers say we can't afford it. They'd rather we beat the bushes the way we did twenty years ago than pay more taxes for updated equipment. Same old song, same old tune, the "Bebop Big-City Cop Blues."

When Samson walked in the door at home, he was met by Shadow's friend. Charlene had the door open before he could get out his key. She looked wild with panic, hair flying haphazardly around her face, eyes blinking so rapidly she might be strung out on speed. "What's going on?" he wanted to know, his heart taking a downward slide. "Is it Shadow?" He thought she must be hurt. Nothing less could cause this kind of behavior in the older woman. She was normally a little crackers, but she wasn't completely weird the way she was now.

"Yes, it's Shadow! She's gone back to the mansion!"

He didn't understand. Why would she do that? "She moved back out?"

"No, it's not that, you have to go out there and help her."

"Help her do what? Why did she leave?"

"It's the copycat," she said. "He told her to meet him there."

Samson reached out and caught the woman by the arms. "Now slow down, tell me exactly what's going on. I don't know what you're talking about. What kind of copycat?"

Charlene began to cry. Her voice was shaky and he could hardly make out her words.

"Shadow . . . she . . . I don't know how it happened, but she . . ."

"What? What is it?" He knew something terrible was coming, some confession he would not want to hear, but he must. He felt Pavlov jumping at his leg, trying to get his attention. He saw everything with such clarity—Charlene's face wrinkled in distress, her eyes wild with fear, Big Mac standing behind them in the doorway of the kitchen, holding her peace, watching and listening with interest.

"She killed some of them," Charlene said finally. "The first ones. The Gulf Water killings."

Then he understood everything. The murders of men who had been in the exotic clubs. The rap sheets most of them had. Shadow telling him her husband had committed suicide. Her cold refusal to show any grief over the fact. The washing up of the bodies not far from where they lived in the big brooding mansion on the shoreline. The *copycat?*

"There's a copycat killer?" He had shouted to make her come to her senses. She was gibbering and trying to tear loose from his hands. "Is there someone else doing the killings, too, is that what you're saying? And Shadow went there to meet him?"

Charlene bobbed her head. "She's going to kill him if she can. But he might, he might . . . and she didn't mean to do these things. The first one, the one who was stabbed, he got into the house one night and tried to . . . tried to . . . he was on top of me . . . and . . . Shadow came . . . and . . ."

Samson turned for the door. Kay Mandel and a copycat killer. Together, working in some kind of unholy tandem, they had killed eight men. He had made love with, fallen in love with a woman who poisoned men. How had it happened? What did it say about him and his perceptions, his investigative abilities, his total *blindness* to where the facts had been pointing all this time? How goddamn crazy had the world become that a beautiful woman would kill strangers and then sleep with a Homicide Detective? How goddamn crazy was *he* not to have had even a thought that she could be involved?

Christ, he'd invited her into his home. He had spent nights with her. He had made love to her in the bed where she might have . . .

He raced to his car and hurriedly got it started. As he backed from the drive, he didn't notice the two older women standing in front of the house watching him leave while Pavlov raced around the yard in circles, yelping with newfound delight.

Son helped the drunk maneuver the spiral staircase in the dark.

"This is creepy shit," the old guy said, slurring his words.

"We'll have a party," Son said, pressing him forward and upward. On the landing he took the man's arm. "What's your name, pal?"

"Ch . . . Cha . . . Charlie."

"Well, come on, Charlie, we have a while to wait. Let's cross this catwalk. On the other side is the living room and a place to sit down."

He swung the beam of the flashlight ahead of them, his other hand to the small of Charlie's back to push him ahead of him. Their footsteps boomed along the metal walkway in the emptiness.

"I ca . . . can't see my hand in front of my fa . . . face."

Son hated the stuttering. It drove him bat shit. He'd had to listen to it in the car all the way across the city. "Just keep going, I've got you. Follow the flashlight."

They exited onto another landing and Son led him down the staircase. In the living room he pushed him onto a leather sofa.

"Ha . . . ha . . . hey. Whatta we doin' here, you said, didn't you?"

"Waiting for a friend of mine. It won't be long. Take it easy."

"You got anything to dra . . . drink?"

Son had a pint of doctored whiskey in his coat pocket, but he couldn't give that to him yet. Not time.

"You'll get something, just wait." He crossed the room to the front door and stood watching. Waiting. She should arrive soon. Until then the show was on hold.

‏❧Thirty-eight❧

She stood at the front door, hands gripping the wrought-iron bars. He stood on the other side with a flashlight, unlocking the deadbolt. She stepped back, felt in her shoulder purse for the gun. She had put it there before leaving the car. She had a firm hold on the handgrip.

Her breath came shallow and her pulse trumpeted until she felt she was on the precipice of a dizzy spell. She had to do it. This should not have felt any different than the other times when she gave the men poison, but it was different, it meant survival. And this man was not bedazzled by her lies. He knew how dangerous she could be. He would be on guard.

He gestured she step inside. She moved past him, heard him closing and relocking the door, imprisoning her, and she was about to turn to protest, but a voice interrupted in the near dark to say, "Oh, guh . . . guh . . . good, you called over a gur . . . gur . . . girl to join the party."

Son moved away from the door and closer to the other man, who Shadow could now see sat on the sofa near the fireplace. "This is our guest of honor," he said to Shadow. "Meet Charles. He has no idea he's here to serve as an object lesson."

"Huh?" Charles turned his head to look up at Son. "I'm a wha . . . what?"

"You're not going to hurt him," Shadow said. She made herself move closer. The shadows in the room hid too much of her target. She still had her hand in the shoulder purse, the gun warm as the palm of her hand now, a real part of her. "I want you to let him go."

"What's this?" Charles asked. "Something ain't right,

now, and I . . . I . . . I think I ought to be get . . . getting on.'' He began to rise from the depths of the leather, pulling himself to his feet by holding onto the sofa arm.

Son reached over and pushed him down again. "Stay put, Charlie. You're not going anywhere.''

"Let him up. Charlie, get out of here. He's going to kill you.''

"Oh, look what you did,'' Son said, but he sounded a little amused. "The guy didn't have to know that. Then again, it may be fun that he does.''

Before Shadow expected a move, Son turned and pushed Charlie sideways onto the sofa and straddled him. He pulled something from his coat and fiddled with it. Charlie began to yell like a man on fire. "Let me ah . . . ah . . . up! Help, don't let him hurt ma . . . ma . . . me!''

Shadow moved as quickly as she could. She had the gun out, felt her hand shaking, tried to hold it steady, and fired, the gun seeming to go off in her hand without her help, leaping up and nearly out of her grasp, causing her to scream.

She tried to see if she'd hit him, but he had rolled to the floor, and something *clunked* and rolled away from him. He came to his feet, muttering. Charlie was off the sofa in a flash, stumbling toward the stairs, running up them, sobbing.

Shadow aimed again, but she couldn't see, could only see deeper darkness and then that dark was moving, streaking toward her. She squeezed the trigger of the gun, tried to brace for the jerk of her hand, felt herself go off balance, stepped backward, trying to right herself.

She spun back, swinging the gun, and fired wildly, hitting the wall. A chunk of plaster fell with a crash to the white marble floor.

She was alone in the room. She heard sounds all over the house, unable to tell where they came from, which direction. She checked the dark near the sofa and saw he was really gone, he had vanished after Charlie up the stairs and onto the landing.

She couldn't catch her breath. She had been breathing so

hard she was now hyperventilating. Her hands shook and she relaxed her finger on the trigger of the gun, terrified that she'd missed him, that now it was a game of hide-and-seek and she would never find him before he found her.

Her foot struck something on the floor. It rolled with a clatter two feet away and stopped. She retrieved it and found a flashlight. She flicked it on and pointed it up the stairs. Emptiness. Silence ringing against her ears like distant sirens in the night.

Where had he vanished to? She had bungled her only real chance of stopping him.

Now she must track him down through the echoing rooms.

She shut tight her eyes and thought of Mitch, of Charlene, of Scott and the children. Of the four victims she had dropped over the side of the motorboat.

She opened her eyes and carefully approached the stairway. There was no other choice. In her life, she thought, there had never been any choices. She did what she had to, what she was compelled to do, and no more.

Son found another stairway at the end of a hallway that took him down to the swimming pool. Overhead little light streamed in through the green glass ceiling. There was but a slip of a moon tonight and clouds covered the stars.

He stood with his back to the wall listening to the sounds of movement in the house. He knew the drunk had crossed the catwalk and gone down the spiral stairs to the garage door exit. He had heard him pounding across the walk, his footsteps fading as he went down in the back of the house. He'd be on his way for help now. The police would come. They couldn't find him here. They'd have to find Shadow. Dead. He hadn't much time left. What he had hoped to be the fulfillment of a dream had turned into a messy nightmare.

He had never shared a murder before. She had ruined everything for him.

It was her fault. He hadn't thought she'd turn on him that way. He knew she didn't want to go through with the

killings anymore, but he had never thought she'd regar
him as her enemy. Didn't she understand that she was th
catalyst, that she had begun it all?

She was furious with him because he had taken the gam
to new heights, he was calling the shots for the first tim
in his life. Didn't his mother just hate that when he did it
Were all women the same?

He felt something dripping from his shoulder an
reached up to find out what. His fingers came away sticky
He touched his forefinger to thumb and the liquid smeare
there was gummy. He brought it to his nose to smell. H
thought . . . He put a finger to his mouth and tasted wit
the tip of his tongue.

Blood.

She had shot him, the stupid bitch. He was wounded. H
felt again and found the hole in the upper meaty portion o
his shoulder just above his socket. The bullet must hav
gone right through him. He hadn't felt the pain. His min
was elsewhere, dealing with catastrophe.

Now he felt it, the burning and sharp shrieking bolts o
pain shooting down his arm and into his chest. Well, hol
Christ. He didn't have anything to put over the hole, to sto
the bleeding. He had to find something, some kind of cloth

He crept from his hiding place in the deep shadow an
felt his way along the wall. There had to be something
down here, a room, a curtain, something. He moved a
quietly as he could and halted, listening, when he hear
footsteps overhead at the entrance to the catwalk.

"Son, where are you? Come out. We can't stay here al
night. Charlie left. He'll bring the police."

He smiled up at her silhouette against the sky overhead
Yes, he thought. You'd like for me to come out so this tim
you can finish me. You'd really like for it to be so easy fo
you.

He watched her while moving along the brick wall, feel
ing with his right hand for a door. Just as soon as he foun
something to pack over his wound, he would go to her. H
remembered his fleeting fanciful thoughts when he had sa
outside this house, watching. How alike he and Shadow

were. How they were equal parts of the same organism, working toward the same ends. She the machine, he the gears. She the darkness, he the light. Killers, compatriots, both engaged in the most meaningful activities of their lives, complementing one another.

Now he knew the truth. She was just another woman. Women could never be trusted. Sometimes they lived just to spite you. Sometimes they died for the same reason. They were never, by God, there when you needed them most.

Shadow turned off the flashlight, afraid suddenly that it made her easy prey. She couldn't see Son, didn't know where he was, but if she used the light, he would know exactly where *she* was.

She became conscious of every sound. She needed to get off the catwalk. She tried to tiptoe off the metal grid, heading again for the front of the house, but she was still making noise. She decided there was no way to silence her passage and finally hurried, shoes ringing on the catwalk, until she reached the landing. When she got there, her heart was racing and she felt perspiration wetting the material under her arms.

She had the gun in one hand, the flashlight in the other. She needed to keep the gun close to her body so that he could not come out of the shadows and knock it from her grasp or twist it out of her hand. She strained to see if anything moved on the landing, down the long hallways, ahead of her on the stairs leading to the front room.

Where was he?

She could leave the house and let the police find him here. That might be the most practical move. But what would they charge him with, breaking and entering? He hadn't really harmed the man named Charlie.

No, she couldn't leave him here alive. As soon as Mitch heard of Charlie's complaint, he would put everything together, and he'd know she had something to do with the murders. He would have them check the house. They might find the spots of blood from her victims on the old mattress still lying on the cast-iron bed in her bedroom. Why hadn't she thought to haul it out back and set fire to it? That small amount of blood was the only evidence of her crimes. As careful as she had been with the plastic covering, when she and Charlene rolled up the bodies and took them from the house, there had always been small accidents, little drips of blood that slid from the plastic to soak into the mattress beneath. When they left the mansion, she had no idea anyone would ever question the few small stains; they wouldn't have had reason to. Mitch would, though. He would know whom to suspect.

From the corner of her eye she thought she saw movement in the shadows in the direction of the hall where Charlene had stayed. She turned and pointed the gun. A vision shimmered there and disappeared, shimmered again, then faded. That couldn't have been Scott. She must be hallucinating. He was long dead and could no longer hurt her.

She heard the sound of a child's voice, softly laughing, coming from behind her where the catwalk began. She turned again, panicked. Were there ghosts here just as Charlene claimed? Had that sound come from her own lost children or from the boys who had played around the pool?

She mentally shook herself, throwing off the notion. She had heard nothing. *Nothing.* She had seen nothing. She was losing it, that's what was happening. She wished she had some kind of tranquilizer so her nerves would stop jumping, her mind stop slipping away into dungeons from the hellish past. She'd give anything to be away from this house and the madman who stalked her.

She had to search him out if he would not show himself. She still had the gun. She still had resolve.

What she didn't have much of was time.

Son found a bathroom with one tiny window set in an outside wall that let through weak light. He felt along the sink counter and found nothing. He opened drawers as quietly as he could and they were empty. He swore to himself. He was bleeding badly, had to find something to staunch the flow.

He opened the lower cabinet doors and felt inside. That space was empty, too. He turned to retreat from the room when he saw there was a closet or pantry door. He opened it and saw folded objects on the shelves. Towels and washcloths. That's what he needed!

He shook out a towel, dropped it. It was too big, too thick. He snatched at the towels, trying to find something smaller. He finally found a hand towel that would do, unbuttoned his shirt, reached up to his shoulder, and lay the towel over the wound, front and back. He rebuttoned his shirt and tucked it into the waist of his pants to hold the towel in place.

Now he could attend to Shadow.

Stepping from the bathroom door into the hall, he saw her coming toward him. He jerked back into the doorway and caught his breath, readied himself to grab her when she neared. He had to watch for the gun, make sure he took her arm and held it away from himself. He would not die because of her. She was no real threat at all. He had taken down much stronger, more intelligent enemies.

He heard her footsteps nearing the open door. He must be swift and sure. The moment she moved into his line of sight, she was his.

❧ Thirty-nine ❧

She saw the car lights shining through the front of the house before she heard the engine of the approaching car. She halted, turned, rushed to the landing again to see if it was the police. She had not heard sirens, wouldn't they have turned on their sirens?

She moved down the curving staircase to the living room and went to the door. When the car parked right before the steps and the car door was opened, she saw Mitch emerge, his face grim in the flooding amber light from the car's interior.

She looked over her shoulder. Where was Son? How could she let Mitch find her here? How did he know she had come back to the mansion? It was Charlene. She knew it. Charlene had told him everything.

What could she do now? He knew she was a murderer. He must know about the Copycat and why she'd been called to return here.

She ran from the door, knowing it was locked, that he could not enter from there. She was beneath the landing and in a long hallway that supplied two exits, one to the swimming pool and the community showers there, one to the chest-high brick maze. She swung right, toward the maze, watching every shadow, imagining a figure leaping from cover to take away her life.

Overhead, on the landing above, she heard footsteps. She paused. It couldn't be Mitch, he couldn't have gotten inside yet. She suspected Son had broken in from the back of the house, through the garage. That's where Mitch would have to come from. So the sounds she heard above her had to be the result of Son, creeping through the dark. She wanted to hide. She wanted to flee. She wanted . . . she wished . . . God, how she wished she had never been born.

It stunned him when Shadow left the hallway. His muscles relaxed and his hands unclenched. He had been seconds away from rushing her.

He came from the bathroom doorway to follow behind. Then he saw the headlights from a car soaring across the walls, spearing Shadow as she stood bathed in the glow on the landing. The river of light moved on then disappeared. Someone was here. He should have killed the drunk, he shouldn't have waited for Shadow, he should have done it right away, as soon as they reached the mansion. The bastard had called the police and they were already here. He had to get out. If they caught him in the house, she would implicate him in the murders. Wasn't he already doomed now that Charlie could identify him?

He might pack up his things and leave Houston. Disappear to another state, maybe another country, before they found out his whereabouts.

And leave Mother? Lying in her bed without a decent burial? He couldn't do that! He wished he had arranged things more carefully now. He must have been mad to let her death go so long without his attention. What would they think if he left and they found her that way, naked and cold, the crocheted pillows propping her up in the bed? They would think he was a poor excuse for a son. He could never explain to them that he had not wanted to lose her totally from his life, that her presence, even in death, in some way soothed his troubled mind. She had been his touchstone to reality, the rock that steadied him during the mental storms that periodically tossed him about in a sea of confusion. He *needed* her, but they would never understand that, never.

When again he looked for Shadow, she was gone. Which way had she gone?

A man stood at the front door, trying the doorknob. Son could not make out his features. He appeared to be alone.

Had the police sent only one man? How terribly odd. How stupid of them.

The man at the door went down the steps again and Son could not see him. He'd try the other entrances now. He'd find the broken door in the garage. That's where he would enter, up the spiral stairs and onto the catwalk.

Son turned his back on the front of the house and put his hand on the catwalk's railing. He'd wait here. It was better that he wait than go hunting. Sooner or later both of them, Shadow and the man, would fall into his hands if only he had the patience to wait for them. He hadn't a gun, his only weapons the bottle of poisoned whiskey still in his pocket and his own two bare hands. Nevertheless, he was not frightened. He would have surprise on his side.

His concentration blocked out everything but the catwalk. The soft throbbing in the tender open wound in his shoulder was hardly noticeable. He focused on the sounds in the big empty house. He breathed evenly, regularly, and a calm filled him. No matter how it turned out, he was prepared to deal with it. He had not succeeded this many years by letting panic and fear overcome him. Death held no terror for him. It never had. He had been the instrument of death for too many for it to hold any supernatural power of dread over him.

He almost sighed in a kind of ecstasy, so sure he was that he would persevere and escape, unharmed, whole, free to plot and kill again.

Mitchell knew Shadow was in the house. Her car sat in the driveway. Another car was parked in the underground garage. He supposed it belonged to the copycat killer, if Charlene had been telling the truth.

The only way he could find to enter the house was at a door leading from the garage. He saw the door had been jimmied and broken from its frame. He opened it and stepped forward. Facing him was a staircase that spiraled up into the darkness to the second floor of the house. He remembered being on the catwalk with Shadow, looking down at the swimming pool. He placed this stairway at the far end of that catwalk.

He had his service revolver from its shoulder holster. He knew he should have called for backup. Why he hadn't was something he didn't want to think about too closely right now. He knew his reluctance had to do with protecting Shadow from involvement. But he couldn't do that, not really, not if it was true she had killed those men.

Yet, Charlene might be wrong. She was, after all, mentally unstable. She might have imagined anything in her fevered state of mind. That Shadow knew something about the murders, he had no doubt, but he could not quite convince himself she had poisoned those men. He realized he just didn't want to believe it. If he did, it meant he had made too many mistakes, he had been willingly duped and perhaps used in a way he couldn't accept. Wasn't it just as likely that there was no "copycat"? That the copycat Charlene had told him about was the serial killer, and he had gotten Shadow mixed up in it in some bizarre fashion? Anything was possible. If he had learned nothing else in his years as a cop, he knew that. The more a thing seemed to be true, the more it must be false.

He crept up the stairs, cringing at the hollow sound the metal steps made as he stepped on them. Once on the catwalk, he'd be an easy target. How else could he cross to the other side, though? That was the portion of the house where Shadow and Charlene had lived when they were here. For some reason he did not think anyone was hiding on this end of the huge house. They were both *over there*.

He must go to them. It was up to him to take the battle to the enemy. He could only hope the killer, who had not used a gun for a weapon in the murders, did not now have one in his possession. If he did, when Mitch crossed the catwalk, he was dead meat.

Shadow crouched in the maze and was unable to see overhead to the middle of the two-story space to the catwalk. She heard footsteps there, but was suddenly afraid to look. Someone might see her. As long as she stayed low and out of sight, she was safe from discovery. She looked both ways in the heavy dark wondering if she could see Son if he came toward her around the sharp turns at either end of the center of the maze where she hid. She held her hand in front of her face and could not see it. She might as well be in a sealed room without window or light source, it was so dark.

She felt a wetness on her cheeks and reached up to feel the tears there. She didn't know she had been crying. She buried her head in her knees and wrapped her arms around herself. She felt five years old again, hiding from her abusive father and the screams of her battered mother. She shut out the sounds on the catwalk and tried with all her might to go away from whatever it was making those sounds. If she was not present in spirit and mind, she would not know what was happening.

She vaguely remembered another time she had done this, and recalled how easy it had been to do. At that time she had escaped seeing her husband and children lying dead on the floor, pieces of their brains and skulls all around, blood splattered in random patterns on the walls, the carpet . . .

No, she thought, admonishing the memories and sweeping them away into corners where they belonged. She would not remember. Not anything.

You just slipped off from the real world and left it behind. When the world was too painful to endure, too threatening to your sanity, you just turned aside from it and embraced the peace and quiet that could be found in the narrow sanctuary of the mind.

Son held himself rigid in deep shadow next to the wall facing the catwalk. He watched with trepidation as the man came across the walk toward him. He could see there was a gun in the man's hand. He had to be a cop. He might not be in uniform, but he was a cop nonetheless. Why he had come alone, Son could not fathom, though he was glad.

The man paused along the way, turning his head, looking over the railing both right and left as he came. Once he looked behind him and, sure he was not being followed, came forward again.

Come on! Come to me before it's too late.

The man neared. He reached the end of the walkway, hesitating again before stepping out onto the landing. Son barely breathed. He still could not see the man's face. He could tell that the man was larger than he had hoped. A man taller than Son, broader in the shoulders, in better shape.

Not that it made any difference. Surprise was the lever that could tip the scales and put the bigger man at a disadvantage. That's what Son counted on. It was what he had always had going for him.

He pressed his back into the wall and waited, willing the other man to come forward just a bit more. A few steps, that's all, and he could lurch from the darkness of the wall and be at the man's back, taking him down.

Samson made it without mishap across the long open length of the catwalk. He could hear nothing moving in the house. There was a vast silence that lay like a pall over the rooms, the swimming pool, and atrium maze below. Where were they? He fought the urge to call out to Shadow, to find out if she was all right. He must be careful and not make the mistake of firing at phantoms. He might accidentally hit her and he'd never forgive himself.

He moved stealthily toward the open landing, wondering briefly if they were in Shadow's bedroom with the cast-iron bed. Could they be lovers, rolling and tumbling on the mattress, sharing a sexual abandon he had thought belonged only to him? Oh God, he couldn't bear it if they were. Such an unholy alliance all but made him go crazy on the spot. Jealousy and fury combined to make him open his mouth to call out to her.

A jolt from behind took him so off guard that he thought he must be imagining it at first. An arm snaked around his throat and took him backward onto his heels. Someone chopped at his gun hand and made him drop the weapon to the floor. He reached up instinctively to grip at the arm squeezing the air from his throat. He meant to grip the hand, tear it away, turn and flip the attacker. He meant to make short work of a deadly situation, but he was being wrestled so expertly backward that he found himself on the catwalk again, flung against the rail. His remaining breath was knocked from his lungs as his stomach connected with the iron rail and he was tipping forward, dizzy, disoriented, unknowing of up from down, and then someone grasped his legs and heaved. He went over and down, head over heels, falling, falling, falling.

❧ Forty ❧

She didn't know if it was the landing of the body on the concrete floor in front of her or Son's wild piercing shriek of victory, but Shadow came to from the world of cotton batting and mental retreat to stare in horrified fascination at Mitchell Samson lying before her, not inches away. She went onto her knees and crawled to him, frantic with the thought he might be dead.

"Mitch, oh Mitch," she whispered. She draped herself over him where he lay unmoving on his side. She felt along his chest to his neck, sliding her fingers up his face, feeling his mouth and nose and eyes as if she were blind. He was breathing, though shallowly. His eyes were closed.

She moved down his body until her face was near his. She felt all over him in the dark, her hands mechanical in the way they searched for protruding broken bones and blood flow. She could not find anything outwardly wrong with him, but he was undeniably hurt after falling so far. She arched her neck and looked up at the catwalk. Son was gone.

The son of a bitch! He might have killed Mitch. He had meant to, she knew that. There was no telling what damage Mitch had suffered. Internal hemorrhaging. A concussion. A broken back. Paralyzation. Dear Jesus, it was all her fault.

"Shadow?"

She flinched. She hadn't expected him to regain consciousness. His voice was whispery and unsteady.

"Are you all right? Where are you hurt?"

"Leg . . . I can't move it, think I broke it."

"I'm sorry for everything," she said, bending over to kiss him lightly on the cheek.

"Stay . . . stay away from him. He'll kill you."

"No, he won't. I'm not afraid."

She stood, uncaring if Son saw her now in the maze's depths. She began walking, taking turns, keeping her eyes on the front of the house where she knew Son waited. She had to get out of here and kill him.

There was nothing that could stop her now.

"It's just you and me," Son called.

He stood close to the entrance of the concrete passageway that had been built beneath the catwalk. He was in shadow, but she could see the outline of his body.

She came from the maze and moved toward him, the gun leveled. She wanted to pull the trigger, but she might miss again. This time she would take no chances. She turned on the flashlight and shined it directly into his face. He squinted and put up a hand against the light. She lowered the beam so it was on the lower half of his face.

"Yes," she said, not recognizing her own voice. It sounded rusty and unused, it sounded like someone else speaking through her. "It's you and me, Son. It's time to end it."

"We don't have to," he said. "I still have poison. We could make him drink it, if he's still alive—he's still alive, isn't he? We could pour it down him and take him out together in the boat. When the police arrive, they won't find us. We'll put in to land somewhere south of here."

"You think I want him dead? Mitch? I cared about him. Everyone I've ever cared about died, did you know that?"

He turned his head to the side and put up his hands. "You have a gun. But you don't want to kill me, Shadow. I'm closer to you than the cop ever could be. He'll put you in jail. I'd never do that. He'll turn on you. I wouldn't."

"You're not my friend or my partner. What I've done I had reasons to do." She hated him with such bright malice that had he been able to see her eyes, he would have run for his life. The cold cunning so useful to her when she murdered the men she had brought to this house was still alive in her heart. She saw Son as nothing more than human excrement, something stinking and vile she must immediately remove from her presence.

"You are *exactly* like me," he said in a high, old womanish voice.

This change made her stop and consider him. "Who are you? What kind of lunatic are you?"

His voice changed again to the one he had used on the phone, the one with the light British accent. "I'm no one and everyone. My name is Son, progeny of Mother and a father I never knew."

"If you think I'm going to feel sorry for you, forget it. I don't give a goddamn about your life. I don't care what your name is. You're Frank, you're Son, you can hide behind a million names, a million faces, but I know you. You tried to kill Mitch. You'd kill me if I let you."

Now his voice changed again, and it was one of a child, a lonely sad little child. "I can mimic anyone, isn't that something?" he said. "I'm very gifted. I have great talent."

For a long moment she was afraid. She couldn't kill a child. She could not pull the trigger on a small helpless baby. Then she knew it was a trick. And she hated him even more for trying to confuse her. "You're a sick, twisted, heartless bastard. I might be sick. I might be twisted. But I'm not like you, nothing like you. I didn't kill anyone who was innocent."

She stepped closer and his hands came down to reach out for her as if to take her gently into the circle of his arms.

She squeezed the trigger of the gun in her fist and the sound of the shot reverberated from the catwalk overhead, it echoed through the hallways and the floors and the dome of green glass that graced the center section of the mansion.

Son stood in place, the flashlight full in his face. He had a look of utter shock and disbelief in his eyes. She squeezed the trigger again. A second shot rang out loud as a sonic boom and Son slumped now to the floor, falling to his knees, his face still turned up to her.

She pulled the trigger again and again, and finally the hammer clicked against empty cylinders. She did not stop pulling the trigger until Son fell forward, grasping her knees before sliding to the marble floor.

She stepped back, dropped the gun beside him.

There was nothing left in this world that she had to do. She had committed all the wrongs and suffered all the wrongs she could stand for one lifetime.

There was still the motorboat, tied to the pier. It would take her away from the dead man at her feet, away from making any excuses for her actions, away from Mitch who had loved her and was ultimately betrayed by that love.

❧Forty-one❧

In the far distance on the shore she saw lights swarming the Shoreville Mansion. As she watched, mesmerized by the twinkling, the house windows glowed, one by one, until all the floors blazed like a fiery multifaceted diamond.

She felt nothing but a small regret that she could not have said good-bye to Charlene. She knew Mitch would see about her and keep her safe, but she would have liked to tell her how much she'd meant to her, how much her friendship had been valued. How much she had truly loved her.

The waves in the bay were gentle swells that came from out of the open sea. The small outboard motor hummed, pushing the boat away from land, from the lights, the dark and jumbled past.

She looked to the sky for a signal of morning. It seemed she had lived for days in the mansion, hiding, searching, alternately afraid and fearsome. It had been but hours. The sky to the east changed from unpolished silver to pearl gray as she watched it. By the time the sun rose, she would be deep into the Gulf of Mexico. Soon after the motor would run out of gas. She'd drift, carried by ocean current past the shipping lanes and into the vast open empty sea.

There, when she had worked up her nerve, she would slip over the side of the boat and let the sea take her down. She knew by then the Coast Guard would have been called to either capture or rescue her, but all they'd find was the empty vessel floating aimlessly over the waves.

She settled back against the ribs of the boat and guided the handle of the motor so that her course would not be altered.

The wake trailed behind her, picked at by flashing divers, seagulls hunting breakfast. She saw a sleek gray dolphin leaping. It came alongside for a time, pacing the boat, accompanying her to sea.

When the sun was just over the horizon she had cleared Galveston Island and was leaving it too behind. She saw a shrimp boat ahead of her, but too far for them to notice she trailed them. Far to the right was a freighter that looked as small as a toy boat in a bathtub. Isolated, it steamed toward a foreign destination.

When the sun had fully moved up the eastern horizon and she could no longer see the Seabrook or Galveston shorelines, when there was no land at all in sight and deep cobalt waters surrounded her, when the shrimp boat and freighter were lost in dawn mist in another part of the Gulf, she waited for the little motor to splutter and die. It obliged her minutes afterward while she spent her last moments immersed in a pleasant reverie of her time with Mitch, loving him as she had loved no other man, even Scott.

When she came to herself and realized the motor was dead and that the bow of the boat was turning, drifting on its own, she looked once at the sun, once at the shadows racing across the water from fat, blue-bottomed clouds hanging low overhead, and then she crawled to the side and lowered herself into the cold, rippling body of blue, hoping, hoping sincerely, that God lived, and that He safely held the souls of all little children in the palm of His hand.